Hadrian's Rage

Patricia Marie Budd

Clink Street

London | New York

Dedication

Hadrian's Rage is dedicated to Vladislav Tornovoi who was raped with beer bottles, tortured, and murdered by two of his friends on Friday, May 10, 2013 in Volgograd, Russia after coming out to them as gay. The world must never forget the violence committed against this young man.[1]

I also wish to dedicate *Hadrian's Rage* to my LGBTI students: in particular my Safe Zone students. Regardless of the daily prejudices thrown your way, you have found the inner strength to be you. You are my inspiration.

#pmb

---

[1] http://www.pinknews.co.uk/2013/05/13/russia-identity-of-man-killed-and-raped-with-beer-bottles-revealed/

Acknowledgements

My initial editing team: William Chappell III and Brindusa-Katalin Poenaru. Your personal responses to what I have written were instrumental in the birth of a new novel.

Robert Wilson, as with *A New Dawn Rising*, your keen eye and editing advice have helped make my fourth dream, *Hadrian's Rage*, possible.

Co-Administrators for *Hadrian's Lover*'s Facebook Page: Allan De Vuyst, James Duncan, Blueyed Angel, and Bartley P. Busse (the hidden admin who sends me links to post on a regular basis).

Garet McKenzie Deusenberry for sharing her story and what it is like to be a transgendered female.

Cody-Liam Blake for reading through chapters that included or referred to transgendered persons.

Christine Marie Scott, your unwavering support and endless fountain of advice have been one of the greatest gifts given to me in this life.

My sister, Michelle Gavigan, for her continued unconditional love and support.

My loving parents, Edith Marie Gavigan (1920–2014) and Keith Jerome Gavigan (1916–2002), who raised me to love and respect all persons!

Most importantly, my husband, Simon John Budd, the man who gives me the strength to write and the will never to give up on myself.

"The sin of my ingratitude even now
Was heavy on me: thou art so far before
That swiftest wing of recompense is slow
To overtake thee. Would thou hadst less deserved,
That the proportion both of thanks and payment
Might have been mine! only I have left to say,
More is thy due than more than all can pay."
— William Shakespeare[1]

---

[1] *Macbeth*, Act I, scene iv, lines 294-300. OpenSourceShakespeare. Retrieved from: http://www.opensourceshakespeare.org/views/plays/play_view.php?WorkID=macbeth&Act=1&Scene=4&-Scope=scene. Retrieved on: August 16, 2015.

Author's Note

When I wrote *Hadrian's Lover*, I created a parallel world to illustrate what happens when an individual's sexual awakenings and sexual exploration go against societal norms and the impact this has on our youth. With *Hadrian's Rage*, I was inspired to develop further that parallel by illustrating the heinous hate crimes committed against the LGBTI[2] community on a global scale. Many chapters have been inspired by very specific acts of hate committed across the globe. Whenever you come across a footnote, click on the live link (or type in the url) and read about the horrors we put our LGBTI brothers and sisters through on a regular basis. *Hadrian's Rage* was sadly inspired by all of this hate.

Please visit my Victims of Hate album on *Hadrian's Lover* Facebook Page and observe a moment of silence to honor those who have suffered most cruelly under the real abomination: HATE.

https://www.facebook.com/HadriansLover/
photos/a.533170636810518/533171296810452/?type=3&theater

For more information on the victims of anti-LGBTI hate, go to Erasing 76 Crimes Blog: 1000s who died in anti-gay, anti-trans attacks:

http://76crimes.com/100s-die-in-homophobic-anti-gay-attacks-statistics-updates/

Disclaimer: I cannot be held accountable for non-functioning website links that may change in the future.

#pmb

---

[2] LGBTI: Lesbian, Gay, Bisexual, Transgender, and Intersex.

To the Reader

Hadrian's Rage is written as a sequel to my previous novel *Hadrian's Lover*. In case you haven't read that novel or have not read it recently, let me catch you up on the story.

Hadrian's Lover opens on the fiftieth anniversary of the country of Hadrian's founding. Its citizens are reminded through *Salve!*, the nation's news agency, why the founding of Hadrian was so important. The world is on the brink of disaster. Overcrowded, poverty-stricken, and with starvation and disease running rampant, there is little hope left for the earth's future. Except for the population of one country: Hadrian. Hadrian has successfully protected itself against immigration and unchecked growth, but it has taken radical and unorthodox measures to ensure its survival. An unusual and progressive law governs the land, one that prohibits heterosexual relationships and natural reproduction. While homosexuality is held up to be the moral ideal, heterosexuality is deemed to be the ultimate ill, one that has led humanity to the dire conditions it now faces. All those who break the law are subject to severe consequences: reeducation or even exile from Hadrian. Although a great majority of Hadrian's citizens conform to these devastating rules imposed by the government, a few are unable and unwilling to adjust.

In *Hadrian's Lover*, Todd Middleton was one such rebel. At sixteen, he has finally come to realize that his sexual orientation will never be accepted by Hadrian's society, and in order to avoid being criminalized, he must do everything possible to keep his intimate life a secret. When Todd falls for a beautiful young woman, he is unable to hide his feelings and is quickly caught being sexually intimate with her and charged by the state for his crime. As a juvenile, Todd is dispatched to a reeducation camp, but his confinement and his separation from the girl he loves prove to be an emotional torture. As his depression deepens, thoughts of suicide run through his head, over and over again. It will fall to Todd's closest friend, Frank, to save his life. As his darkest hour finally passes, Todd begins to see that Frank's intentions are not as innocent as they first appear. Even the man who loves Todd like a son, Dean Hunter, cannot save Todd from the despair created by a society that abhors him for his sexual orientation.

Hadrian's Rage begins not long before *Hadrian's Lover* ends. As the Hunter family (Geoffrey, Dean, Frank, and Roger) struggle to heal the wounds incurred by Todd Middleton's death, the country, too, is feeling a rip in the social fabric. The country of Hadrian has become polarized on the issue of sexual equality. With heterosexuals no longer fearing the threat of exile if exposed, some have dared to live openly in a world that abhors them. Anti-heterosexual laws spring up that refuse heterosexuals the right to promote their way of life to anyone under the age of twenty-one. Regardless of continued restraints being placed on the lives of those who live outside society's sexual norms, the more conservative citizens of Hadrian feel their lives threatened by the growing acceptance of bisexuality and heterosexuality. The country is besieged with internal violence as people physically lash out at those perceived abnormal.

Characters from Hadrian's Lover

Crystal Albright: Best friends with Todd Middleton and Frank Hunter, she was one of the three stars of Pride High's b-ball team, the Pride Panthers. Although she had seduced Todd Middleton and was sexually intimate with him she did nothing to defend him after they were exposed. Though she never stated the fact, she never denied her aunt's insinuation that Todd raped her.

Stephanie Chatters: Trans woman, member of Hadrian's re-ed class. When still identifying as a man, she was Matthew Molloy's guardian at the Northwest Reeducation Facility. She had been Gideon Weller's favorite and had adopted his brutal approach.

Melissa Eagleton: News Anchor for Hadrian's Nation News Service *Salve!*

Sissy Hildebrand: Jeremy Stoker's little sister; a closeted heterosexual, who runs the sheep ranch just north of the Cattle Ranch.

Dean Hunter: Originally a member of the founding Stuttgart family; married to Geoffrey Hunter, currently separated. He is confused about his sexual orientation, though claims to be straight. He is attending Augustus Uni and is President and founder of Augustus Uni GSA.

Frank Hunter: Geoffrey Hunter's eldest biological son; a private (penal restriction) in Hadrian's National Army.

Geoffrey Hunter: Dean's husband, CEO of Hadrian's National Detritus Fisheries (detritus fisheries serve Hadrian by salvaging all reusable waste from Hudson Bay as well as ecologically disposing of all toxic and non-re-usable waste).

Roger Hunter: Geoffrey Hunter's youngest biological son, attending Antinous Uni.

Todd Middleton: A seventeen-year-old heterosexual whose death pro-voked change in Hadrian's sexual reform laws. After Frank Hunter's trial for Todd's murder and the trial of Gideon Weller (Warden of the Northeast Reeducation Camp) for rape and physical and emotional abuse of reedu-cation students, the country of Hadrian no longer exiled heterosexual men and women unless proven they participated in penile vaginal intercourse.

Matthew Molloy: Detritus fisherman for Hunter National Detritus Fisheries; member of Hadrian's re-ed class.

Cantara Raboud: Faial Raboud's biological daughter, heterosexual; a student attending Augustus Uni; Vice President of Augustus Uni GSA.

Faial Raboud: Hadrian's top defense lawyer.

Devon Rankin: Todd Middleton's old boyfriend; Roger Hunter's old boyfriend; a lieutenant in Hadrian's National Army.

Ms. Sterne: Crystal Albright's biological aunt. Math teacher at Pride High. Also, the teacher who exposed Todd Middleton and made sure authorities suspected him of having raped Crystal.

Elena Stiles: President of Hadrian. Her non-biological daughter, Crystal Albright, is bisexual.

Jeremy Stoker: A closeted bisexual man, and co-owner of the historic Cattle Ranch. Geoffrey and Dean spent their second anniversary at the Cattle Ranch.

Destiny Stuttgart: Dean's grandmother (mimi) and the last of the founding family members living (one of five families) of the country of Hadrian.

Jason Warith: Todd Middleton's guardian at the Northeast Reeducation Camp. Responsible for Gideon Weller's arrest. Promoted to head of Hadrian's Reeducation System.

Gideon Weller: Former warden of the Northeast Reeducation Camp; his use of corporal punishment and taunting of young men who had had sex with women was so brutal six boys committed suicide under his watch. He was eventually charged with causing unnecessary trauma to the wards in his camp and with rape. He was found guilty of all charges and elected to drink Black Henbane rather than face exile for his crimes.

humanity is
one separated being
open your arms soul
tara may fowler

Prologue

A Plague of Prejudice Threatens to Undermine Hadrian's Society

Submitted to Professor Cora Politis
Sociology 100
By Tara May Fowler

What is the greatest evil that befalls Hadrian today? Some have suggested our inability to curtail wild climate change that has besieged our planet for nearly two hundred years. Many would suggest it is the constant threat of insurgents battering against our walls due to the outside world's inability to curtail the plague of human population. Underlying each of these theories is one that many of Hadrian's citizens believe (perhaps even the majority): all the evils of this world, from those we suffer inside Hadrian to those suffered by the supposedly barbarian masses outside our walls, land firmly on the shoulders of heterosexuals—the strai—"knives" as we like to call those males and "stabs," our preferred insult slung against the females. And yet, all of these theories would be wrong. The real ill that sickens Hadrian to its very core is prejudice, plain and simple.

What form of prejudice, one might ask? It is the overwhelming hatred Hadrian holds against heterosexuals. Bigotry will be our country's undoing. We must, as a nation of enlightened people, find a way to reconcile and accept all forms of human sexual expression by consenting adults. Without this basic understanding and acceptance of humanity, Hadrian will never be able to develop and grow as a healthy society for all its citizens.

Let us begin first with climate change. How is it that we have managed to create the misconception that it is the result of heterosexuality? Some say that overpopulation lent itself to industrialization. As humanity's numbers grew, so too did the need to mine for the materials required to create energy. Not only must we keep ourselves sheltered and warm, but we need to eat. Thus began the excessive raping of the land for agriculture and stock. There is no doubt that as the human population grew, man's respect for nature diminished at an equal, if not exponential, rate. But why must heterosexuals be blamed for all of this? Is it not wiser to consider man's greed as the greater ill? The need for power, money, control—these were, and *still are*, the greater motivators for man's abuses of this earth. Yes, the human population must be restrained, but history has proven that, with the use of proper birth control, a heterosexual family need not exceed that of the expected size dictated by Hadrian's government.

Then there are the outsider barbarians trying to break through our front line of defense: Hadrian's Wall. As much as Melissa Eagleton, propagandist extraordinaire for Hadrian's National News (HNN), would like us to think, not all of these people are heterosexual. In fact, I will go so far as to say they are no different than us. They, too, can be seen in light of the Kinsey scale. Kinsey was, after all, a part of this outside society some two hundred years ago. According to Kinsey, over 10 percent (14 percent based on my calculations of his point scale of 0 to 6) of the human population across the globe is heterosexual. Another 10 to 14 percent or so are homosexual. For the purpose of this essay, I leave out transgendered individuals, accepting their unique status and assuming each to hold his or her own sexual orientation according to his or her true gender. Everyone else, therefore, is somewhere in between, identifying at varying degrees of bisexuality.

Now, Hadrian's scientists claim to have eradicated 14 percent of the human gene that is heterosexual, but those citizens, like Todd Middleton, who only experience opposite sex attraction, know this propaganda to be sheer nonsense. Hadrian's citizens have been fooled into believing any opposite sex attraction is merely a teenage phase or limited to bisexual tendencies that are to be repressed and ignored.

Every Hadrian citizen knows full well what to think of heterosexuals. We hear the expression, "That's so strai," daily. A day doesn't pass when someone doesn't jokingly, or seriously, insult a friend by saying, "You're acting strai." If a man gets too friendly with a female friend, even just the simple act of falling against her by accident while laughing, he will be accused of being a "cunt-hammer"—an insult verging on bad porn! That is certainly not one of our kinder put-downs. A woman perceived to be straight is condemned as "a breeder." She is also called a "sagging hole" or a "flapping vagina." I don't think there is another community of people in Hadrian that suffers as much extreme verbal abuse.

Let me give you an example. As a youth attending junior high school at the Virginia Woolf Children's Academy, my peers ruthlessly pushed me into the coat stalls of my seventh grade classroom. Tauntingly, I was asked whether I was strai. Not having heard the word before and unsure of its meaning, I declined to answer. When I enquired as to the meaning of this word, fearing somehow it wasn't meant to be nice, my classmates insisted I answer the question first. "Just say, 'Yes,'" they insisted. "Just say, 'Yes.'" Finally, I caved to their aggression and replied in the positive, which resulted in one of the most negative moments of my early life. I quickly learned what a strai was, and from then on, I was identified as such amongst my classmates. That they had cajoled this so called confession out of me made no difference at all in their minds. I had admitted to being a strai, so it was now open season on little Tara Fowler.

Proof actual was given the day our seventh grade art teacher told us we could draw any animal we wanted. Earlier that week, my mothers had taken my little brother and me to Hadrian's Zoo. I had watched with fascination as Lucy the elephant sucked water into her great trunk and then sprayed it all over her body. In retro art class, we were given pencil crayons and paper to draw. It was always exciting to be able to work with our hands, so it was a class I especially looked forward to. On one particular day, shortly after our family's visit to the zoo, I decided to draw Lucy just as I remembered her with water spraying all over her back. I began with the trunk lifted high in the air with water spraying up. Before I was able to draw any more, Colin McMasters saw my picture and starting screaming, "She's drawing a dick! She's drawing a hard dick, and it's squirting!" He then began laughing while all the other children gathered round to peer down at my elephant's trunk deemed penis. Mr. Walton soon arrived at the desk and shooed the other children back to their desks. He glanced at my drawing, took a voc shot, and then grabbed my elbow and led me into the principal's office. My mothers were contacted, the image of a "penis ejaculating" was immediately sent to them, and home life proved unbearable thereafter. Not even my own mothers would believe I was drawing a picture of Lucy the elephant!

Verbal abuse soon escalates into physical abuse. We've all heard the horror stories of what happens at reeducation camps. Frank Hunter's trial for the death of his lover, Todd Middleton, revealed the extreme depths of this cruelty. The bloodstained paddle wielded against this youth and numerous other items hang in the main hall of the Ministry of Education as a stark reminder of our hatred of strais. I, too, suffered cruelly from the violent abuses of my peers: chases home, being bumped into, pushed aside as well as being laughed at. I watched boys believed to be straight picked on and attacked by gangs of boys and girls. It seems like there is nothing more disgusting in the minds of Hadrian's citizens than the heterosexual male. I feel this is truly unfortunate because I am lucky enough to have befriended a heterosexual man. He is loving, generous, kind, and defies all of the stereotypes we have placed on straight men of being dirty, violent, and sexually aggressive. My friend shows no signs of being a sexual psychopath roaming the alleys of our good country to find women to rape or little girls to abuse. He is simply a hardworking man who wants to be accepted for who he is in this world. Instead, we mock, berate, and bully men like him as well as any women sexually attracted to men. I was saddened by the news the other day when, on HNN, Melissa Eagleton reported how a middle-aged man, a detritus fisherman, was beaten to death and then had his body set on fire after he admitted to having never been successfully reeducated. And although there was no evidence of his being sexually active, he was sought out and murdered.[3] Even though heterosexuality was decriminalized shortly after Gideon Weller's trial, the hatred of heterosexuals continues.

It is this extreme abuse that I see as Hadrian's illness. Not only is 14 percent of our population condemned simply for being born—and no, being straight is not a choice—but at least 72 percent of all of Hadrian is bisexual. These figures come from Kinsey's 0 to 6 point scale,[4] which has created

---

[3] http://uk.reuters.com/article/2013/06/03/uk-russia-killing-gay-idUKBRE9520A120130603
[4] Kinsey, Alfred Charles et al. *Sexual Behavior in the Human Male*. W. B. Saunders, 1948.

the most demeaning of insults, "Heterosexuals are ZEROES." Parents are the worst for using this slur. I can't tell you how many times I heard my parents and the parents of friends utter the phrase, "There are no Zeroes in my family." I wonder whether it has ever occurred to these people how many of their own children, or their children's friends, they are hurting with such a trite dismissal of at least 14 percent of our population. And what about those children who are a 1 or a 2? They, no doubt, identify more with heterosexuals than they do with homosexuals. Should we not be cognizant of how we make our children feel whenever we unwittingly and blatantly abuse the heterosexual population?

It isn't just those on the scale from 0 to 2 that I worry about. The 3s, 4s, and, on rare occasion, even 5s will experience opposite sex attraction. Each person who feels this sexual energy feels the stigma of hate our society has cast upon the damnable het'ros. As a nation, we place up to 86 percent of our population at risk of psychological stress due to this deeply imbedded hate. And, ironically, it is those who have experienced opposite sex attraction who are most likely to repress those feelings and convert them into hate. Thus, Hadrian citizens lash out against one another in a desperate attempt to deflect any suggestion of their own opposite sex attractions.

So how do we end the hate? By ending Hadrian's official stance that heterosexuals are a danger to society. By closing reeducation camps that do more damage than good, and most importantly, by no longer denying heterosexuals access to higher education. Parents need to accept their children regardless of whom they love, and, most importantly, bisexuals should not be forced to "pick a side," but, rather, be allowed to love whomever they fall in love with regardless of gender.

BOOK 1

THINGS FALL APART

Frank's Mantra

The first day of Frank Hunter's official incarceration is held in Lieutenant-General Pauloosie's office at the Southwest Gate. As the circumstances surrounding Todd Middleton's death were unique, Judge Julia Reznikoff, Hadrian's top judge, made a precedent-setting decision surrounding Frank Hunter's sentence. Instead of being required to choose between exile or death for murdering his best friend and lover, Frank Hunter is required to serve a life sentence in service to his country. No longer the wiry, vibrant young man who had longed to study cosmetics and become a makeup artist, Frank Hunter is now Private Recruit Hunter, Penal status.

"Step up on the desk, private." It is Lieutenant-General Pauloosie who gives the order, but the desk in question is not his own. A smaller desk has been brought into the room for this purpose. Frank does as ordered. He is cold, rigid, unbending in thought and emotion. *Look directly ahead. Do as I'm told. Think nothing. Feel nothing at all.* This has been Frank's internalized mantra from the moment Judge Julia Reznikoff sentenced him to a lifetime of service in the army. Stunned by the knowledge that he would be forced to live after he had already decided he would drink Black Henbane, the young man now puts all his energy towards voiding himself, emptying his mind, heart, and soul. If he must exist, he will do so, but in body only, reminding himself over and over with yet another mantra: *No family! No lovers! No friends!*

As Frank stands on the desk, he feels a hand lift up his pant leg—a dull khaki since he is already in uniform—and lower his sock. "Lift your foot," a voice orders. It is not the general. Frank doesn't care who it is. He will not acknowledge anyone except his senior officers and then only to salute and to obey.

The general seems to understand Frank since he repeats the order, always with an edge of command, but in this case, not unkindly. "Lift your foot for the tattoo artist, private." Frank does as instructed, and the tattoo artist removes the sock from Frank's foot (he had removed his boots as instructed when he first entered the general's office). Frank feels the cool antiseptic wipe followed by a series of pin pricks of the needle as the bar code for his tactile tattoo restraint is slowly being etched into the skin above his left ankle.

Being one to talk while he works, the tattoo artist tries to engage Frank in conversation. "They told me you didn't want any fancy images. This barcode's, quite frankly, boring. I'm quite skilled with the tactile tattoo. I can make all kinds of designs around the coding so that it doesn't have to look like late twentieth century merchandise." Frank ignores the man. Not one to work in silence, though, the tattoo artist rambles on. As he is getting nothing out of the private, the artist turns his attention to the only other person in the room. "Now, General, you look like the kind of man who could do with some nice ear design or neck art. Tactile tattoos are for vocs, you know, and the reception from one of these babies is ten times better than any piece of jewelry." When the general points to the right side of his head, the artist, catching on, tries another pitch. "My tactile tattoos even rival the most sophisticated micro-chip implants. Why settle for an implant when you can get the same or better from a little body art?" Stopping now to look over his work, the artist adds, "You know, I do believe this is the first time I ever heard of one being used to control a man's movement."

The general, not wanting time wasted on idle chat, grunts and motions for the artist to get back to work. Ensuring his point is clear, he adds, "Done?"

"Patience, my good man. Tactile tattoos are a fine art, even when the design is as mundane as this one. I still have to input the micro-chips. You want it to work, don't you? Otherwise, your prisoner private could just prance away at his leisure." Finally sensing that neither man in the room is willing to be audience to his thoughts, the tattoo artist lapses into silence and completes the job at hand. "There, done. Now, all you have to do is scan his ankle barcode with your voc, blink activate, and this boy will be contained to a three-mile radius extending from this office." Grimacing slightly at the agony that awaits the young soldier, the artist still asks the general, "Care to test my work?" Both the general and the tattoo artist note the lack of reaction from Private Recruit Hunter, the one who will soon be feeling just how painful it will be for him if he ever attempts to cross the threshold of his three-mile barrier.

"Yes." He grimaces slightly and almost looks apologetically Frank Hunter's way, but he catches himself in time to avoid looking sentimental towards one who is not only his subordinate, but also prisoner.

The three-mile walk seemed but a moment for Frank. He refuses to register time and distance. Without thought, another mantra pops into his head to help him distance himself from the world and everything in it: *Do what I have to do. Go where I have to go.*

"You needn't step over the line, private; just reach your hand forward."

The instant Frank's hand passes the three-mile line, his body is wracked with pain. It is as if someone has ignited his blood, which is now pumping scalding hot throughout his veins. No longer in control, Frank's body threatens to fall forward into the forbidden zone, which would continue to sear him through with enough pain to knock him out cold, even kill him. Luckily, the general catches Frank before this can happen. "That's enough of a test." The general speaks these words kindly as he helps to steady Frank, whose seizure has dropped him to his knees. After helping the private to stand, the general thanks the tattoo artist before half-leading, half-carrying Private Frank Hunter back to the barracks. There are no doubts about it; the tactile tattoo ankle restraint will be successful in keeping Private Recruit Frank Hunter contained within his three-mile barrier.

* * * * *

Frank's Evaluations

**Initial Entrance Evaluation—Frank Hunter
(Private) {penal restriction}
Guillaume de la Chappelle, Colonel-HDF Training/Logistics
Dated this day, July 4, 21__.**

I met Private Frank Hunter two days after his sentencing to "life service" defending "the Wall." I was immediately struck by his stolid composure. He didn't have any "chip" on his shoulder about what had happened with the late Mr. Todd Middleton. There were no signs of remorse or grief. His expression remained blank throughout the interview—the perfect poker face—giving me the impression I was looking into the eyes of a cold-hearted killer, qualities no doubt useful in a soldier, but not in a soldier who wishes to retain his humanity. This unique trait is rather disconcerting when witnessed in one so young. Private Hunter was also taciturn— another useful trait in a soldier, but one also reflecting a lack of any social skills. I was assigned with other command training officers to evaluate his ability to integrate into the Hadrian Defense Force, become a soldier, and to find out what abilities and talents could be used in training him in the right areas of said training. We know he is willing to kill strais, so I am suggesting we train him as a wall sniper. His full physical evaluation reveals to us a youth in prime condition; his school report identified him as an athlete in track, basketball, and volleyball, thereby collaborating that fact. His height, 6' 4", was, and is, a clear advantage. He has a sturdy, muscular physique so no "whipping into shape" is needed. Instead, we will allow him the opportunity to create his own physical regime to maintain the necessary weight and strength required of a wall soldier. Unfortunately, he was not a member of the wrestling team in high school so he will need the basic training required for hand-to-hand combat.

Devon's Fury

Tryouts used to be such an exciting time for Devon Rankin, but this year, he can't help but wonder why he even showed up at all.

The previous year's tryouts had certainly been exhilarating, for Devon Rankin had spent the summer leading up to his grade eleven year training with his then boyfriend Todd Middleton. With Todd Middleton's guidance and advice, Devon was finally senior team material. Not only had he made the team, but he had earned the coveted position of first string along with Pride High's top players, Todd Middleton, Frank Hunter, and Crystal Albright.

This year's team is not so winning. Only two players from the first string remain, Devon and Millicent. Millicent is good, but of the five starters from last year, she was the weakest, and from the look of the extra weight she has put on since the last season, Devon sees little hope for his senior year b-ball team. Todd Middleton is dead, and that bastard Frank, who murdered him, is incarcerated at the Southwest Gate serving a life sentence in Hadrian's military. And Albright, *Crystal fucking Albright*, she gets to prance around the school as if nothing bad happened, as if her perfect little world had no impact on the lives of others. Every time Devon sees her in the halls, he has to fight back the urge to strangle her.

Devon goes through phases of wishing they'd let Frank drink henbane, exile him and—oddly, Devon can't figure this one out—feeling glad Frank suffered neither of the only two fates doled out in Hadrian's criminal justice system. Confused and rankled by Frank's sentence, Devon couldn't help but sneer. Though true that Todd Middleton had asked Frank to help him commit suicide, and also true that Todd had been raped and put through an incredible amount of emotional torture while in reeducation, Devon still saw Frank's act of suffocating his boyfriend—his?—mine or

Frank's?—as murder in the first degree. Devon was always angry these days. Not just because it appeared that Frank got away with murder, but Todd's girlfriend, Crystal *fucking* Albright, the girl Todd was accused of raping, though never proved, the girl who helped expose Todd and who refused to deny the accusation of rape, is also getting off scot-free. Devon scoffs, the same morning after Todd was pulled from class, Ms. Sterne, their math teacher (and Crystal's aunt) brought in Hadrian's prosecuting attorney, Graham Sabine, to warn the class about the need for secrecy. *Man,* Devon remembers, *he gave us quite the song and dance about protecting the victim, and boy did we fall for it. Crystal was playing it up, sitting there in her desk, bawling her pretty little eyes out with all the girls cooing and comforting her. And we all signed those fucking waivers. I can't even tell my moms without breaking the law. That fucking little bitch,* Devon thought then and still believes now, *is the main reason Todd Middleton is dead and I can't tell a God damn soul! I hate her, but she sure as fuck isn't worth getting exiled over. That fucking little—*

Devon hasn't even the time to finish his internal curse because Crystal Albright walks into the gym dressed for tryouts. Devon stares incredulously. The coach, who was just about to blow the whistle to get everyone's attention, has also stopped dead in her tracks, her whistle poised ready at her open mouth. Silence strikes a deafening blow in the gym as all the students gape at Crystal's entrance.

"What?" she queries defensively.

Crystal's anger and derision slam into Devon like a punch in the stomach. He grunts and, after gaining composure, swears. He had been taking practice shots prior to Crystal's entrance and is now holding one of the b-balls scattered around the gymnasium for tryouts. Swiveling on his toes, he throws the ball with all his might across the gymnasium, slamming it into the far wall, the smacking of the ball reverberating throughout the gym and the ball bounces until it rolls and comes to a stop on the opposite side of the gym. The ball remains the only movement and sound as everyone stares at Crystal. Some look at her with a mixture of pity and disgust, one or two smile at her audacity, and one, Millicent, Crystal's girlfriend in their grade ten year, looks upon her with pity and remorse. Devon's expression is hate; seething hate! The feelings he has for this girl and the role she played in the demise of Todd Middleton cannot be expressed in words, more so the pity for Devon, for if he could at least articulate how he was feeling, then his emotions wouldn't be rotting away and corroding him from the inside. With anger boiling deep inside, words burst out of Devon like a geyser exploding. "What the fuck is she doing here?" Turning now to the coach, he expostulates, "There is no fucking way I'll play on the same team as that bitch!" The last thing Devon expected was for Crystal Albright to presume she was still a part of Todd Middleton's team, for Todd's team it was and will be as long as Devon Rankin has any say in the matter.

Although this attack was expected and Crystal appears to remain calm and in control, her insides have turned to jelly and her knees feel weak. In as cool and controlled a manner as she can muster, Crystal reminds Devon, "You don't get to make that decision, Rankin."

Crystal's words stir up something inside of Coach Miller who, instead of sanctioning Devon Rankin for his outburst, takes one determined step towards the young woman before saying, "That's right." The coach cannot help but study the face of the young woman who destroyed the life of her star player, and, although she only surmises the young woman's role, Rankin's outburst confirms her suspicion. The students in Ms. Sterne's math class may have signed waivers and none will risk exile by revealing the truth, but that hasn't stopped the rumor mill from turning its wheel over the river gossip. Coach Miller has heard much and believes all. "I do. And Rankin and I are like-minded. I will not coach a team with you on it."

Crystal is stunned. She never dreamed her coveted role on the team could be swiped from her. "But I'm your best player."

"Was, were, one of my best players." She stops momentarily as if to ponder, "The other two, hmm, where are they?" Now with sarcasm thick and dripping, Coach Miller adds, "Oh, yeah, Todd is dead and Frank is imprisoned in the military!" Glaring at Crystal with hate enough to rival Devon, she concludes, "No, Miss Albright, I will not be coaching you."

"You have to," Crystal sputters. "My mothers…"

The coach now bears down on the girl. "I don't give a rat's ass who your mothers are." Few people know that Crystal Albright's mama is President Stiles. "They can fire me for all I care. I will never coach you again."

Stunned by this violent outburst against her, Crystal backs up, tripping slightly on her heels before turning and running out of the gym.

No one saw Crystal Albright again. It was rumored that she had transferred to Virginia Woolf High, following her aunt, Ms. Sterne, who had taken a job teaching math at the illustrious high school, but when Devon later investigated Crystal's whereabouts, he had some odd sadistic need to know what had happened to her; she was not registered, and no one, not even Millicent or Lolita, Crystal's exes, had any idea where she had gone. It was as if Crystal Albright had vanished off the face of the earth. She had effectively hidden herself deep inside the bowels of Hadrian. The only upside to this horrible experience was that the coach had somehow managed to escape dismissal.

* * * * *

Six Month Evaluation and Review—Frank Hunter (Private) {penal restriction}
Guillaume de la Chappelle, Colonel-HDF Training/Logistics
Dated this day, January 2, 21__.

As my transfer to the Midwest Gate was recently approved, I requested that Private Frank Hunter be transferred with me so I can continue working with this extraordinary youth and participate in his reviews. Although Lieutenant-General Pauloosie was reluctant to release the private, General Birtwistle considered my request and readily agreed. It took little convincing considering Private Hunter was amongst the first of the recruits to complete effectively phase one of his marksmanship training. He has become the fastest in his company at disassembling, cleaning, and reassembling his weapon. He has excelled in all safe handling procedures as well as skillfully loading and unloading his weapon.[5] During his arms training, Private Hunter surpassed the required scores, with very high marks in both close range pistol shooting and long range rifle shooting. He is a "natural" marksman and has completed his training with Expert status. Private Hunter is also seen and respected as a leader. His fellow recruits often turn to him for advice and assistance, and Private Hunter has never been known to refuse aid to any of them. Combined, these behaviors put him in an elite group for consideration in Defense Sniper School training, to include physical training, hand-to-hand combat (offense/defense), combat tactics, defense strategy planning, and emergency medical care. He is excellent officer material (with one obvious exception: Private Hunter refuses to interact with anyone when not on duty), though present laws and the sentence given to him do prevent his promotion to officer rank.

---

[5] http://www.military.com/join-armed-forces/army-weapons-qualification-course.html

One Year Evaluation and Review—Frank Hunter (Private) {penal restriction} Guillaume de la Chappelle, Colonel-HDF Training/Logistics Dated this day, July 2, 21__.

As one of twenty-six gate area-training officers at HDFA, I have assigned Private Hunter to Gate 4 Defense Area (Lt-General Birtwistle, Commander). Though Private Hunter is restricted by the tactile tattoo restraint, he has performed said duties well. He has excelled in marksmanship (pistol and rifle), guerrilla tactics, and strategy planning. He works well with others and is highly thought of as one of our best Defense Snipers. Regardless of the overall respect held towards Private Hunter, some fellow defenders of Hadrian's Wall, due to his "penal restriction" status, often avoid him. It is also noteworthy that Private Hunter in no way seeks camaraderie amongst his fellow soldiers. When off duty, he isolates himself from others. When not engrossed in historical texts found in the military library museum, Private Hunter is often seen running long distances, and putting himself through continued, extensive physical training. Private Hunter recently scored the highest award in physical combat training in the Advance Defense Sniper School at the Hadrian Defense Academy for Enlisted Personnel. During the annual physical training evaluation (running, strength, endurance, offense, defense, arms/weapons), he was awarded the second highest score possible. Again, I would recommend him for promotions in rank were it not for the "penal restriction" limiting him to private.

Geoffrey and Dean

Dean knows he is being cowardly, yet he cannot bring himself to say the words face-to-face. They had fought again last night. Dean told Geoffrey that he hated him, and the look of anguish that sprung onto his lover's face was unbearable. Dean had to turn and look away. The last words that Geoffrey spoke were soft and bitten with remorse. "Well, then, Dean, if that's the way you feel, I guess you better leave me." Geoffrey turned and left the living room. Dean kept his back turned but waited quietly for Geoffrey to return. Self-recrimination swirled within the delay. *What must Geoffrey see in me?* he wondered. *What must he be feeling? Anger? Hatred? Remorse?* Turning now, Dean walked towards the hallway to stare down what now appeared to be a vast emptiness towards their bedroom. The door was closed. Dean hadn't even heard Geoffrey shut it. Dean suddenly realized it wasn't their bedroom anymore. Knowing he could not go back in there, he had chosen to sleep in Frank's bed last night.

Even knowing the words he had uttered the night before were lies, Dean cannot bring himself to take them back. *Geoffrey is angry and rightfully so*, he reminds himself. Just as he had tried to talk Dean out of testifying at Gideon Weller's trial, Geoffrey was now trying to convince Dean not to pursue suing Hadrian's government for damages committed against heterosexuals incarcerated at the Northeast Reeducation Camp. That Geoffrey keeps trying to talk him out of taking legal recourse is hurtful, and Dean isn't sure whether he can forgive the man. In his heart of hearts, Dean knows Geoffrey's reasoning is out of love. *He doesn't want me to have to relive the horrors of reeducation.* But the way Geoffrey worded his concern was inappropriate. "There are," he had said, "plenty of men crawling out of the woodwork willing to testify." Geoffrey never should have worded it that way; those words, they suggested Dean and the other men abused by

Gideon Weller were somehow acting in an unseemly manner, even though Dean knew that was not what Geoffrey had meant; he had even tried to take the words back, but to no avail. Some things said can never be unsaid. *All Geoffrey really wanted to express,* Dean suggests to himself, *is his fear that I'm putting myself through a hideous emotional trial.* Geoffrey even attempted to express this when he had shouted, "How can any man live with so much anguish, despair and hate?" Dean shudders as he remembers his reaction, a wild scream having emerged from his breast, "But I need to do this!" *Why can't Geoffrey understand? I need to heal and I won't be able to until that bastard is finally exiled and the government acknowledges its role in the wrongs committed against Hadrian's heterosexual citizens.*

Dean feels an insurmountable amount of hatred towards Gideon Weller, and although justified, it is beyond the bounds of reason. Gideon Weller had been the warden of the Northeast Reeducation camp where Dean had been sentenced after being caught kissing a girl. It was also the camp where Todd Middleton had been incarcerated for having been a sexually active heterosexual as well as accused of—but never proven—rape. Todd Middleton was the sixth supposedly active heterosexual youth who had been accused of rape who had successfully committed suicide while under the command of Gideon Weller. The reason why these young men had committed suicide came to light during Frank Hunter's trial. Gideon Weller had raped each one under the auspice of having performed "medicinal intercourse." In every case, he had claimed the youth in question had requested sexual intercourse to help him learn to accept Hadrian's chosen sexual orientation, but Dean knew better and so did Weller's henchman, Darrell Jeffreys. Faial Raboud, Frank's lawyer, had successfully got the man to confess the truth at Frank's trial. This confession was the basis for Gideon Weller's trial, and Dean felt obligated to testify against the man who had made his own life a living hell and who had intentionally worked to destroy the boy Dean loved like a son, his best friend Will Middleton's boy, Todd Middleton. Dean had promised Will on his deathbed to look after Todd, but he had failed. Now Todd was dead and Dean felt responsible. He had to make sure the man who really killed Todd, not Frank, but Weller, suffered the severest penalty of the law: exile or assisted suicide. In Hadrian, there are only two sentence options for anyone convicted of a crime, and for Dean, not even death was good enough for Gideon Weller. Now that Weller had been convicted, the country waited with bated breath for his decision: exile or death. Dean did not want Weller to choose death, to drink the poison Hadrian's government cultivated for those who could not bear facing life outside Hadrian's Wall. He wanted Weller to be exiled. Government propaganda was clever enough to have everyone, including those who saw holes in the system's management, convinced that life outside of Hadrian was nothing short of hell. With a planet overflowing with human population, it was relatively easy for Hadrian's satellite system to collect countless horror stories about the squalor of life for billions living outside Hadrian's Wall. Images of skeletal bodies, wasted corpses, warring over life-sustaining land, even cannibalism have made their way into Hadrian's propaganda machine, leaving little room for doubt that the citizens of Hadrian are living in an enclosed utopia and anyone who fights against its rules is a fool deserving of death or exile.

Too many thoughts are running through Dean's mind, rendering him incapable of making sense of who he is, what he wants, or what he needs to do. All he knows is that he can no longer live a life of lies. As a result, he has decided to leave Geoffrey, the man he has been married to for twenty-four years; the man he loves but will no longer allow himself to hold. He must go. Dean's grandmother, Destiny Stuttgart, or "Mimi" to Dean, has offered him a home. He will take her up on this offer. She lives in Augustus City, having moved there during the city's rebuilding. Using her status as a founding mother, Destiny Stuttgart helped the fraught and careworn city raise itself up out of the ashes—nuclear ashes—like the phoenix reborn. Even with Mother Stuttgart's presence, Augustus City continues to suffer the stigma of that fateful day, 6-13, when a Christian fanatic drove across the border and exploded a dirty nuclear bomb, destroying most of the city and killing Hadrian citizens in the hundreds of thousands. One victim was Dean's best friend, Will Middleton. He had been working just south of Augustus city when the bomb exploded. Though he suffered no immediate damage, the cancer came shortly after. Years of battling the wasting disease had sucked his family of all financial resources until at last he died, leaving his son to be raised by a bitter, discontented man unable to bear the loss of his partner. And though Dean had done all within his power to protect Todd, he had failed the youth. The boy ended up suffering the same fate he had, being incarcerated in the Northeast Reeducation Camp under the tutelage of one Gideon Weller.

And now, with all these thoughts muddied over the love he once felt for

Geoffrey, Dean chooses to leave. He chooses to leave while Geoffrey is at work. He made no mention of this the night before when they had fought. His last words being "I hate you" and Geoffrey's being "You better leave me." And this morning when he woke up, Dean knew that was exactly what he was going to do. Blinking open his vocal contact lens, Hadrian's main means of communication, and staying connected to the country's information wave, Dean selects the timed pin messaging system. This allows him to record a message to Geoffrey and "pin it" to Geoffrey's messaging system but with a time delay so Geoffrey isn't notified immediately. Most people use this system for sending birthday cards, congratulations, and the like; rarely is it used to send someone bad news. Dean, aware of this incongruity, knows the "pin" will cause his lover even greater pain, but he simply cannot summon up the courage to tell Geoffrey to his face, so, Dean chooses five o'clock for the message to be received. The message simply states, "I took your advice. I'm leaving." Feeling that is too curt, he decides to add, "I'm going to stay with Mimi. She thinks she can get me into Augustus Uni. I always wanted to study medicine." He wants to say "Love, Dean," but that just feels cruel, so he doesn't even sign off. By the time Geoffrey reads the message, Dean will be on Hadrian's Public Tram, making his way south to Augustus City, where he will begin to reconstruct his life.

* * * * *

**Second Year Evaluation and Review—Frank
Hunter (Private) {penal restriction}
Guillaume de la Chappelle, Colonel-HDF Training/Logistics
Dated this day, July 3, 21__.**

In Private Hunter's recent evaluation and testing (physical, arms, education, abilities), he revealed he has embarked on an independent study and research of Hadrian's history, including border defense and outside infiltration tactics, such as guerrilla warfare training (with a list of improvements for better Wall defense, tactics, and offense warfare as needed). {REDACTED—His recent tests in leadership, tactics, strategy planning, and combat analysis show an advanced knowledge and awareness of several areas recently assessed by the HDF Command (classified-restricted access)}. The recommendations made by this youth should be taken into advisement. His "penal restriction" status should not be a reason to ignore his advice.

It is this officer's belief that Private Hunter would serve our country far more effectively if he were no longer restricted to private status. His tactile tattoo restraint should be removed and he should be duly promoted to lieutenant. His exemplary work over the first two years of service has surpassed that of the majority of military career officers.

Third Year Evaluation and Review—Frank Hunter (Private) {penal restriction}
Guillaume de la Chappelle, Colonel-HDF Training/Logistics
Dated this day, July 2, 21__.

Private Hunter continues to improve his skills in leadership, tactics, strategy planning, and combat analysis. As well, Private Hunter continues to excel in marksmanship (pistol and rifle), guerrilla tactics, and strategy planning.

All recommendations made by Private Hunter have thus far been overlooked due to his penal restriction.

All recommendations made by this officer to remove Private Hunter's tactile tattoo restraint and revoke his penal restriction status have thus far been overlooked.

Private Hunter has not been promoted. Regardless of continuously being overlooked, Private Hunter continues to excel as a soldier in Hadrian's National Army.

BOOK 2

HADRIAN'S RAGE

Salve!

Hadrian's Rage!
HNN—Melissa Eagleton Reporting

Almost three years have passed since President Stiles signed government bill 657—the Heterosexual Legalization Act—into law, making it legal for heterosexuals to live openly in our country. The HLA states that no man or woman will suffer exile if caught in compromising circumstances including such acts as kissing, walking arm in arm, hugging, etc. Also, the HLA clarifies the private sexual acts an opposite sex couple can engage in without penalty under the law: all forms of coitus being permissible with the exception of penile vaginal intercourse. Many supporters of equal rights for straight men and women claim this law is no different than the one it replaces since men and women were only ever exiled after the state could prove they did indeed have opposite sex intercourse used in the act of procreation. There is a key difference, though, as prior to the HLA, any of our youth caught in any compromising position were required by law to attend reeducation, whereas HLA now stipulates that registration for reeducation is at the parents' discretion. Nor will Hadrian's quadrant officials and peace officers incarcerate a same-sex couple on "suspicion of heterosexual behavior." HLA stipulates that concrete evidence of the man's penis having penetrated the female's vaginal region must be presented prior to arrest.

Regardless of its similarity to the law it replaces, HLA, not even three years old, has caused a seismic uproar in our small country. It is as if Hadrian has gone mad! The events that led up to this monumental change in our laws started with the death of Todd Middleton, built in force with the sentencing of Frank Hunter, and culminated into a class eight tremblor with Gideon Weller's decision to drink henbane rather than face exile.

Most, I'm sure, remember Gideon Weller's trial. It lasted well over a year and was the key focus of every *Salve!* for over nine months. Charged on multiple counts of rape, torture, and abuse of the many youth registered under his care at the Northeast Reeducation Camp, Gideon Weller ultimately confessed while being interrogated by Hadrian's National Prosecutor, Graham Sabine. Gideon Weller was also charged with inciting suicide in no less than six boys at his camp, the last being that of seventeen-year-old Todd Middleton. As a recipient of an early entrance sports scholarship at Antinous Uni, Todd Middleton's exposure, followed shortly by his traumatic murder, which many suggest was assisted suicide, truly was the beginning of the chaos our country is now suffering. As well as having been Hadrian's "golden boy," Todd Middleton was the son of Hadrian's most famous agricultural engineer, Will Middleton. Will Middleton was the man who successfully genetically modified the soybean plant to grow in our northern climate. Considered a hero to our nation for helping Hadrian achieve close to 90 percent sustainability, it was revealed at Frank Hunter's trial that Will Middleton, like his son, was heterosexual. In the years since these devastating events took place, our good country has become polarized—split in its opinions regarding its founding values. Although everyone agrees to the necessity of keeping Hadrian's population at the ten million maximum, opinions differ as to the best means of maintaining that optimum. Let me begin by explaining to you the nature of these opposing factions.

There are those who firmly believe that heterosexuality is the central ill that has caused humanity to be in this fix in the first place. These people we all know as Hadrian's Conservative Right. They claim that heterosexual lustful ways and a propensity for power and greed are what propelled mankind into its current horror. This sect also blames religious heterosexual supremacist fanaticism for suggesting that the planet and all its natural resources belong to humanity to do with as we choose. Their mission statement: "to return Hadrian back to its founding principles by criminalizing all forms of heterosexual behaviors as deemed necessary by our founding families."

A second, equally vocal, group has emerged, and although the Conservative Right sees it as pandering to the heterosexual agenda, the leader of this opposition says it has but one goal, to educate Hadrian, and then the rest of humanity, of one simple fact: that we are all one. This pro-strai faction believes that if we are to rectify the damage we have done to this planet and diminish the excess of human population, then we must work as one. It is interesting to note that this group is being led by none other than our founding mother, Destiny Stuttgart. And, according to our founding mother, too many unfortunate incidents have begun to molest the true beauty of Hadrian's culture.

Anger, violent anger, has swept our nation, with much of that anger directed towards our heterosexual and bisexual citizens. Just over a year following the trial of Hadrian versus Hunter, the body of a middle-aged man was found burned beyond recognition inside his bubble vehicle. He had been murdered, stabbed multiple times, according to the coroner's report, and died before he was put inside his bubble. It was then set on fire. Presumably, the killer, or killers, as may be the case, set the man's bubble on fire to destroy any evidence of their crime. And these killers were successful. Had there been any of the offending party's DNA on the victim's body or his bubble, none remained after the vehicle had been set ablaze.[6]

Two years ago, we saw the Face of Heterophobia[7] when Georgeta Serban was beaten in Riverside Park where she and her partner, Zagor Petrovich, were walking arm-in-arm. As with most hate crime attackers, Serban's abusers remain unidentified. They were wearing masks and gloves so none of their DNA was found on the victim, nor could they be identified. Zagor believes their attackers were men who were wearing some sort of device that had changed the sound of their voices. He said one attacker held him down while the other beat on his girlfriend. They were shouting out anti-strai slurs like "F'ing Breeder" and "Stab."

And then last year—I'm sorry; sometimes it is difficult to remain impartial in the light of such a crime—four-year-old Fredrik Mustonen was beaten to death by his mother, Hanna Mustonen, because he "walked and talked strai."[8] If you recall, the details of the case included her having hit him in the abdomen so hard his intestines broke. She did not deny her crime. She, in fact, was the one to rush Fredrik to the hospital when he was rendered unconscious by her beating. As you may remember, she had been beating this poor child for some time, and it was this last attack that ended it for him. Hanna Mustonen chose to drink henbane rather than face exile.

Recently, yet another detritus fisherman was allegedly fired because he is straight—sorry—this has not been confirmed and an ongoing investigation into these allegations continues—I have been asked to remind our

---

[6] http://www.pinknews.co.uk/2013/06/03/russia-second-man-in-a-month-killed-for-being-gay-was-stabbed-to-death-and-had-body-burned/

[7] http://www.thelocal.fr/20130408/the-face-of-homophobia-in-france

[8] http://www.dailymail.co.uk/news/article-2608174/Oregon-mom-25-sentenced-life-prison-savagely-beating-four-year-old-son-death-walked-talked-gay.html

viewers that currently in Hadrian, it is legal to fire an individual who is straight. This, of course, dates back to when heterosexuality itself was illegal. The sexual reform laws put in place over forty years ago are in flux as members of the government continue to argue over which aspects of these laws need to be retained and which need to be eradicated. Some believe it essential to wipe away all of the sexual reform laws—of course, no one wants anything that radical to occur. We must continue to preserve the very foundation upon which Hadrian was founded. Even if being heterosexual is now legal, certain heterosexual acts, such as penile vaginal penetration, must remain illegal. Those laws are the very premise upon which our good country was founded.

Hadrian's four cornerstones are critical: Hadrian's chosen lifestyle is homosexual; Hadrian will be a safe haven for homosexuals from around the globe; Hadrian's central focus is the creation and maintenance of a stable human population; Hadrian will create an ecologically sound balance between humanity and nature. The only cornerstone Mother Stuttgart's faction wishes to address is that of a "chosen" lifestyle. The basis of this faction's argument is that one does not choose to be straight just as one does not choose to be gay. Mother Stuttgart proposes rewording this cornerstone, returning it to what she claims to be its original version: Hadrian embraces the diverse spectrum of human sexual expression. Hadrian's Conservative Right argues the dangers of such a flexible representation of human sexuality, claiming we will be opening the floodgates to rampant acts of heterosexual fornications resulting in a massive increase in Hadrian's population. In return, Mother Stuttgart's faction ironically claims its battle is no different than the battle continuously being fought by our LGBTI brothers and sisters condemned by birth to live out their lives in the outside world. Perhaps our founding mother is right—but that is something Hadrian's citizens have to decide—ultimately, though, no matter where you may stand on the legal status of heterosexuality, surely no one, not even the Conservative Right, can condone these heinous acts of violence and murder. In the wake of the violence that has hit our country over the past few years, I believe it is fair to say that our country needs an amendment to its hate crime laws.

Vale!

Humanity's Sun

Dean's shoulders ache, but that does not deter him from bending into his work. It isn't his anatomy text doc he desperately needs to study; rather, he is mired in the difficult task of trying to create...design...some kind of symbol for the essence of humanity. Surrounding him are the scant few members of the GSA[9], an organization he established in his first year of uni, all trying to help him come up with some sort of symbol they can use to represent the heterosexual members of Hadrian's population. They have been batting ideas around for over an hour, but no one has come up with anything viable. Tara Fowler restates her original suggestion, "I still think we should go with a blue and pink striped flag, kinda like the rainbow flag, but with traditional boy/girl colors."

"Too cliché," says Cantara.

Dean smiles; Cantara is the only one able to disagree with Tara and not spark her self-defensive and argumentative nature. "Besides," he adds, "those colors have only been gender specific since the twentieth century, and only for the outside world. We don't want to go back to stereotyping."

Siddhartha Seshadri, whom everyone calls Sid, tries another approach. "Why don't we just use the joined male and female symbols? That would be easy and everyone knows it already."

Dean cocks an eyebrow. "That could work, I suppose." Although Dean is not crazy about the idea, he, like nearly everyone in the group, feels the need at least to consider, if not always agree, with Sid.

"Boring," says Cantara, who, unlike everyone else, is not so easily swayed by Sid's unintended influence. Cantara is extremely difficult to please and has no qualms uttering her opinion, regardless of how curt it

---

[9] GSA: Gay Straight Alliance

is or whom it might displease. "We need something colorful, something exciting. Something everyone can relate to. Something everyone loves, you know, to help make us more endearing. Right now when people think of us, all they think of are things like gross and despicable. We want them to see us as beautiful beings, just like every other human."

"That's the key, Cantara." Dean turns and smiles her way. Cantara flushes with joy. "Somehow, we've got to get across the idea that we are just like everyone else. It doesn't matter whom a person is attracted to so long as we respect one another as humans."

Sid laughs. "It sounds like you're talking about the gay pride flag, all the colors of the rainbow."

"Well, we can't use the rainbow flag; that's just for homosexuals," Tara objects.

"Why not?" Dean asks. The idea intrigues him. "I mean, the original pride flag was really meant to reflect the different colors of human sexuality, and we're one shade of that."

"Yeah, but in the outside world, het'ros mock homosexuals and their pride flag."

"Do they? Do they all?" Dean questions. "No, seriously, people, think about it. Most of us in this room are either straight or bi, except for Sid." Everyone turns and smiles Sid's way, even Cantara. So far, Sid is the only gay person willing to associate with the group to make it a real GSA. "According to the media, straight people don't exist in Hadrian." Smiling, Dean adds, "Well, we know better. Will Middleton was straight. His son, Todd Middleton, was straight. I'm straight. Tara and Cantara here are both straight." Continuing with his reasoning, Dean says, "So, if the media is wrong about us, then no one really knows what people outside our walls might think. All we have extolling strais' evils, and most certainly not any virtues, is HNN, and there are days when I doubt its veracity." No one can deny Dean's censorship of *Salve!* and Hadrian's National News. In the past year, HNN has undergone a major shift in management, and Melissa Eagleton has often contradicted herself in many of the *Salve!* episodes.

"I know," Prasert Niratpattanasai adds. "It's like she starts saying things that sound supportive, and then suddenly, she pulls at her ear and begins backtracking and spouting shit."

Sid agrees. Prasert and he are roommates and having been dating for over a year. Prasert is bisexual and his last lover was a girl. When Sid learned of their affair, he proved to be the best of friends. Rather than expose his companion, he sat and listened when Prasert explained the way he felt about Edit and why. Sid never pretended to understand, but since Prasert had become his closest companion, he couldn't bear the thought of ending their friendship. Sid understood why he had stood by Prasert shortly after Prasert's breakup with Edit. Their friendship had grown much deeper than "just friends," and Prasert was unwilling to deny their connection. He ended his affair with Edit, and when he told Sid why, Sid readily embraced him. "Prasert's right," Sid says, and then considering for a moment, he adds, "and so is Dean."

"Thanks, Sid." Dean appreciates Sid's vote in his favor because Sid's voice carries a lot of weight in their little group. "You're absolutely right, Prasert; we really can't depend on anything Eagleton and HNN have to say. They are running the Conservative Right Party line, and even if Eagleton wants to back us, clearly she can't. Either way, this part of our discussion is moot since our real concern is to decide on an appropriate symbol that reflects all of humanity so we are no longer promoting ourselves as heterosexuals against homosexuals. We need to promote ourselves as humans opening our arms to other humans."

"We could have a circle of men and women holding hands." Tara cringes as soon as she suggests it. Looking to Cantara, she apologizes. "I know, too hokey, right?"

Feeling like she has hurt her best friend's feelings, Cantara back-pedals. "No, it's not hokey at all. I kinda like it. What do you guys think?"

"It's one idea," Dean mutters. Blinking open a new doc and keyboard, he types the idea down. He then opens a design page. Blinking a holographic pencil mid-air, Dean reaches for it and attempts to draw out a rough sketch.

"We could make each person a different color of the rainbow," Prasert suggests.

"Maybe," says Dean, not sounding convinced. Even so, he taps the toolbar for colors and begins using the eyedropper tool to color in the stick bodies he's created. He shakes his head in disapproval.

Cantara laughs. "It's a good thing your vocation is nursing because you make one hell of a lousy artist!"

Dean joins the others in a chuckle at his expense. His digital design really sucks. Sitting back in his chair, he stares critically, then issues the vocal command, "Trash." The holographic image disappears. Turning grim before the others' jocularity has subsided, Dean gathers the group closer to him.

Cantara feels worried because Dean seems so solemn. "What is it, Dean? What's wrong?" The rest of the group gathers in closer, concerned, too.

"Nothing. I just hate remembering this man."

"Who?" Tara's curiosity is piqued. Dean is so amicable it seems odd he would express dislike towards any human being.

"An acquaintance from my past. He worked in the black market. He taught a friend and me a very important skill."

Prasert leans in closer. "What's that?"

"How to make sure your trashed items really get destroyed."

Cantara looks pale. "You mean just trashing doesn't trash?" She turns her worried look onto her friend.

Tara responds, "Dean taught me already." Cantara's sigh of relief is audible. "Apparently, anything you type is saved in the government's archives, so if you type something you don't want anyone else to see, you have to trash it, then retrieve it from the archives, and then destroy it completely."

"Show us." Sid's request sounds like a command. More than curious, this is a skill this group really needs to know.

"No item is really trashed. Like Tara said, everything you type is saved instantly to Hadrian's National Archives. There are different storage files like individual citizens, businesses, uni admin, uni profs, uni students..." Dean trails off. "See what I'm getting at? Even though I just trashed my design, it is still out there inside the Augustus Uni student folder deep inside HNA's cyber world. We have to hack inside, retrieve the file, and disintegrate it before anyone else discovers it there."

"How would anyone know it's even there?" asks Prasert, questioning the necessity of such an extreme action. "I mean, it could sit there for centuries, and no one would even notice it amongst so many other files. It's like a virtual warehouse filled with hundreds of billions of files."

"Yes, but all information is filed there, so if anybody ever wanted to find something out about you, something that could be used against you, well, that would be the place to look." A collective shudder ripples through the room.

"Wouldn't so many files overburden the system?" Prasert remains skeptical.

"Yes," Dean replies. "You're right. I asked my friend the same question. The government has sweeper programs that delete anything inconsequential like grocery lists and the like. Even things like children's journals, if all is innocent. The sweeper files scrub the system every morning sometime around 4 a.m. That is also when the system retrieves any sensitive information and then forwards it instantly to gov security. So," Dean warns, "whatever you type for the GSA, print and then destroy all files before 4 a.m. Understood?" Everyone nods in agreement.

"So," Sid asks, "how do you do it? Hack in to disintegrate your files?"

"Watch close." Dean may not have an instructor's finesse, but his serious demeanor makes up for that. All eyes and ears are attentive. "Step 1: Access hgov forward slash voclink. Step 2: Scroll down to the bottom of the link. Step 3: Here in small print—" Dean zooms in so the others can read—"is gov security. Tap. Step 4: Up pops verification code. Insert the following password: hgs6669." He pauses briefly before saying, "My friend's a sick bastard."

"I don't get it."

Tara laughs. "For a horny little thing, you sure are naive."

"The number 666," Sid explains, "is an old Christian superstition—"

"Hey," says Prasert, hitting him. "Some of us believe in God, here!"

"Sorry, babe." After an apology kiss, Sid recommences his explanation. "The number 666 is said to stand for the devil. And sixty-nine—" He smirks as Cantara blushes.

After a lengthy laugh at Cantara's expense, Dean continues with the lesson. "Now that we're in, we begin the search." Dean begins typing "Augustus Uni Dean Hunter student access—"

"Hunter?" Cantara is oddly disturbed by this. "Why not Stuttgart?"

Dean pauses; confusion passes over him. "Ah—I'm not sure. I was still going by Hunter when I registered and, ah—I guess I never changed it."

Quick to smooth away tension, Sid launches in with an explanation. "Too much of a hassle; damn near impossible, I'd think, to change every single point in the system with your name attached." Cantara relaxes. So does Dean.

Back in focus, Dean finds his digital design. He opens the file to ensure it is the right one—colorful stick men holding hands—and then issues a vocal command, "disintegrate file." It breaks into particles of light and vanishes.

There is a collective murmur: "Cool!"

Cantara utters her approval, "I like this friend of yours."

"He abandoned his son because he was straight."

Admiration turns sour and Cantara spits out, "Bastard!"

There is a moment of silence. Everyone knows the name of the boy in question: Todd Middleton.

Prasert, ever the pragmatic, gets the group back on track. "Okay, so the file's gone. Now what?" Apologetically, he adds, "We still need a logo."

"It's okay, babe." Turning now to Dean, Sid asks, "What are you thinking?"

"Well, I was hoping we could come up with something to reflect Tara's haiku 'Humanity's Sun.'"

"Oh, I love that one." Cantara smiles and, even though everyone has heard it before, she recites it for her peers: 'We are each of us/rays of light shooting forth from/humanity's sun.'"

"If we could come up with an image for humanity's sun, that would be ideal."

"Well," says Sid, turning to kiss Prasert on the cheek, "we'd love to stay and help, Dean, but we have a sociology class. Tara, coming?"

Tara's eyes brighten. "Yes!" She lets out a little laugh and there is a sudden spring in her step as she joins the two men. "Cantara," her voice is bubbling over with excitement, "meet us for supper so we can celebrate."

"Okay." Cantara's smile stretches over the whole of her face. She knows why Tara is excited. Her sociology professor is going to read her essay about what it is like growing up straight to the class. Tara was practically dancing on air when Professor Politis asked for permission to share it. "I'm hoping it will open a few minds to understanding others," the professor had said. She also promised not to expose Tara by keeping her name anonymous. Sid and Prasert are the only students in her class who will know it is Tara's essay. Waving as Tara and the two boys exit their small GSA office, Cantara shouts, "See you later!"

After the pack leaves, Dean inquires, "What was that about?"

"I promised Tara I wouldn't tell anybody, but I think you're safe. Her professor is going to read her essay about what it is like being heterosexual in Hadrian."

"Whoa," says Dean, his brow contracting, "that could be dangerous." He knows the essay; he proofread it for Tara, and although he fully agrees with everything she has to say in it, he warned her not to hand it in. Tara seemed to believe her professor was more open-minded than Dean was willing to give her credit for. Clearly, Tara was right, but still, if others learn who authored that piece, Tara could be in for a lot of ugly treatment by her peers. Augustus Uni may be the first in Hadrian to admit openly bi and straight students, but that doesn't mean that all of the faculty or its student population are accepting of their presence. Most bi and straight students remain in the closet. Even the office for their campus GSA is a well-kept secret. Or, at least, so Dean hopes.

"You worry too much, Dean," Cantara chastises. "Politis promised not to share her name. I think it's great. I mean, someone is willing to share our story and actually hopes to open the hearts and minds of our fellow students."

"Yes, I just…" Dean pauses; he can't help but fear the worst, having experienced a lifetime of prejudice. "I just hope no one discovers Tara's the one who wrote it."

"They won't; there's no way."

"Well, if you say so." Rubbing his forehead to ease some tension, Dean politely asks Cantara to leave. "Anyway, I've got to get to work and try to do something with this."

"And then you have to study your ass off for your anatomy test!"

"Yes," Dean admits, "so, if you don't mind…"

Before he can finish, Cantara acquiesces. "Okay, I will leave you alone." But Cantara doesn't want to leave. She likes being in close proximity to Dean. When they first met, he couldn't be in the same room with her unless his grandmother was with him. *His mimi sure has done wonders with him,* Cantara muses. Now she can be alone in the same room with Dean and he hardly has any negative reaction at all. She stands there by the door for a time, quietly watching Dean work, fantasizing about the day when he will hold her in his arms and kiss her.

Thinking Cantara has left the room, Dean begins musing out loud. "Humanity's sun—humanity's sun—rays shooting forth—" Blinking, Dean opens a new design doc. He begins with a circle to represent the sun. Using the eyedropper, he colors in the circle with a creamy yellow. Picking up the holographic pencil tool, he begins drawing thick rays shooting forth from the sun. He paints each sunray a color of the rainbow. Above the image, he types the title "Humanity's Sun," and beneath it, he types in the haiku. "It's not great," he mutters, "but it'll do." He prints a copy of the design and then goes through the arduous process of deleting, retrieving, and destroying the image. He will share this image with the group next time they meet, and if it meets with everyone's approval, he will create a new one and spread it over the wall screens at the uni using an ad virus. Dean smiles; he hasn't shared all of Mike Fulton's secrets with these kids. Assuming Mike is right, Dean should be able to encrypt his poster design with enough security that it will take even the best of Hadrian's hackers to decode it prior to the 4 a.m. deadline. All he has to do is make sure to trash the viral doc every day at the same time and then reload it with Fulton's modulating security program. The plan is simple: create, blast, trash, erase—recreate, blast, trash, erase for as long as he can get away with it.

Finally, Dean opens his anatomy files and begins to study. He is having trouble focusing, though. The stress of exams, running low on credits, and having to hide everything they do as a GSA is starting to wear on Dean. With pain shooting up the sides of his neck and down the front of his collarbone, he stops studying to attempt self-massage. Fortunately, he doesn't have to struggle to reach his back shoulder muscles because Cantara enters the room and takes over for him. "Here," she says soothingly. "Let me do that for you."

"I thought you'd left." After a few moments of her hands rubbing into his neck muscles, he smiles. "I'm glad you didn't."

Cantara gently chides, "Hadrian's Lover, Dean, your neck and shoulder muscles are tight. It's like trying to soften rocks." Then worried, she adds, "I'm not the cause of that, am I?"

"No." Dean does not want her to stop. Her hands may not be as strong as Geoffrey's, but the digging into his muscles is exactly what he needs right now. "No, I'm fine. I'm just stressed about getting our logo done. I want to flood the campus screens with our image to start spreading awareness."

"Yes, but you can't do everything. And, you have midterms coming up. You don't want to fail your anatomy class, do you?"

"No, you're right." Dean moans. "By all that's gay and glorious, that feels good." *But not good enough*, Dean winces as he realizes the hands he really wants massaging his neck are Geoffrey's. "Could you press a little harder?"

"I'll try, but I don't want to hurt you."

"Trust me; you're not hurting me at all."

Cantara smiles. "Does it feel good?"

"Yes, thank you."

Suddenly, Cantara is in front of him, settling down on his lap. "Dean," she whispers.

The room starts to feel close. Dean's throat tightens. Cantara smells good. Her breathing enhances her breasts. She leans in for a kiss. Dean's lips reach for her mouth as his heart pounds against his chest. Try as he might, his body begins to rebel and he pushes her away. "I can't; no, Cantara." He gets up from his chair and begins pacing the room, trying all the while to control his breathing and hold back the ensuing nausea. "Mind over matter. Mind over matter," he whispers over and over.

"Dean, I'm so sorry."

"It's okay, Cantara. I'm the one who's sorry." Trying now to ease her hurt, he says, "It's not a good idea for us anyway. You are much too young—"

Angered, Cantara counters, "That's absurd!"

"I'm forty-four, forty-five next month, while you're only—"

"I'm twenty-two years old. That makes me a consenting adult. I can sleep with a ninety year old if I want."

Dean can't help but laugh. "Yeah, I suppose you could. I just," he says, wiping the sweat off his brow, "I can't. I've tried. I want to be with you, but every time we try, I feel residual shocks, and then the nausea sets in." Breathing more slowly now, he adds, "I'm sorry, Cantara; it's just not going to happen. Not now. Maybe not for a long, long while. Re-ed has taken its toll on me." Turning now to face Cantara, hoping to discourage her, Dean concludes, "Don't wait for me. Find someone you can be with, someone who can make you happy."

Ignoring his advice, Cantara changes the subject. "Show me what you've come up with." Dean readily acquiesces; it is easier to be around Cantara when their focus is business. Reaching into his back pocket, he pulls out the print out of the logo he has created.

Cantara unfolds his work and immediately expresses pleasure. "I love it!"

"Really?" Dean remains unsure.

"Absolutely. It's perfect. It's just what you said you wanted. Humanity's sun!"

The two smile. The tension between them has subsided. For now.

* * * * *

Salve!

An Interview with Greatness
HNN—Melissa Eagleton Reporting

"Viewers, it is both an honor and a pleasure to introduce to you today's guest, Hadrian's Founding Mother, Destiny Stuttgart. Mother, thank you so much for joining us today."

"Call me Destiny."

"Oh, I don't think I can. Forgive me, Mother, but it doesn't feel right referring to you on such an informal level. You have done so much to help make our country great."

"And that's why I agreed to come here today. I want to keep our country great and not let it fall deeper into the hands of hatred."

"Why do you say that?"

"You know why. You reported about the many abuses committed against our heterosexual brothers and sisters—not just through reeducation but in the series of hate crimes polluting our culture of love and peace."

"Oh, I know, those violent hateful crimes. Mother, how can we stop them?"

"By educating our citizens. Letting them know heterosexuals are not evil people—Why are you pulling at your ear?—And now you're wincing. Explain yourself, dear."

"But—there is the Heterosexual Agenda that we must be aware of. You must agree, being a founding member and having helped write the four cornerstones. The first cornerstone is very explicit about Hadrian's chosen sexual identity."

"Yes, I am fully aware of that wording, but I argued ardently against it. Which is why I am fighting so hard for its revision, back to its original wording when I first drafted the constitution for Hadrian."

"But why?"

"It saddens me that you have to ask that, dear. Look at me when I talk to you. Sexual identity is not a choice. No one chooses to be gay. No one chooses to be bisexual. No one chooses to be straight. No one chooses to be intersex. And no one chooses to suffer from gender dysphoria."

"Yes, but our scientists have done wonders with the human genome, eradicating the heterosexual gene—"

"And what right do we have to do that?"

"To avoid procreation."

"We don't want to avoid procreation. All we want to do is reduce human population in the most peaceful, loving, and humane manner possible."

"I think we've done that here in Hadrian; don't you?"

"Do you call the list of hate crimes you shared with us on your last *Salve!* peaceful? Do you call the murder of a four-year-old boy loving? Do you call the numerous beatings of our heterosexual citizens humane?"

"No, of course not, but—"

"There you go, grabbing at your ear again. What does that mean anyway?"

"No, hate crimes are not peaceful, but…heterosexuals shouldn't flaunt themselves in public, giving our children the message that it is okay to be straight."

"It is okay."

"No, Mother, it isn't—Mother, why did you sign the constitution? Why did you agree to its wording?"

"I was outvoted. Oh, dear, you are going to pull that earlobe off if you're not careful."

"And now—you are using the current political climate and your power as the last founding family member to—to—"

"Just say what you have to say, dear."

"—to corrupt our constitution."

"The word corrupt does not fit this context. No, dear, not corrupt—amend."

"I'm sorry, Mother, but our time has run out. I hope you will join us again."

"That's not very likely, is it? And dear, see a doctor about that ear. Oh, oh, oh, let me say it. I've always wanted to…

Vale!"

A Detritus Fisherman's Fiasco

Although the role of a detritus fisherman is a dangerous one, it is deemed as critical to Hadrian's existence as that of the military. Even so, it is a life seldom chosen out of want, or altruism; rather, such positions are filled out of desperation and need. Few willingly put their lives at daily risk, a risk, if statistics were ever revealed publically, that is actually greater than those known to the military. One need not fear having a bullet piercing his flesh; no, when one fishes out the refuse floating in the Bay, built up over centuries with human waste, one fears contamination. As well as radioactive materials, many dangerous chemicals and biohazards litter the world's oceans, and much of that litter has found its way into Hudson Bay via its estuaries stretching down from the Arctic Ocean and east from the Atlantic. The average life expectancy of the detritus fisherman, colloquially referred to as "DF," is said to be anywhere between forty-five and fifty years of age. The oldest known DF died at the ripe old age of fifty-eight. This is why over 90 percent of all DFs are from the re-ed class—that unwanted class of Hadrian citizens that has been discovered experimenting with heterosexual behavior before the age of twenty-one; that unwanted member of society that has required reeducation.

The detritus fisherman is really nothing more than a glorified salvage-man, but no one working in this capacity feels any sense of glory in his or her work. It is simply a dangerous life, one compounded with difficult times and hard labor. Wolfgang Gaidosch, known by close friends as Wolf, is no stranger to hard times and backbreaking labor. Backing away from his post for a minute, Wolf presses his knuckles between his shoulder blades and cracks his back. Glancing about him circuitously to ensure no pier manager is looking his way, Wolf stealthily removes a half-smoked cigarette from his pocket and lights up quickly. After a few drags, he carefully extinguishes it, hiding the remaining butt in his coverall pocket. He had been employed as a level one DF, first by Hunter Enterprises and now with Hadrian National, and never once has he been offered a promotion or even heard back from any of his applications. *So much for fifteen years of service!* Bitterness is a hard pill to swallow, and Wolf no longer even tries. He just chews on it and spits when his mouth gets that all too familiar foul metallic taste. Unfortunately, he has been doing this for quite some time. *I'd change jobs*, he muses, *but to do what?* This is the only low-end job out there that actually offers benefits thanks to Geoffrey Hunter's intervention when the fisheries was still a family-owned company. *And sadly*, he ruminates, *things have only gotten worse since they legalized heterosexuality.* No one is forced to go to reeducation camps any longer, but parents still have the authority to send anyone under twenty-one, so the camps still run at full capacity since no one wants a child who acts on strai tendencies. With a harrumph, Wolf spits. *No one wants to believe that someone in Hadrian might actually be born straight! Irony*, he thinks with a grim chuckle, *when nobody in the outside world wants to believe people are born gay.* Shaking his head in disbelief, Wolf mutters, "I hate irony." Walking back to the edge of his pier, Wolf resumes hauling in more of the refuse within depth and reach of his pole.

Wolf's pier is the third one out on the northern water border of Hadrian. The border is lined with detritus piers to which DFs are assigned. Every ten minutes, a kilometer or two into international waters, the water patrol boats pass by. Occasionally, one passes close enough to allow male guards to toss a few taunts Wolf's way. Today is one of those days.

"Hey, sexy fisherman," one of the older guards calls out. It may sound like an admiring catcall, but Wolf knows better. There is nothing sexy about a DF in uniform. Muddy fishing boots, with chest high waders, jacket, and hat are all baggy and designed to protect one from the contaminated waters of the Bay. In actuality, a DF looks like little more than a big, yellow, slimy lump covered in grime.

"Ah, Leon," the other guard cries out, "leave the little strai alone." The other man's shout is just a little too loud to be construed as supportive. Ignoring them, as usual, Wolf plunges his pole as deep as it will go into the Bay before dragging it along the edge of the pier. As always, he snags something. At first, Wolf anticipates more illegal fishing nets—composed of strong synthetic polymer that Hadrian makes good use of by converting it into spools to be later used in the weaving of shoes and clothing.[10] The feel of this catch is different, though. The net seems to be caught on something. Tugging, Wolf begins to pull upward on the pole in an attempt to free whatever intractable object this net has latched onto. Whatever it is, it is stuck hard. Wolf releases the pressure he has placed on the pole and dips it deeper, bending deep at the knees so he can place hands and arms deep into the rancid water. Feeling the net under the object, Wolf uses his legs to help him lift the item whilst pushing down with his right arm and pulling upward with the left. Wolf grunts as something silver dangles from a long chain knotted up inside his net. Sunlight sparkles off the water dripping from both chain and object. It is unimpressively small, tubular; it must be the chain in which it is entangled that bears the bulk of the weight. Mustering all of his strength, Wolf lifts his catch high enough to toss it and the chain up into the large bin next to him. *Ugh.* Whatever it is, it has a rancid stench. Of course, everything Wolf pulls out of the Bay has a reek, but whatever is in his net is particularly pungent. It speaks volumes when a stench can trigger disgust in the nostrils of a DF. *No doubt,* Wolf reasons, *this object must be extremely toxic.* "Damn," he mutters. "I'll have to report that." This spells disaster for Wolf: paperwork, detoxification showers, followed by numerous medical tests (the bulk of which are at his expense even with the addition of medical benefits). "Fuck," Wolf mutters. "I hate this shit!" Before climbing the side of his bin to look inside at his newly acquired catch, Wolf's attention is averted to rasping, begging off in the distance. "Fuck!" Wolf spits. Nearing the edge of his pier is a small refugee boat. *How the fuck did they get past the water patrol guards?* he wonders.

"Please," a voice begs. "Please let us in."

Wolf's head drops in shame. He can't even bring himself to look up at this week's latest starved and desperate refugees begging for mercy and salvation inside Hadrian's borders.

"Please!" The voice is so desperate Wolf glances up momentarily, regretting instantly this fatal mistake. It is the rhetoric drilled into every detritus fisherman's brain from day one until the day he or she dies. (No one has ever lived long enough to retire.) *Never look at them; never engage them. If you do, you will fall prey to sympathy, and Hadrian can't afford to extend any aid to the outside world!*

---

[10] https://ca.news.yahoo.com/blogs/daily-buzz/adidas-creates-a-shoe-made-from-illegal-fishing-171835933.html

Wolf tries to warn them off. "The water patrol guard will be returning shortly." The pleading voice, he notes, is that of a dark-skinned older man. *Probably African*, Wolf muses. *For the love of Hadrian*, Wolf spits, *he looks to be fifty or sixty*. Wolf suddenly considers as he shakes his head, *He's probably no older than me*. (Wolf is a mere thirty-three years old.) *Fuck, who am I to judge?* Wolf considers. *No doubt I look fifty years old or more myself.* The years have not been kind to men and women like Wolf. Age lines crease his face, his skin is tanned to thick leather; his work, however, has given him a very strong, muscular body. Even so, a small belly protrudes, from the overconsumption of beer and junk munch. The beer medicates the psychological pain, and the junk munch, well, junk munch is simply more affordable than healthy food. And although every home in Hadrian is built to accommodate home gardens, either in a yard or on the roof, the twelve-hour shift work, coupled with the long bus ride to the docks, followed by an even longer boat ride to the piers and back again, can make Wolf's work day anywhere from four-teen to eighteen hours, so Wolf has little, if any, time for gardening. And since his job is so low paying, Wolf, like many other detritus fishermen, fights for the luxury of working overtime on his days off in the hopes of a little extra pay.

"Dear God, please," the older man's voice rasps. "Help us. We can't go home."

Wolf quickly looks down at his rubber steel-toed boots. Sludge has stained the right toe. He spits on it and tries to rub it clean on the leg of his coveralls. "They'll kill you," Wolf warns. "You're too close to the pier."

"They'll kill us if we go home. We're gay," the man begs.

They'll fire me if I help you! Wolf reminds himself. *Who knows? I might even be punishable with expulsion. Would I drink Black Death?* He wonders. Squeezing his eyes tightly, Wolf desperately fights back painful memories. Every level one DF has a story like his, and every DF hates to talk about it. Wolf is aided in his attempts to forget by the return of the older man's raspy voice.

"We had to leave because the penalty for gay sex is death. They will stone us if we go back!"

Wolf shudders. These words, this very real threat to their existence, is one with which he can relate. *Leona*, he groans inwardly. The thought of Black Death followed so quickly by the mention of a death penalty made it impossible for Wolf not to remember her. Leona was thirty-one, he nineteen. Long black hair, hazel eyes, rich caramel-brown skin, lush lips, and breasts he could hide his face in. They had met at the Midwest Gate where both were stationed. Wolf, like all eighteen-year-old citizens of Hadrian, had been conscripted into military service on the first Monday following the last day of high school. Hadrian's government dictates that all Hadrian's citizens serve in the army in order for all its citizens to gain a clear understanding of the dangers threatening them from the outside world. *Not everyone,* Wolf grimly reminds himself. A very lucky few win academic or sports scholarships, exempting them from military duty. These fortunate individuals are deemed Hadrian's intellectual and physical elite. Each of Hadrian's eight unis offers one full academic scholarship and one full sports scholarship per annum. The lucky recipient of such a prestigious award must maintain a 75 percent average if a sports beneficiary or 85 percent for the academic scholarship. Failure to maintain this standard means a loss of scholarship and immediate conscription into the army.

Wolf had not been so lucky as to win a scholarship. His 88 percent average was insufficient, though high enough to ensure entrance into the uni of his choice after his years of service. Wolf had planned to go on to college after the army, until he met Leona.

Leona de Bruijn. Wolf was still a virgin when they had met. They had fallen so deeply in love they had even plotted out how they might be able to escape Hadrian. In the end, they realized the only thing to do was wait until Wolf was twenty-one, and then they would simply have to walk up to the gate and ask for it to be opened. But that was still two years away and, although the couple had been circumspect, they had been found out— caught in the act. Leona was exiled instantly by her commanding officer. She chose Black Death. Wolf, being but nineteen, was shipped 100 kilometers east to the Midwest Reeducation Military Facility. All members of the military discovered as strai are sent there. The military feels it best that it run its own reeducation camp since all the strai sent there are trained soldiers, thus their potential to become dangerous foes is too great. Wolf had heard that the military reeducation camp was the least abusive of all the camps. This notion always causes Wolf to shake his head in wonder. Perhaps that was the reason why he was able to survive over two years inside that prison. Wolf had only succumbed to the denial of his sexual orientation a few days before his twenty-first birthday when he knew his only other choices would be exile or Black Henbane. The years spent inside a re-ed camp had taught him to give up on death, but they never helped him deny who he was or made him choose to be gay. *It is hardly a choice to deny who one is*, Wolf thinks. *And these poor buggers can't do it any more than me.* Wolf looks up and holds the old man's eyes in his. For a brief moment, their spirits unite. "All right!" he shouts back. "I'll talk to my foreman. But you gotta move back a good ten kilometers, or they'll shoot you on sight."

"How will we know? How will we know?" Their pleading becomes even more desperate.

Wolf spits. Taking a small knife out of his pocket (also fished out of the Bay), Wolf opens it and stabs it into the pier. "Back off ten kilometers from this point. That way, if they let you in, they'll know how to find you."

"How long?"

Wolf grimaces, spitting once before lying. "Two days, three at most." *More like hours*, he shouts inside his mind.

The small boat heeds Wolf's warning and begins to back away from the pier. Soon it is out of sight. Knowing what he is about to do is utter folly, Wolf feels obliged to try at least. He has, after all, given his word.

* * * * *

Matthew Molloy pulls his fingers through his dirty, matted red hair, ripping through a few knots in the process. Shaking what he is allowing to turn into dreadlocks, Matthew gets rid of most of the wet grime that had settled there from a long day of slugging through the slimy muck of the Bay. After zipping off his overcoat and kicking off thigh high water boots, Matthew steps out of his coveralls. Turning to toss them in the laundry bin, he spies a lone figure leaning against the pier railing, looking out towards the shore.

"Will that fucking boat ever get here?" Wolfgang mutters.

"Hey, Wolf," Matthew observes, "you're cleaned up awful early; I hope it's not a medical appointment." Matthew works the morning shift, which overlaps the evening shift by an hour. To see Wolf standing and waiting for the boat home when his team works nights is odd.

Wolf spits between his teeth into the water. "Nope," Wolf grumbles. "The fucker fired me."

"What?" Matt is truly dismayed. Everyone knows Wolf to be a hard case, but he always does his job with no slacking. "Why would Malco fire you?"

"Because he's a fucking dick; that's why."

Matthew crosses over to Wolf and puts a hand on the older man's shoulder. "I know you're pissed, man, but come on; what happened?"

"It's simple; he called me a dirty strai, threatened to expose me, and when I told him he couldn't get me exiled anymore, he decided the next best thing was to fire me."

"But," Matthew stammers, "he can't do that, can he?"

"Oh, yeah," Wolf grimaces, "he can and he did. There ain't no law protecting us, you know. Just because the government passed a law saying it won't exile us or try to force-feed strai rats henbane anymore doesn't mean we can't still be legally fired just for being straight!"

"Yeah, but," Matthew feels almost stupid saying this, "you did the re-ed thing, too, didn't you?"

"Fuck, yeah, I did that shit. Fat lot a good it did, too, except scare the emotional shit out of me for life." Scowling now, Wolf adds, "You, too; don't fucking pretend otherwise, *Matty*, me lad. Me little paddle me backside leprechaun."

Matthew had confided in Wolf shortly after taking on this job. He told the older man about Gideon Weller's treatment and that horrible day he had suffered a second paddling, by Gideon Weller's hand, and his having passed out mid-beating. Although he never saw it, he was told how the paddle dripped blood when the vicious beating was over. "Don't—" Nearing tears, Matthew barely manages to hold them back. "I meant, well, he can't claim you're still straight, not after graduating re-ed and all."

"He says I confessed—fuck," Wolf mutters. "I almost practically did." Seeing deep concern in Matthew's eyes, having mentored the youth when he first came to the docks to work, Wolf softens some and explains. "There was a boat of refugees, a small group of gay men. Fuck!" Near exasperation, Wolf utters "fuck" with a guttural grunt. "Ten of them—there were only ten of them. They had escaped persecution, I don't even know from what fucking country. They said if forced to go back, they'd be stoned. In their country, being gay is punishable by death. I guess, in those countries, they bury the poor fuckers up to their chests and then pelt them with rocks until rescued by death."[11]

Matthew shudders. "I'd rather drink henbane."

"Yeah, that sounds more merciful, doesn't it?"

---

[11] http://www.huffingtonpost.com/2013/03/21/gay-teen-stoned-somalia-sodomy_n_2916655.html

The acerbic slurring slaps Matthew as if he were to blame. "Gee, Wolf, come on."

"I'm sorry, kid; this whole thing's got me messed-up in the head, a real mind fuck. I have no fucking idea what I'm gonna do now. It's hard enough getting hired as a re-ed, but to be a fired re-ed, fired for being straight—I might as well drink the fucking henbane anyway."

"Tell me what you said—everything, exactly like it happened."

Matthew's earnest plea makes Wolf feel compelled to comply. "I felt something for these men, you know, living a similar sort of persecution. I figured, 'Why the fuck not? They're gay, there's only ten of 'em, and shit, it's not like the country's busting at the seams with people like the rest of the planet,' so I took their petition to Malco. I thought he might listen, talk to bigwigs, maybe do something to help them." Sighing now, Wolf continues, "I sure as hell never expected what happened. Next thing I know, he's spitting in my face all kinds of rhetoric about population control, diseases of the outside world, and they're not really gay but a bunch of fucking strai liars trying to play on our sympathies to get inside our borders." Then, shaking his head in dismay, Wolf cuts his story short. "I don't know what the fuck was said after that except a bunch of yelling and him calling me every fucking het'ro slur he could muster, and he threatened to expose me. He even blinked open his voc call display so I could watch him place the call. That's when I told him to go right ahead, that they don't exile heterosexuals anymore." Sighing deeply, Wolf concludes, "He took that as a confession and fired me on the spot for being straight."

"Well," Matthew responds confidently, "I'm gonna help you get your job back."

"How?" Matthew's assertion is so strong Wolf is almost inclined to believe him. Cynicism, however, quickly quells any stirrings of hope.

"You remember that kid, Todd Middleton?"

"Yeah, the b-ball star."

"And a confessed strai. I was in re-ed with him. I met his father and his papa at his funeral."

"Middleton's?"

"No, fuck, I mean Hunter's—that Hunter kid that killed him."

"Hunter?" The name comes out in a whisper. Understanding begins to dawn. "You met the big guy, Geoffrey Hunter?" Wolf allows some feeling of hope to prevail. "You think...you think he might help...might help me?"

"Well, I'm gonna fucking try and ask him," Matthew asserts with conviction.

Too easily swayed by bitterness, Wolf spits out, "They won't even let you talk to him."

"I'll tell 'em I knew Todd Middleton; that'll get his attention. I'm sure of it."

"Well, fuck, why not? You try, why not? Try for me, kid. It probably won't work, but I appreciate you trying."

"It'll work," Matthew reassuringly promises. "It'll work."

A horn sounds off, signaling the arrival of the return ferry. Wolf offers the youth an appreciative nod, clasps Matthew's shoulder, and then play-fully shoves his young friend towards the boat. They ascend the ramp together, both men almost smiling.

* * * * *

Salve!

Discrimination in the Workplace
HNN—Melissa Eagleton Reporting

As many of you are aware, there is an ongoing debate regarding the treatment of the reeducation class in the workplace. Those who graduate from reeducation often find themselves working in less desirable positions, the least of which is the lowly one of the detritus fisherman. These men and women toil endlessly to clean Hudson Bay by retrieving reusable wastes and disposing of toxins pulled from the heavily polluted waters. Stats indicate that at least 65 percent of all detritus fishermen are re-ed. This, of course, is due to Hadrian's previous education policy that denied re-eds uni entrance. At the request of the Dean of Augustus Uni, the policy was revised after President Stiles signed the bill making heterosexuality legal. This once fine institution has suffered greatly due to the stigma of the nuclear attack against that city on that fateful day of 6-13—Ironically—the uni's decision to be inclusive of heterosexuals has hindered the uni's growth, which is now associated with nuclear radiation and—and—rampant—heterosexual orgies.

Excuse this divergence as the focus of tonight's *Salve!* is workplace discrimination. While many argue that no such discrimination exists, members of the re-ed class, feeling emboldened by President Stiles's recent change in laws regarding heterosexuality, have come forth to register complaints. Pazima Zulu, Quadrant Four's Ombudsman spokeswoman, has reported a significant increase in complaints from re-eds employed as detritus fishermen. Quadrants Four and One, as you know, are the home to the majority of our re-ed class as, besides Antinous City, the majority of detritus fishery factories are housed nearest to the Hudson Bay waters. Zulu believes our re-ed citizens, especially detritus fishermen, need greater protection under the law. One recommendation she makes is that management, especially of the detritus fisheries industry, undergo sensitivity training to better help employers understand the individuals who work in one of our most dangerous industries. "Not only do these workers suffer from numerous medical issues due to the exposure to chemical pollutants, they also have to incur discrimination on a daily basis. Even after having been reeducated, many of them still suffer the stigma of being considered straight." Her reasoning is sound a—I'm sorry?—Yes—I said, yes!

Humph. I've been asked to remind our viewers that all of Hadrian's citizens are employed—but no one wants to be forced to work alongside heterosexuals—which is—understandable. Employers simply ask that you use common sense and not reveal any unseemly attractions to persons of the opposite sex. Individuals are urged to repress offensive sexual inclinations. If you do not act upon repugnant desires, you will have no issues to deal with at work.

Va—

I'm sorry—it is also important to remember—What?—Heterosexuals are—are—dangerous members of society—if you think—no—if you believe—a coworker might be—strai—report him—to your employer immediately.

Vale!

Messages

Geoffrey's late return home from work follows a very similar routine. He quietly calls on the living room's lights and wall screen. As Roger is already in bed, likely having been asleep for over an hour, Geoffrey never wants to wake him. Waking Roger might result in a conversation. Roger always insists they talk at dinnertime, but Geoffrey never feels like talking. He comes home for supper every night, though, because a teary-eyed Roger would constantly voc him to please come home. Still, Geoffrey is always able to find a reason to return to work. *I'm a fucking horrible dad!* Geoffrey mutters to himself, another regular aspect of his late night routine.

The first thing Geoffrey does when he enters the living room is to toss his suit jacket towards the couch, miss it as usual, and ignore that the jacket falls to the floor. As he stretches and attempts to crack his back, he calls up his messaging system: "Voc mail on." Although he could simply blink and pull up a small screen for his eyes only, Geoffrey is always too tired at this time of the night; he never gets home before 11:30 p.m. He needs the wall screen in order to blow up images for him and to increase print size if necessary. "Messages. Vocal, please."

The voice of Geoffrey's voc message system is Dean's. He had Dean record his voice to use for his voc a few years back. Even though Dean has been out of his life for almost two years now, he can't bring himself to change it. Geoffrey shudders briefly as he hears his ex-lover's voice: "You have two messages."

"First message?"

"Destiny Stuttgart."

"Play."

Destiny Stuttgart's image appears on the screen. Even at eighty-eight, she is quite alert and perky. Her hair is completely white, thinning some, but she successfully combs it up and curls it in such a way as to hide her bald spot. She is smiling and her eyes twinkle, complementing her wrinkles. "Hello, Geoffrey. I hope this message finds you well. I had hoped you would be home. It is, after all, 8:30. Who spends the evenings with Roger? I know Dean worries about him. You leave the boy alone far too often. Is being CEO of Hadrian's Detritus Fisheries really that important? I know you make a decent wage and are using it to help pay for Dean's uni and saving up for Roger's—"

Geoffrey mumbles amidst Destiny's speech, "I can't believe he's going to graduate this year, and so early." For Roger, the best way of coping with his father's workaholic nature, his fathers separating, and Frank being sentenced to a life of servitude in the military was to become a workaholic just like his dad. He began fast tracking as soon as he started grade ten, and now, in the first semester of his grade twelve year, Roger is able to graduate early. In fact, as his grades are exceptionally high, always mid to high 90s, Roger has successfully convinced Pride Administration to let him write his finals early so he can begin uni at the start of the new year. It was his counselor at Antinous Uni, Joel Lipmann, who came up with the idea. In fact, Professor Lipmann contacted Pride High on Roger's behalf, which helped ensure the young man could finish his last semester of high school one month early. Roger will graduate from grade twelve on December 20th, the last day of school before the New Year holiday season begins.

Mimi's voice shakes Geoffrey out of his reverie. Mimi, used to Geoffrey shutting down during their voc calls, will often intersperse her messages with a curt reminder, "Geoffrey, are you listening? I hope so." Geoffrey always shudders when this happens because Mimi always seems able to time these reminders at just the right moment. *Every time that woman vocs, I swear by Hadrian's Lover she is standing in this very room!* "As I was saying, Dean tells me you are more than financially able to fund Roger's uni education. He worries that you work too much—"

Speaking over Destiny's voice, this time, Geoffrey grumbles, "Worries so much he never bothers to voc me."

Again, it's almost as if Destiny is in the room with Geoffrey. "I know he hasn't voc'd you yet—"

"For over two years." Geoffrey struggles to control his emotions.

Again, Destiny responds with foresight into what she knew would be Geoffrey's response. "—and that it has been two years, but please try to understand that Dean has been through a lot."

"And I haven't?"

"As have you." Geoffrey shudders. It really does feel as if Dean's grandmother is in the room with him and not just an image on the wall screen.

"I remember how difficult it was for you during the trial, having to deal with both Frank and Dean being so distant. Their refusal to talk or even look at one another after you told Dean—Oh, Geoffrey, I don't think you should have told Dean. How will he ever learn to forgive?"

Geoffrey steps closer to the wall as if he is actually addressing the woman. "Oh, yes, it's all my fault!"

"I don't mean to blame you; really, I don't. It's just, well, sometimes certain things are better left unsaid."

"Dean had a right to know!"

"I know you believe it was important, but—ah, well, all that is water under the bridge, as they say. We need to move forward, and we can, Geoffrey, if you have faith."

"Faith?" The incredulity in Geoffrey's voice is the result of Destiny's use of a word that holds no meaning in his life and the fact that it really does feel like he is having a face-to-face conversation with the woman. "What are you," he shouts to the wall, "a fucking psychic?" Realizing he has raised his voice, Geoffrey immediately starts whispering again. What Geoffrey doesn't know is that Roger is startled by the sound of his voice and has stumbled into the hall. He restrains himself from entering the living room, though, as it really does sound like his father is talking to someone—or rather having an argument, so he stops short and quietly listens. His father is so elusive these days that spying on his conversations is sometimes the only way Roger gets any news about Geoffrey's life.

"At any rate, Geoffrey," Destiny replies, "the reason for this call is to ask you to transfer 12,000 credits into Dean's uni account. Oh, Geoffrey, he is doing so well. I am so proud of him. He is always in his study. I have to pull him out for dinner and breaks, but uni is very demanding. He feels so overwhelmed at times. The workload and pace required of him leave him quite exhausted. There's a reason why we do uni in our youth. It really is a lifestyle designed for the young. Just listen to me; my thoughts wander far too often these days. What was I saying? Oh, yes, 12,000 credits. He doesn't want me to remind you of this since he's already feeling guilty about allowing you to help pay the costs, but you did insist and, well, I agree with you. We both know I can carry the cost easily myself, but this one gesture on your part does help maintain a connection between the two of you—"

"Some connection."

"It may not be much, but it ties Dean to you, and I do believe he still loves you. Please be patient with him. We often talk about you—"

Destiny isn't allowed to finish because Geoffrey can listen to no more. "Delete message." After rubbing his eyes, wiping away the tears he struggles so hard not to release, Geoffrey stands erect; he tightens his torso before releasing a deep breath. "Open credit account." Geoffrey's arms cross, his hands in fists, as his right hand taps his thumb against his mouth. "Transfer 12—No, make it 13—transfer 13,000 credits into Dean Hun— correction, into Dean Stuttgart's uni account."

Still hiding in the hall, Roger smiles. His father still loves Dean. He worries about him and wants to make sure he doesn't find himself short of credit. Just as Roger is about to enter the living room, he hears his father open a second message and listens to Papa Dean's automated voice recite, "Second message from Matthew Malloy."

"Who?" Geoffrey looks at the wall screen, his inquiry prompting the voc messaging system to retrieve Matthew's image. "The boy looks familiar." Chewing now on his thumb, he ponders the image for a minute until recognition dawns. It is the young man who was Todd Middleton's roommate at the Northeast Reeducation Camp. "Open."

Appearing on the wall screen is the vid image of Matthew Molloy. *For such a young man—he can't be more than twenty-one*, Geoffrey thinks, *—his face is so withered. Hadrian's Lover, he looks thirty.* Geoffrey sighs as he realizes this could have happened to Dean.

> *Hello, Mr. Hunter. I'm not sure if you remember me. My name's Matthew Molloy. We met at Todd Middleton's funeral. I told you then he and I were bunkmates at re-ed. I am really sorry to call you and cause what I am sure are unpleasant memories, but this is really important. I remember your husband is also re-ed—sorry, but, well, if he is, then you might understand. They say you created most of the reforms that have helped us re-ed workers and, well, I'm hoping you might help out my friend and probably one of your most loyal detritus fishermen, Wolf Gaidosch. You may even recognize his name...*

Geoffrey didn't.

> *He started with Hunter Fisheries and transferred over to Hadrian's Fisheries when the company went national. Anyway, he was just fired. After fifteen years, to just be let go like that. And the reason is prejudice plain and simple. Our manager has never liked Wolf. Since heterosexuality was made legal, Wolf came out as straight, and the manager has harassed him ever since. He used Wolf's wanting to help a boat of gay refugees as an opportunity to fire him. But the real reason he fired him is because Wolf is straight. He told him right to his face, called him a "Fucking strai"; sorry, sir, but those were the manager's words, and he said he was done putting up with Wolf's "strai bullshit." I hope you will look into Wolf's case. I would never have used my slight connection with your family if I didn't believe Wolf was a decent honest man who doesn't deserve to be treated this way. Anyway, I'm sorry to bother you. Please help Wolf. And, well, goodbye, sir.*

And then Matthew Molloy did something quite strange. He knuckled his forehead. Geoffrey paused the vid image at that point. *Why is he doing that?* And then Geoffrey remembered Dean telling him how knuckling the forehead used to be a sign of respect expected from the lower class after addressing someone of a higher class. Dean had done that when they first met at the Northeast Reeducation Camp. Gideon Weller had imposed this on the young men in his camp to instill in them their new place in society. Geoffrey's tears begin to flow freely as he whispers, "Dean, Dean." After a time, Geoffrey brings himself under control. Looking up at Matthew Molloy's image, he decides to respond. "Open reply link." He pauses briefly to collect his thoughts. "Matthew, yes, I remember you. I will look into Wolf Gaidosch's case." He takes a moment to study the young man's face one last time. "Send reply."

With the messages taken care of, Roger assumes his father will head to his room. This is his usual routine, so Roger moves to the center of the hall to greet him, but tonight, something different happens. Maybe it was watching Matthew Molloy knuckle his forehead, coupled with the reminder of Dean with Destiny Stuttgart's message, that solicits Geoffrey's inner longing for his lost lover. Roger turns to stone when he hears Geoffrey mutter, "Voc mate. Full flesh sensitivity." Voc mates are the latest fad in

Hadrian. You can design a holographic partner who will interact with you sexually. With full flesh sensitivity, it can feel like having sex with a thick bowl of jelly. Kids at school had been talking about using these and how bizarre and fun they could be. As one friend put it, "It takes masturbation to a whole new level!" The last thing in Hadrian Roger ever expected to learn was that his father had created his own voc mate. Leaning forward just enough, Roger sees that his father's voc mate is Papa Dean. Then his father chooses a position. "Hands and knees." Suddenly, Roger feels like a voyeur. The last thing he wants to do is listen in on his father's—masturbation. He quickly turns around and scuttles back to his room without ever letting his father know he has awoken.

* * * * *

Salve!

Fired Detritus Fisherman Claims Discrimination!
HNN—Melissa Eagleton Reporting

Early last week, one of HNF's detritus fishermen was fired for having attempted to smuggle in a boatful of refugees. He claimed these men were homosexuals who feared returning to their home country. The manager, Malco Neumann, responsible for terminating Wolfgang Gaidosch's employment, claims otherwise. These men, he says, were in fact heterosexual terrorists looking to find a way to infiltrate our border. This is a—far more believable story than that of a—of a strai trying to save the lives of gay men. Wolfgang Gaidosch claims that Malco Neumann is using the refugees as subterfuge, an excuse justifying dismissal. According to Gaidosch, Neumann concocted this lie to hide the real reason for his dismissal: discrimination. Look to my right and watch our screen as Gaidosch lashes out with unfounded allegation against his former boss. "Malco knows that Geoffrey Hunter, the CEO of Hadrian National Fisheries, is strai-friendly, so Malco doesn't want him to know the real reason for firing me. He called me a ***BEEP*** strai and then fired me."

At the center of this heated debate is Geoffrey Hunter, former CEO of Hunter Fisheries, who is now CEO of Hadrian National Fisheries. Geoffrey Hunter has taken sides with the detritus fisherman. His comments, too, were recorded: "The real reason for Wolfgang Gaidosch's termination is Wolfgang's sexual orientation. He is openly straight. As soon as Wolfgang told me his story, I knew he was telling the truth; I could see it in his eyes." Using his position as CEO of HNF, Geoffrey Hunter has not only rehired Wolfgang Gaidosch, but promoted him to manager of Wharf 12. This was the position of the manager who had fired Mr. Gaidosch. When questioned, Hunter had this to say about Malco Neumann: "He has been transferred to the main office in Antinous to assume a position he applied for previously." When asked whether he would have rather fired Neumann, all Hunter had to say was: "There are no grounds for firing Neumann. He acted in accordance with the law. It is within his right to dismiss a man who is straight, just as it is within my right to rehire and promote the said individual." As you are aware, Geoffrey Hunter is famous for his marriage to Dean Stuttgart, an openly strai man. Hunter's ex-husband, according to confidential sources, seems to support the contention the two men have divorced, and they hid—his founding family status until—until advantageously—revealing it at their son's murder trial. It is believed that as a result of his marriage to this strai, Geoffrey Hunter has always been a strong supporter of his re-ed workers. Many speak of the reforms he brought in when he owned the company and even more after he sold controlling interests to HNF. Due to Geoffrey Hunter's tireless efforts, all detritus fishermen, the majority of whom are from the re-ed class, receive medical benefits. HNF detritus fishermen are the only DF workers in Hadrian to receive medical benefits. It is perhaps—a dangerous precedent to set—suggesting greater value be placed on—the work of re-eds over—natural citizens.

Geoffrey Hunter, CEO of Hadrian's Detritus Fisheries, disagrees, believing the number of abuses against heterosexual employees to be much higher than we realize. Malco Neumann's firing of Wolfgang Gaidosch, Hunter said, opened his eyes to the profuse discrimination against the straight detritus fishermen under his employ. "We are so used to an acceptable standard of hate that we don't even notice when we say something hurtful or discriminatory against our straight brothers and sisters." As a result, Mr. Hunter has decided to run a series of sensitivity workshops for all of his employees, including higher management. Viewers, you may remember from the previous *Salve!* that such workshops were being recommended by Quadrant Four's Ombudsman spokeswoman, Pazima Zulu. Mr. Hunter had seen that episode and contacted Zulu for more information. The incident involving Neumann and Gaidosch, he said, helped to expedite the sessions. When asked why he was going to such extremes to protect strai employees, his response was simple: "Everyone deserves to feel safe in the workplace. When employees are accepted for who they are in their work environment, productivity cannot help but improve."

Not everyone agrees with Hadrian's National Fisheries CEO, Geoffrey Hunter. The newest addition to HNN, *Salve!*'s production manager, Darien Dumas, sees "sensitivity training" as a waste of Hadrian's tax fund. Our money, he believes would be better spent ensuring the successful reeducation of our youth rather than pandering to the hurt feelings of a few strais.

Vale!

Call Him!

"Mimi, I can't."

"Why not?" Mimi sighs. "Oh, Dean, how did you become so stubborn?"

As Dean leans back in the blue plush reclining seat in his grandmother's living room, he covers his face with his hands. Mimi, seated next to him in her rocker, shakes her head. "Look," she points to the wall screen. She and Dean are watching *Salve!* and, using a remote ("My eyes are too old for a voc," she claims), Mimi pauses the show on Geoffrey's image. "Weren't you listening? Didn't you just hear him? Even without you in his life prodding him, he is standing up for the reeducated. He rehired that man. He doesn't care that the man is straight. He just sees a loyal worker who has worked hard for his company for fifteen years. Granted, he should have fired the other man, but that would have been deemed prejudice. That's the irony of the bigoted world."

"Mimi, I know. I saw. I see." His face is still in his hands, but his elbows are now on his knees, as if his head were a weight too heavy for him to bear.

"And on top of that, he is planning sensitivity training for his staff. Now that's got to be a first for Hadrian!"

"I know. I know."

"He still loves you. It's so obvious."

"Mimi, please."

"Do you love him, Dean?"

"Of course I do. You know I do. I always have—I just can't—"

"Can't what, dear? Tell him?"

"I've changed. I can never go back to pretending. I need to express this other side of me."

"I understand, dear, but—"

"No buts, Mimi. I spent the first forty years of my life pretending to be someone I'm not. I can't go back to that now. Geez, Mimi, you're always quoting Shakespeare. Wasn't he the one who said, 'Be true to yourself.'"

Mimi nods approvingly, "'This above all: to thine own self be true, / And it must follow, as the night the day, / Thou canst not then be false to any man.' *Hamlet*, Act I, Scene 3."[12]

Dean laughs, shaking his head. "Line numbers?"

"Oh, don't be silly; of course I don't know the line numbers." Looking upwards coyly, "Or do I? 72, 82, 92?" After, laughing at her own jest, she adds, "I'm just kidding; of course I don't know the line numbers." Serious again, she says, "That was Polonius to Laertes; a father's advice to a son. Another lovely bit of irony, Polonius, such an underhanded government worm, actually saying something profound. But that was Shakespeare; he certainly had his finger on the pulse of man's paradox."

Dean smiles and reaches for his grandmother's hand. "I am being true to myself, Mimi."

"Are you, really? I know everyone thinks you're straight. That's what you've told all of us—"

Dean refuses to let her finish. "Yes, Mimi, I'm attracted to women. I've always known that."

Sensing Dean's irritation, Mimi decides to lighten the mood with a little cajoling. "And that little girl? Are you dating her?"

"Cantara and I are just friends. Besides, you know she's only twenty-two."

Now posturing annoyance, Mimi says, "Oh, you make me sound like an ageist." Coyly, she adds, "I've dated younger women in my day, too, you know." Looking up at the ceiling, tapping an index finger on her front tooth, Mimi tries to remember. "The youngest was—a good twenty years my junior."

Dean blushes. "Mimi, please."

"Oh, don't be silly. She's a consenting adult, and if she wants you, why not?"

"I'm—ah—" More than embarrassed, Dean finds this conversation has him in knots. It's hard enough talking about sex, but to have this discussion with his grandmother is downright disconcerting. Unable to come up with

---

[12] Shakespeare, William. The Tragedy of Hamlet, Prince of Denmark, Act I, scene iii, lines 564 to 566. OpenSourceShakespeare. Retrieved from: http://www.opensourceshakespeare.org/views/plays/play_view.php?WorkID=hamlet&Act=1&Scene=3&Scope=scene.

a reasonable explanation, Dean murmurs, "I'm just not ready for a relationship. I mean, I don't have time, and then re-ed—"

Mimi, no longer posturing, becomes quite stern. "Stop using that excuse. I know being around women still makes you uncomfortable, but you can work through that. It's just an excuse—unless you're still lying to yourself."

Perturbed, Dean enquires, "What do you mean?"

"Quite simply, love, there is no shame in being bi."

"Mimi, you don't understand."

"Yes, I do."

"*No*, you don't!" Dean winces; he hadn't meant to be harsh. "Sorry, Mimi." Sighing deeply, wiping his eyes dry, Dean explains, "I've taken up a cause. My being straight is a part of that."

"Seriously, Dean, do you have any idea how stupid that sounds? I've taken up this cause, too, and I'm gay."

"I, know, but—"

"But what, darling? Are you afraid people won't take you seriously enough if you're *only* bi?"

"Why is your voice like a whip?"

"Oh, my, dear; I wasn't that curt." Smiling slyly, she adds, "Or is it just the truth that hurts?" Mimi gives Dean a moment to calm himself. "Did I ever tell you my wife was bisexual?" Dean looks up, surprised. "Oh, yes; we didn't always used to be so uptight sexually in this country. Gender fluidity was the basis upon which this good country was founded. It was okay to be gay; it was okay to be bi; it was okay to be transgender," and smiling, she adds, "and, yes, it was even okay to be straight. Those crazy laws only came in after the Birtwistles and the Nassers managed to convince the rest of us—" pointing to her sternum, Mimi raises her eyebrows as if to say, "Me excluded," and harrumphs, "that an alliance with heterosexuals would be our downfall." Sighing now, she adds, "And somehow excluding heterosexuals meant excluding bisexuals as well." Shaking her head in disbelief, she continues, "It didn't help that attacks against the Wall were relentless in those days. And then 6-13 happened! I thought we'd never see the light of reason again." Mimi sighs. "With all of those radical changes over the past forty years, well, that's all people know now. It seems like everyone has forgotten the ideals we really founded this country on." Shaking her head, she asks, "Can you believe people actually believe the story that Mark and Julie Reiner were the only heterosexual couple to join us and that they sacrificed their sexual love for each other? Humph. Well, let me tell you, they *weren't* platonic." Chuckling now, Mimi says, "I guess all this ranting is just my way of saying it's okay to be bisexual. You can be bi, Dean, if you are. And then," she pauses briefly to allow Dean to let the thought sink in, "choose to be with the person you love."

"I wish it was that easy, Mimi."

"It's as easy as it is difficult. It always is when it's the right thing."

"I love you, Mimi," Dean says, and looking up at the screen, he adds, "And I love Geoffrey." But shaking his head, he concludes, "I'm just not ready to go back." Looking Mimi's way, he adds, "And when I finally am, I'm not sure whom I'll choose to be with, if anybody. I'm—needing this independence."

"That I understand. Just don't deny yourself the opportunity to love again."

"I promise, Mimi, I won't."

"All right, I guess that's the best I can get out of you for now." Dean stands and turns towards the den. "Time to go study again?" Smiling, she adds, "I so admire your dedication." Clucking her approbation, she concludes, "You're going to make a fine nurse."

Dean turns and laughs. "How do you know that?"

"By the way you take care of me, dear. You should consider geriatrics."

"I might at that, Mimi. I might at that."

"All right, then." Mimi picks up her remote and shuts off the wall screen. Rising slowly, hindered mostly by stiffness and pain, she crosses over and kisses Dean on the cheek. "Goodnight, my beautiful grandson; I'm off to bed."

"Goodnight, Mimi." Dean watches her hobble down the hall. Her body has deteriorated quite a bit over the last two years. "But you're still smart as a whip," he mumbles to himself, "still smart as a whip!"

* * * * *

Salve!

Reeducating Reeducation: A Salve!
Interview with Jason Warith
HNN—Melissa Eagleton Reporting

"Parents, before we begin, it is incumbent upon me to warn you of the delicate nature of tonight's special. We will be discussing the new anti-heterosexual laws and the impact they have on Hadrian's youth. Our producers have rated it PG 14—parental discretion is advised.

"With that said, welcome to another *Salve!* interview special. Tonight's guest is the Golden Boy of Reeducation himself, Jason Warith. He was hand-picked by President Stiles just days after her inaugural ceremony as Head Director for Reeducation. His first commissioned task was to run a series of reviews and evaluations at each of Hadrian's ten camps: both girls' and boys' Northwest, Northeast, Southwest, Southeast, and the military Midwest camp. Jason Warith has visited each camp and scrutinized the standard procedures used by each to reeducate our youth. Subsequently, the first unwarranted method to be abolished was the use of corporal punishment. We all saw the bloody paddle Gideon Weller wielded against those poor boys, and few amongst us regret the loss of that disciplinary tool; some still believe it was necessary—the majority of the population, however, does not. Next, Jason Warith banned electric shock therapy. This decision didn't go down without a fight from many medical practitioners who quickly pointed out its success rate at deterring opposite sex attraction. Warith responded by citing numerous anecdotal stories and research studies that clearly demonstrate men and women still feel opposite-sex attraction after shock treatment protocols. In spite of the overwhelming evidence, his opposition still insisted upon the return of its usage and contends that electric shock therapy has rendered opposite-sex attractions and activity difficult, if not impossible. More importantly, though, we'll discuss the new anti-heterosexual laws in place as well as Bill 52 proposed by Senator Nasser and General Birtwistle. So, without further adieu, allow me to re-introduce all of Hadrian to the Head Director for Reeducation, Mr. Jason Warith.

"Mr. Warith, welcome back."

"Thank you, Ms. Eagleton. I'm honored to be invited back. May I call you Melissa as I did the last time I was on the show?"

"Yes, and, if I recall correctly, you said I could call you Jason. I wasn't sure whether I should take such a liberty now that you hold such a distinguished governmental position."

"Please, I'd prefer Jason. I'm still not comfortable wearing shoes ten sizes too big for me."

"Now, why would you say that? I think President Stiles was right in choosing you for this position. Who better?"

"A great many. I am only too aware that President Stiles chose me for this position due to my association with the Middleton case and my role in the Frank Hunter trial."

"That's not the only reason she chose you. According to Adrian Adams, Director of the Southwest Reeducation Facility, the President couldn't have chosen better."

"Adrian's being much too kind. In fact, the President would have chosen better had she chosen Adrian Adams. He's open to change and recognizes the dangers inherent in our role as reeducators. I'm lucky to have him as my mentor."

"You speak as if you are still in practicum under him."

"In many ways, I still am. I may be Head Director for Reeducation, but Adrian Adams has the years of experience and wisdom required for this job. That's why I asked President Stiles to make him Assistant Director. I need his wisdom and experience to guide me if I'm to reeducate reeducation effectively."

"Yes, I love your catch phrase. Reeducate Reeducation. What made you come up with that?"

"I think we all know the answer to that. After the horrors of the Northeast Reeducation facility were revealed, we'd no choice but to rethink how we go about reeducating bisexual youth."

"Not all bisexual youth—only those who insist on experimenting with opposite sex attractions."

"True enough, Melissa, but even you must agree that the majority of our youth in reeducation are in fact bisexual. Cases like Todd Middleton, pure heterosexuals, are rare."

"Touché. Our geneticists have seen to that."

"Assuming they truly can detect the heterosexual gene and eradicate it like they claim."

"Why question that?"

"I was in court the day Faial Raboud examined Geneticist Avery Gillis. He couldn't guarantee that every child born in Hadrian has the homosexual gene."

"But they're so close, Jason; surely we can safely say that being straight is a choice in Hadrian."

"Melissa, our greatest geneticists can't provide us with 100 percent accuracy; that means some members of our society are born straight."

"Well—"

"Well, nothing, Melissa! Who in their right mind would choose to be straight? What could such a choice bring other than misery, the threat of exile, peer abuse, and loss of family?"

"Of course, when put that way, I can't see why anyone would want to be straight. So why do you think bisexual youth choose to act on their heterose—strai tendencies?"

"Quite simply, because they experience them."

"Yes, but they also experience same-sex attraction."

"Of course they do, but asking a bisexual (anyone between a 1 and 5 on the Kinsey scale) to ignore his or her opposite sexual attractions is just as futile as asking someone to ignore his or her same-sex attractions."

"Surely any 4 or 5 on the Kinsey can ignore them. What's so funny, Jason?"

"The Kinsey scale was a behavioral scale, which means—"

"I understand that, Jason, but here in Hadrian, we use Kinsey's scale to refer to the level of attraction a person feels, which would correspond with behavior if such behavior were allowed."

"I'm certain most 4s and 5s can and do ignore their opposite sex attractions. It's probably easier for them than it would be for the 1 to 3s."

"Whether it's easy or not, it remains imperative that bisexuals deny and avoid opposite sex environments and attractions."

"Not necessarily."

"Jason, please. Opposite sex attraction leads to het'ro sex, which in turn results in unwanted pregnancy."

"Not always."

"Okay, sometimes, *but it does*, and that's the central point. Het'ro sex *is* designed for procreation, whereas homosexual sex isn't. It's safe sex when it comes to avoiding pregnancy. The prohibition on heterosexual sex allows and empowers society to curb and ameliorate the threat of overpopulation."

"You see, Melissa, that's the intellectual foundational base upon which reeducation must be founded: the stabilization of human population. Rather than claim opposite sex attractions are wrong, we need to acknowledge their existence. This is the only way we can then begin to educate our youth effectively on how to control their sexual desires so our same-sex attractions can take precedence for the good of humanity. We can't beat sexual attraction out of a person. We can't terrorize individuals, forcing them to be gay. All we can do is reason with our youth and help them better understand the principles upon which Hadrian was founded: not just Hadrian as a homosexual community; not just to provide a safe haven; not just to reclaim the natural balance of the planet; but also to ensure a stable and sustainable human population. We can no longer tell people that they can't be straight. Rather, we must return to the first principles upon which our country was founded and encourage responsible citizenship that respects the need to avoid sexual acts leading to procreation—we all know there is only one sexual act that causes pregnancy; penile vaginal intercourse."

"Thank you for bringing us to that point, Jason, since it leads right into my next question. What do you think of Dean Stuttgart's comments urging heterosexual sex be made legal?"

"Dean Stuttgart is asking for something straight citizens already have. Nearly all forms of heterosexual sex are already legal, with the exception of one act: penile vaginal intercourse. It is that one sexual act that I believe must remain illegal. All other forms of coitus are harmless."

"Yes, but we all know what happens in the heat of the moment. Sexual energy builds, partners get carried away, and the next thing you know, they're procreating—Seriously—?"

"Are you still talking to me?"

"No—Yes—All right. Jason, all forms of het'ro sex need to be illegal. There's no point debating it. Our time is limited, and we still have a number of issues to discuss. Another controversial topic is the new law that allows mandatory medical examinations and procedures on het'ro women accused of having had penile vaginal intercourse. Should this be done?"

"No."

"No?"

"Absolutely not. No one should be forced to undergo any medical examination or procedure without his or her consent."

"Yes, but if she's had strai sex, she could be pregnant."

"Possibly, but it's not fair to impose testing based on a supposition. You have to prove the girl had penile vaginal intercourse and has missed her period. Additionally, it is imperative to respect due process and the rule of law."

"Oh, but you know as well as I do that no woman would admit to being straight given the stigma and consequences surrounding heterosexuality. That leaves our government very little choice but to act on Hadrian's behalf—and that of humanity. Next question: Should we allow for opposite sex marriage in Hadrian?"

"Why would you even ask that after our previous discussion? If heterosexuals are not allowed to have sex, what is the point of marriage?"

"So you think marriage is only about sex?"

"No, Melissa, I do not. I do, however, believe sex is an integral part of marriage. Two people choose to partner for life because they love *and desire* each other."

"True enough. Next question:—"

"I feel like you're shooting me with a Gatling gun."

"Sorry, Jason. We have so many questions to get through. I will try to slow down. Next question: What about Bill 52 and the proposed penalties for anyone running a GSA (Gay Straight Alliance) for citizens under the age of consent?"

"Many have rightfully called Bill 52 the anti-strai propaganda law."

"Yes, well, Senator Nasser's new bill proposes all persons found guilty of promoting the heterosexual lifestyle to our youth should be sentenced to no less than five years of forced military service."

"It seems to me, Melissa, that Senator Nasser and General Birtwistle, his most prominent supporter, are more interested in creating ways to increase Hadrian's military than they are distressed about the 'heterosexual menace,' as they like to call it."

"They also recommend a five-year military sentence for anyone who 'offers premises and other related, fixed, or movable assets for purposes of heterosexuality or promoting heterosexuality,' including landlords who rent space to GSA groups."

"Even against parents who support their children? I assure you, Melissa, I'm not impressed—"

"And then, there are the first two citizens, Alicia Graham and Tikaani Cloud, who are on trial under these new laws. It's alleged they participated in carnal knowledge 'threatening the order of nature'[13]—"

"What does that even mean, 'threatening the order of nature'?"

"Aiding and abetting the population explosion. If Alicia and Tikaani are found guilty, they'll be exiled or offered Black Henbane. Do you feel this is appropriate?"

"I would rather see—"

"But they're heterosexual. That's illegal."

"Let me be very clear, Melissa; being heterosexual is not illegal in Hadrian. It never was, and I pray it never will be. Even the new anti-heterosexual laws don't make being heterosexual illegal. In fact, ironically enough, this new law is less harsh than the original one that denied any heterosexual contact, including hugging, kissing, and walking arm-in-arm. All this new law does is specify penile vaginal intercourse, 'aggravated heterosexuality,'[14] as illegal. It's this act, as we all know, that's punishable with exile or assisted suicide."

"So you must agree with their sentence, then?"

"I may not like it, but *if* they're sentenced, *if* they're proven guilty, that will be their fate. But how's that to be done?"

"If they'd pass Bill 52, then a forced medical examination would quickly determine the presence of sperm inside the woman's vagina."

"Only if the medical exam occurred within a reasonable time limit. If the two haven't had sex for at least five days before the test, there's no sperm left alive. Alicia and Tikaani have been in military custody for over two weeks. If you can't definitively prove they had penile vaginal sex, you've no right to exile or impose assisted suicide."

"The condition of her hymen—"

"Don't even go there, Melissa. To do so is to put every woman at risk. There are numerous nonsexual activities that can cause the hymen to

---

[13] https://www.hrw.org/news/2014/04/28/double-threat-gay-men-syria
[14] http://76crimes.com/2014/04/18/2-ugandan-men-face-trial-on-gay-sex-charges/

break. Accusing all women with a broken hymen of penile vaginal intercourse is dangerous, uninformed, and misleading."

"You're right, Jason. I apologize. Let's move on. What about Alicia's brother, the young man accused of having sheltered the couple? As you know, viewers, Alicia's brother, Jacques Provencher, is also on trial, having been charged with offering 'premises and aid to active heterosexuals.' Under the new law, 'to harbor active heterosexuals,' turning a blind eye to their dangerous activities, is punishable with five to seven years' service in Hadrian's military. Since Hadrian has no penal system, nor is the government looking to form one ('to do so,' according to President Stiles, 'would be to waste tax dollars on crime when it is needed to capture carbon and save the planet'), all those convicted of 'aiding and abetting the destruction of the planet through the willful act of shielding procreators' will be required to make amends through mandatory military service. And what about the government's plan to sweep the sewers of Hadrian for heterosexual youth?"

"Melissa, please, you haven't allowed me even to answer your last question."

"Sorry, Jason, but we're running out of time. The upsurge in runaway heterosexual youth attempting to avoid reeducation, or those who have been kicked out by parents, has increased. Do you think this is the unfortunate result of legalizing heterosexuality?"

"Humph. Many of these youths, the majority of whom are bisexual, are fighting back against the necessary restrictions placed on their sexual desires. When parents, friends, or educators discover they've opposite-sex attractions, they bolt."

"Too many of these youth are spotted hiding in Hadrian's sewer systems. It is really disgusting when you think about it."

"Melissa, these poor kids have nowhere to go. They've set up makeshift homes down there to live in absolute squalor."[15]

"Some citizens believe these youth get exactly what they deserve. Considering their chosen lifestyle, it does seem an appropriate location. Due to heterosexual sex, our planet has been turned into a sewer. What do you say to that?"

"I say no one deserves a life like that. We must remember that

---

[15] http://76crimes.com/2014/04/17/jamaica-youth-minister-to-develop-plans-for-lgbt-homeless-youth/

sexuality is a fluid reality. Many of us, the majority of Hadrian's cit- izens, whether we like it or not, are bisexual. Less than 15 percent of our citizens are fully homosexual. If our scientists are as accurate with genetic coding as they claim, even fewer are fully heterosexual. That renders the majority of us bisexual. That doesn't even take into account the transgendered."

"Yes, the issue of transgendered individuals is tricky. We've always accepted gender dysphoria, but by the same token, we do need all our citizens to conceive one child to maintain a stable population."

"I see no problem there. Most transgendered women donate to Hadrian's sperm bank before transitioning. After transitioning, the transgendered female is sterile so her sexual activity isn't a threat to human population."

"Yes, but what about transgendered men?"

"When these men are still in female bodies, Hadrian has provision for them either to give birth before transitioning or to donate eggs pre-transi- tion in order to have a surrogate goddess give birth later."

"Yes, but most of these women—"

"—men—"

"—yes, yes, men, choose transitioning at such a young age—"

"—with parental consent—"

"—yes, yes, with parental consent—transitioning at such a young age, they're not able to donate eggs. Once fully men, they expect Hadrian to provide them with sperm, eggs, and surrogacy for free."

"Of course. This also happens with our transgendered women who transition early in youth and are no longer able to donate sperm."

"Yes! They also expect free sperm, eggs, *and* surrogacy based on birth male status. That is a very heavy burden on Hadrian's tax dollars."

"I see no problem, Melissa. Hadrian's tax dollars are designed to sup- port gender fluidity as well as the restoration of our planet."

"Don't forget education and the military. With such expensive strains on our tax dollars, shouldn't individuals who transition bear the financial burden for their choice."

"Melissa, please. You know as well as I that one does not choose to be gender dysphoric. Hadrian doesn't condemn anyone for having been born in the wrong body. We accept and embrace all forms of sexuality and gender expression. There's only one form of sexual expression that we can't allow and that's heterosexual penile vaginal intercourse. We ban this solely due to the current state of human population and the disastrous environmental conditions our ancestors left to us."

"Yes, Jason, that is the key point. We must ban heterosexual sex 'due to overpopulation and environmental chaos.' It was so wonderful hosting you on our show again. Thanks again for coming."

"Thanks for having me, and for occasionally letting me speak."

"Well, that's all for tonight, folks. Stay tuned for our regular *Salve!* newscast."

Vale!

What in Hadrian's Name…?

As soon as the studio lights click off and room lighting is back to normal, Jason stands up and addresses Melissa Eagleton. "What in Hadrian's name was that? You call that an interview. I felt like I was being bombarded with a Gatling gun."

Melissa, too, stands. Her eyes shoot daggers Jason's way. All the anger seething inside her is projected at him for the moment. Through gritted teeth, she curses before uttering, "Not now, Mr. Warith."

"Not now?" he shouts back. "If not now, when?" Having turned away from him, Melissa refuses to look back. She quickly walks out of the studio as motion sensors slide a portion of the wall open for her. Jason follows at her heels, gripping the door's frame as he calls out to her, "I thought you had more integrity than that Ms. Eagleton!" Seeing she is ignoring him, Jason turns and promptly leaves the studio.

Jason Warith's remark has not gone unnoticed. It stings Melissa, and she flushes with anger and shame, knowing full well the accuracy of his critical comments. "So did I," she whispers to herself as she walks down the hall towards the production manager's office. As soon as she enters Darien Dumas's outer office, she is halted by his secretary, Tam Tuan, who is annoyed at being interrupted in his act of preening before his handheld mirror. He quickly ceases his grooming in an attempt to deter Melissa's passage into his boss's central office. "Out of my way, Tam," Melissa orders.

"He's not going to take well to you barging in on him. He's in the middle of a voc conference."

Melissa turns on her heels and stares down the young man. "Really? Well, he had loads of time to interrupt me during my broadcast. I think it only fair I cut him off during his voc con!" With that, Melissa swivels back to the door, but she is stopped when the motion sensor doesn't open it for her. Melissa bangs on the wall to no avail. As with all the doors in the studio, Darien Dumas's door blends in with the wall, the camouflage so perfect that if you didn't know a door was there, you would never notice it.

Tam immediately responds to his voc. "I'm sorry, sir. It's Ms. Eagleton. She insists on seeing you." Glaring Melissa's way, Tam triumphantly relays his boss's message. "He said to take a seat. He'll be with you in a moment."

A moment turns into forty-five grueling minutes with Tam refusing to acknowledge her existence, ignoring her every request, and not even bothering to offer her a beverage. Finally, he looks up and smiles, "Mr. Dumas will see you now."

Incensed, Melissa refuses to say, "Thank you." Cringing, she walks through Dumas's door with Tam's snide remark "Rude bitch" shot at her from behind her back.

As soon as she enters Dumas's office, Melissa marches straight to his desk and launches into her harangue. "Would you please explain to me what that was all about?"

Dumas doesn't even look up from his work; he has a series of files projected in front of him and concentrates all his attention on them. To Melissa, he gives just a series of backward waves. His voice is cold, calculating, and very business-like. "My voc cons are none of your business, Ms. Eagleton."

"I am not interested in your voc calls—"

"Conferences," he reminds her without once looking up from his work.

"Fine, conferences, whatever. I want to know why you kept interrupting me and imposing all those ridiculous questions for me to ask Jason Warith?"

Finally, Dumas blinks off his work. His grey eyes bore into her like ice. "Ridiculous questions? Now, you see, Ms. Eagleton, that is the very negative attitude that is affecting *Salve!*'s ratings."

"*Salve!*'s ratings were just fine until you upended things."

"'Ridiculous' and now 'upended.' You think quite poorly of Hadrian's National News Agency."

"Hadrian's National News—*Salve!*—is my baby! Andrzej Sobieski and I made this news show what it is today: the most watched, most respected newscast in all of Hadrian!"

"That may have been the case at one point, Ms. Eagleton, but the ratings tell a very different story."

"The ratings were just fine—"

"Until you changed."

"Me?"

"Yes. You changed and you are trying to drag Hadrian down with you. Well, I won't let that happen. Hadrian is not a liberal country; it never has been. We are conservative for a reason. Our planet demands we be conservative. The very safety of Hadrian's citizens depends on our controlling individuals who have crazy opposite sex urges; urges that rebel against our very being. You and your subversive het'ro advocacy are not wanted here. I took over Andrzej Sobieski's position as production manager at the insistence of our stockholders and viewers, who are fully aware you are intentionally dismantling this nation's ideals, leading us into the very gutter where those strai rats have taken up residence." Melissa, who is too stunned even to respond, stares at Dumas, her mouth hanging open. "Quit gaping at me like a moron. Aren't you listening? You're out! You're fired!"

Stammering at the realization of what has just happened, Melissa attempts to speak, "B-but—"

"But what? Wasn't I clear enough? You. Are. Fired."

Finally finding her voice, Melissa retorts, "I'm the face of *Salve!* I bring Hadrian the news."

"Let me correct your misconception—you were the face of *Salve!* You are no longer. The face of *Salve!* must be a true lover of Hadrian. You do not love this country. You want to see us descend into a state of abomination. No, Hadrian needs a new face. The face of *Salve!* must be Hadrian's lover!"

"Hadrian's lover? Are you insane?"

"I might ask that question of you, but I don't care enough to want to."

Desperate now, Melissa blurts out, "You can't replace me."

"I already have. My voc con was with Danny Duggin—"

"Danny Duggin? That actor who—"

"That's right—that actor who portrayed Antinous in the docudrama *Hadrian's Lover.* Who better to be the real face of Hadrian than Hadrian's lover himself? He's young, he's handsome, he's loved, *and* he's moving into your office today. Security will accompany you as you clear out your belongings, and then it will escort you off the property." Looking up to the right to register the time display on his voc, he orders, "You have one hour." Indicating that their meeting has ended, Darien Dumas blinks up his work files and resumes reading. Looking up briefly, he waves her away with a curt, "Good day, Ms. Eagleton."

* * * * *

Salve!

The New Face of HNN
HNN—Danny Duggin Reporting

Good evening, Hadrian! Yes, I know, "What's this?" you say. Well, I, Danny Duggin, am the new face of Hadrian's National News Source, *Salve!* I am confidently hopeful you will come to know me as a dedicated news host, and I look forward to serving you with hard-hitting journalist interviews. Many of you may remember me from my role as Antinous in the mini-series that aired a few years ago, *Hadrian's Lover*. After retiring from acting, you can imagine my surprise when Darien Dumas, the production manager for *Salve!*, cast me as Melissa Eagleton's replacement. I assure you I felt most deeply honored to accept this new challenge. And now, here I am today, beginning my new life journey as your host to all things newsworthy in Hadrian.

First, no doubt, you are all wondering what happened with Melissa Eagleton. There is very little news on that front; there simply were irreconcilable differences between Ms. Eagleton and HNN. To elaborate further, as Mr. Dumas said, would bring dishonor to one who has served Hadrian so well for so long. So, let's leave it at that, shall we? I don't know about you, but I loved Melissa, so I would never want to say or do anything that might damage that good woman's reputation. I just hope I am capable of stepping into her shoes, metaphorically so to speak, though she did have good taste in footwear.

Oh, oh, my ear is speaking. I'm plugged in to our production manager. He has promised to help guide me through the first few *Salve!* episodes since there was no time for any training. It seems I need to move on to more newsy stuff. I am here, after all, to present to you hard-hitting, cutting-edge information about all things interesting in Hadrian. HNN's mission has always been to keep Hadrian's citizens informed about key events—everything from the daily machinations of President Stiles's government to the fun and frolic of everyday citizens' lives. That's right; we want you to be a part of the new *Salve!* Please voc us your stories, everything from the sublime to the ridiculous. Let's share and have fun in Hadrian! What better way to reduce the tension in our lives by laughing at all our silly little human follies?

In fact, just to get the ball rolling, my partner Ricky volunteered to share the first short excerpt of daily life humor. I am so embarrassed, but if we are going to ask you to send in your silliest moments, I guess it's only fair to share with you one of mine. Last Sunday, Ricky and I spent the day meandering through Hadrian's Zoo. Oh, it is such a beautiful location, but you still have to be careful. These animals are, after all, mostly wild. The zoo trainers are very careful to ensure the most dangerous animals are kept securely locked away and pose no harm to humans. Still, there are one or two locations at the zoo where you can walk amongst the more gentle creatures. One such place is Monkey Mountain. Oh, folks, I am so embarrassed. I could positively kill Ricky for having voc cam'd this. Anyway, there I am on screen; you can't see Ricky in the shot since he's the one recording. Now, you may not know this about me, but although I'm dedicated to being trim and in good shape, I am absolutely addicted to junk munch. Prior to entering Monkey Mountain, I positively loaded up on the junk munch. Now, there are numerous signs—oh, look; Ricky even zoomed in on one—that warn zoo visitors not to bring any food items onto Monkey Mountain, and Ricky even reminded me, after the fact, of course. *Significant others!* Additionally, the zoo brochure I had downloaded to my voc also provided the same warning. Needless to say, I failed to heed those warnings—perhaps I should say, failed to read them. Oh, here it comes. As you can see, I'm thinking these cute little monkeys are just wanting to play with me, but, oh no, there it is—the attack. They made a beeline for every pocket I had stuffed with food. Oh, and there goes the shirt pocket, and the whole front of my beautiful green garden of hope silk shirt. I loved that shirt! We recycled the material, of course, but it will never be my beautiful green shirt ever again. Oh my, and my entire front torso is exposed. Well, it is a good thing I keep in shape; otherwise, I would be displaying belly fat to all of Hadrian right now. Well, all I can say is thank Hadrian that's over.

But it wasn't that painful, really, and I must admit it is fun and cathartic to be able to laugh along with others at myself. So, now that I've exposed my soft underbelly, so to speak, it's your turn, Hadrian. I can't wait to see your vid cam entries!

Vale!

Catastrophe!

"No!" Cantara is adamant. "Politis didn't out you, and she wouldn't want you outing yourself."

Sid reaches over and holds Tara in his arms. She is crying and refuses to listen to reason. "Cantara is right." Dean nods in agreement.

Tara starts ripping at her hair in agitation. "It's my fault, people. They're going to fire her!"

Dean and Cantara join in on Sid's embrace of a frantic Tara. "You can't beat yourself up over this." Cantara, too, is crying. The group sways slowly as they attempt a collective soothing caress. It is not working.

"Why did I ever write that piece? Why did I let her read it? I thought I was only putting myself at risk. I had no idea they'd can her for it."

"She's been suspended," Dean reminds her. "She hasn't been fired."

"But they're talking about it." Had she not been tightly wrapped between three bodies, Tara would have run from the room and found herself a straight-edge; all she wants to do right now is cause herself pain as some form of ameliorating penance. Self-harm is a sad condition suffered by many in the bi-strai community. For Dean, it was punching himself in the legs. For Tara, it is cutting.

Cantara knows what Tara is thinking. "You don't want to cut yourself, girl." Tara's forearms and wrists are covered with scars and archaeol inscriptions—obscene reminders of past episodes and suicide attempts.

"It's my fault," Tara sobs. "Why was I so cocky? Who the fuck do I think I am?" Tears now streaking her makeup, Tara looks into Cantara's eyes. "They're going to fire her, and it's all my fault."

"Listen," Sid attempts to reason with her. "She's been suspended, but they won't fire her. She's tenured."

"They said—they said—" Tara hiccups between gasps.

"It doesn't matter what they said," Dean whispers.

"What did they say?" Prasert asks as he enters the room. He is still in the dark about the catastrophe that has shattered Tara's life. Seeing the scene before him sends shivers up his spine. "Hadrian's Lover," he cries, "what's happened?"

Sid answers. "The Dean has suspended Dr. Politis for reading Tara's essay out loud in class." Tara moans. Cantara and Dean soothingly coo to calm her. Sid continues, "Some students complained."

"Higgins and Godoy, no doubt." Prasert is angry. "Those fucking bitches, such bigots."

"Angel and Grace are my friends," Tara shrieks. "They wouldn't turn on me."

"Didn't you hear what Angel said in class when Politis was reading your paper?"

"She didn't know it was me; she didn't know it was me." Tara is almost spastic in her defense of her friend. Angel, Grace, Sid, Prasert, and she had formed a study group for Sociology 100. Tara is convinced that their bigotry is simply what they were raised with, and all they know, but with subtle hints and the right kind of prodding, she can bring these two around to accepting heterosexuals. At the very least, she believes they are capable of tolerance.

Sid silences Prasert with an angry glance. Of the five, Prasert is the least susceptible to emotional turmoil. He prefers to look at everything with unveiled, pragmatic logic. The last thing Tara needs right now is realism. She needs love, support, and yes, to have her friends help her put rose-colored glasses back on. Prasert concedes to this need. Sid has argued with him over this point, and this is a moment when he decides Sid is probably right.

"Well, we don't know who complained. Their names are a guarded secret." Sarcasm drips off Sid's tongue. "But they don't want Tara's name to be a secret—"

Shrieking in agony, Tara says, "I have to tell. I have to turn myself in or they'll fire her."

Sid, Dean, and Cantara respond in chorus, "Absolutely not!" Their voices now overlapping, they continue, "Politis wouldn't want it." "She's protecting you." "They're not going to fire her!"

"Please, Tara," Cantara begs. "They are trying to expose you. Don't let them win."

"Cantara's right." Prasert's voice is soothing. "You have to wait this out." Prasert joins in on the group hug. "I agree with Sid. They're not going to fire her." The other three utter their agreement. Although they are all in doubt of the veracity of this declaration, each one knows how critical it is to convince Tara in order to keep her from harming herself. Softly, slowly, five bodies sway insecurely, desperately feigning confidence.

Finally, Sid breaks their silence. "Sweetie, don't think me cruel, but you have to let this incident go, put it aside. We have finals. We all have to study."

Unable to bear her own pain and needing to lash out at someone, Tara yells, "Go! Go! All of you! Leave me alone." She struggles to break free of the group. Sensing imminent danger, her four friends almost crush her inside their collective, supportive grasp.

"That's not what I meant, sweetie." Sid is now kicking himself inside for bringing up what everyone must surely be thinking: *Finals wait for no one.*

"Hey, Tara." Cantara pulls her friend out of the collective and hugs her tighter. "He didn't mean it that way." She pulls back just enough to look into Tara's eyes but to retain a solid grip on the girl. "And you know he's right. We all have finals." Sensing Tara is about to explode again, Cantara cuts her off. "I've got an idea. Let's let the guys go and you and I have a voc conference with your mama."

Tara shivers. "They don't want to talk to me."

"Your mom is the unreasonable one. You know Mama Cecilia still cares. She vocs me all the time to ask how you're doing." When Tara flashes an accusing glance Cantara's way, she defends herself. "You know that. I've told you every time."

"And I told you not to voc them."

"I don't. Your mama vocs me." Shaking her head at what she knows Tara is going to say, Cantara continues, "I refuse to be rude and ignore her. Besides, I really think she is attempting, you know, really trying to come around."

Tara gulps, "You think?"

Cantara smiles. "Yeah, I think." Sensing Tara no longer wants to bolt or harm herself, Cantara relaxes her grip. "So," she adds, now nodding in the direction of the three men, "how's about we let the boys leave, let them do some studying, and you and I voc Mama Cecilia?" When Tara first came out to her mothers, both women were shocked. Her mother took it hardest off all, refusing to believe that someone with her genes had "strai blood." Her first method of retaliation was to kick Tara out of the house. Her next move was to cut off her financing of Tara's voc. When she tried to close Tara's credit account, rendering her thumbprint (the means by which individuals transact business in Hadrian) null, she was stymied. Once a youth begins any form of employment and begins depositing his or her own money into the account, the parent no longer has complete legal control over it. All Tara's mother could do at that point was to cease depositing credits into Tara's account. Since Tara has a part-time job, her employer continues to deposit her earnings into her account, keeping it open. Tara may not have much in terms of spending money, but she is managing to stay in uni. "So what do you say?" Cantara asks, trying to be jocular for Tara's sake. "Shall we voc up Mama Cecilia?"

Still shivering, Tara nods, "Okay."

Cantara gives the boys leave. "You guys go. I'll take care of her. I promise."

"Are you sure it's okay, sweetie?" Sid is still feeling the sting of guilt. "We'll all gladly stay if you need us."

Dean and Prasert chime in, "Of course we'll stay."

"No," Tara smiles weakly. "It's all right. Cantara's right. If Mama Cecilia—if she—" The hope combined with the fear of rejection is too much for Tara to bear.

"She will. I know she will," Cantara says with more confidence than she truly feels.

Tara begins nodding successively. "Mama's what I need. Connect me, please."

The three men take this as their cue to leave. After their hugs and good-byes, Dean asks Tara to be sure to let them know how the call with her mama goes. She promises as they repeat their final goodbyes.

* * * * *

96

Salve!

Tenured Uni Professor Suspended[16]
HNN—Danny Duggin Reporting

Hello, fans and viewers. Thank you so much for embracing me as your new host for *Salve!* I was thrilled to read so many positive comments in favor of the change. John Dunson commented, "What a delight to have such a handsome face reporting the news." Thank you, John. Imran Kumar said I was refreshing and "far more relaxed than" our previous host. Adnan Shakiri's comment made my day: "Danny, I loved you as Antinous, and I LOVE you as the new face of Hadrian. In *Hadrian's Lover*, you made me cry. As the new host of *Salve!*, you make me laugh." Thank you, thank you, thank you all, so very, very much. I wish we had time to read all your wonderful comments but, as you know, we must get on with the meat of the show.

Earlier this week, Dr. Cora Politis, a tenured professor of Augustus Uni, was unceremoniously suspended from her duties as an instructor of sociology. The president of the uni, Archibald Hoffstetter, and the chair of the sociology department, Dardana Jashari, are deliberating whether or not to terminate the tenured professor from her post. She was suspended from duty shortly after she read a student's paper out loud to her Sociology 100 class. Apparently, this student wrote about what it feels like to grow up strai in Hadrian. The essay was handwritten on paper—an atrocious waste. When requested, Professor Politis refused to hand over the student paper, which contains the young woman's name, as she does not wish her student to suffer any negative consequences or ramifications. Of course, the writer should suffer negative ramifications if for nothing other than abuse of the environment. The professor needn't worry that this particular student would be expelled as she herself said this was that student's first and

---

[16] Inspiration for this *Salve!* entry comes from: http://chronicle.com/blogs/ticker/s-c-house-keeps-penalties-on-colleges-that-assigned-gay-themed-books/74099

only abuse of the environment. As we all know, Hadrian's environmental laws work on the baseball principle of three strikes and you're out! Even so, Politis claims to have shredded the document. Apparently, she chose to omit the student's name during her in-class read to maintain the writer's anonymity. Professor Politis claims the student's name must be protected against the anti-strai sentiments running high at Augustus and, apparently, throughout Hadrian. This, of course, all stems from the legalization of heterosexuality and this particular uni having opened its doors to openly strai and bisexual students.

You bisexuals…excuse my sneer, but please…all you do is confuse everyone with your hurtful ways of playing both sides of the field. Pick a side already and stick with it—and if you have any sense inside your heads, you will make sure that side is with the same sex! Sorry, people, but bisexual behavior is one of my pet peeves. I knew a bi once—he left me for a lady! I so wanted to expose him, but it was his word against mine, and I had no evidence except what he had said to me. I should have voc recorded it. Those were the days when he would have been exiled! But today, his actions are technically legal.

Oh, dear. You see me tapping my ear because the production manager is directing me to get back on track, given I have digressed too much.

Currently, the president of Augustus Uni and the chair of the sociology department are deliberating whether to terminate Professor Politis's contract. Politis was suspended after an outpouring of complaints from her Sociology 100 students as well as letters from concerned citizens about Augustus Uni educating its students with strai propaganda. Both the uni president and a coalition of fifty students from Sociology 100 have laid charges against the professor. If she is found guilty of presenting strai propaganda, Professor Politis's sentence will be that of banishment. Of course, the nation will provide her with Black Henbane to drink if suicide is her preference.

Faial Raboud is Professor Politis's defense attorney. Ms. Raboud is famous for having convinced Judge Julia Reznikoff to revert Frank Hunter's exile to that of a lifetime of military service. For those who may not remember, Frank Hunter was found guilty of murder. He had suffocated his lover, Todd Middleton, who was a confirmed heterosexual. Ms. Raboud's line of defense for Professor Politis is based on the reasoning that the Anti-Strai Propaganda Law only prohibits the sharing of heterosexual information to youth under the age of twenty-one. "As all of Professor Politis's Sociology 100 students are age twenty-two and older," Raboud said, "she cannot be convicted under this new law." Well, that was rather redundant of her. Of course, we all know that most uni students are twenty-two or older. Everyone had to serve in the military for four years before heading off to college, but that's not the crucial point! Hadrian's Federal Prosecutor, Graham Sabine, correctly points out that every uni in Hadrian offers two special scholarship awards to high school graduates. These lucky recipients do not serve at the Wall like the rest of us. And, as Prosecutor Sabine rightly adds, all high school graduates are under twenty-one, some as young as seventeen; there are always at least seven or eight students on any given campus under age. Any dissimilation of intelligence in a first year uni course is then likely to make its way into the ears of these youth. Currently, there are no scholarship students under twenty-one attending Augustus Uni. Although the campus offers scholarships, no one has applied for one since 6-13. Regardless, it is important to note that there is a seventeen-year-old scholarship winner, Roger Hunter, attending Antinous Uni. Sabine's argument is that no uni professor be allowed to instruct students regarding heterosexual behaviors in order to protect Hadrian's youth.

Well, Hadrian, what do you think? Should Professor Politis have been suspended? Should the uni dismiss her? Should she be held accountable under Hadrian's new Anti-Strai Propaganda Law? Voc us your views at **HNN#RE-AUP-ASL**.

Vale!

Salve!

HNN—Viewer Wave Link
@HNN#RE-AUPS-ASL

Aaron Whyle
fire the BITCH

April Bolger
Uni students are old enough to understand strai concepts. To punish intellectual inquiry and discussion by censoring not only limits academic freedom but also undermines the intellect and education in general.

Derrick Defrock
Isn't uni supposed to be a place where all ideas are explored? There should be no censorship at the uni level. We aren't high school students.

Angel Higgins
@ Derrick Defrock—No ideas were explored! I'm in that class. It was blatant heterosexual propaganda! I want that woman fired *and* exiled! We have no room in our good country for deviants, perverts, and their hoodwinked supporters.

Derrick Defrock
@ Angel Higgins—Ideas were explored after you and your bigoted friends left us. You weren't willing to listen and consider other perspectives.

Dean Stuttgart
@Angel Higgins—I agree with Derrick. Uni is the place to discuss controversial views. Those who graduate uni are the ones who go on to lead this country. We need people in government who aren't blinded by prejudice and understand that humanity is a spectrum and not a harsh, blinding light.

Angel Higgins

@ Dean *Hunter!*—No doubt you're the strai rat that essay spoke about. How dare you flaunt your founding family heritage! You should have stayed dead! Your poor father! The shame you bring to your family. I read somewhere about some religion having honor killings. Maybe your father should look into it.

Sissy Hildebrand

@Angie Higgins—You sick excuse for a human being! His poor father? His poor father abandoned his son! His poor father faked his own son's death! His poor father is as much a pathetic excuse for a parent as you are for a human being! Shame on Gordon Stuttgart! Shame on any parent who would abandon a child for any reason! And as for Dean Stuttgart flaunting his founding family status, it was his grandmother, our founding mother, Destiny Stuttgart, who revealed Dean's founding family status to Hadrian! As well as being pure evil in spirit, you are also ignorant and repugnant. I read about those "honor killings" you wrote about. You fool! The people murdered by those families were often women who refused to obey religious laws as well as GAY MEN AND LESBIANS!

Guillaume de la Chappelle

@Derrick Defrock; @Angel Higgins—A thorough education must include all sides of discussion and debate, in order to have informed opinions, and also to correct the behavioral and social patterns of unrest and prejudice. One doesn't "censure" and/or fire qualified instructors/teachers for showing all sides of issues, as that promotes unfairness and lopsided/one-sidedness in thoughts, actions, deeds, and laws. Reading a submitted paper in class is an effective teaching tool. It teaches discourse, discussion, and peer opinion and evaluation, and no teacher should be threatened or treated with disrespect for doing what the particular course requires for education purposes.

Andreas Contreras

these strais have an hell-inspired agenda! its like my pastor says the strai agenda wants to take over the family forcing us all to register strai! just for making babies and we know how making babies is the *real strai agenda!* its what landed human into all this mess! in the first place we got to stop them there are trying to try to take over education workplace environment governemt they want it all! they gonna destroy all! hadrian augustus uni is their base of operations that prof needs to go and augustus uni needs to expel all the strais!

Sissy Hildebrand

Does bad grammar and bigotry go hand in hand? @Andreas Contreras—Might I suggest you learn how to use capital letters, and punctuation, and spelling **AND** then add a little human decency into the mix.

Adolf Gaafar

See what happens with the legalization of strais; they think they own the country now! (@Sissy Hildebrand—is my grammar good enough for you?) I agree with Aaron Whyle—fire the BITCH!

Fernando Pereira

Heterosexuality has never been illegal in Hadrian. The law simply made it mandatory for anyone under twenty-two to attend reeducation so they would not make the wrong lifestyle choices. What is, and always has been illegal, is heterosexual sex. The new law simply outlines exactly what qualifies as heterosexual sex, that being penile vaginal intercourse. The new law also only encourages parents to send a child to reeducation if he or she displays or admits to having opposite sex attractions. It is in that child's best interest. That being said, heterosexuals of any age can now kiss, pet, walk arm-in-arm, etc., without fear of banishment. However, I wouldn't recommend any heterosexual going around flaunting his or her sexual preference. No one in Hadrian needs to or wants to see that!

Roger Hunter

I am that seventeen-year-old scholarship recipient. I am completing grade 12 at Pride High and, yes, when I attend Antinous Uni next semester, I will still only be seventeen. Even so, I think it's ridiculous that people out there believe that my, or any other person's, sexual orientation can be so easily swayed by one student's personal essay. I am a gay man. I have always known I am gay, and I have only ever been attracted to men. Nothing anyone can say or do will ever change that fact. Fernando Pereira, you say the parents of children who experience opposite sex attractions should be encouraged to send their child to reeducation camps. Well, my Papa Dean—*Dean Stuttgart*—was forced to attend one of those camps and the stories he tells are harrowing. I would not wish that on anyone! Be careful what you ask for, for one day it may be your child suffering under the tyranny of prejudice! I, for one, would like to see all of these camps shut down!

Guillaume de la Chappelle

@Roger Hunter—well said, young man. It is clear why you won a scholarship award—academic, no doubt!

Qadria Flore

@Roger Hunter—you love you're papa and that good but he is openly bi and men like him are danger to Hadrian. you should encourage him to forget bi feelings. bi men are really het'ro in disguise. At best they are hedonistic to the core.

Emile Nelligan

Professor Politis should be whipped for sharing something like this! I know many, including myself, willing to volunteer to wield the whip. Let the press record and film it and then show that to uni students and let them see the "natural consequences" the perverts have brought upon themselves and fully deserve due to the filthy choices they have made. This should be used to deter future youth making such choices. Any good parent would take their children to view the whipping—although this is harsh, reality is harsh, and we should not hide this from our children; they must see us confront het'ro evil!

Bromek Sobranski

They should interrogate every student in that class to uncover who the strai is!

Brindusa-Katalin Poenaru

It saddens me to read all this hate. I thought we were better than that, Hadrian.

* * * * *

Mama Cecilia

When Mama Cecilia receives the voc link from Cantara, she instantly leaps up from her chair at the kitchen table. Her wife, Angelina, and their son, Hardeep (Cecilia's birth child), both look up, shocked.

"What is it, babe?" Angelina asks. Cecilia is usually the calm and centered one. To see her react so suddenly is odd.

"Nothing, nothing," she says as she sprints out of the room. Knowing Angelina's inquisitive nature, Cecilia judiciously elects to take this call outside. "It's just an important message from work."

Seeing Cecilia head towards the door, Hardeep begins to whine, "Where are you going, Mommy? I want to go too!"

"Hush, you," Angelina reproaches the child softly. "Mommy has work to do."

Now pouting, Hardeep protests, "But she promised to take me to the park."

"Mama will take you. Would you like that?" Angelina tries to compromise. Pouting even more, he replies, "You never play with me."

"I'll play with you, I promise. But first you have to finish all your soup." Hardeep smiles. "Can we go now?" he asks after swallowing a spoonful. Angelina inspects the boy's bowl. "Three more spoonfuls first."

By this time, Cecilia is seated on the yard swing. It is early evening and the cool of this late spring nightfall has yet to settle fully. Still, she has brought a shawl out with her because she is hoping this will be a long call. "Cantara, what's happening? How are you doing? Is everything okay? How's my baby?"

"Hey, Mama Cecilia. Tara needs to talk to you. She's going through a rough patch, and I told her I believed you would listen and—"

"Link us up! Link us up!"

"Please don't judge her."

"I won't. I swear I won't. I just want to talk to her. I just want to see her."

"Okay, here she is." Mama Cecilia watches as Cantara steps back and Tara comes into view. At that same moment, Mama Cecilia's image comes into focus on the wall screen in the small office of Augustus Uni's GSA.

"Hi, Mama." Tara tries so hard not to be emotional, but she blurts out her words between sobs anyway.

"Hey, baby. How's my little girl?"

Tara half laughs. "I'm not so little, Mama; you know that."

"I know." Mama Cecilia stifles a sob by placing her hand over her mouth. "It's been so long."

"You heard what Mom said."

"I know," Cecilia replies mournfully. "But I don't feel that way. I still love you, baby. I may not agree with you. I may not like it. But I still love you."

"I love you, too, Mama."

"What happened? Tell me."

"They're gonna fire my teacher because of me."

Mama Cecilia's sudden intake of breath shows she has seen the most recent *Salve!* "Oh, baby, that was you?"

"I need to turn myself in. Dr. Politis won't tell them my name, and they've threatened to fire her if she doesn't."

Cantara steps back into view. "Mama Cecilia, tell her she can't do that. Tell her it's too dangerous. I know Professor Politis. She wouldn't want her to."

"Your friend's right, baby." Remembering the *Salve!*, Cecilia tries desperately to reassure her daughter that anonymity in this situation is her safest move.

Tara sighs deeply, her breath wobbling. "But it's not fair to Dr. Politis."

"Who asked her to read your paper? Did you?" Mama Cecilia has turned pragmatic.

"No," Tara concedes. "She asked me if she could read it."

"And whose idea was it for you to remain anonymous?"

"Hers."

Mama Cecilia's sigh of relief is audible. "That means she wants you to stay anonymous. She didn't have to read your paper. You didn't ask her to read it. She asked you to stay anonymous because she wants to protect you. She knows what she is doing. She is standing up for your rights as a strai—heterosexual individual." Tara smiles at Mama Cecilia's effort to avoid an anti-heterosexual expression. "She decided to risk opening up discussion on this issue, not you." Breathing deeply, tilting her head to the left as she so often does when asking for a favor, sucking closed lips between her teeth, her eyes now those of an innocent doe, Cecilia says, "Baby, please; revealing yourself as the author will not help your professor. All it will do is make your life impossible to bear."

"Mama, will you—" Beginning to believe there is a chance for reconnection, Tara ventures out on a limb, exposing her frail psyche to great risk. "—will you come visit me after finals?"

Without hesitation, Mama Cecilia answers, "Yes, baby, I will."

* * * * *

Hadrian's Real News

Real News for the People, about the People
HRN—Melissa Eagleton Reporting

Good evening, fellow citizens. I am pleased to be reporting for you once more. Tonight's episode is the first of what I hope to be many on *Hadrian's Real News* station. That's right, Hadrian will now have access to another voice, another perspective when it comes to news reporting. When I left HNN, my camerawoman, and life partner, Alsoomse Lund, came with me. Together, we have pooled our life savings and have begun *Hadrian's Real News, HRN*. After experiencing the micro-managing of Darien Dumas' totalitarian control over Hadrian's news at HNN, I decided our country needed a more impartial look at events as they occur in our nation. *HRN*'s mission, therefore, is dedicated to providing Hadrian's citizens with as truthful a dissimulation of the news as possible. I am aware of my human frailty, so feel free to call me on any presentation I give about events that you feel are given in a biased manner. What I have to say about the current happenings in our country will be radically different from the perspective you will receive from HNN, but I will endeavor to give you facts-based reporting. Unlike my old show *Salve!*, my goal with *HRN* is to bring you the truth.

No doubt—*no doubt* you have all seen the *Salve!* or have at least heard reports about HNN introducing you to the new voice and face of Hadrian's News: Danny Duggin. On that *Salve!*, Danny mentioned that I left HNN due to "irreconcilable differences." That is very true. I, however, have no scruples sharing with you what those irreconcilable differences are. But, first, I need to give you some of the background that led up to my dismissal. That is right, folks; I did not resign. I was fired. You see, a few years back, Hadrian was hit with some very shocking news: one of our elite high school students, Todd Middleton, son to famous agricultural engineer Will Middleton, had been exposed as straight. He confessed to being an active heterosexual. We were later to learn that his father, the man who genetically redesigned the soya bean so we could cultivate it here in our northern climate, a man to whom all of Hadrian is grateful, was also heterosexual. This news alone should have been enough to shock some sense into our government, making it recognize the need to treat our straight brothers and sisters with the same level of equanimity we offer to ourselves. But there is more to this sad story. Shortly after Todd Middleton was exposed by the woman he loved, whose name remains a profound secret, although the reason for the need for secrecy has never been explained—sorry, Hadrian; I digress, but rest assured, I intend to do a great deal of digging into the identity of this girl.

As I was saying, shortly after Todd Middleton was sent to the Northeast Reeducation Camp, his best friend and lover, Frank Hunter, murdered him. Although the judge rightly found Frank Hunter guilty of murder, she acknowledged his unique circumstances. His boyfriend, Todd, had been brutally raped while inside reeducation, and Frank believed Todd when he said he would never be able to live a happy and fulfilling life as a gay man. So when Todd asked Frank to help him die with dignity, Frank Hunter agreed.

What does all this have to do with my sudden dismissal from HNN as host of *Salve!*? Quite simply this: I agreed with President Stiles's decision to reevaluate the laws regarding heterosexuality. She rightly had the wording changed so that someone over the age of twenty-two who identifies as straight or bisexual will not be summarily exiled, nor are parents now required by law to register their child, anyone twenty-one or younger, at a reeducation facility. As President Stiles said, the choice regarding the reeducation of our youth belongs to the parent. Parents are still free to choose and encouraged to do so, in fact, which is why, as many had feared, our reeducation system has not collapsed but continues to prosper. Our nation also continues to provide services for parents to use at home, but it is no longer mandatory that a straight or bisexual child be sent to one. The decision is now that of the parent.

When this report first hit the news, HNN fully backed the President's move. There has, however, been a change in management since then. I find the new production manager, Darien Dumas, and his team to be far too right of the current politics for my tastes. Darien Dumas and his team are anti-strai. All attempts on my part to report impartially regarding heterosexual issues were thwarted at every turn. My last *Salve!* episode was likely the worst example of this. You may recall I was interviewing Jason Warith about the new direction reeducation is taking and, well, Danny Duggin makes this easy for me to explain. He told you that his production manager is helping him through his first few episodes of *Salve!*, that he was training him in essence, and that is why Danny sometimes refers to his right ear. That lovely piece of jewelry Danny wears is actually the microphone for his voc, which is connected directly to Darien Dumas. Darien is telling Danny what to say just as he had been instructing me to cut off and counter everything Jason Warith had to say. Danny Duggin, I'm sorry to tell you that "temporary voc connection" to Dumas is not going away. I am a seasoned news anchor, ten years' experience under my belt. When I told Dumas I would not have him vocing me during a *Salve!*, he promptly fired me. HNN now has an agenda, not to provide Hadrian with real impartial news, but with a slanted propaganda that is designed to perpetuate prejudice and hatred of heterosexuals and, as you heard with Danny's little tirade, bisexuals. I have since learned that Darien Dumas is a member of Hadrian's Conservative Right.

So, as I said earlier, this is why I am airing *Hadrian's Real News*. My camerawoman, and life partner, Alsoomse Lund, supports me in this endeavor. Together, we pledge to bring you honest and impartial news. Real News for the people, about the people!

Before I close, I must extend my sincerest apologies to Jason Warith for that debacle of an interview I held with him. He was given no chance to air his views or explain how he is working to restructure Hadrian's reeducation system. Every time he attempted to respond to the many questions I hurled at him, Darien Dumas ordered me to cut him off and change the subject. Complying with my then superior's requests showed me in the most unprofessional light. And as I stand here today, Hadrian, I give you my word that I will never again treat a guest in that manner. I give you my word I will give a voice to the voiceless in our nation.

I also owe our transgendered citizens an apology. During my interview with Jason Warith, I made some very disparaging comments about them. The insinuation that our trans brothers and sisters are bleeding Hadrian's wealth through necessary transitional medical procedures was both cruel and unfounded. I have come to recognize that our trans brothers and sisters, though we claim to accept and support them fully, are not given the same level of respect that Hadrian's gay citizens receive. Shortly after my dismissal from *Salve!*, I went to Hadrian's Support Center for Transgendered Citizens—HSCT—and offered my apology in person. While there, I learned that far too many of our transgendered citizens don't even take advantage of the medical services at their disposal for transitioning due to the prejudice of our society against heterosexuals. I was dumbfounded by this statement and asked why this was the case. Daoina Leifsson, President of the HSCT, explained that transmen attracted to women or transwomen attracted to men often fear being mistaken for heterosexuals. In some cases, they fear losing their partners if they do use surgical transition. Not only are the numbers of trans men and women low in our country, but the percentage of those who access the free medical services offered to them is less than 15 percent. My trans brothers and sisters, you are not a drain on the system. *Au contraire*, it is Hadrian's backward attitudes towards human sexuality that are clearly a hindrance to you.

Now that I am to sign off, I'm at a loss for what to say. *Vale!* was my signature for *Salve!* and continues to be used by that news service. *Vale!* sadly is no longer my signature, so I will end my episodes with a new word, a word I believe you need for a real news station, what all of Hadrian needs:

TRUTH!

The Past Resurfaces

Wolf proudly appraises his new office. It's small, yes, but it is his. He has a window overlooking pier three and an exterior office for his assistant and a secretary, as soon as he hires one, that is. He still can't believe his good fortune. One day he's being fired for being a "fucking strai" and the next he's being promoted to pier manager. "The kid really came through for me," Wolf mutters in admiration. In return, Wolf offered Matthew Molloy the job as his assistant pier supervisor. "Shit," he keeps reminding himself, "that's the least I can do after all this." His arms wave around, following his body in a complete circle as he takes in his eight by ten office, desk included. The reception and waiting area and cubicle for his assistant are slightly smaller in size. It also contains a small fridge for storing food, a sink, and counterspace for food preparation lined up against the back wall next to the door for the washroom/storage room.

Matthew Molloy, leaning against the doorframe of Wolf's office, is watching his new boss with amusement. He can't help but laugh. "Sorry, boss, but you look ridiculous dancing around like that in the middle of your office."

Wolf blushes, embarrassed at being caught mid-private rejoicing. "I'm not dancing; I'm just…taking it all in, is all." Sighing deeply, experiencing contentment beyond his wildest dreams, Wolf ejaculates, "I still can't believe it's real."

"Well, you earned it." Matthew, too, is sporting a grin wider than anything he's experienced since before his time in reeducation.

"Oh, I don't know," Wolf muses. "That's awful kind of you to say, but it's really all due to you and the big guy's soft spot for us strais."

"It's more than that, and you know it. You've been here fifteen years. You know these piers better than anybody. A hell of a lot better than Malco ever did. At least you can tell the difference between junk that's reusable and junk that needs to be disposed of." Remembering the last time he pulled up something poisonous, Matthew adds, "And that idiot couldn't tell toxic waste if it hit him in the face." It's Matthew's turn to sigh, a sign of relief. "Finally, we'll have some common sense prevail around here."

"Thanks, kid." Wolf truly does appreciate the approbation.

"And my name's not 'kid'; it's Matthew." Now, considering his new position, he adds, "Besides, how am I going to carry any weight around this place if you keep calling me 'kid'?"

"Yeah, yeah, I know, but 'Matthew' is too formal for me."

"Then call me 'Matt.' I'm okay with that."

"All right, kid, I'll call you, 'Matt.'" Matthew just rolls his eyes. Wolf grins, "Okay, let's get this place cleaned up. I'm interviewing for secretaries this afternoon."

"Cleaned up?" Matthew is confused. "What in Hadrian's name is there to do?"

"Watch your language," Wolf chastises lightly. "We're in the office now."

"Sorry, but seriously," says Matthew, gesturing first to Wolf's office, "you got your desk." Now to the reception/waiting room, "There's the secretary's desk. Two chairs and a coffee table for whoever the hell—heck—comes up here to wait to talk to you," gesturing now to his cubicle space, "and I got my work area." Looking around, convinced all is fine, he concludes, "There's nothing for us to do but sit down, call up our new office programs, and get to work." Matthew slaps his hands together in anticipation and begins moving towards his cubicle.

Wolf grimaces. "Look at this place!" Disgusted, he wipes his finger over his desktop and then wiggles black grime in Matthew's face. "I doubt Malco ever once took a rag to this place." Now assuming what he thinks is an authoritative stance, he orders Matthew to get out a broom and dustpan and start sweeping the office floors. Still having trouble seeing his coworker in a senior role, Matthew makes a mock salute before heading towards the bathroom to retrieve the necessary cleaning tools.

"Don't be such a smartass, ki—Matt. I'm still getting used to my new role. And I'm nervous."

Wolf purposefully ignores Matthew's laughter. They are both feeling good-natured these days with such good fortune having come their way. He can let the young man have his guffaws. Wolf crosses over to his desk and sits down. Blinking, he brings up the office program Matthew spoke of. It waves slightly in the air. Finding it a little hard to view, he blinks up the image of an old-style computer screen, which Wolf believes stabilizes the text. Both he and Matthew were issued vocs as part of their new position. Geoffrey Hunter set both men up on a three-year, no interest loan, allowing them to pay off their vocs through a monthly deduction from their work credits. Even with these monthly payments, both men are now earning more than they ever dreamed possible in their lifetimes. After opening up one of the manuals Mr. Hunter sent for him to study, Wolf calls out to Matthew, "Matt, can you start in here? My first interview is at one o'clock, and I want to make a good impression."

This time, Matthew's laughter is so robust the red dreadlocks dance around his face as his whole body shakes. His green eyes twinkle as he turns back to lean inside the doorframe of Wolf's office. "What in Hadrian's name have you to be worried about? You're the boss! You're the one doing the interviewing."

"Yeah." Wolf blushes again, aware of the absurdity of his remark. "It's just I never interviewed anyone before. Mr. Hunter gave me some tips, but it still feels weird."

Matthew's pleasure at Wolf's discomfort actually causes Wolf to squirm a little. "My first interview is going to be with a woman."

Matthew turns grim. He knows the discomfort that comes when a re-ed man is forced into a woman's presence, especially when the man spent two years in the re-ed system like Wolf did. Matthew was lucky. He had only a couple of months under the torture of Gideon Weller, the notorious Warden of the Northeast Reeducation Camp. Gideon Weller was known for the use of corporal punishment and electric shock therapy. That all ended after Jason Warith had the man arrested for abuses against re-ed youth, as well as raping six victims, all of whom committed suicide while under his care. "Do you have to interview women?" Matthew asks gently. He knows how hard this will be for Wolf. He's heard the horror stories of how effective reeducation is; he, being a product of the same camp system, albeit for a much shorter period of time, also finds himself feeling queasy when around a woman he finds attractive.

"Mr. Hunter said that no court would back me if I refuse to interview a woman. It would be seen as discrimination." Not wanting to make Mr. Hunter out as the villain, Wolf quickly adds, to the man's defense, "He said he understood, that his husband suffered from the same thing, but Dean, his husband, never had to work with women; he was a stay-home spouse." Sighing, Wolf rubs his forehead, removing some of the nervous sweat buildup. "Me, on the other hand, well, I'm a pier manager, so I've got to work with the public, in a sense. Whether I like it or not, I've got to interview the woman if she puts in an application and her CV is noteworthy." Blinking up the girl's resume, Wolf has to admit, "And this woman's CV is definitely noteworthy."

"Maybe she won't be your type," Matthew suggests. He finds it much easier being around women to whom he isn't sexually attracted.

Wolf laughs. "Me? I was a real horn dog before I got caught. I don't remember a single lady out there I wasn't interested in. All women are beautiful in my mind."

"Even the homely ones?"

Wolf studies the young man. "Homely, Matt? There are no homely people. Get to know the person and the beauty of the soul shines out of her eyes and through the smile."

Matt chuckles. "You're a hopeless romantic." Twirling the broom he was using in his right hand, he asks, "What time you say she would be showing up?"

"One o'clock."

"You want I should be out of here then?"

"No," Wolf determines judiciously. "You would have to share a workspace with her, assuming she gets hired, so I think it best you at least meet her and see how you feel around her, too."

Still spinning the broom, Matt attempts to respond in a blasé manner, "All right, boss. You know best." But he, like Wolf, is discombobulated at the prospect of having to spend a substantial amount of time in the woman's presence, maybe even working in tight quarters next to her.

Wolf knows what Matt is feeling. He thinks, *Get him working; that will help get his mind off the looming possibility of the upcoming, and most likely, unpleasant experience.* "Stop spinning that broom," he orders, "and start running it over the floor like you're supposed to."

* * * * *

When Stephanie Chatters walks into the reception area of Wolf's new office, Matt is nowhere in sight. He has just slipped into the washroom to put away the last of the cleaning tools and is currently relieving himself. So when Wolf steps into the doorway of his office, he greets the young lady, completely oblivious of the role she once played in Matthew Molloy's life.

Wolf smiles, extends his hand, and welcomes her inside his small office space. "Hello, Ms. Chatters." Directing her to the chair opposite and facing his desk, he says, "Please have a seat." He closes the office door behind him so they can hold the interview in private.

* * * * *

The interview went better than Wolf had expected. Still, he listened to Mr. Hunter's advice about not hiring the first person who walks through the door. "Let the prospective employee know you have other applicants to interview and that you'll get back to her after the interview process is finished." Wolf remembers Mr. Hunter's smile. "You may well end up hiring the first person in the end, but you don't want to make that decision until you have considered all the applicants." Wolf grimaces, wondering whether he is really management material. Sensing his sudden frown is disconcerting the young lady, Wolf resurrects his smile and gently leads her from his office into the reception waiting room. His hand on the back of her waist feels comfortable, and only now does he realize she hasn't caused him to feel queasy at all, which Wolf finds amazing considering how attractive Stephanie Chatters is. Her breasts are the perfect champagne glass full, her lips are plump, and her makeup is impeccably applied. The perfect lipstick lesbian, he decides, *and if I were a woman*, but he instantly lets that thought disintegrate. Once in the waiting area, Wolf gestures for Ms. Chatters to sit in one of the chairs next to the small, round coffee table. "Ms. Chatters, if you wouldn't mind taking a seat. I would like to introduce you to my assistant. If you get this job, you will be working with him almost as much as you will be working with me. I think it wise you two meet."

Stephanie's smile widens. She sees this as affirmation that the interview went well and she might land this contract. Sadly, her hopes are dashed as soon as Wolf calls his assistant and Matty Molloy, her ward from the Northeast Reeducation Camp, steps out from inside his cubicle. There is a silent explosion of tension as their eyes meet. Wolf remains ignorant of this as he begins introductions. "Matthew Molloy, I'd like you to mee—"

Matthew finishes the sentence for Wolf. "Stephen Chatters!"

Wolf blinks, a little confused.

Stephanie straightens her back. Her initial reaction had caused her to shrink and drown inside a whirlpool of guilt and desire. But if there is one thing she always finds inner strength for, it is insisting others accept her for her true gender. "You know my name, Matty. It is Stephanie."

Matthew's eyes flare in rage. His voice rises to a shout. "I'm not calling you Stephie or Stephanie or any other bullshit name like that! I know you for who you are, so don't try playing your pretending games with me."

Tears burgeon, and though Stephanie begins to shake, she refuses to back down. "I am a woman. I've always been one. I didn't understand that when we were inmates at—"

Matthew pushes his face right up against Stephanie's. "I was an *inmate*— you were the camp warden's little pet!" The spit that flies from his voice into Stephanie's face accents Matthew's disgust—and hatred. She quickly backs up and trips back into the chair Wolf had offered her. Glaring Wolf's way with his index finger pointed at Stephanie, Matthew screams, "He is not a she. He is a he!" Turning now to stop any defensive remark from Stephanie, Matthew yells in her face, "I know you're a man because you made me suck on it, and you raped me with it, so don't even try to pretend otherwise." Turning now to Wolf, Matthew declares, "I will not work with this man ever! Hire him and I quit! I don't give a shit if I have to go back to the piers. As Hadrian is my witness, I'd rather beg in the streets than ever work with *IT*!" On that note, Matthew storms through the door, slamming it behind him before pounding down the outer stairs to the dock.

Wolf stands amazed. This is not what he had been expecting, though he suddenly realizes why he doesn't feel the usual discomfort around Stephanie. The male body she was born into does not give off the same pheromones as a female body. Reeducation focuses on pheromones as much as it does image. When Wolf was in the Midwest Military Reeducation camp, he had undergone treatment where he would be hit with electric shock therapy even without a woman present. Female pheromones that specifically indicated a woman's body was ready for mating would be sprayed in the room, and when his body reacted, he suffered the extreme pain of electric shock therapy. The pheromones are clearly a lot stronger than the physical appearance because Stephanie is really very beautiful and sexually attractive. This is when it dawns on Wolf that, although she identifies as female, Ms. Chatters has yet to undergo physical transformation.

Watching Ms. Chatters crying, slumped over in her chair, clearly devastated by her encounter with Matthew, Wolf crosses over to bend on one knee in an attempt to comfort her. Being virtual strangers, Wolf only reaches for her hand to hold. Too much physical contact might make them both uncomfortable. He tries to soothe her with calming hushes, but Stephanie continues to sob and shake. "Please, Ms. Chatters," Wolf says, desperate to defuse this situation, "allow me to apologize for Matt." Wolf cringes slightly after saying this, wondering whether Matthew really owes her an apology. Matthew opened up to Wolf when they first met, having shared all the horrors he had endured at this woman's hands when Ms. Chatters was still identifying as male. Still, the situation is delicate, so he needs to handle it carefully.

Stephanie sobs louder when Wolf apologizes for Matthew. Then she states, "It's not Matty's fault. He's right. What I did to him in that place is unforgivable. I'm the one who needs to apologize." At this point, she looks bleary-eyed, her once impeccable makeup now streaming in rivulets down her face. "But he will never give me that chance, now, will he?"

Wolf shrugs his shoulders as if unsure, but he knows the answer as surely as Ms. Chatters. Matthew Molloy will never allow Stephanie the opportunity to repent and, even if he does and she apologizes with all her heart, he will refuse to forgive. "Matt's pretty bitter, Ms. Chatters. I don't think waiting around to try to apologize is a good idea."

"No, I know." Now looking desperate, she begs, "But you'll tell him for me, won't you."

"Of course," Wolf agrees readily. "I'll tell him you're sorry. I'll tell him anything you ask." Wolf pauses, wondering how to broach what are the most worrisome and pressing subjects on his mind. Will Ms. Chatters be pursuing her application, and will she be planning to press charges of abuse against his young friend?

Stephanie seems able to read Wolf's mind. "You set your mind at ease, Mr. Gaidosch. I couldn't work anymore with Matty than he can work with me."

Wolf's sigh of relief is audible. "Do you plan to press charges against him for what he said about you—your not being female?"

Stephanie opens the latch to her purse, perfectly matched to the paisley dress she is wearing, and retrieves a small flowered handkerchief. After wiping her eyes and dabbing her nose, she removes her compact and attempts to clean up a little of her makeup. For a moment, she stares at her reflection in the compact lid. After snapping it shut and returning it to her purse, she shakes her head. "No, Mr. Gaidosch. What Matty said was wrong; he clearly doesn't understand what it means to be transgender—"

"Maybe he's never heard of gender dysphoria."

"Maybe, but like you said, he is bitter. And—" For a moment Stephanie has to fight back more sobs. "And," she begins again, after struggling to regain composure, "I was cruel. I believed everything Gideon Weller told us. I thought it was all for the best. Oh, Mr. Gaidosch. I was horrible." Stephanie cannot help but gasp at the pang of self-recrimination. "I—I understand why he hates me."

Again, Wolf breathes a sigh of relief. The last thing he wants is to have to fire Matthew—not after everything the young man has done for him. "Thank you, Ms. Chatters. Thank you."

Stephanie now stands and walks quickly to the door. Before pulling it open, she turns briefly to remind Wolf of her request. "You will remember, won't you, to apologize to him for me. At least try to make him understand." Her voice trails off as she knows what she is asking for is hopeless, but Wolf reassures her that he will do his very best. "Thank you," she mutters as she reaches for the doorknob and then quickly exits.

* * * * *

Salve!

Armageddon Is Upon Us!
HNN—Danny Duggin Reporting

Hadrian, I must warn you. A dangerous time is approaching. The threat no longer lies solely beyond our walls. There are those amongst us who wish to demolish the very cornerstones that make our country great. In just three days, Hadrian's governing council will vote to legalize opposite sex marriage, thereby allowing these reprobates of our society to procreate at will. Soon our good country's population will swell, breaking down our border walls and forcing decent homosexual citizens to mix with the outside world, a world rife with the sins of heterosexuality, overpopulation, and abuse of our beautiful planet. What little beauty that remains here inside our walls is now at risk of utter destruction. Do not allow heterosexuals back inside our walls, for, Hadrian, we will rue the day of their acquisition of power. Unless we are vigilant, they will utterly destroy us and our small clean corner of the planet.

God has abandoned heterosexuals, and so must we! Their lascivious ways, excessive copulation, and procreation are both sinful and damaging—damaging to the planet and to the human psyche. The heterosexual barbarians used God's name to perpetuate violence and hate. How many of our homosexual brethren suffered brutally under the "holier than thou" heterosexual supremacy! Our history books are riddled with documentation of men, women, and, yes, even children brutally murdered in God's name until finally God's voice thundered from above, demanding, "Enough!" In God's infinite wisdom, the founding families were delivered unto the land—the land of plenty—a land still virginal and untainted by the polluting hands of the heterosexual. Laws forbidding the existence of heterosexuals inside our walls were created for a reason. We live in God's light. We live in love and peace and prosperity, all because we heeded God's warning to banish the heterosexual from our sight—nay, not just our sight but, ultimately, from the entire planet. We must abide by God's will and eradicate heterosexuals from Hadrian's soil or God will rain justice down upon us—we too will suffer and starve and die by breeding ourselves into extinction! God has spoken! Give no sway to the heterosexual barbarians. Allow them no quarter. Round them up and dispose of them before their heinous ways contaminate the pure life of God's chosen people, the homosexual. For God knows we are the only ones dedicated to preserving the planet and ensuring the survival of the human species.

Vale!

Tara's Coming Out Party

It's Friday night. Tara wrote her last final this afternoon so she is longing to celebrate. Cantara has just refused her offer of cruising and carousing the bars because she still has one major final to go.

"But your English exam isn't until Wednesday," Tara laments. "Come on; let's have some fun."

"I can't, Tara, I have to read Leo Tolstoy's novel *Anna Karenina* in its original form and compare it with the Hadrian-released version. The original book is no simple read, let me tell you, but, oh, Tara, the romance, the love, and all between opposite sex individuals. It is truly stunning. To actually read, for the first time, a piece of literature that deals with het'ro themes is so refreshing and exciting. I just can't put it down, even if I wanted to. And I don't. In its original form, the book deals with three central couples, not just two, and I swear it's over a thousand voc pages long!"

"Why don't you just read the uni notes version? That's all anyone else does."

"Oh, Tara, how can you even ask? Even if the notes weren't riddled with anti-strai propaganda, they could never achieve what reading the real book is like. Oh, I wish I could hold the real print book in my hands."

"You might as well wish for a thousand dead trees."

"Oh, I don't know. Did it really take more resources and energy to produce books than it does to produce all our technology?"

"I don't know, Cantara. All I do know is that we abandoned books and the excessive use of pen and paper for ecological reasons."

"Well, you cheated." Cantara's wide smile reveals that she approves.

"I had to. You know I did. If I had submitted that paper over the wave, anyone and his dog could have read it. What if it got into the hands of my mother?"

"I know, I agree. There is no security on the wave, especially with the anti-pseudonym laws. If we could at least keep our identity secret, we could express ourselves more freely without fear. Thank Hadrian that Dean taught us that little trashcan trick." Grinning now, seeing how her friend has effectively deflected the topic, Cantara adds, "I haven't changed my mind, you know."

"About what?" Tara asks coyly.

"About going out, or about reading a real book someday. I do wonder what it would be like. The wave links I've read suggest books have a dusty, musky smell to them, especially after they have aged."

"Ugh. Sounds gross."

"I think it sounds romantic."

"You and your romance. Romance doesn't exist if you can't love the person you love."

"Oh, but we're getting there. Progress has been made."

"Off the bones of six dead men!"

"Well, at least we can be open about who we are now without the threat of exile."

"Oh, sure, they won't exile us if we admit to being bi or straight, *but...*" the elongation of the vowel with the crisp slamming of the final consonant helps to emphasize Tara's frustration, "if we have sex, now that's a different matter. There is still the anti-strai sex law that criminalizes opposite sex intercourse."

"And the Anti-Strai Propaganda Law that gags us!" Cantara is being swept up into the political discussion.

"All of which do little more than perpetuate hate. They act like lighter fuel sprayed over sparks."

"True enough, but," Cantara counters, "it is our first victory since the sexual reform laws enacted in year ten."

Year ten is bitterly remembered by all heterosexuals and bisexuals as the year prejudice revealed its ugly head inside Hadrian's Wall. As the young country struggled to maintain the ideals established in what is known today by Hadrian's citizens as the four cornerstones, many powerful members of Hadrian's government were beginning to foresee difficulties in restraining heterosexual couples from those nasty accidental pregnancies. Bill 33 was set before the Senate putting all propagation under government control as well as severe limitations on heterosexuality. Fear of overpopulation and emulating the lives of the outside world was strong enough to push through very stringent restrictions on all forms of heterosexual behavior. No one was allowed to reproduce except through Hadrian's Reproduction Clinics. The propaganda chant of the time was "Say YES to IVF and NO to het'ro sex!" Once Bill 33 passed, defending the logic of other anti-strai bills was easier. The sexual reform laws outlawed heterosexual intercourse, and with the ever-growing fear that the law was, in itself, not enough, reeducation camps were created to ensure all of Hadrian's youth were guided towards the only acceptable, normal, and safe form of sexual behavior, that of same-sex couples. This draconian law also meant that anyone twenty-two years of age or older was summarily exiled. The extreme Conservative Right, which was currently in power, had used the need for extreme measures to ensure population control as its central argument. It wasn't long after that the most damning attack against the Wall occurred, where all the soldiers both on and off duty were slaughtered and the women raped and tortured. When 6-13 happened, the setting off of a dirty nuke at Augustus's city border gate only added fuel to a fire that had been burning into white-hot coals for far too long. All Hadrian remembers 6-13; it cemented the general population's mistrust of outsiders and everything strai. When a straight man drives across your border and ignites a dirty nuke, it doesn't take too big a push to convince the majority of citizens to abhor all things heterosexual.

"Even you have to admit," Cantara added, "getting rid of the threat of exile just for being who we are is astonishing and wonderful."

"But not good enough," Tara lamented. Ironically, when alone, Tara is the more outspoken of the two, but when in the company of others, Tara's abusive background takes over and silences her, leaving Cantara to act as her mouthpiece. But, here, in the relative safety of her dorm room with her most trusted friend, Tara feels free to express her deepest thoughts and feelings. "Six men had to die in those camps before the law was softened— softened, Cantara; not removed." Here Tara gets deadly serious. "How many more of us have to die before real changes are made—the kinds of changes that will allow us to walk the streets arm-in-arm without the threat of abuse or ridicule, the kind that would allow me to write a paper on being straight through the voc without fear of reprisals? And then they fire Politis—"

Cantara is shocked at this news. "I knew they had suspended her, but I didn't think they'd go so far as to fire her. Oh, Tara, I'm so sorry."

Tara is nearing tears. "I should have exposed myself. I shouldn't have let her take the fall." Giving her friend a sheepish little smile, the one that always wins Cantara over, Tara sweetly begs, "Please come out for a drink with me. I really could use one with all this business with Politis and shit."

"Oh, Tara, I want to—really, I do. But I can't. I have way too much reading to do, and then I have to work on figuring out what my thesis strategy will be on the day of the big exam."

"Are you sure there is no way I can convince you to come out with me? The Blue Chair is said to be strai-friendly." The Blue Chair is Antinous Uni's Sonic Music Nightclub. "We might even be able to secretly hook up with some guys. How exciting would that be?"

"Hadrian's Lover, that would be awesome!" Now, using her hands like a hatchet, cutting the air with each word, Cantara concludes, "But. I. Can't." Exasperated, Cantara turns her back to her friend and pulls up a visual screen of the book she is reading as if to emphasize her need to study.

"All right, read your book. Be a good little student and study. I'll ask Angel and Grace. They're both done with their finals, too." Sighing now, she adds, "I won't be able to meet any guys with them, but at least I can get drunk."

"I don't like them," Cantara warns. "Remember, they walked out when Politis was reading your paper?"

"Yeah," Tara replies in their defense, "but they didn't know I was the one who wrote it. They still always say 'Hi' when we meet, and Angel even offered to buy me a drink once."

Cantara isn't mollified. "I don't trust them. They were behind Politis being fired; you know that, right?"

"Yeah, I do. But everybody's gone. They're the only ones around, and you won't party. So they're not my favorite two to hang out with, but what's a girl desperate for fun to do? You're clearly determined to stay in, and I'm clearly determined to go out."

"What about Sid and Prasert? You could still meet a man hanging with them." "They took off on a spontaneous romantic getaway this weekend. And, I know, then there's Dean, but Dean—"

Cantara cuts her off. "Don't you dare say he's too old!"

Tara retracts quickly. "Of course he's not too old; he just doesn't like to party—I mean *really* party!"

"Please don't get so drunk I have to clean up your puke in the middle of the night, again."

"No promises, girlie," Tara laughs as she walks through the door of their dorm room.

Cantara shakes her head in mock censorship, an action she will later regret.

* * * * *

That night at The Blue Chair, the three women are drinking quite heavily. Angel is standing behind Grace with her arms wrapped around her. She is swinging Grace from side to side in her embrace. Every so often, Angel attempts to caress Grace's private regions. Grace giggles at Angel's provocative advances, but she skillfully deflects her lover's aim. Even drunk, Grace isn't willing to let her lover get carried away sexually in public.

"For the love of Antinous, you two get a room." From behind the bar, the bartender can be heard laughing at Tara's remark. He even tosses her a wink. This sets Angel off.

"What the fuck's your problem, Tara? Pissed your little girl wouldn't come out with you?"

Grace laughs robustly at that. "Like anyone could get that fucking breeder to do anything." Angel appears to concur and rewards her girlfriend with a tighter hug and a kiss on the back of the head.

"What makes you two think Cantara's straight?" Tara asks noncommittally.

Angel responds, her head now resting atop Grace's, "I saw the stupid bitch going into the strai office."

Tara acts amused. "Strai office? They have an office?"

Angel is miffed. "You know what I mean—that stupid GSA room."

Feigning ignorance, Tara asks, "What's a GSA?" Had she been seen entering the GSA office space, too? The location chosen for the GSA to meet is quite discreet. Very few on campus know of its existence, so Tara wonders how these two learned of its location.

Grace answers, her drunken slur destroying her attempt at sarcasm, "Gay Straight Alliance." Both Angel and Grace laugh at how stupid Grace sounds.

"Oh," Tara replies, trying hard not to show any signs of worry.

"You know," says Grace, stepping forward to get in closer to Tara and slipping out of Angel's embrace, "I'll bet that little bitch was the one who wrote that crybaby 'How it sucks to be a strai' paper."

Angel agrees instantly. "Yeah, what a fucking piece of shit that was."

Both girls chime in sync, "So strai!" They laugh uproariously at their joke.

"Don't be ridiculous, she wasn't even in our class. Besides, Professor Politis obviously thought it was well-written," Tara says, the phrase popping out before she realizes it.

"Yeah, well," Angel begins suspiciously, "we know what happened to her." Grace giggles. Angel responds by wrapping Grace inside her arms again. "I suppose someone might like that paper if she were strai," Angel ponders. She eyes Tara briefly and then cuts the tension with, "Maybe old Politis is a closeted strai."

Tara forces a short laugh. "Yeah, maybe." Then trying to be onboard with the other two, she adds, "She couldn't help but coo over the paper; that's for sure." Shaking slightly inside, Tara reaches for her drink and gulps it all back.

"Whoa there, girlie," Angel laughs. "If you keep drinking like that, you'll end up drunker than Grace." To which Grace begins to giggle uncontrollably in Angel's arms. Angel is clearly enjoying the vibration effect. While Tara is ordering another drink, Angel whispers something in Grace's ear. At first, Grace appears upset, but after a few more soft whisperings, Grace begins to giggle uncontrollably again. She is also nodding her head in aggressive agreement. "Hey, Tara," Angel says, "get that bartender back. I think we three need to get rip-roaring drunk!"

"What can I get you, ladies?" the bartender, a young man of mixed Asian and African descent, asks. He is close enough to Tara that she can smell his strong, musky odor. Large, dark eyes and thick curly hair add to his physical attraction. She tries not to show just how much she longs to kiss his lips or embrace his tall, lean body.

Angel snaps Tara out of the bartender's magical allure by slapping her on the shoulder. To do this, she has to lean forward and push Grace's face into Tara's bosom. Grace giggles in ecstasy as her face gets squashed between Tara's abundant breasts. Angel then addresses the bartender. "Bring us three tequila shooters. Don't forget the salt and the lime. You guys do have lime, right?"

"No, sorry," the bartender says apologetically. "Imports have been tighter than usual."

Tara feigns interest to keep the young man close. "Why? We haven't had any major attacks since 6-13."

The young man smiles as he replies, "There've been extreme droughts down south, you know, in what used to be tropical regions."

For a brief moment, Tara imagines herself on a beach, lying next to this dark-skinned, handsome young man.

Turning his attention back to Angel, he offers up the next best option. "But we do have some very tart chock cherry juice that tastes even better."

Angel slaps her hand down on the bar and orders. "Screw that, then! Get us three Mindbender shooters." The bartender nods and turns to prepare the concoctions. While they wait, Angel leans into Grace's ear and whispers again. To Tara, it simply looks like Angel is seducing Grace, as usual. When the Mindbenders arrive, Angel releases Grace and stands between her and Tara. She takes on a solemn pose and turns to face Tara. "Tara, I have a confession to make." She reaches her hand behind her to grab Grace and stifle the silly girl's laughter. In a tight whisper intended only for Grace and Tara's ears, she announces, "I'm bisexual." At first, she was going to say straight, but as she and Grace are clearly a unit, she opts for the next best thing, pretending to be bisexual.

Tara is stunned by this sudden declaration. She looks over to Grace, who is struggling so hard not to laugh that she is doubled over from the effort. "Grace, is this true?" Grace is only capable of nodding.

Angel immediately hushes Tara, who has spoken at normal volume— much too loud for such a delicate conversation. Looking back now at Angel, Tara complies and lowers her voice. "But what you were saying about the paper? I thought—"

Angel cuts her off. "Uh, uh. I was only saying that because I wasn't sure about you and, you know…" She uses her head to point around the room at the various other carousers. "But I think I know you're strai, too. Am I right?" When Tara doesn't respond right away, Angel reassures her, "It's okay. Grace and I are cool."

Tara is sucked in. "Oh, wow. I never would have thought it of you. But you—I mean, you walked out of class after Politis read the paper."

"Of course I did! I'm closeted." Leaning in now, she whispers, "I didn't want anyone to suspect me, you know."

"Yeah," Tara ponders, slightly confused but far too drunk to distinguish between falsehoods and truth. Turning now to her other friend, she inquires, "What about you Grace? Are you bi, too?"

"Nope," Angel replies for her as the combination of alcohol and laughter has left Grace incapacitated. "Grace is lesbian through and through. But it's cool; she's an ally, aren't you, Grace?" All Grace can do is nod her assent. "So, am I right? Or did I just shoot myself in the head by telling you?"

This is the line that works its way into Tara's trust. "Yeah," she smiles, feeling free and unburdened. "It's true."

"And you," Angel adds, "you wrote that paper, didn't you?"

"Yeah, that was my work."

"Brilliant!" Angel adds. Grace nearly falls flat on her face with giggling. Angel sighs, "Poor Grace; I better hold her up again," which she promptly does, using her right arm, only leaving her left hand free for the shooter. "All right, then," she says as she picks up her shot, "to allies, bi, strai, and gay!" Angel watches as Tara throws back her shot. Then as Tara shudders in convulsions, Angel quickly dumps her shot off to her right. She shoves Grace, slightly reminding her to do the same, too. "Barkeep," she calls out, "three more." Angel repeats this pattern two more times, ensuring that Tara is so intoxicated she almost falls flat on her face. Angel catches her laughing. "I think you're done for, girlie. Come on, Grace; we better take Tara back to the dorms."

But they don't take Tara to the dorms. Instead, they lure her into the alley behind The Blue Chair. Once there, they proceed to strip Tara of her clothing. When Tara resists, Angel punches Tara so hard in the head she drops to her knees. Angel tears at Tara's blouse, ripping if off her body. Grace, after unzipping the back of Tara's skirt, effectively wrenches it down around Tara's ankles. "Put her in a headlock," Angel orders. Grace complies. Tara now retrieves the beer bottle she had smuggled out of the bar. "So you're a fucking strai, are you? Do you know what it feels like to have a strai man stab a hard dick into you?" Angel's voice has become menacing. "Well, it feels like this, you fucking strai bitch." When Tara cries out, Angel orders Grace, "Shut her up!" To do so, Grace shoves Tara's blouse into her mouth, deep enough into her throat to make her gag. Now muffled, all Tara can do is groan. When Angel is finished, she tosses the beer bottle aside and begins to beat and kick Tara unconscious. "Let her go, Grace; she's done for."

Grace does as she's told and allows Tara's limp body to fall to the ground. Standing back, the two women stare down at their work. They are both struck by the horrifying wonder of what they have done. Suddenly, Grace squeaks out, "She's still breathing, Angel." Looking into her girl-friend's eyes, the terror of the moment causing tears to streak down her face, Grace whispers, "What if she wakes up and tells someone?"

Angel's mind turns cold and calculating. She sees an old brick lying against the building wall. Picking it up, she shows it to Grace. "This will prevent that." Grace watches in horror as Angel smashes the brick three times into the back of Tara's skull. The brick, now stained red, falls from Angel's hand. She doesn't look up to address Grace; she merely mutters, "She ain't telling nobody nothing now."[17]

* * * * *

---

[17] This chapter was sadly inspired by the murder of Vladislaw Tornovi: http://www.pinknews. co.uk/2013/05/13/russia-identity-of-man-killed-and-raped-with-beer-bottles-revealed/"

BOOK 3

THE FALLOUT

Salve!

Murder at Augustus Uni
HNN—Danny Duggin Reporting

This is a special *Salve!* News Report. This just in—the body of Augustus Uni student Tara May Fowler was found in the alley behind the uni's student lounge, The Blue Chair. Although full details of the story are yet to come in, some say she had allegedly tried to seduce young men while drinking at The Blue Chair. Apparently, this establishment is well-known as a strai bar. I've spoken with a witness from The Blue Chair, and my source suggests that whoever murdered Ms. Fowler was likely a male. Apparently, Ms. Fowler was making unwanted advances towards many of the young men in the bar. It may be that one of these young men, disgusted by her overtures, may very well have killed Ms. Fowler.

If the murderer truly is a decent, hardworking gay man, then I can honestly say I feel for him. I can't imagine the horror and disgust he must have felt by having a strai come on to him like that. It would have been very shocking, and then, under the influence of alcohol, anything can happen. I hope when they do find this young man that the courts go easy on him. A life sentence of military duty, like that given to Frank Hunter, the man who murdered a straight male five years ago, would be reasonable.

Another conceivable scenario is that the young man who killed Ms. Fowler is another strai. We all know what these heterosexual barbarians are like, especially the male. The primal beast comes out in them when sexually aroused. It is entirely plausible that he murdered her as part of some sick het'ro sex thing.

One thing is for certain—the young woman was beaten and raped before being murdered.

Either way, this story is a clear warning to our youth who like to play with strai fire. Het'ro public displays of affection are not wanted in our society. Strai guys and gals, you better learn to control your sexual urges. Whether this death resulted from a decent citizen who snapped at unwanted solicitation, or from the brutal act of het'ro lovemaking, what you are playing with by pretending to be strai is clearly deadly.

Nobody likes to hear about acts of horror. No one wants to condone murder, but strais need to take a lesson from these events. Your ways are not welcome in Hadrian, and there are those willing to act outside the law to rid our good country of your disease-ridden ways. Remember, being straight is a choice. Choose wisely and reject those disgusting opposite sex attractions.

Stay tuned to HNN for more on the murder of the Augustus Uni strai.

Vale!

Cantara

Jason's bubble rides so smoothly that he feels as if he is floating on air, which helps to ease the tension. He is a little nervous about tonight because he will be dining at Faial Raboud's home—and they will be alone for most of the evening. Ever since their work together during the Hunter trial and their success at getting President Stiles to legalize heterosexuality, Jason and Faial have formed a strong friendship. Jason Warith squints his eyes as he approaches Faial Raboud's home. Being pre-dusk, the sun's rays are hitting the solar panel siding at the exact angle that reflects the strong light back into his eyes. Even the Ray Ban sunglasses he is wearing fail to stave off the worst of the glare. It is this incessant glare occurring post-dawn and pre-dusk that is the most annoying quality of life in Hadrian, even with the mandatory anti-reflective coating. Along with Ray Ban glasses, the parasol is an ever-popular accoutrement in Hadrian fashion. To help reduce the glare factor, Hadrian's city engineers designed all homes to face the same direction so the sun would not reflect into a neighbor's house or yard, with one line of houses per street. However, glare remains an issue when the sun's rays hit the panels at those crucial angles, post-dawn and pre-dusk. An added advantage to this unique design feature is that no one lives directly across from, or immediately behind, someone else, thus making for an expansive city and large backyards, the latter of which are necessary for home gardens and fowl as livestock since many of the wealthier citizens raise their own chickens, geese, or ducks.

Passing through the bright reflection, Jason turns into the side driveway and around to the parking stalls in the back. All entrances to a home in Hadrian are at the rear. Housing in Hadrian has very little diversity. A house's front and roof consist of solar panels. The only signs of wealth in a family home are its size and the presence of glass windows. Faial Raboud's home has three small glass windows. Jason surmises correctly that each window is for a bedroom, the slightly largest of the three most likely the family room. Reaching over to the passenger side of his small bubble (not being married and having yet to bring his own child into the world, Jason only owns a small, two person bubble), Jason retrieves the small bundle of flowers he picked fresh from his garden prior to leaving for Faial's. Jason presses the button to release the bubble door, but only after taking one deep breath of the flower's scent. Pausing with one foot out of the bubble, Jason begins to question himself. Maybe the flowers aren't such a good idea after all. Faial might misconstrue. *No*, he reminds himself, subconsciously shaking his head along, *it isn't inappropriate to give the person who invited you to dinner flowers*, and reassures himself that nothing sexual will be construed. Faial is in a solid, loving relationship, so to think she might misinterpret his intentions was just foolishness on his part; he is, after all, the head of Hadrian's reeducation system. Stepping confidently out of the small vehicle, Jason walks towards the door with a spring in his step.

* * * * *

Faial and Yuusi's home is small but luxurious. The living room, which also serves as the dining area, is decorated in ancient Persian. There is a large stone fresco hanging on one wall showing a line of bearded men in long robes, each with a dagger sheaved at his side. Its grandeur and size is all that is needed to decorate that wall. On the adjoining wall, a small statue, a woman seated wearing a headdress and veil that drapes over her shoulders, sits atop a marble pedestal. Above it on the wall is a small oval window offering illumination. Furniture is also sparse. In the center of the room is a low oak table placed atop a Persian tribal rug decorated with squares of multiple colors. Upon the table, a beautiful crystal vase is now home to the flowers Jason has brought. Surrounding it are glasses and a bottle of red wine, open and breathing in anticipation of consumption, as well as a few plates of hors d'oeuvres: pork and lemongrass meatballs in lettuce cups; small bites of roasted cucumber sandwiches; and Faial's favorite, hummus with home-baked pita chips for dipping. Faial, her partner Yuusi, and Jason sit sprawled on large pillows scattered around the table, each a different color to match the squares on the rug, with varying shades of yellow, orange, blue, green, and red.

Although the appetizers and cocktails began without incident, it didn't take long before all the pleasantries were over. Faial's lover asked to be excused to take their youngest daughter to a small birthday party for the little girl's friend, leaving Faial and Jason alone. There is nothing awkward about the moment. Faial treats Jason as she would any houseguest—with respect, ensuring his wine glass is always full and the vintage to his liking. When she notices he has yet to try one of the hors d'oeuvres she set out, she begs him at least to try the baked pita chips and hummus. "Really," she smiles, "the hummus is quite mild, and the spices baked onto the pita are not too pungent. I'm sure you will like it." She lifts the plate with both hummus bowl and chips atop and brings the victual offerings closer for him to reach.

Jason politely refuses. "No, really, Faial." He takes in a deep breath to luxuriate over the smells emanating from the kitchen. "Whatever you've got cooking in there smells so fantastic I want to save all my appetite for that."

Faial's laughter is as beautiful as the full lush lips it emerges from. Jason catches himself admiring them. Faial redirects his attention to her eyes. "Really, Jason, I must be honest. I did not prepare the meal for tonight. That's Yuusi's handiwork we smell, not mine. She prepared the hors d'oeuvres and our meal. All I had to do was open a bottle of wine. I'm afraid I'd burn the pot if I tried to boil water."

"Well, whoever cooked it, and whatever it is, it smells delicious. I'm dying to sink my teeth into it."

"You'll have to be patient; it's a pot roast, all the trimmings but the salad cooking inside with it. That," she says, while blinking her right eye to check the time, "I can fix, and—" Faial draws out the word, "—Yuusi said it won't be ready until the meat reaches 75 degrees Celsius. Before leaving, she said that would take at least another hour, and that was half an hour ago." Shrugging apologetically, she adds, "I'm sorry the meal isn't tradi-tional Persian, but Yuusi is very fussy when it comes to preparing fancy meals for guests. Since she couldn't stay, she decided to create an all-in-one dish for us." Then, fearing she has underplayed the quality of tonight's meal, Faial assures Jason, "It really will be delicious, I promise you."

Jason smiles. "Oh, I've no doubt. It smells too good not to be delicious. And," he says as he reaches for the pewter plate Faial holds before him, "I have these wonderful Persian appetizers to enjoy while we wait." As Jason dips a pita chip into the hummus, he asks, "How is your daughter doing? Cantara, right?"

"Yes, good; she's doing well. Spring finals are coming up, so she's busy studying."

"Good for her. How old is she?"

"Just turned twenty-two. She served her four years in the military and then started uni as soon as she got out. She's an April baby, born on the 19th. She spent her whole birthday voc complaining about having to write a final exam on her birthday."

"Which uni is she attending?" Jason asks to keep the conversation flowing.

"Augustus Uni. I wanted her to go to Antinous, but she insisted on Augustus."

"Why is that do you suppose?" Jason is curious, as would be anyone. The Uni of Augustus suffers from the stigma of being in the city where the dirty nuke exploded that fateful day of 6-13. An extreme evangelical Christian, one Jeremiah F. Butler, drove into Augustus City and exploded the nuke, killing himself whilst simultaneously destroying most of the city and the surrounding southern grasslands in the process. Even though Augustus was rebuilt more than one hundred kilometers north of the old city, many people still view it as an unhealthy place to live.

Before Faial is able to answer Jason's query, Cantara opens the door and calls out "Mom, Mom!" Her voice is high-pitched and filled with sorrow. Faial turns in the direction of the kitchen. Hearing the distress in her daughter's voice and not having anticipated a visit at this time causes her to rush into the kitchen where the two women crash into each other's arms. "Mom! Mom! Oh, Mom!" the poor girl wails.

"What is it, honey?" Faial cradles Cantara in her arms and begins to rock her from side to side.

"They killed her—they killed her. They beat her and raped her and killed her. They murdered her!"

"Hadrian's Lover," Jason mutters. He has followed Faial into the kitchen, being drawn by the terror of Cantara's voice.

"Who was murdered?" Faial asks.

"Tara," Cantara wails. "Oh, Mommy, they killed her."

"Tara," Faial is stunned. Tara and Cantara had been friends all through high school, even planning to go to the same uni together after their time in the service. Until learning their daughter was straight, Faial and Yuusi had assumed the two girls were a unit. "Calm down, baby; tell me what happened."

"Dean Stuttgart came to my room—he came and told me. They found her body. We had to identify it. Oh, Mommy, it was horrible. She was all bloody and bruised and pale."

"What happened, baby? What happened?"

"Tara went out drinking. She wanted me to go, too, but I had to study. Oh, Mommy, I should have gone. Maybe then those bitches wouldn't have killed her." Gasping between sobs, she explains, "Oh, Mom, they killed her because she was straight."

Faial's grip on her daughter tightens. "Oh, dear. Oh, baby."

Jason places a hand on Faial's shoulder. "Maybe we should do dinner another time. I think you've got your hands full here."

Faial looks over her daughter's shoulder to smile weakly Jason's way. Tears are streaming down her cheeks. "Thanks, Jason; another time, another time."

"Jason?" Cantara pulls away from her mother to turn and see through blurry eyes Jason Warith, the Director of Reeducation. "Jason Warith? What is Jason Warith doing here?" All sorrow and terror churn inside Cantara, spilling out in wrath. "What is Jason Fucking Warith doing in our house?"

"Baby, I know you're upset, but that doesn't give you the right to attack my friend."

"He's your friend?"

"Yes, he's my friend. I voc'd you dozens of messages about him, but you don't read my messages, do you?" Seeing the wounded look on her daughter's face, Faial regrets having chided Cantara at such a sensitive moment. "I'm sorry, baby, but we have talked about him from time to time, too."

"Yeah," Cantara mutters her discontent, "and I told you what I thought about him then."

"And I told you," Faial says in her friend's defense, "that he was the man who helped me change the laws. Without his help, heterosexuality would still be illegal."

"Well, with his help," Cantara's voice drips with venom, "heterosexuality's still illegal and a fucking stigma! He runs those fucking camps and publically says straight people should never have sex!" Turning now to face off with Jason, Cantara demands, "Where do you get off?"

"Cantara, please." As much as she feels for her daughter's loss, Faial cannot allow her to take all of her pain out on Jason.

"It's okay, Faial. Your daughter is upset. I should just go."

"Yeah, that's right," Cantara hisses. "Just go!"

Faial Raboud glares at her daughter. "Baby, I know you're hurting, but you're taking liberties you've no right to." Before Cantara can protest, Faial puts a finger to the young woman's mouth. After silencing her daughter, Faial turns to face her friend. "I'm so sorry, Jason. She doesn't really mean it."

"Don't say what I don't mean. I know what I'm saying and I mean it!"

"Enough, Cantara!" Faial's struggle to avoid getting angry with her daughter is failing. "This attack against Jason is unwarranted. You can't use your grief as an excuse to abuse another."

"But he's—he's—we both know what he is!" Cantara's anger reaches a breaking point as each word bursts out of her like successive thunder crashing. "I. Will. Not. Submit. To. His. Authority!"

Faial grabs her daughter by the arm and quickly pulls her away from Jason. "You've got it all wrong, young lady."

"Oh, do I? Do I?" Cantara pulls her arm loose from her mother's grip before storming back to confront Jason, Faial trailing at her heels. "Who in Hadrian's name do you think you are?" Cantara demands of a clearly befuddled Jason Warith.

"Ah," Jason stammers. "Fa-Faial, what is going on here?"

"Hadrian be damned, I will not go to one of your reeducation schools."

"You're—" Looking now to Faial, Jason asks, "Your daughter is straight?"

"Straight as an arrow, you Vibia bitch!" Cantara shouts.

Faial and Jason wince. Many consider such an insult to be the worst one can give to another in Hadrian. Vibia Sabina was the name of Hadrian's wife. History suggests she was a plague to the Roman Emperor.

"Okay, back off," Faial demands. "Jason didn't come here to talk you into attending reeducation. We weren't even expecting you. In fact, he had no idea you were straight until you so rudely announced it to him."

"Then what's he doing here?"

"I invited him for supper."

Cantara stares at her mother, dumbfounded. "What in Hadrian's name possessed you to invite *him* to dinner?"

"We have become good friends since the Hunter case. You would know that if you ever read any of my voc messages." Faial is no longer worried about wounding her daughter. "As I said, he was instrumental in helping me amend the law that made heterosexuality legal."

"He may've helped change the law, but sure as Vibia was a bitch, this man is a hypocrite!"

Faial is mortified by her daughter's cruel treatment of her guest. "Take that back, Cantara."

"NO! You must've heard him. Remember when he was on *Salve!?* To say—well, to say that it is wrong for heterosexuals to have sex is like—well, we might as well go back to making it illegal again." Cantara is near to tears. "Attitudes like his just pave the way for people to do what they did to Tara."

Jason Warith feels some sympathy for the girl. But as much as he wants to commiserate with her, she has gone too far with this accusation. He may have been taken aback initially by the young girl's brutal attack, but this is his political arena, and he is comfortable and secure in his stand. "I've never countenanced the abuse—and especially not the murder of heterosexuals. I'm sorry for what happened to your friend. As for making heterosexuality illegal again, your mother helped prove that's ridiculous. One can't make illegal the way a person is born. Here in Hadrian, we are fully aware that the spectrum of human sexuality is diverse. We can accept nearly all forms of gender and gender expression—"

"Except heterosexuality!" Cantara bursts in.

"Heterosexuality is no longer illegal, *but,*" Jason quickly stops Cantara from interjecting, "the fact is heterosexual intercourse is just too dangerous an ill for the future of humanity."

"Too dangerous an ill," Cantara mimics, causing her mother to cringe.

Jason ignores her mockery. "We have to curtail human population. Calling for heterosexuals to choose celibacy isn't the same as making it illegal."

"Yes, it is." Cantara's voice rises to near hysteria. "Don't you see? It was never illegal to *be* straight; it was acting on it—kissing, walking arm-in-arm, not just the having sex. All of it was illegal, but now you are asking us to give it up willingly just when Hadrian says we can make love if we want to."

The two become a cacophony of voices riding over each other's attempt to speak.

"You can still make love to any man you want—"

"Why in Hadrian's name should I have to give up any form of sexual pleasure?"

"—you simply cannot indulge in procreatory intercourse. That style—"

"No one else is asked to give up any one *style*?"

"—of heterosexual sex is designed for procreation."

"Bullshit!"

"It's not bullshit!" Jason having passed beyond reason is now angry with the girl. "We have to curtail human population."

"What? You think heterosexuals can't prevent pregnancy?"

"Heterosexuals have to sacrifice their sexual desires for the betterment of man."

"Never heard of birth control?"

"The government must remain in control of all procreation; thus, penile vaginal intercourse must remain illegal."

"What about sixty year olds?"

By this point, Faial's head is spinning. She can barely hear her own thoughts above their deafening roar. "Stop it, you two. Stop it."

Jason complies with his friend's request, but Cantara rages on. "A sixty-year-old woman can't get pregnant, can she?"

"Cantara," says Faial, beginning to rub her temples. "I said stop."

Jason is pulled right back into the fight. "Maybe not, but a sixty-year-old man could still knock up a woman." Jason is relentless. "Do you suggest we put age restrictions on heterosexuals, specifying who can love whom and at what age?" Ever since being placed in charge of reforming reeducation in Hadrian, Jason has begun to see the issue in another light. Although he still maintains that heterosexuality is natural, he believes he can see even more clearly why procreatory sex is a danger to mankind. As willing as he is to accept heterosexuality as a natural human condition, he is not willing to accept that heterosexuals be encouraged to be sexually active. In many ways, he wishes all sexual contact between heterosexuals was still illegal, but he knows better. Trying to make any natural sexual act illegal is pure folly. Rather, he surmises, what is needed is better education of our youth. "Instead of seeing yourself as straight," he suggests, "try considering you're bisexual."

"I know I'm bisexual," Cantara cries, "at least a little." Faial raises a brow at this. This is the first time Cantara has ever willingly admitted to some attraction to the same sex. "I had a girl crush once and, maybe, if she had liked me too, well, who knows? We might have dated, but nothing ever came of it, and I've never been attracted to another woman since." Faial can't help but wonder whether Cantara means Tara.

"You see," Jason responds, just a little too enthusiastically, "I knew it. This is the very thing we need to nurture in you and our youth. There's really only 10 percent of the human population that's fully heterosexual, and then, with our scientists fixing the human genome, Hadrian's percentage is even lower."

Jabbing her index finger into Jason's face, Cantara begins shouting, "That's the very sort of thing that pisses me off! How dare you bastards fuck around with human DNA?"

Jason grabs the girl's hand and holds it tightly against the kitchen table. "How many people are there on this planet?" Cantara begins to struggle against Jason's grip. Faial wonders whether she shouldn't intercede, but she decides Jason is not physically harming her daughter, only restraining her from harming him. "You don't want to answer, do you? Well, I'll tell you—"

"I already know," Cantara spits out whilst still struggling against Jason's grip. "Over twenty billion."

"That's right." Loosening his grip, but not releasing Cantara's hand, Jason continues, "And how many of us can the earth sustain?"

Giving up on her struggle, even with a lighter grip, Cantara still can't free her hand. With a harrumph, she answers, "Less than ten billion."

"That's right, less than ten billion. So whether we like it or not, humanity has to be responsible for decreasing its numbers—and fast. Hadrian's doing everything it can to keep our population stable, and heterosexuals have to—"

"—pay the price," Cantara finishes for him.

"It's a necessary evil." Jason is adamant. "And we are only asking it of less than 10 percent of our population."

"It's way more than that and you know it. Everyone who's bisexual has opposite sex attractions. That makes it 80 or 90 percent!"

"And bisexuals," Jason says, pausing for a moment to consider whether his revelation will help, "people like you and I who experience opposite sex attractions, are asked to control those urges for humanity's sake." Yes, Jason realizes, his confession did soften the young lady some.

Faial, too, raises a brow at this admission. Stunned by what she hears, Faial reaches for the nearest chair and sits down. *I wonder how many people in the government know of Jason's bi status?* Faial quickly dismisses this concern. Everyone in Hadrian accepts that the majority of its citizens are most likely bisexual. The expectation placed on these citizens is that they choose to act only on their same-sex attractions, dismissing and/or repressing any opposite sexual attractions that they have.

Cantara refuses to allow a feeling of kinship to exist between her and Jason, though, so she lashes back contrarily. "You can't stop a person from falling in love!"

"You can't. Nor do I wish to. You can love anyone you want, just not sexually. Hadrian simply asks that all opposite sex love be kept platonic."

"Sacrificed on the altar of human population." Feeling bitterness rise in her throat, Cantara lashes out at Jason, "Do you love my mother?" *Let's play a little hardball, you bastard,* she figures. Ever since her mother defended Frank Hunter four years ago, Jason Warith and Faial Raboud have spent a substantial amount of time together. Having just realized the depth of their friendship, Cantara decides to throw Jason a curveball.

Clearly stunned, Jason doesn't know how to respond at first. Faial jumps to his rescue. "Cantara, how dare you insinuate—"

"No, it's all right. The girl has asked a fair question." Though Cantara is a bit too smug, Jason allows the girl her victory. "Yes, I do love your mother."

"And are you sexually attracted to her?"

"Cantara!" Faial has had enough and begins insisting this line of questioning cease. As well as being inappropriate, it is beginning to make her very uncomfortable and may well endanger her friendship with Jason Warith.

Jason raises his free hand slightly (still holding on to Cantara's). He has learned from past work with recalcitrant youth who do not wish to accept their bisexuality or shed their same-sex attractions that honesty is the best approach. "There have been times when I have felt some—" Jason can't help but cough; he had never intended to make this admission before Faial. "I have felt sexually attracted to Faial, but," he adds a little too quickly and a bit too ardently, "I have never once considered acting on those feelings." Now looking directly at Faial, he says, "I would never put you in such an awkward circumstance. I would never even have mentioned it if your daughter hadn't dragged it out of me. Please, trust me."

"It's okay, Jason," Faial says calmly, more calmly than she feels. "I believe you."

"Oh, you don't have to worry about Mom," Cantara adds. "She's 100 percent pure lesbian. I can assure you, she's never once thought of you that way." Cantara throws that last little bit in just to be hurtful.

Jason, however, takes the words as a balm, giving him a strong sense of relief. If Faial had been bisexual, the temptation to act would have been so strong he would have had to end their friendship and never see her again.

"So," Cantara asks, secure now in having gained an upper hand in the debate, "why are you still holding my hand?" Now being coy, "Do you like me, too?"

"No." Although Jason's admission was not intended to hurt, Cantara can't help but feel some sting. Jason Warith is an attractive man, the quint-essential tall, dark, and handsome. In other circumstances, she would have liked to seduce him. "I want," he continues, "to look at your fingers." Jason releases his grip on Cantara's hand. Curious as to his request, Cantara turns her palm face up and her fingers spread open.

"My fingers?"

"Yes, if I may?" Jason places both his hands beneath hers. His have formed a cup holding her hand as if it were life-giving bread or water. "Close your fingers for me." Cantara obeys. "Look," he says, pointing to her index finger. "Your index finger is shorter than your ring finger."

"So?" Cantara is baffled.

"What does it mean?" Faial, who has avoided much of the conversation, is also flummoxed by Jason's observation.

"Now let me see your hand, Faial." Although Faial extends her hand forward, palm up, fingers closed, Jason avoids touching it. "You see," he says to Cantara, "it is the same with your mother."

Exasperated now, Cantara flexes both hands open on each side of her head. "*So?*"

"It's the mark of the heterosexual man and the lesbian. The index finger is shorter than the ring finger.[18] With gay men and heterosexual women, the opposite occurs."

"Rubbish," Cantara exclaims.

"Medical fact," Jason rejoins.

---

[18] http://media01.commpartners.com/AMA/sexual_identity_jan_2011/index.html, slides 26 & 27

"All that really proves is that I'm bisexual and I've already admitted that."

"Yes," Jason agrees, "and that is the material point. You *are* bisexual, meaning you have same-sex attractions and those are the attractions upon which all your sexual desires and energies need to be placed."

"And what about you?" a snide Cantara iterates. "I suppose you have long delicate fingers. No doubt your index is longer than your ring finger."

A long, scintillating pause evokes tension—scintillating for Cantara, that is. For Jason, it produces excruciating pain. Suddenly, without warning, Jason slams his hand on the table, fingers pressed tightly together. Cantara screeches with joy. "By all that is gay and glorious, Jason, your index finger is shorter, too!" Then far too jubilant, she adds, "Way shorter!" Snickering gleefully, she adds, "Isn't that the mark of the lesbian *and* the heterosexual man?"

Faial simmers. She has let this fiasco go on far too long. "That is enough out of you, Cantara."

"Oh, no, it's not." Cantara giggles ecstatically. She has guessed the truth. She can see it in his eyes. "You're not even bi; you're 100 percent, fully, a big fat ZERO on the Kinsey scale heterosexual. Oh, Antinous loves me." Then with a smirk, "I can hear him giggling. You got yourself big ol' fat stubby there, don't ya"

Faial stands. Glaring at her daughter, she demands, "Stop mocking the man!"

"Oh no, Mother. He's not getting away with this! How dare you," she derides, "How dare you counsel young men to deny their sexuality when you're straight!"

Jason's hand forms a fist that trembles against the table. "That. Is. Exactly. Why. I. Can. Counsel. Them." His eyes close tight.

"You hypocrite!"

"Cantara, I said enough!" Faial has never felt more impotent in her life.

"I am no hypocrite." Jason struggles against his inner emotional turmoil. "I happen to be celibate." Jason spits out the word "celibate" much like the hiss of Eden's snake.

"Cantara, leave him alone. This is going too far." Faial's love and respect for Jason as a dear friend has strengthened immensely as a result of her daughter's attack on the man.

"Oh, for the love of Hadrian, Mother, the man denies himself!" Cantara's mood switches instantly from sardonic to joie de vivre. Turning back to taunt Jason, she asks, "So what does that make you—Hadrian's equivalent of the Catholic priest?" Tears stream down Cantara's face as she partakes of joyous laughter. Unable to control her laughter, she sputters a few times before spilling out, "*Chriss du calisse, Mamma,*" more shaking and sputtering followed by knee slapping along with an outright burst of jocularity, "*il est un vierge!*" Noting the look of confusion in Jason's face Cantara translates for him, "I said, 'Jesus Christ, Mom, he's a fucking virgin!'" She was going to add, "Of course, that's not an exact translation," but she is too busy falling into a chair in a spasm of mirth.

Jason's fist, no longer shaking, slams into the kitchen table, resonating its boom throughout the Raboud household. Faial cringes, but then, thankfully, she remembers that her partner, Yuusi, and their young daughter, Kaafiya, are out for the evening. Jason takes no note of Faial or even Cantara's reaction (even more merriment) to his sudden, violent outburst. "I live this life for a reason. For a purpose greater than merely having sex. I happen to believe in what this good country stands for. I happen to believe—" His breath expels itself and Jason slumps down in the nearest chair. He breaks down into tears. Cantara, taken by this sudden burst of emotion and distress, is finally able to control her outbursts. His sorrow rekindles her own grief over Tara's death. Emotions begin to surge and sway inside her as she dives down from her high into agony. She, too, collapses into sobs.

Faial stands, caught between the emotional anguish of these two. Her mother's instinct kicks in and she chooses first to kneel beside Cantara. As soon as her hand touches Cantara's shoulder, though, the young woman bursts up and out of the room. She exits, screaming something about het'rophobes, murderers, and Jason Fucking Warith. Shaking her head in dismay, Faial crosses to Jason's side, crouches beside his chair, and gently rubs his shoulder. "It's okay, my friend. The life you lead is truly noble."

Slowly, Jason stutters out his conviction. "I—I really do believe—believe in Hadrian's four cornerstones—the n-need for humanity's population to decrease. Hadrian is on the right track." His eyes meet Faial's, imploring her to understand, or at the very least, believe his sincerity. "It's just, prejudice—prejudice, can't be part of the picture."

* * * * *

Cantara stands in the entrance to the kitchen, the soft light of the living room creating a glow around her form. Her face is wretched. After a high-pitched squeal, Cantara screeches, "Agony is shredding through every fiber of my being, and you're comforting him!"

"Go to her," Jason mumbles. "I'm okay."

Faial is unconvinced, but before she can utter her thoughts, Cantara retorts, "No, Jason, you're not okay." Now looking her mother in the eye, she adds, "And neither am I."

Faial quickly stands and reaches for her daughter. "Baby—"

Cantara refuses to let her mother in. Slapping away her outstretched arms, Cantara demands, "Leave us!"

"Go," Jason whispers. "We need to do this." Faial is stunned. Everything is wrong, suddenly backwards; her loyalty to her friend has suddenly superseded her loyalty to her daughter. *What happened to my mother's instinct?* Jason nods his head as Cantara stands back, giving her mother room to leave. Sarcastically, she waves her past. Jason chides her with, "You are being too rough on your mother."

Cantara stares down at Jason. "My best friend just died."

"I know. I'm sorry."

"She. Was. Murdered!"

"I know. I'm sorry."

"Because she was straight!"

"I know. I'm—"

Cantara mimics him. "*I know. I'm sorry. I'm know. I'm sorry. I know.* Do you? Do you really?"

Jason stands, angered by this attack. "Yes! I know! I understand! That's why I'm in this business. To help kids like Tara and you!"

"And you?" Her question is dripping with pity.

Jason takes the query like a slam to the gut. "Yes," he coughs out, "like me."

"How? By telling us we don't belong?"

Regaining his composure, Jason begins to fight back. "No, by helping you find a way to belong. By teaching you how to blend in and be a part of our society."

"Why?"

"Because I believe in our good country."

"Good country, my ass."

"Yes, good country. In many ways, Hadrian is a paragon amongst the countries of this planet."

"Not when it comes to treating everybody equally."

"Everybody is treated equally!"

"Not if you're strai, or actively bi!"

"The values our country stands on are critical—values like population control and reclaiming the natural balance of our planet. These are critical, and to this end, we have to work together!"

"YES!"

Jason smiles slightly, cautiously, fearful of a verbal trap. "You see, you do understand."

"No. I see things differently." Jason sighs and closes his eyes. It was too good to be true. Too easy. Cantara continues, "I see humanity working together as a whole."

"You can't mean outside, too?"

"Ultimately. But we can't reach out to them until we've healed ourselves." Shaking her head discriminatorily, she states, "You can't keep doing what you're doing, Jason. It's wrong and you know it."

Jason recoils with momentary self-doubt and then, reining in his terror, he lashes back at Cantara with full force. "It is not wrong to try to keep our country solid. It is not wrong to try to help children fix broken lives."

"YOU CAN'T FIX WHAT ISN'T BROKEN!"

"Their lives—"

"Strais, bis, transgendered, pansexual, gender fluid, every beautiful colorful stream of the sexual light spectrum. Does Hadrian even remember the rainbow? NO! And you know why? I'll tell you why! Hadrian has forgotten about us—ALL OF US!" Cantara is beyond yelling, her voice now too hoarse. "They are not broken. We are not broken. No one, not one of us is broken. We are all born whole. It's society that does the breaking. Society that does the destroying." The tears are streaming, her nose is dripping, and Cantara collapses to her knees. Jason kneels in front of her. He reaches his arms around her as she wails, "My best friend's dead!" Now crumbling into his arms, she weeps, "Dead, Jason. Dead."

"I know," Jason murmurs softly.

"They murdered her." Cantara's voice is now a jumble of sobs. "They murdered her."

All Jason can do is rock the young woman gently in his embrace. She is right. Deep in his heart, he knows she is right.

* * * * *

HRN

Hadrian's Disgrace
HRN—Melissa Eagleton Reporting

Just moments ago, *Salve!* aired an emergency broadcast to inform the populace of a cruel and brutal murder. Danny Duggin's representation of what Tara Fowler suffered at the hands of her murderers, and the victim-blaming he focused on as opposed to the known facts, was badly done. That is not professional reporting, Hadrian, and you have the right to hear truths told about such events, not ridiculous rumors that have no basis in reality. Having just spoken to the head of Augustus Uni Security, I have learned that Tara Fowler's murderers were not, in fact, male. Nor had the young woman solicited these two in any way. Rather, they are two female uni students who knew Tara Fowler from her Sociology 100 class. According to the bartender at The Blue Chair, they had appeared to be friends, laughing and drinking the way most college students do on a Friday night. They appeared to have left the bar amicably, if not exceedingly drunk. The bartender noted that the two women had to help Ms. Fowler up and out the door since she was too drunk to walk on her own.

The names of the two women responsible for Tara Fowler's death are being withheld until after their confession has been heard, but the details of her death have been released—I'm sorry, Hadrian, but what they did to this poor girl boggles the mind. She was stripped, beaten, raped with beer bottles, and had her head smashed in with a brick. There is no excuse for this sort of behavior—no justification. No "decent citizen," to quote Danny Duggin, would ever "snap" like this. Nor was this a deranged heterosexual male acting out some sordid sexual fantasy. This murder was an act of barbarism. What was done to this poor girl is not only a sign of the times but Hadrian's *disgrace*.

And, for the record, Danny Duggin, your "source" just happens to be one of the murderesses. The Head of Uni Security saw you speaking with her just prior to her arrest.

TRUTH!

Jeremy Stoker's Mistake

Jeremy Stoker and Jake Matonabee's ranch house is small and cozy. Neither man goes in for ostentation, so their home only has a kitchen that doubles as their living room, one bedroom, and a bath. The kitchen is their favorite room, and though small in comparison with other homes, it is the largest room in the house. It is a Sunday evening and the two men are relaxing over a simple meal of fried steak and mashed potatoes after a long day's work.

As he always does during mealtime, Jeremy is reading HNN's newsblog voc'd up in front of him. "Sweet Hadrian's Lover!" Jeremy mutters in dismay.

"What is it?" Jake asks over a mouthful of potatoes. Jake never wears a voc, getting all his news from Jeremy.

"A young girl was murdered just outside Augustus Uni." Jeremy Stoker gasps, raising his hand to cover his mouth.

"What is it, babe?" Jake reaches a hand across the table to caress Jeremy's arm.

Jeremy's eyes continue to scan over the voc doc he is reading. "Hadrian help us, Jake; they raped her first!"

"What?" Incensed, Jake's hand, holding his fork, turns into a fist. "What sick fucking strai did that?"

Tears begin to burgeon. "It wasn't a strai, Jake; it was the poor girl's two female friends." He shudders. "Her two best mates murdered her because she was a strai."

Jake lets go of Jeremy's arm. His eyes close as he breathes deeply. Resting his head in his hand, Jake begins to shake it slowly. "How did this happen?"

Through choking sobs, Jeremy relays the story to his lover. "Her name was Tara Fowler. Apparently, she had come out to her friends Friday night while they were having a few beers in the student uni bar."

Jake pounds his fist on the table, then tosses his fork away. "That fucking uni, opening its doors to strais."

"Please, Jake," Jeremy murmurs. Jake doesn't know about Jeremy's little sister, Sissy Hildebrand. Nor does he know about Jeremy being bi and having had sexual relations with her. Sissy and Jeremy only became brother and sister after their fathers' registration, a registration that occurred when Jeremy was seventeen, only one year before he was conscripted into the army. The two never did grow to see each other as brother and sister, especially since no genetic bond connects them.

Jake softens long enough to witness Jeremy's distress. "Hey, hey," he coos. Reaching out once more, Jake begins caressing Jeremy's arm. "What's wrong, babe? I know any violent crime is disturbing, but you're acting as if you knew the woman." Pausing for a moment, he asks, "Did you?"

Jeremy shakes his head. How can he tell Jake why this murder is so upsetting? How can he possibly explain his worry over Sissy's safety, even his own?

"Then what is it?" Jake asks softly.

"It was how——" Jeremy's voice chokes inside a sob.

"It's okay," Jake coos. Trying very hard to soothe his lover, Jake begins to hum softly.

"Don't! Don't!" Jeremy insists. "That's not going to work for me today."

Whenever Jeremy gets anxious or upset, Jake resorts to cradling him and humming softly. Jake never even realizes he's humming; the action has become so automatic. Leaning back in his chair to give Jeremy a little space, Jake responds without choler. "It's okay, babe. I'll stop." He holds both hands palm up to show the sincerity of his expression. "Just tell me what happened that's got you so upset."

Jeremy takes a moment to calm down and catch his breath before beginning the harrowing tale of Tara Fowler's death. "Tara was at the student's bar, The Blue Chair, Friday night. She and two of her mates were having a few drinks. I guess with the legalization of heterosexuality and the new strai gay club there, Tara must have felt emboldened. "It says here," he points to the air a few inches in front of his right eye, and even though Jake can't see the article inside Jeremy's eye, he knows what Jeremy is referring to, "she had confided in her companions that she was strai. The bartender didn't notice anything untoward between the three women so Tara must have thought they were okay with it. I guess when they left the bar, the two women stripped Tara naked and commenced beating her. They dragged her into an alley behind the uni where they raped her with beer bottles. Apparently, they had beaten her unconscious, and one of the girls, fearing Tara might wake up and report them, decided they needed to finish her off."[19]

When Jeremy fails to continue, Jake urges him on. "Then what happened?"

"The girl picked up a brick and smashed in Tara's skull with it."

"Hadrian's Lover, that's awful." Even Jake, who has no love for heterosexuals, is appalled by the violence of Tara Fowler's death. "And those two women, her friends—how did the authorities catch them?"

"They spent the evening sitting at the bar with her; and they left with her; the bartender said all three girls were laughing when they left. He said it couldn't possibly have been them, but when quadrant officials went to interview the women and take samples of their DNA to compare with the spit they found on Tara's body—can you believe they spat on her body after killing her?—the one girl's DNA matched."

"That is sickening." Jake can't help but feel disgust for anyone who would act as these women had. "Even so, you can understand their motivation."

Jeremy shudders and shakes at Jake's words. "W-what? How could you possibly understand their motivation?"

Jake remains oblivious to just how deeply shaken Jeremy is by this murder. He takes a moment to muse over his philosophy. "Well, being het'ro is no longer illegal so they couldn't expose her and have her summarily exiled, so they did what they thought necessary to rid Hadrian of the het'ro plague."

Jeremy is incensed. "The het'ro what?"

Jake takes a moment to scrutinize Jeremy's mood and posture. His lover is oscillating through numerous emotions, including fear, grief, and rage. "Take a moment to control your emotions, Jeremy. I understand that this was a violent crime, unacceptable, but these girls were acting on what they felt was in our country's best behalf."

"It is not in our country's best interest to rape and murder someone just because she is straight!" Jeremy breaks down, no longer able to hold in the excessive fear. "Hadrian, please protect her."

---

[19] http://www.pinknews.co.uk/2013/05/13/russia-identity-of-man-killed-and-raped-with-beer-bottles-revealed/

Jake stares at his lover, at first dumbfounded, but slowly, his mind begins to put the pieces together. Jeremy isn't asking Hadrian to watch over the dead girl's soul; he is asking Hadrian to protect his little sister. At first, Jake's declaration is a whisper. "She's a fucking open hole"

Jeremy hears every word as if it were a series of thunderous explosions. "W-who?"

"I knew it!" Incensed, Jake stands, pushing his chair back, roughly scraping the wood against the rough stone floor in the process. Pointing an accusing finger Jeremy's way, Jake demands to know, "She is straight, isn't she?" Jeremy responds with further tears. There's no point asking anymore; Jeremy knows exactly whom Jake is talking about, and in his current emotional state, he is no longer able to dissimulate. "Fucking knew it! Fucking knew it!" Pacing back and forth in the small kitchen space, Jake wheels on Jeremy. "She is off this ranch."

Jeremy looks up at his long-time lover, stunned. "But you never see her. She lives on the north quarter, takes good care of our sheep. What possible difference could it make letting her stay there?"

Jake is having none of Jeremy's excuses. Deep-seated suspicion has rooted itself, and now it is beginning to grow inside, suggesting what he has always denied. Instead of expressing his fears, he shouts, "My great-great-grandfather started this ranch, started it even before Hadrian was a country! I will not have the likes of her living and working on my ancestors' soil." Suddenly, spinning, Jake reaches a conclusion, a slightly more preferable conclusion than the one he is desperately running from. "That man, that man she hired over three years ago, he was her cunt-hammer? He was, wasn't he?"

"I—I have no idea." Jeremy is flabbergasted by Jake's aggressive onslaught of verbal violence against his little sister and the man she loved. Suddenly, Jeremy sees a whole new side to his partner. Sissy's lover had been brutally murdered two years ago. Although members of the bi and strai community cried hate crime, it was never proven. All details surrounding Quinton's death were dismissed as his parents insisted that claims their son was straight were blatant lies and dishonoring his memory. Quinton's family had their suspicions, though, and Sissy was not allowed to attend her lover's funeral.

"Oh, you know, you know, you know!" Jake's voice rises in intensity. He knows Jeremy knows because Jeremy hasn't been riding north to visit his little sister anywhere near as often as he used to. "I want her gone!"

Jeremy stands. He stops Jake from pacing by grabbing his lover by the shoulders. "Jake, she's my little sister. We can't just throw her out in the cold."

"She is a fucking het'ro, Jeremy! A breeder!" Jake spits out the word "breeder" with so much vehemence and hate Jeremy is frightened of what he might do if Sissy were in the room—or if he knew. Now standing, Jake shoots his finger like a bullet towards Jeremy's face, pronouncing Sissy's fate. "I want her off my ranch, tonight! Her and any fucking cunt-hammer she may have with her!" Shivering with rage, he adds, "You voc her, and you voc her now."

Jeremy knows now exactly what he has to do. He nods his head, stands, and gets ready to leave. "Okay, Jake, but she's not on your ranch; she's on my fathers' sheep farm, which they left to both Sissy and me. You can't legally kick her off her own homestead."

"You're siding with that bitch." Jake is now circling Jeremy like a wildcat circles its prey. "You've known all along she's a stab. You and she have been lying to me all these years. And that fucker we hired to help her out up there, he was a strai too, wasn't he?" And then with a sneer that sends shivers up Jeremy's spine, Jake adds, "That's why they murdered him." Jake begins pacing the kitchen like a panther, his glaring eyes burning with hate. "You voc quadrant officials up in Peace River—" Peace River is the small farming community nearest the Cattle Ranch. "You voc 'em now and you tell 'em, you tell 'em she's a strai. Strais got no legal rights in Hadrian. You can get them to sign her share of the land over to you."

"What?" Jeremy can't believe what he is hearing. "I will not steal from my own family! She's my sister!"

Jake isn't fooled. He's been suspicious of those two for quite some time. "She's more than that to you, ain't she?"

"What are you talking about?" Jeremy knows exactly what Jake means, and though he tries to remain calm, a slight quiver marks his voice.

"You fucked the bitch, didn't you?" When Jeremy reddens and fails to deny the accusation immediately, Jake comes to his own conclusion and punches Jeremy in the face, slamming his back against the refrigerator. Jeremy's knees weaken, but he regains his balance quickly. The advantage of being Peace River's bucking horse rider is that Jeremy can take quite a beating without getting knocked down.

After stepping away from the fridge, Jeremy wipes the blood Jake drew from his mouth and shakes his head sadly. "I'll pack and be out of here in the hour." As he turns to leave the kitchen, he lets Jake know, "I'll voc Sissy that I'm coming up to live with her."

The last words Jeremy ever hears his lover say are, "I don't ever want to see you or that fucking breeder again!"

* * * * *

Salve!

Heterosexuals Are Waging War!
HNN—Danny Duggin Reporting

It is absolutely absurd that President Stiles is even considering allowing more laws to support and create freedoms for heterosexual citizens. Heterosexuality is a behavior, not a civil right. If one chooses to be straight and participate in sexual activities that continue to augment the human population explosion on our planet, then these people should expect, at the very least, to be denied basic civil rights. The call for job security, laws to protect strais against discrimination, laws that would force ethically-minded and loyal Hadrian businesses to serve strais, even a law allowing them to register with all the rights and privileges given to same-sex couples, is preposterous. That President Stiles is even willing to listen to these seditious radicals is horrifying. Well, we're going to block this law the same way we blocked strai marriage!

Be warned, Hadrian; our current government is pandering to the demands of a very dangerous minority. We know the perils of strai relations; we live in an overpopulated world. The only reason our country isn't bursting at the seams like the rest of the planet is Hadrian's respect for our founding principles, in particular, the cornerstone that indicates we are a homosexual society. We do not copulate like rabbits out of control. Hadrian's citizens are dedicated to reducing the human population on this planet, and if that is to happen, then people have to stop having het'ro sex. By ensuring that all citizens procreate through government controlled IVF, we have maintained a stable human population. Our past laws of exiling anyone who is openly het'ro proved very successful in keeping that unwanted element on the outskirts of our society where it belonged. But with the law Stiles signed into effect three years ago, making breeders legal, we must now endure individuals who are openly strai taking to the public airways, spreading their debauchery amongst our youth like a viral plague.

Thank goodness for all the right-minded folk who are working in the government, circumventing Stiles from getting too carried away with all her "philanthropy." These individuals, like Cooper Johnston, who, last year, resigned his position in Stiles's cabinet in order to form the Conservative Right Party, were at least able to ensure the Anti-Strai Propaganda Law was signed and sealed when all this folly began. Now there is a man with foresight!

And then there is the alternate media, *HRN*! Melissa Eagleton should be ashamed of herself for spreading its lies and supporting its agenda, which is to pull down the cornerstones of our society and have us descend into madness like the rest of the planet. She better be careful because she is walking a very fine line between presenting the news and spreading strai propaganda! Tsk, Tsk. It would be a sad day indeed if she were to be exiled.

What is truly frightening, though, is to see how the strai agenda is tearing apart one of our greatest families. Gordon Stuttgart is suffering a great deal, having both his son and his mother working in cahoots with strais. To have his son come out as het'ro has put a huge strain on the poor man. We all know that Dean Stuttgart was said to have died when he was still a teen, but it turned out that he had been caught sexually accosting a young woman. It is understandable why Gordon Stuttgart would like to sever any connection with his son. Of course, Dean Stuttgart entered the reeducation system. It appeared to have worked for him since he married and seemed to have lived happily with his husband, Geoffrey Hunter, until the trial of their eldest son. It seems that Frank Hunter being found guilty of having murdered a confessed strai and the young man being sentenced to a life of servitude in Hadrian's military destroyed the façade of love these two men had been projecting. Dean Stuttgart cruelly reclaimed his name and family status. He then worked his charms on a senile, little old lady, somehow convincing his grandmother to take him into her home and pledge herself to his insane cause. No founding-family member would stand behind such a hideous plot to destroy our good country, but as we know, Mother Stuttgart is close to ninety years old. She is no longer in her right mind, and dementia is steering her away from the country she once fought so hard to form.

This is it, Hadrian. The heterosexuals are now waging war against us from inside our Wall. This is not the petty fear-mongering the pro-strai movement accuses us of. No—we leave that sort of devilry to the het'ros outside our borders—those who claim homosexuals are the agents of the underworld, here to wreak havoc upon the planet by causing all the natural disasters resulting from global warming and the overpopulation of our planet. No! What we at *Salve!* bring you are facts—pure and simple facts. The breeders have overpopulated our planet, burgeoning human numbers beyond that which the earth's natural resources can sustain. There is only one way to counter this unholy human explosion, and that is to curtail—nay—halt all heterosexuality, ideally bringing it to its well-deserved end across the whole of the planet, but as our reach doesn't extend that far, we can, at the very least, stop the progress of heterosexuality, abort its very presence within our borders! We must fight back against this insidious insurgence, this friendly-faced form of protest, this attack of "Love us; we're your children" crap! Or, as William Shakespeare would have said it, those who "look like the innocent flower" while "being the serpent under't."[20] The ethical and moral foundation of our good country is at stake! Do not allow the strais to destroy all we have worked for here in Hadrian. Do not let them destroy our sanctuary and the only hope left for our planet!

Vale!

---

[20] Shakespeare, William. Macbeth, Act I, scene v, lines 420 to 421. OpenSourceShakespeare. Retrieved from: http://www.opensourceshakespeare.org/views/plays/play_view.php?WorkID=macbeth&Act=1&Scene=5&Scope=scene. Retrieved on January 1, 2016.

Ripe for the Shaking

Destiny smiles. Fading before her eyes is the shimmering countenance of Danny Duggin. *Vizard*, she muses, is a far more apt word to describe the lineaments of this man's facial features. *So smug, so confident, so self-assured— so bigoted!* "Yes," she decides, speaking out loud, regardless of being alone. "An interview with this man is essential." And yet, she knows Duggin—or rather, his puppeteer, *Salve!*'s new production manager, Darien Dumas, will not be so eager to grant her one, regardless of the assured higher ratings. *No*, she thinks, *Darien Dumas will not be so eager to pit me against his real-life Pinocchio*. Destiny giggles at the sudden image of Danny Duggin with a foot-long nose. It is at this point that Dean walks into the room, arms overflowing with books. Seeing her grandson with what is deemed contraband in Hadrian, she chastises him, demanding, "What are you doing with those antiquated items?"

"None of these are new, Mimi. I borrowed them from the uni's historical library. I'm curious to see whether any of our historical medical texts have been tainted by propaganda."

"Hmm." Destiny's eyes mist. "There was a day when no one would have ever considered that sort of conspiracy theory happening in Hadrian."

"Sorry, Mimi, but times aren't like they were when Hadrian was first founded."

"I know." This concession saddens her further.

"Gee, Mimi, I'm sorry." Dean sets the books down at his feet; then briefly relieved of the weight, he takes a moment to crack his upper back before sitting next to his mimi. Dean gently caresses her arm. "You looked so happy when I walked in, even a little mischievous, and I go and bring a damper to your mood." The reminder of her previous decision causes Destiny to chuckle gleefully. "There's my irreverent granny." Pleased that Mimi is back to her jovial self, Dean smiles. In fact, Mimi is more than a little jocular. She now looks downright fiendish. "Okay, Mimi, now you're scaring me." He can't help but smile at the thought of what his grandmother has planned. Whatever it is, he knows she's up to no good—or, rather, a lot of good, the kind of good that can get a person into trouble when living in a corrupt society. "What's brewing inside that mind of yours?" Dean wants to know out of pleasure as much as out of worry.

"Well, before you walked in here and scared the beejeebers out of me—"

"Oh, Mimi," Dean protests joyfully, "I did not."

"Damn near gave me a heart attack." Mimi enjoys teasing her grandson.

"That old ticker of yours," says Dean, always joining in on her little game, "has a good twenty years or more left to it."

"Oh, dear," she replies quite decidedly, "let's hope not."

"Don't talk like that, Mimi." Their teasing has become serious again.

"Twenty years or more; why that'd make me well over one hundred. By then, I'd very likely be suffering from the senility Danny Duggin just accused me of. I want to die before I lose my mind." Looking Dean straight in the eye, she adds, "And I'm counting on you to make sure of that."

Completely ignoring his grandmother's request, Dean hones in on the mention of Danny Duggin and his false accusations laid against his grandmother. Appalled and incensed, he immediately replies, "Danny Duggin called you senile? On a *Salve!* episode?"

"Yes, sir. For all of Hadrian to hear."

"That miserable little sycophantic son of a Vibia bitch!"

Destiny tries to hold back her smirk. "Oh, Dean, I've never heard you swear like that."

Dean blushes. Ever since the news of Tara's death, Dean has been a swirling vortex of emotions. One moment he is grieving, the next he is lashing out, trying to hurt whoever is next to him, and other times, he suffers immense waves of guilt for having just felt happy. "Sorry, Mimi. This just makes me so mad. Anyone who knows you knows that that is utter balderdash."

"Thank you, sweetie." Patting his cheek reassuringly, Mimi adds, "Well, we can say Danny Duggin was the mouthpiece, but the voice behind the insult was really Darien Dumas." Noticing the look of concern on her grandson's face, Mimi seeks to reassure him. "Oh, sweetie," she says, smiling, "you don't need to feel sorry for me." Her smile widens and is tinted now with a wry expression. "Save your pity for *Salve!* and little Danny Duggin."

With his grandmother's eyes now ablaze, Dean can't help but laugh in anticipation. "Okay, Mimi, what's the plan?"

"I plan to entrap that man."

"Dumas?"

"And I'll get to him through his little sycophant, Danny Duggin."

Intrigued, Dean's smile widens. "How?"

"Do you remember when Melissa Eagleton asked me in for a second interview? This time for her new show *HRN*?"

"Yeah. Why did you refuse?"

"Oh, that first interview was a real kerfuffle. I was still a little miffed at her." Admitting a weakness only her grandson will ever hear, Mimi adds, "Sometimes, it's hard for me to forgive."

"I understand, Mimi." Even though the conversation is about Eagleton, Dean knows she's really referring to Dean's father. Gordon Stuttgart had done more than just abandon a son; he lied to his country *and* his mother. Dean still isn't sure Mimi will ever forgive him. Nor is Dean the one to act as intermediary between them. He knows his own weakness well. His father will never hear the words "I forgive you" from his son. But Gordon Stuttgart is only the subliminal element of this conversation, and Dean is curious how Mimi might, in fact, get back at Dumas through Duggin, so he asks again. "What does this have to do with getting back at Dumas and Duggin?"

"I'm going to agree to the interview."

"Really?" Regardless of his grandmother's status in Hadrian as an original founding family member, Dean still questions whether or not a second interview was possible after having rejected the offer.

Mimi answers Dean's silent query. "Oh, she'll take me up on it. My presence will ensure higher ratings for her, and though she is a proponent of the truth, human nature is more interested in human folly as humor than it is in its ghastly truth." Sighing, she adds, "The truth, when it reveals how sordid humanity can really be, ends up repulsing one's audience. That's why she is still struggling to bring her voice into mainstream focus."

Nodding a little acquiescence, Mimi acknowledges her newfound interest in *HRN*. "I know if I call her up now, I could have her in this very room tomorrow morning, no matter what show she had on the go." Chuckling in a fiendish manner, Mimi continues, "She'll be more than happy to help me taunt Dumas's little lover boy into interviewing me." With a wicked grin, she adds, "And then 'I'll do, I'll do, and I'll do.'"[21]

Trust Mimi to quote the Bard, especially a line from the Scottish play referencing the first of the weird sisters. Dean smiles, fighting back the stinging guilt over feeling joy at this moment.

Sensing her grandson has "harp'd" her meaning "aright,"[22] Mimi giggles, adding "Danny Duggin is 'ripe for the shaking.'"[23]

* * * * *

---

[21] Shakespeare, William. *Macbeth*. Act I, scene iii, line 12. OpenSourceShakespeare. Retrieved from: http://www.opensourceshakespeare.org/views/plays/play_view.php?WorkID=macbeth&Act=1&Scene=3&Scope=scene. Retrieved on: August 15, 2015.

[22] Shakespeare, William. *Macbeth*. Act IV, scene I, line 74. OpenSourceShakespeare. Retrieved from: http://www.opensourceshakespeare.org/views/plays/play_view.php?WorkID=macbeth&Act=4&Scene=1&Scope=scene. Retrieved on: August 15, 2015.

[23] Shakespeare, William. *Macbeth*. Act IV, scene iii, lines 244 to 245. OpenSourceShakespeare. Retrieved from: http://www.opensourceshakespeare.org/views/plays/play_view.php?WorkID=macbeth&Act=4&Scene=3&Scope=scene. Retrieved on: August 15, 2015.

Hadrian's Real News

The Founding Principles of Our Nation
HRN—Melissa Eagleton Reporting

"I would like to begin by thanking Mother Stuttgart for accepting my invitation for a second interview with me. Had I been her, I would have flatly refused. Mother, please allow me to apologize for the horrendous treatment you received during our last interview when I was still host of *Salve!*"

"You are right, dear. Had you still been hosting *Salve!* and I had not been following your progress with *HRN*, I most certainly would have declined this offer, but I must say you have more than atoned for your previous stand on political issues. I always knew you to be a woman of integrity, even if much of what you touted while on *Salve!* made me cringe."

"Those last few episodes on *Salve!* were eye-openers for me, Mother. I had no idea just how backwards our country had become and how much I was pushing an agenda of hate. The mortification I felt during our interview and what Darien Dumas forced me to say—"

"Blame him all you want, but you still said the words he fed to you through the link, and that remains your responsibility. The biggest mistake we make as humans is to constantly find someone else to blame for our own stupidity: 'He talked me into it.' 'It was her idea.' 'He made me say it.' Well, it doesn't matter how much another person influences you. What matters is how much you allow him to influence you. But don't worry, dear; you regained your honor when you vacated that post and began your own newscast. I respect what you are trying to do here."

"Thank you, Mother."

"I do wish you'd call me Destiny. This Mother title is so vexing. It reminds me of Catholicism and Mother Superiors. I'm not religious, nor do I see myself as superior to any other human being. I'm just a woman who joined forces with other humans to try to create a loving environment where all of humanity is accepted."

"That doesn't sound like any of Hadrian's Founding Principles, Moth—I mean, Destiny."

"Thank you, dear. Well, that was the wording of the first of many drafts. Unfortunately, the collective opted for segregation and separation over accepting all humanity. I wish I could have made them understand that segregation, regardless of how necessary the reasoning may seem, does not heal the breach between opposition. All it does is foster resentment and hate, cutting even deeper trenches for the bigots to sink their boots into while arming and aiming their weapons against us. Unfortunately, the aggressive attacks against homosexuals on a global scale, then and now, and the continued abuses of our gay and lesbian brothers and sisters even in those countries that claimed acceptance convinced the majority of the families that we had to isolate ourselves from the heterosexual world. What this meant, I reminded them, was that by excluding everything hetero-sexual, we would also be excluding bisexuals, the transgendered, and the intersex. No one could see how this was possible. They argued vehemently against the idea that we would ever become prejudiced against our own. 'Diversity,' I remember distinctly Mildred Stiles, my mentor and friend, claimed, 'is the very foundation of our culture. It is the reason we have come together to found Hadrian.' 'Yes!' I replied. 'Which is why we cannot cut off any one segment of that which makes us all human.' Sadly, I was out-voted, even by Mildred. Don't get me wrong; I stand behind much of what is written in Hadrian's Four Cornerstones. Population control and creating and maintaining a stable balance between nature and humanity are both critical. I also approved the wording that Hadrian would be a safe haven for homosexuals from around the globe—that at least here in our small part of the world, we would never have to fear verbal or physical abuse for simply being who we are. Nor would we ever have to fear vio-lent torture and death at the hands of those who continue vehemently to hate us. But I have never approved of the wording that homosexuality is Hadrian's chosen lifestyle."

"And why not, Mo—Destiny?"

"Because no one chooses to be gay. No one chooses to be bisexual. No one chooses to be transgender or cisgender. No one chooses to be intersex. No one chooses to be straight. We are all who we are when we are born. This was an understanding I believe we all had when we first came together to found Hadrian, but fear—well—fear does strange things to people. It occupies their psyches and convinces them that the very real dangers we see around us need to be combated by reacting against them in the extreme. And that is what happened here in Hadrian. We took extreme measures to make extreme changes, and by doing so, we have taken on the very characteristics of the people we are fighting against."

"That is a very scary thought, Destiny."

"Yes, yes, it is."

"What do you propose we do?"

"At the very least, I propose a rewording of the cornerstone that dictates one sexual orientation on the population. It doesn't work in the outside world, and it doesn't work here inside Hadrian. Hadrian's first cornerstone needs to express how our country is home to sexual diversity and understanding."

"And what about the anti-strai laws still upheld by our government; laws that allow for employers to fire an employee who is straight[24]; laws that deny straight persons complete sexual freedom[25]—"

"Yes, the Anti-Penile Vaginal Intercourse Law!"

"—laws that require a woman to have an abortion for an unplanned pregnancy even if it is her first; and, of course, the most recent being the Anti-Strai Propaganda Law[26] that restricts heterosexuals from promoting their lifestyle to our youth?"

"All those laws need to be struck down."

"That is a very radical suggestion, Mother."

"Those laws came into place after the founding of our country, and they came into place at the hands of bigots. Somewhere, at some point, we have to learn how to accept humanity for who we are, every single one of us. Until that day, we will continue to hate and destroy one another."

"Thank you, Mother; this has been a very insightful interview."

"Destiny. Don't forget, Destiny."

"Sorry, Destiny."

"Oh. Oh, oh, let me say it, please. This is even more exciting than saying *Vale* because this sign off is infused with meaning."

---

[24] http://www.upworthy.com/29-states-can-fire-you-for-being-gay-is-your-state-one-of-them
[25] http://www.bbc.com/news/world-25927595
[26] http://www.globalequality.org/newsroom/latest-news/1-in-the-news/186-the-facts-on-lgbt-rights-in-russia

"As you wish."

"Truth, Hadrian.

"TRUTH!"

Geoffrey, Please!

Dean opens his eyes. He has no idea when he closed them. He sits peering at Mimi's backyard through a blurry veil of tears. *I haven't accomplished a thing*, he realizes. The vegetable garden he is sitting in remains molested by spring's first growth of weeds, and all he has done for the last hour and a half is to continue to dig into the same small patch of ground, digging so deep that his fingers are now clawing through clay. *What am I doing?* he asks himself as he wipes his hands over his chest and down across his thighs, not concerning himself about the old shorts and T-shirt he has donned for a day of gardening. Dean is not concerned about what the mud is doing to his clothing, nor can he feel the numbing grow in his buttocks, a numbing caused by the stillness and the damp.

Dean is numb. He has taken Zolam for the first time in nine months. He remains on the Seroxat and has accepted that he is likely to be dependent on the medication for the rest of his life. Although it has been an emotional, uphill battle, Dean has finally come to terms with needing it—his life having been one filled with anxiety and stress, resulting from hiding his sexuality, struggling to be someone he's not, only to embrace the identity of someone he is not. It's like his mimi always says, "Humanity lacks balance," and all Dean has done so far is go from one polar extreme to the next.

"There is balance in there somewhere," he mutters, but looking for that balance right now seems incomprehensible. Not now, not so soon after Tara's death—Tara's murder.

"Oh, Hadrian, why?" Dean cradles his face inside his hands, hands muddied with topsoil, fertilizer, and clay. Mimi's backyard has the potential for great beauty and bounty, but it is relatively untended. Unlike the garden Dean had tended when he went by the name of Hunter, Mimi's garden is prairie flat. Her yard has been divided into four quadrants, each like a piece of the pie mirroring Hadrian's layout. The center oval where each quadrant meets up is home to a very old crabapple tree. Mimi loves crabapple jelly and canned crabapples. Each quadrant of land is dedicated to growing its own unique genre of foods. This year Quadrant One is the vegetable garden; Quadrant Two is for berries; Quadrant Three is for grains while Quadrant Four is for fallow. Even as little as two years back, Mimi rivaled the best with her backyard farm, but today, the arthritis in her fingers makes the task unbearable. Dean volunteered to get her garden back in order for her. It was intended to be his summer hobby between shifts at Augustus Hospital's emergency ward, but with Tara's murder, Dean was granted a two-week hiatus from his first residency. He was even exempt from his last final in Human Biology: Anatomy and Physiology. This right was granted to all of Tara's closest friends—Cantara Raboud, Prasert Niratpattanasai, and Siddhartha Seshadri. Tara's death, the sheer brutality of the murder, coupled with their ability to feel the horror she suffered in the remaining hour of her life, rendered these four friends emotionally and psychologically catatonic.

"Dean." Mimi's voice startles Dean out of his shock.

"Mimi, you scared me."

"I'm sorry, but you had me worried. You haven't moved from this spot since you first ventured out here."

"I just…" Dean's voice trails off and he stares through his tears into space again.

Mimi gives Dean's shoulder a shake. "Dean."

"Huh? Oh, Mimi. I'm sorry."

"Oh, baby, I wish I could help you."

"You do. Just by…" But Dean cannot finish. His head drops and his shoulders heave from sobs.

"No," Mimi says gently but with resolve. "You need the arms of a lover—someone who can surround your soul, hold you tight with both physical and spiritual love." Sighing now, speaking the words Dean knows to be true but is too afraid to acknowledge, she adds, "You need—Geoffrey."

Between shudders, Dean nods his head in agreement. Mimi sighs her relief, pats Dean's shoulder, and then retreats back inside. Rather than avoid stalling, Dean blinks open his voc immediately. Any delay and he knows he will chicken out. Sadly, rather than reaching Geoffrey, he merely gets the man's answering machine. "Hello, you have reached the voc of Geoffrey Hunter. Geoffrey is not available to take your call, but if you leave your name and voc contact after the chime, Geoffrey will reply as soon as possible." Dean is stunned. Not having voc'd Geoffrey since their breakup, Dean had not expected to hear his own voice on the machine. When the two had been together, married for twenty-two years, Dean had taken it upon himself to record both his and Geoffrey's voc answering messages. Geoffrey was always too busy to worry about non-essentials like this and, pre-Dean's influence, had always used the sterile vocal voice provided with the vocal contact program.

With the sound of the chime, Dean somehow manages to stutter, "Geoffrey, please." No one is ever away from the voc in Hadrian. Though there are the odd few who remove the voc from time to time, just to avoid the mass clatter of being constantly connected to the wave, but not Geoffrey. Geoffrey wears his voc twenty-four hours a day. A few years back when he was working out a deal with Hadrian Fisheries, he purchased the vocal mini-disc and had it implanted into his cerebral cortex. This unique feature allows the wearer to have full access to the wave and vocal contact twenty-four hours a day. Most businessmen, like Geoffrey, are digitally tagged in this manner. Thus, the only reason someone like Geoffrey doesn't answer a voc call instantly is due to work or, as Dean knows is the case in point, because he simply doesn't wish to speak with you.

Since it is Sunday, Geoffrey is not required to be at work. Though no laws identify Saturday and Sunday as required days off, the custom of the previous millennium is a part of Hadrian's ritual. Everyone acknowledges the human need for rest and recreation, and these two days also meet the spiritual needs of the various religious faithful who are part of Hadrian's population. Dean knows he is purposefully being ignored. "Please, Geoffrey, I need—" *What*, Dean wonders, *what is it I need?* "I—I need you." And yet, still no reply. At least Geoffrey hasn't severed their connection. Comforted by this lone thought in the void of his agony, Dean reaches out one more time. "My friend was murdered." There is a slight pause as Dean sobs with abandon. "She is the girl who was raped and murdered."

A connection is opened. Geoffrey's holographic image kneels down in front of Dean. Taken out of context, an onlooker might assume the older man was about to propose marriage. Geoffrey's right thumb wipes over the tears in Dean's left eye. Being holographic, he fails to wipe the tears away, but the gesture is registered. A small electric shock occurs with the touch of the holographic thumb upon the dampness of Dean's face. Both men feel the tingle. Geoffrey leans in to cradle Dean in his arms. Dean becomes immersed inside the holographic waves of his old lover, the bodies of the two men becoming one.

* * * * *

Salve!

Mother Stuttgart
HNN—Danny Duggin Reporting

"Well, Mother, what a treat to have someone as auspicious—"

"—and senile."

"I'm sorry, Mother?"

"I'm sorry; did I say something? My apologies; please continue."

"Yes, well, as I was saying, it is a real honor having you back on my show."

"'Bow wow says the dog.[27]'"

"Huh?"

"Oh, I'm sorry. Did you interview me already?"

"No, no, Mother. Not me, but you were on *Salve!* once before back when we had—"

"Oh, yes, that sweet little lady—what was her name again?"

"Melissa Eagleton, Mother. As you know, she now runs her own show. In fact, you were on it last week."

"Oh, was I? 'Mew.' Silly me for forgetting."

"That's okay, Mother—"

"'Quack, quack.'"

"—Yes—As I was saying, it's expected at your age."

"Oh, and how old am I?"

"To be honest, Mother, I'm not quite sure, but I think you're close to ninety."

"Ninety? Really. Oh my, that is old."

"Yes, it is. But don't you look beautiful? Why, you don't look a day over seventy."

"Oh, aren't you a sweet kitty, kitty. But seventy's pretty old, too, isn't it?"

---

[27] http://www.online-literature.com/dickens/mutual/48/

"Not so old, Mother."

"Oh, no, not so old as me."

"Well, let's not worry about that, shall we? As I was saying, you look so beautiful."

"Do you like my outfit?"

"It's lovely. Where did you get it?"

"I'm not sure. I think in my closet at the geriatrics ward."

"Oh, Mother, you're so funny."

"And you, look at you, so handsome. No wonder they cast you as Antinous."

"You remember, Mother."

"Oh, if something's important, I'll remember it."

"Selective memory, huh?"

"You might say that. 'I know a hawk from a handsaw.'[28] But you must let me admire you."

"Who am I to say no to a little admiration, especially coming from the last surviving founding family member."

"I absolutely adore your earring. May I have a closer look at it?" Mimi's eyes twinkle in delight, giving Danny Duggin the impression she really does love his earring.

"Of, course."

"Lean in a little closer, son; I can't see from here. Closer. You forget I'm old. My eyesight is fading even faster than my memory."

"Here, Mother; why don't I just hand it to you?"

"Oh, isn't that just lovely."

"An original Gale J. Greenlea."

"Oh my, that means these beautiful emeralds and diamonds are real. Look at how they sparkle in the light. It's so dangly and—oops."

"Be careful, Mother!"

"Oh my, my fingers are a little shaky, too. It's so hard getting old. And then—Oh, no! Did I just step on your original Gayle J. Greenlea earring? Oh dear, oh dear. Look at you. You're so pale. Was that your voc—your voc thingy—what do they call it?"

"Transmitter."

"Does that mean no one can voc you while we are on live television?

---

[28] Shakespeare, William. Hamlet, Act II, scene ii, lines 1460 to 1461. OpenSourceShakespeare. Retrieved from: http://www.opensourceshakespeare.org/views/plays/play_view.php?WorkID=hamlet&Act=2&Scene=2&Scope=scene

Nod for yes. Shake for no. Good! Now, start asking me some real questions. Think fast boy or I'll start interviewing you! Perfect. What made you think I was senile? What's wrong? 'Cat got your tongue'?"

"Ahh, I—"

"Surely you can say more than that! How old are you anyway? Twenty?"

"T-t-twenty-five."

"Well, you'd think our ages were reversed. I'm the one who's almost ninety and senile, but you're stuttering like Mel Tillis when he wasn't singing."

"M-M-Mel who?"

"I wouldn't expect you to know him. I didn't even know who he was until I asked my grandson to look up the names of famous people in history who stuttered. I figured I'd catch you u-u-unawares."

"I—I'm confused, Mother. W—w—what's going on?"

"It's quite simple, sonny. You are going to interview me using your own head, or the man who likes to use you as a mouthpiece can walk right on stage and interview me himself, instead."

"I—mouthpiece?"

"I don't see him walking through the curtains, so you better get ready to start acting professional. Fine, I'll take the lead on this one. Why do you think I am senile?"

"You're ah—almost ninety."

"So your bigotry knows no bounds. You're also an ageist."

"A what?"

"Ageist, son; learn it! It's a simple word. It means you treat the elderly as second-class citizens simply because they are older. You also treat our bisexual, straight, and transgendered brothers and sister with contempt. You and your intrepid leader seem to think you can abuse anyone who isn't gay and treat him or her like second-class citizens. You spread fear-mongering and hatred like a con artist selling land to fools in the neutral zone. For those viewers who don't know what the neutral zone is, it's a fifty-mile radius between Hadrian's Wall and the rest of the world. Much of it is wasteland due to numerous chemical explosions, or it is still glowing from radiation resulting from 6-13.

"Still unprepared to say anything? How about this? What makes you think you have the right to judge anyone?"

"I—ah—"

"You know, I owe Mel Tillis an apology. He may have stuttered, but he had a beautiful singing voice. You clearly can't sing at all. Only lip sync. Oh, how do I know Mel Tillis had a great voice, you ask? Well, Danny, my grandson, found a few old recordings on the wave that he played for me. So lovely.

"Next question, you say? How do I feel about my country having gone from an all-inclusive, all-loving community to an exclusive, xenophobic country club for the elite of the homosexual community? Well, Danny, I'm saddened, sickened, and dismayed. Think about it. The five families who purchased this land from old Canada did so out of a need to create a safe haven, not just for homosexuals, but for all the oppressed across the globe. Our first hue and cry was that all were welcome because all were human. Then what happened? Well, Danny, maintaining a controlled population of ten million was difficult at first; needless to say we stumbled and found ourselves topping our desired number. With a little patience and persistence, I've no doubt we would have been successful over time. The people who joined our collective came here knowing our purpose was to reduce human population and the early education programs for planned parenthood and easy and inexpensive access to IVF clinics were starting to work, but some of the founding members and a few concerned citizens felt we weren't moving forward fast enough. Suddenly, the rhetoric became 'The Planet is Dying. We Must Act Now.' I tried talking reason with these people, but, alas, I was quite young, so my opinion was viewed as foolish and radical. And, today, people like you claim my opinion is foolish and radical because I'm old. Will the world never learn?

"So, you see, Danny, the original intent of our constitution was not to exclude heterosexuals from our community or demand that all our bisexuals repress their opposite sex attractions. Rather, we had earnestly hoped to form a human collective that desired peace, not war, a healthy planet with a clean environment and an intelligent approach to population control. That does not mean, nor did it ever mean, that heterosexuals are evil. The only evil that has ever existed in this world is fear and hate—the very fear and hate that leads to bigotry—the very fear and hate that leads to war.

"Oh, you wish to thank me for being on your show. Well, it was a pleasure. Thank you. Oh, no, don't say it, Danny. I want this episode to end as all news shows should end, with the—

"TRUTH!"

"Ah—ah—

"Vale!"

HRN

Viewer Views
@HRN#MS-SENILEorPoliticalGenius

Dean Stuttgart

Mimi, I'm so proud of you.

Siddhartha Seshadri

Mother Stuttgart, thank you for being an ally for our heterosexual and bisexual brothers and sisters.

Reni Bouchard

Mother, you are so not senile. You were amazing. I love how you shut that bigoted fool down. You set "la Duggin" up, and "pitter-pattered" the senility scenario like a pro. Stepping on his voc earring was so nicely done! Spot on! I LOVE you.

Maxence Nogoev

I love how you slam dunked the truth down that fool's throat! There is a lot more about Hadrian's founding that the government is clearly unwilling to share with us. Thank you for refusing to stay silent.

Sissy Hildebrand

CLANG, BANG, BOOM! Our Mother's words were no warning shot across the bow. Nothing so easy for the opposition. Not from Mother Stuttgart. Hey, Duggin, how's the egg on your face taste?

Reeta Adolvsson

You people make me sick. Listen to yourselves. Everyone one of you making fun of Danny Duggin like he was put in his place or fooled. Well, let me tell you, he did what any decent, respectful Hadrian citizen could do when being attacked by an original founding family member. He HAD to defer to her. No one would ever dishonor one of our founders! And, I'll tell you, that wasn't Mother Stuttgart speaking either. No, sir! She is old. There is no way someone her age could demolish an opponent that way. Sadly, it is our founding mother who has been turned into a mouthpiece for her grandson. Dean Stuttgart knows no one will take him seriously, so he has her doing all the talking for him. There is no doubt in my mind that she was wearing a voc implant, and everything she said he said first! It is so sad to see one so honored by our country being used by degenerate breeders to promote their wicked ways. Gordon Stuttgart needs to rescue his mother from his son!

Dr. Patrick O'Donnell

@Reeta Adolvsson—As Mother Stuttgart's attending physician, I can assure you she is not senile, nor does she wear a voc. I've known this woman for over 30 years and believe you me, she did all the talking. No one was prompting her. At 88, our founding mother may no longer be spry, but she still has all her wits about her.

Earl Higgins

Strais are sick, selfish sones of anarchy! they are controlled by their groins and believe they own the planet. As far as strais are concerned, everything and everyone is here to serve them. @Cantara—you and others like you ARE the enemy! If you people were given full reign again the whole world would be dead!

Duncan Fraser

@Earl Higgins—Let's be reasonable. History has shown that Planned Parenthood does reduce the number of pregnancies between heterosexual couples. Heterosexuals are just as capable of controlling the number of children born in this world as homosexuals are.

Earl Higgins

@Duncan Fraser—yeah, that's why the planet is overrun with humans—because strais are so good at controlling themselves. They've got access to birth control and abortions, but they choose not to use them! They just keep pumping out babies, overpopulating and overpolluting our planet! The only good strai is a dead strai!

Fernando Pereira

I love Mother Stuttgart last of the original founding family members. I am grateful for all she and other original founding family members did to form our great country and ensure humanity survive against itself. But she is wrong. We can't align ourselves with het'ro's, bis do have to repress opposite sex, and transys need to be known dangers of presenting self as het'ro couple. We need to re-criminalize heterosexuality and remake, mandatory reeducation for youth.

Todd Starn

@Fernado Perira—Agreed. We have to strop the heterosexual monstor in its tracks. They may control the outside world but we can't let them spread their tentacles get inside our walls.

Sarah Rios

Is Mother Stuttgart senile? No. Is she right? No. Is she misguided by her love of a grandson she thought she had lost and then found again? Yes!

Cantara Raboud

This overwhelming hatred of heterosexuals has to stop. Please, people, come to accept us as your brothers and sisters. We are not the enemy.

T'Neal Cantos

@Cantara Raboud—You're wrong. We don't hate heterosexuals. But more importantly, we love humanity. And we love our planet. History has proved that heterosexuals have created overpopulation. And excessive human population caused excessive pollution. Our planet can no longer afford to tolerate heterosexual supremacy any longer.

Derrick Defrock

We simply can't ignore the fact that procreation is a basic human physical need. Heterosexuals have always lived amongst us and they always will regardless of all our attempts to quell their existence. They are just as much a part of humanity as we are.

Charles Johnston
@Derrick Defrock—het'ros are the cancer of our society—of our planet! They are killing us with excessive human population and excessive human waste. We need to take radical surgical procedures to reduce their numbers, cleanse our planet of their existence. If nothing else, we need to put Hadrian back into remission.

Bronek Sabonski
@Charles Johnston—Agreed! Maybe one day, when the overall human population of the planet is reduced to a reasonable number, maybe one billion, maybe then we can reconsider accepting heterosexuals back in our midst, but until then, het'ros need to be illegal again!

Emile Nelligan
Mother Stuttgart has to be senile to say shit like she did on *Salve!* and *HRN*. "Bow wow says the dog," WTF? There is no way she believed this crap when she was young!

Sissy Hildebrand
@Emile Nelligan—"'Bow wow,' says the dog. 'Meow,' says the cat. 'Quack, quack' says the duck" is a direct quote from Charles Dickens's classic novel *Our Mutual Friend*. It was said by a character who wanted people to think he'd gone mad in order to prove a point and achieve a positive goal. You might try picking up a book now and then.

Mauvourneen MacMahon
Poor Gordon Stuttgart. First a strai son and now a traitorous mother.

April Bolger
@Sarah Rios—Mother Stuttgart is neither senile nor wrong. @Mauvourneen MacMahon—Mother Stuttgart is no traitor. She loves *ALL* humanity: gay, lesbian, bisexual, pansexual, transgender, intersex, or straight. She doesn't care. Nor does Race or Faith make any one person better or less than another. Every human being is beautiful in Mother Stuttgart's eyes. She will only ever stand against you if you oppress another of humanity's children. We all need to be more like Mother Stuttgart.

Earl Higgins

Nutcases, all of you. Don't any of you give a shit about our planet? Sure, let's just follow the senile little old lady back to the days before Hadrian when our people suffered under the tyranny of heterosexual supremacy and had to fight for crumbs with twenty billion other people.

Sarima Adeyemi

The people who think Mother Stuttgart is senile are desperate. They don't want us to believe she is making any sense because what she has to say will change the way our country is run. Accepting heterosexuals as a part of Hadrian's family is the first step towards opening our borders. We would go from xenophobic to embracing all of humanity. We could no longer ignore our brothers and sisters outside our border.

Earl Higgins

@Sarima Adeyemi—We are at war with heterosexuals! My daughter, Angel, is a casualty of that war.

Cantara Raboud

@Earl Higgins—Your daughter raped and murdered a woman. She is not the casualty her victim was!

Earl Higgins

@Cantara Raboud—You strai slut—strais are the enemy! My daughter merely did what the government used to do. Remove strai rats from our presence. Strais are dirty, polluting rats, and like rats, we need to exterminate them!

Cantara Raboud

@Earl Higgins—the apple doesn't fall far from the tree. You and your daughter are NUTS! Heil, Higgins!

* * * * *

First Date

The first thing Wolf does when he contacts Stephanie Chatters is to apologize for using her contact information from her job interview. "I know how inappropriate this is," he says, "but I'd really like to see you again." Wolf winces instantly, knowing how feeble he sounds.

Stephanie Chatters smiles serenely. She is delighted by this voc, but she does not want to show too much emotion in case her hopes are dashed too soon. Seated in front of her government-installed wall screen, Stephanie takes a moment to smooth her skirt to avoid giving away any expression. Unlike Wolf, she does not have a voc; they are too expensive for the average individual in the re-ed class. Stephanie may have held a privileged position in the Northeast Reeducation Camp under Gideon Weller, but that shattered like glass when the warden was removed from his post, arrested, and tried on charges of rape and abuse. To assuage Wolf's worries, Stephanie replies, "No harm done, Mr. Gaidosch."

Wolf flushes red. Having Stephanie refer to him as Mr. Gaidosch is like being slammed in the head with their age difference. He immediately regrets having made the call. "I am so sorry, Ms. Chatters; please forgive me. I never should have voc'd."

Now playing coy, Stephanie asks, "Would you please explain to me what you mean by 'seeing me again.'"

Wolf is quite flummoxed. Not knowing what to say, he fumbles, "Ah, I was, ah, hoping, maybe, ah—"

Stephanie begins to feel sorry for the man. "Are you asking me out on a date, Mr. Gaidosch?"

"Not if you call me Mr. Gaidosch." Suddenly shocked by this bold response, Wolf begins to stutter again. "I mean, ahh—"

Stephanie can't help but giggle in delight. She has the poor man off balance, and she knows now he really likes her. "Should I call you Wolfgang, instead?" She remembers his full first name from the job advertisement.

Wolf sighs with some slight relief. "Well, my friends just call me 'Wolf.'"

"Wolf," Stephanie repeats. "I like that. May I presume to call you 'Wolf' then?"

"Please." Wolf is starting to calm down and even smiles. "Please."

"You have a nice smile, Mr. Gaid—I mean, Wolf." Against Stephanie's own better judgment, her smile widens. Her past disappointment has been bitter, and she fears entering into a relationship with anyone—Wolfgang Gaidosch even more so than others as he has a clear connection to Matty, the one man she had devoted her entire soul to back in the Northeast Reeducation Camp. *Had we but met at another time, in another place, but no*, she reminds herself, *what happened at re-ed can't be erased. Matty can never forgive me, and I can never forgive myself*. But Wolf's smile, his willingness to approach her, Stephanie finds it hard to resist. Everyone wants to be loved, and Stephanie is no different. "So, were you going to ask me something?"

"Yes." Wolf clears his throat first. "I was hoping you might like to go out for a cup of coffee on Sunday?"

"Coffee? Do you mean real coffee?"

Wolf is smiling now; his idea of a coffee date is working. "Yes, I was thinking we could take the Jane Addams nature walk, and at the end, there is this new little coffee shop. They have their own greenhouses where they grow their own coffee and cocoa beans."

Stephanie's eyes darken. "But, Wolf, something like that would take up so many credits. I couldn't possibly—"

Wolf smiles. "You forget I've just been promoted and my first paycheck was downloaded. I have no idea what to do with all these credits, so I thought of you and how it might be fun and—" Once again, Wolf blushes.

Stephanie is thrilled. "I would love to go out with you. A nature walk followed by a cup of real coffee sounds wonderful."

"That's great, great." Wolf is so happy Stephanie didn't reject him that he forgets to mention the time he plans to pick her up.

"Don't sign off yet, Wolf." Stephanie can't help but giggle at his expense. "Don't you need to tell me when and where we'll meet?" Wolf turns an even darker shade of crimson. "You look good in red, Wolf. Maybe you should use a few of those credits to buy yourself a red shirt."

Wolf joins in on the laugh at his expense. "Sorry." Thinking about the best place, he suggests they meet at the HTS (Hadrian's Transit System) terminal nearest where Stephanie lives.

"Thank you, Wolf; that is very thoughtful of you. And what time?"

"How about 12:30? It will take us an hour by train to get to the Jane Addams Nature Interpretive Center. We have all kinds of nature walks to choose from, all of which will bring us to the International Tea and Coffee House sometime around 4 p.m. We could take a late tea. I hear they have a nice menu."

"Wolf," says Stephanie, smiling. "You're not British. How did you know about that tradition?"

"I looked it up on the wave. I figured since you have British heritage, you might appreciate an English-style first date."

"Well, then..." Stephanie is now beaming. This man is so thoughtful she is now anxiously awaiting the arrival of Sunday. "Sunday at 12:30 it is then."

* * * * *

The train ride was just under an hour. The line is only a few kilometers south of the northern border wall separating Hadrian from the northern country of Nunavut. Before the collapse of old Canada, Nunavut had been one of its northern territories in which resided mainly the indigenous population known then as the Inuit. Today, Nunavut is a country as over-populated with immigrants from around the globe as any other country outside of Hadrian, the Inuit long suffering the status of minority in their own home. Some say this is no different from when it was old Canada, while others see circumstances definitely worsened.

Stephanie and Wolf get off at the station next to Hadrian's northern-most tourist site: the Jane Addams Nature Walk Interpretive Center, which is nestled in a small inlet of Lake Addams, renamed shortly after Hadrian's founding in honor of Jane Addams, an American human rights activist of the late nineteenth and early twentieth centuries. Wolf uses his thumbprint to transfer the credits necessary to pay for their entrance fees. Stephanie acquiesces all financial control to Wolf since the date he has planned for them exceeds her personal budget. Inside the park, they begin in the information center. Here they learn about the history of the Inuit people who used to reside in this area. Wolf reads from the digital voc brochure he downloaded in preparation for this date. "The Inuit are a people whose ancestors date as far back as 2500 BC.[29]"

"Isn't this amazing," Stephanie sighs in awe. "Such an ancient and cultured people."

"Yes," Wolf agrees, "and their artwork is amazing." He points to an enclosed glass shelf with a variety of stone-carved sculptures on display. Stephanie's eyes twinkle as she spies "Raven Sparkle," a spiral-shaped oval forming the bird's head and beak. "Oh, Wolf, look at this one." Wolf smiles; Stephanie's enthusiasm is contagious.

"Yes," he replies, "it is beautiful."

"The artist's name was John Sabourin." She sighs deeply, "Oh, it is just so lovely."

Stephanie spins on her heels to face Wolf. They are standing so close Wolf can feel her breath tickling his cheek. "Which one is your favorite?"

Wolf takes a moment to peruse the sculptures on display. There is one that looks like a school of fish and another with two whales that are either interlocked in war or mating. Finally, his eyes land on "Inukshuk" by Qavavau Shaa. Its elegance is in its simplicity, a series of stones stacked to form a sculpture that makes Wolf think of a man. "I like this one the best," he says as he points its way.

"I'm not surprised," Stephanie replies. "It's simple, almost clumsy, but strong, and although it looks quite fragile, like a little push could topple it over, it also seems quite strong." Smiling, she looks at him again. "It makes me think of you, in all its fragile strength."

Wolf is so moved by Stephanie's words that he leans in and kisses her on the lips. It is as quick and simple as the artwork that inspired it. For a brief moment, the two look into each other's eyes. Fortunately, they are alone in the nature center, so no one notices their public display of affection. Wolf smiles and nods to the nature walk maps. "Which walk would you like to take?" The two cross over to the wall screen and debate over which walk is likely to be the most scenic at this time of year. Being mid-June, many of the flowers are in full bloom so they elect the most notable walk that stretches south of the interpretive center along the banks of the lake. Although everyone simply calls it the Spring Blossom Tour, The Mary Rozet Smith Stroll is actually named after Addams's life partner. Both

---

[29] http://www.nunavuttourism.com/about-nunavut/people-of-nunavut

Wolf and Stephanie are cognizant that the shrubbery and flowers have been mostly cultivated, but the naturalists at Jane Addams, having studied the natural flora and fauna of the area, were able to give it a very natural look, as if these plants truly did spring up of their own accord.

Wolf, having downloaded the tour pamphlet into his voc device, is reading the pamphlet verbatim for Stephanie. Like most of the re-ed class, she does not own a vocal contact lens and relies on government-installed wall screens for all her wave information. "We are now standing on what was once the tundra. Look at this old map of Manitoba. This is Hadrian. Here used to be boreal forest, and here used to be a coniferous forest. Notice our current map of Hadrian. The deciduous and coniferous forests have overtaken most of what used to be boreal." He blinks up a map of old Manitoba, Canada, and reverses the image so Stephanie can view it, too. "See here." He points to the holographic image to the northern tip near the Hudson Bay. "This little black spot is where we are standing. All this and everything north of here used to be tundra." He traces his finger down and around where the tundra once existed.

"This entire area?" Stephanie asks dismayed. Even though everyone in Hadrian studies about how climate change has altered much of the earth's landscape, it remains difficult for the mind to grasp when presented with the evidence of such large-scale devastation. "All this used to be tundra?"

"Uh, huh." Wolf's reply is a little too nonchalant. It is really hard to affect the sensitivities of a Detritus Fisherman who has seen firsthand the results of man's havoc. "Now, as you can see, it is nearly all boreal forest mixed in heavily with northern coniferous. In fact," Wolf adds, using his own knowledge from grade school, "most of Hadrian's northern and western forests are a blend of the three, though the common nomenclature is simply to call it the boreal forest. And, as we all know, the tundra no longer exists."

"That's why the polar bear went extinct, right?" Stephanie inquires, her eyes a little shiny from emotional distress. The once mighty polar bear that roamed the northern tundra has become symbolic in Hadrian for humanity's vast greed and cruelty in destroying the natural habitat for most of the planet's wildlife.

"Sadly, yes," Wolf replies. Wanting now to cheer his date, he points out much of the plant life that has survived and been reclaimed through Hadrian's extensive natural reclamation project. "We may not be able to recreate the tundra, and temperatures are now too warm for that climate, but look at the trees and flowers we've managed to help regrow naturally here. Look," he points, "that's a spruce; next to it is poplar; over there are some birch, jack pine (the most hearty of all), aspen, even a little balsam. It is really amazing how many species of trees we've managed to save here in Hadrian."

"And the flowers, Wolf," Stephanie pleads. "Don't forget to name the flowers. They are so beautiful."

"This one is probably the most common," Wolf answers immediately as he points to a tall tubular purple flower with multiple blossoms that grow up the long stem. "It's called a fireweed. It blooms all spring and summer. You can tell the change in season by where the blossoms sit on the stem. Right now they are quite low, indicating it is still spring, but when the very top buds open, it will be fall."

"That is so interesting." Stephanie's eyes sparkle. Her excitement is infectious, so Wolf quickly scrolls through the pamphlet to see whether he can identify another flower for her. Finally, he spots one that is in the pamphlet registry. "Here's one," he says, pointing to an unassuming flower. "It's called a Woodland Horsetail." Stephanie smiles, even though the flower doesn't impress her; the petals are so tiny and the flowerets so numerous from a distance that it just looks like a blob. Wolf kneels down to get a much closer look. "It is really quite pretty when you get in close enough to see its intricate detail." Stephanie, not wanting to kneel down and get her skirt or nylons dirty, decides to take Wolf's word for it. "Look at that one, over there!" she exclaims. "It's quite pretty with its little purple petals and yellow stamen. What's it called?"

Wolf has to do a bit of scrolling before he finds the answer, but finally, he satiates Stephanie's curiosity. "It's Blue-Eyed Grass."

"How lovely."

Their walk continues on in much the same vein with a warm spring breeze carrying the sweet scent of the freshwater lake to their nostrils and the soft spring sun shining down on them until they come at last to the little tea and coffee house Wolf has promised Stephanie. It is exactly one tram station away from the interpretive center, so after their meal, they will simply catch the train back to their respective stops.

The International Tea and Coffee House (named to commemorate Jane Addams's role as a world-renowned feminist whose work stretched across the globe to help women and the unfortunate) overlooks Addams Lake. The teahouse is nestled in a small alcove of poplar and birch with the front entrance open towards the lake. There is no sign of the mighty greenhouses the park purports to have in order to grow the coffee, cocoa, and tea plants. "Just as long as they serve the coffee they promise in the brochure," is Stephanie's response when Wolf notes this curious omission. "Perhaps they keep the greenhouse farther off so it doesn't ruin the ambiance of a rustic cabin on the lakefront." Wolf nods in agreement since Stephanie's rationale makes sense.

The interior is as rustic as the exterior. The International Tea and Coffee House was a log cabin recreated in the style of the eighteenth century. An old Hudson Bay blanket decorates one wall while copies of Inuit wood and stone sculptures for sale are lined up on a series of shelves against the other. Wolf places one hand on Stephanie's waist and leads her to the table in the corner farthest from the door. After sitting, Wolf waves to the waiter and asks him for the address of the link to the menu and drink options. The young man eyes Wolf and Stephanie circumspectly before crossing over. "All right then," he exclaims as he blinks up the image of a traditional waiter's notepad. Sighing now, he looks first at Wolf, then at Stephanie. "Which one of you is trans?"

Stephanie places her face in her hands. Wolf blinks, taken aback by this sudden bizarre inquiry. "Excuse me? What business is it of yours?"

Now holding a holographic pencil in his hand, the waiter motions to the room around them, "This is my business."

"So?" Wolf still cannot understand why this person is asking about their gender expression.

"There is no, 'So' about it," the young man says testily. "This is my business, and I don't serve strais here. So you were either both born with a willy or both born without one. Either way, I don't care, but if you are, as you so clearly appear to be, of the opposite sex, we'll have nothing to do with you and you can walk your sick strai bodies out of my establishment."

Wolf lowers his head; that familiar metallic taste fills his mouth, urging him to spit. Stephanie leans across the table and touches Wolf's hand. Wolf looks up, noting the tears forming in her eyes. Their hands clasp. The waiter snorts in derision. Stephanie says, "Wolf, I'll—"

"No, Stephanie." Wolf cuts her off before she can announce her transwoman status. "It's none of this bastard's business. Let's go."

The waiter steps back and points towards the door, yet remains firmly in their way so Wolf and Stephanie have to circumnavigate around him. He continues to weave back in front of them so he can fully berate them with his tirade. "That's right; you go. Get your strai rat bodies outta here! Hadrian may have made being you legal, but that doesn't make your presence acceptable to honest citizens like me. Breeders are a disgrace to this planet. Overpopulating, breeding like rats, and then swarming all over each other, committing obscene acts of cannibalism. You people are disgusting. And the pollution! What you've done to this planet! That's right, you go. You just march right on out of here. The very sight of you makes me sick. You know what bugs me the most about you people? That two decent Hadrian citizens are probably going to be exiled for killing the likes of you. Why, they were just doing what the law should do. If I had my way, we'd go back to exiling the lot of you or offering you henbane to choke on. In fact, I'd like to see a real reform to that law; we should take out exile as an option altogether. Why should we let people like you live so you can further spread your contagion around the planet! That's right; get out! Get Out! GET OUT!"

Once outside, Wolf embraces Stephanie, knowing how hurt she is by this whole ordeal. The owner of this fine establishment, seeing their public display of affection, rushes out screaming. "Get away from here now. Don't you do that sick strai stuff in front of my teahouse; you'll scare away potential customers. Nobody wants to see you people touching like that."

Before walking towards the tram station, Wolf turns and flips the man off, eliciting another vicious tirade, including the ironic comment, "Oh, sure, aren't you mature?"

* * * * *

The tram ride home is quiet. Sitting across from them, two young women are canoodling. To their right, two men are hanging on to one of the poles, swinging around and occasionally kissing one another. Stephanie and Wolf sit apart with an empty seat between them, neither willing to risk eye contact. They don't even say goodbye when Stephanie gets off at her station.

* * * * *

Salve!

To Serve or Not to Serve?
HNN—Danny Duggin Reporting

Should conscious-minded businesses be forced by law to serve heterosexual citizens? That is the question on many of Hadrian's citizens' and entrepreneurs' minds these days. Just last Sunday, an allegedly heterosexual couple was denied service at The International Tea and Coffee House, beautifully situated in an alcove of birch and pine overlooking the picturesque Addams Lake in the Jane Addams Nature Park on the northeast border of Hadrian. This scenic park has one of Hadrian's finest campsites and cabins for rent. You should seriously consider taking your next spring, summer, or fall vacation up there, but back to our story. According to Ashur M'Bala, co-owner and headwaiter at The International Tea and Coffee House, the couple in question was far too brazen in their public display of affection. He wanted assurances that they were not the heterosexual couple they clearly appeared to be. Look now to the right screen and you can watch my interview with him.

* * * * *

"Mr. M'Bala, I understand you asked a heterosexual couple to leave your business the other day. Would you mind explaining why you refused them service?"

"I have no intention of encouraging strai behavior in my establishment. I believe fully in the cornerstones our country was founded on, especially the one that rejects heterosexuality. Our good country was founded on the principle that overpopulation is bad. That hasn't changed. The world out there is still over twenty billion. Heterosexuals know no boundaries when it comes to having sex. They continue to reproduce at a terrifying rate."

"That is very true, Mr. M'Bala. You are so right. Now, you mentioned

192

earlier that when the couple first came into your establishment, you had wanted to give them the benefit of the doubt. Could you please explain what you mean?"

"I am aware that some of our transgendered citizens transition so successfully that you cannot identify them for their real gender. So, instead of simply assuming these two were strai, I first asked if one of them was in fact trans. When they refused to answer, I asked them to leave."

"That was very generous of you. Not as many citizens are as accepting of our transgendered citizens. And really, transi bros and sisses, you need to make sure your fellow citizens know what your real sex is so we don't mistake you for strais. That's your responsibility. So, Mr. M'Bala, what happened next?"

"Well, they left, but as soon as they were out the door, they started making out like two horny little strais. It was sickening. So I told them to take their disgusting PDA someplace else."

"For my viewers who may not be aware, PDA is the acronym for Public Display of Affection."

"And that it was. So I told 'em, their kissing and groping is going to frighten away decent customers."

"And it would have. No one wants to watch that sort of thing. Yes, okay, you heterosexuals, it is now legal, and no one is going to exile you anymore—unless you have that "special" strai sex—that act is so disgusting, why would anyone want to overpopulate—enough of that. I don't even want to think about it. Don't go showing off. We don't need to know you're straight. Have some common sense and a little common decency, please.

"So, tell me Mr. M'Bala, were you aware this couple is really a gay couple and that the girl is in fact a boy, or transwoman as they like to call themselves?"

"No, I didn't. I don't understand why he didn't say anything about being trans then. Really, how stupid."

"Indeed. Clearly, they are strai sympathizers and foolishly identify themselves in that way. Listen, 'transyman' and 'transygirl,' and also your supposedly 'opposite sex partner,' you need to acknowledge your real gender in our community. Be transy all you like, date a transy all you want, but if you're a gay couple, you're a gay couple. And if you go around letting people think you're straight, well, you're just setting yourselves up."

* * * * *

And there you have it, folks. My advice to our transgendered citizens needs to be taken into consideration. Do not align yourself with the breeders of this world. Any decent business in this country is going to deny you service if you appear to be heterosexual and refuse to prove otherwise. There are no laws protecting strais, and a good business will turn any potential strai customers away.[30] Hadrian's entrepreneurs are not in the business of promoting procreation and population explosion. Rather than serve heterosexuals, we need all our businesses to turn them away, sending a very strong message that it is not okay to choose to be strai!

Vale!

---

[30] http://www.huffingtonpost.com/2015/04/07/marc-benioff-indiana_n_7017032.html

Frank's Evaluation

**Fourth Year Evaluation—Frank Hunter
(Private) {penal restriction}
Guillaume de la Chappelle, Colonel-HDF Training/Logistics
Dated this day, September 3, 21__.**

Private Frank Hunter has done some remarkable work in the HDF Training Program. Had he not been restricted to "penal status," Private Hunter would have surpassed the rank of lieutenant by now.

Facts and Observations as follows:

-----Scoring first in the annual Sniper Competition for a second time, and with a score of 997/1000. This score is an amalgamate scoring in three areas: pistol competition, standard issue rifle/target competition, and sniper weapon competition.

-----His efforts in promoting team cohesion and enhancing each team member's abilities in his specific areas says much about his leadership ability and potential. Though he is not "officer rank" (though it is this colonel's opinion he should be), Private Hunter shows an amazing ability to step aside when needed, and at the same time, he will not back down to those who do have the rank.

-----As the present chief evaluation/promotion board officer for this period, I was able to gather reports from HDF Training Center, medical records (psychiatric), and physical training team leaders, and a listing of all sources accessed through the Hadrian Archival Records. Private Hunter's ability to garner and process past enemy actions against Hadrian, collate them, and then initiate and practice new defense scenarios bodes well for Hadrian's future defense. With my encouragement, Private Hunter is designing a series of war games to use as training scenarios for new recruits, though he feels all field soldiers should be required to take this training too, for, as he puts it, "We have all become too complacent, believing we can repel any possible enemy attack. Everyone anticipates victory at every turn, and that is precisely when defeat is bound to happen." I approve of Frank Hunter's proposal for upcoming Hadrian War Games.

It is my recommendation that General Birtwistle agree to Private Hunter's proposal and allow the private to be in command of the games.

-----Private Hunter has earned the highest marks in class instruction, including Tactical Planning/Defense, Strategic Planning/Defense, and National Defense Instruction. These high marks and course evaluations have earned him specific considerations with the Midwestern Gate Force commanded by General Egbert William Birtwistle.

-----Lastly, Private Hunter is still restricted by his tactile tattoo restraint. If his restraint is never to be removed, at least heed my recommendation to disengage it during the War Games. Private Hunter deserves to be the one to head these games.

Hadrian's Real News

Hadrian's Wall
HRN—Melissa Eagleton Reporting

"As you all know, the original Hadrian's Wall—named for the Roman emperor who ordered it constructed, and for whom our country is also named—was built across northern England in a desperate attempt to keep the northern barbarians from crossing over and attacking the Roman occupational army. A similar reasoning was used for the construction of our country's Wall. It acts as a barrier between our country and the outside world. And according to our military and all-known propaganda, hetero-sexual barbarians overpopulate that world. Well, it turns out a third wall is about to be erected today.

"As you can see, I'm standing in front of the Atheist Think Tank. Inside, members are preparing for the farewell ceremony being held in honor of Tara May Fowler, the young heterosexual woman who was brutally murdered last week. As you can see, many of her friends and allies to the straight community have gathered to protect her family members and clos-est friends from being harassed as they enter the Atheists Guild.

"To my left, you can see the centurions of Hadrian's army, better known to us as Hadrian's Conservative Right. They are here, as promised, to picket the gathering in honor of Tara Fowler. Their signs scream hate with sayings like "Go Away, Mr. Strai" and "Die, Breeder, Die." One sign even demands Hadrian's government bring back expulsion of all straight individuals. Adjacent to all this hate, we have Augustus Uni's GSA setting up its version of Hadrian's Wall.

"Mr. Stuttgart, may I ask a few questions of you while you work?"

"Oh, ahh, hi. Yes. Please just give me a moment to get strapped in."

"What Mr. Stuttgart is referring to are two back straps attached to wooden poles. There are two poles per person along which has been sewn red, flowing fabric with the design of bricks handpainted on them.

Once Mr. Stuttgart and all the others are strapped in, we will watch the unfolding of Hadrian's Wall. And there it goes—the opening. This is truly impressive. Six persons wide on each side with a good two feet between each person, this wall effectively stretches the full length of the pathway leading from the sidewalk to the building doors.

"You look fully secure now, Mr. Stuttgart. May I ask you a few questions about this wall that you and Tara Fowler's friends have just erected? Or, rather, I should say opened wide."

"Of course. As you know, Tara Fowler was a member of our Augustus Uni GSA. She was our secretary, in fact."

"And you, sir, are its president, correct?"

"Yes, I am the founder of our little union and was duly elected president."

"Would you please explain the purpose of your representation of Hadrian's Wall to our viewers."

"Of course. Hadrian's Wall, the original built during the Roman occupation of England, was designed to protect the Romans from incursion by the northern barbarians, as they called them. Our country's Wall was designed for similar reasons. It is believed that we are in constant jeopardy of raids by outsiders. These outsiders, the majority of our citizens believe, are heterosexual barbarians bent on destroying our peaceful culture and clearly established homonormative society. It is not the heterosexuals we need fear from the outside world, only the uncompromising militants who hate us. Sadly, that also includes the fanatics who live here in Hadrian amongst us. These are the haters of our world—the extremists who cling to their beliefs so tightly they are willing to kill anyone who thinks or believes differently. This is true whether the society is heteronormative or homonormative, founded on religious principles or secular ones. It will always be the haters from without and within whom we will need to defend ourselves against."

"Interesting. But why this wall, here, now? What does it represent for you, the family and friends of Tara Fowler?"

"Hadrian's Wall was designed to shield all within from the damaging practices of haters. We erect this symbolic Wall to shut out the haters who want so very much to cause pain to Tara's family and friends. In a few moments, two bubbles will arrive with Tara's mothers, her little brother, and the Raboud family, the Fowlers' closest friends. We have chosen to protect them from the hate surrounding this place with our own version of Hadrian's Wall."

"That is a beautiful gesture, Mr. Stuttgart, but even though you block out the sight of these people, how do you hope to block the sounds of their hate-filled chants?"

"When the Fowlers and Rabouds exit their bubbles and walk towards the Think Tank, we plan to sing 'Amazing Grace' so the sounds they hear will be ones of love and not hate."

"'Amazing Grace'? Isn't that a Christian hymn? I thought the Fowlers were atheists. This is the Atheist Think Tank. Why a Christian song, Mr. Stuttgart?"

"Being an atheist does not mean being closed minded. The lyrics of this particular hymn speak of one who was dejected and lost but found again. That reflects Tara, a young girl who struggled with her sexual identity for many years until she finally found the courage and strength to be who she truly is—was, before she was brutally murdered."

"And what will happen after the farewell ceremony? The centurions announced their intention to remain outside this building during the ceremony and continue their chants and demonstrations when it is over."

"Yes, I am well aware of their threats. That is why we will return to our posts after Tara's farewell ceremony to protect her loved ones when they leave here to attend Tara's cremation."

"The location of her cremation is a carefully guarded secret I've been told."

"Yes, it is our hope that the haters will not be able to find out where it is to occur. They have threatened to picket that, too, if they find out its location. Just in case, we plan to bring our wall with us."

"Thank you, Mr. Hunter—Oh, I'm so sorry; Mr. Stuttgart, I mean."

"That's okay. No need to apologize. I am not offended by any connection with my husband's name. As you can see, he is one of our wall guard posts."

"Yes, of course. But if I may, just one more question, please."

"Certainly."

"Where did you get this idea—creating a barrier between Tara's loved ones and the haters picketing her farewell ceremony?"

"Are you familiar with the historic figure Matthew Wayne Shepard?"

"That name sounds very familiar; please remind me."

"He was a young gay American, brutally tortured and left to die for being gay. His murderers left him to die tied to a fence in a farmer's field near Laramie, Wyoming, of the old United States. He was found twelve hours later, and after three days of fighting between life and death at a nearby hospital, he passed away. There was a Christian church at the time, Baptist I believe, whose members picketed the young man's funeral. Since the Shepard family was Christian, Matthew's friends dressed up as angels and used their wings to block out the haters picketing Matthew's funeral. I went onto the wave and found heart-wrenching stories about how this poor boy died and the way his friends chose to protect Matthew's family. The people picketing his funeral were carrying signs that said, 'God Hates Fags' and 'Fag Matt Burn in Hell.' Who does such a thing? But we see here today that fanatics come in all shapes and sizes. When I read about what Matthew Shepard's friends did for him and his family, I knew we had to do something similar for Tara's family."[31]

"Yes, of course. Thank you for sharing this with our viewers, Mr. Stuttgart. I appreciate your time during, what I am sure, is a most heart-breaking and difficult experience for you and all here to endure.

"Viewers, what we are witnessing here today is the juxtaposition of love and hate. Now, I am sure some of you watching this perceive the Conservative Right justified in their actions, but I hope the number of you who feel disapproval are much greater. Please take a moment to con-sider the ramifications of not only Tara Fowler's murder, but the actions of those picketing her farewell ceremony. Listen to them shouting hate-ful curses against the bereaved. Is this really the kind of society we want Hadrian to be like? Dig deep into your souls, citizens of Hadrian. It is my sincerest hope you will choose love over hate.

"TRUTH!"

---

[31] https://thispositivelife.wordpress.com/2011/10/09/thinking-of-matthew/

Tara's Eulogy

Xenophobia
boils hate o'er human fire
steaming violence

That powerful haiku, written by the deceased Tara May Fowler, exemplifies the very foundation upon which our country was built and is crumbling. At but twenty-two years of age, this young woman had gained a sense of maturity and understanding of human nature beyond the reckoning of most. Perhaps this was due to her having to live in this world as an outsider condemned to looking in as opposed to being allowed to act as a participant. You see, Tara Fowler was straight. Her sexual orientation, something decided by her body in utero, is deemed a plague by our society. Yes, our President has signed the bill making heterosexuality legal, no longer requiring adults to be expelled or our youth necessarily forced into reeducation camps, but that alone hasn't stemmed the tide of hate. In fact, it is as if all the haters are now crawling out of the woodwork, desperate to force those brave enough to come forth with our true identities back into hiding.

Tara had a unique philosophical outlook on life. She was not religious. She, like her mothers, was an atheist. She did not look to any deity to justify and condemn the good and evil of this world. "All that is man is man," she would say, "and every man is man." She explained these odd notions by stating that humanity was more than just one race; we are the human race. According to Tara, all of mankind is one man splintered and at odds with humself. Humself? Oh, how we all laughed when she said that. "What in the name of all that's gay and glorious is humself?" we queried. "Humself," she replied quietly, "is my word for the human pronoun.

We are all a part of hum." When we asked her why she didn't just use the pronoun Mx[32], she replied, "That's for the intersex and transgendered. 'Hum,'" she insisted, "is for everyone." She had odd ideas, but they were beautiful. Hum, as Tara explained it, is humanity—not he, not she, not trans, not intersex, but a blending of everyone. When we pushed her to explain this further, she claimed that hum had been splintered and that now we are separate entities. Hum is shattered, and every part of hum is splintered into separate beings: intersex, transgendered, women, and men. Her dream was for humanity to embrace "humself" once again. It saddened her that the focus of humanity was so separate and destructive. In the end, she best expressed this idea in another haiku:

humanity is
one separated being
open your arms soul

Curious as to how she had come up with this philosophy, I asked her to expound. She pondered for some time, as was her way. Tara was never one simply to spout out notions. She considered her ideas, allowed them to ferment and formulate, and then she'd smile when understanding finally came to her. "I guess it dates back to my welcoming ceremony."

You may well wonder what a welcoming ceremony is. Christians have a similar ceremony with baptism. Unlike baptism, which offers the child up to God, this ceremony welcomes the new child into the pentagram of life, or the five elements. Tara explained the ritual her mothers performed when she was but a few months old. Family and friends had gathered, and Tara was dressed in a small frock the colors of the rainbow. She was laid upon the kitchen table, which had been placed in the center of the room. There were no chairs; everyone gathered around the table to watch the proceedings. First, Tara's mother lit a candle and placed it at Tara's head. "This candle, my daughter," she said, "is to bring you the light of wisdom and understanding. May it guide you through the darkness of this life." Next, she placed a bowl of earth at Tara's feet. "This earth, my daughter, is for you to stand firmly upon. Stand tall. Love your planet. Honor her. Treasure her. Protect her." Next a bowl of water was placed by Tara's

---

[32] http://www.dailymail.co.uk/news/article-3066043/A-new-title-transgender-people-join-Mr-Mrs-Miss-used-driving-licences-bank-details-government-departments.html

right hand. "Water, my daughter, is the blood of life. Drink of it deeply. It will heal and cleanse you. Share this gift generously with others." Lastly, a toy windmill was placed by Tara's left hand. First, her mother blew on the wings to allow it to spin and show its power. "Wind, my daughter, is the breath of life. It represents strength. The wind is your breath and your soul." At this point, Tara's mother stepped back, allowing her mama to step forward. Mama Cecilia then lifted the infant Tara from the table and held her high for everyone to see. "You, my child, my lover's heart's desire, are the fifth element; a human amongst humans. Live for one. Live for all." We were all in tears by the time Tara finished that story. Her mothers, I know, suffer grievously now. They brought this woman into the world. They welcomed her to life, and now they must say goodbye. It is not for the parent to bury the child, but that is what the prejudices of our society ultimately dictated for them.

So, why did Tara come out? Why did Tara not just pretend to be someone else? I have heard many people asking this question through the wave. "She set herself up for this abuse," they claim. "She never should have told anyone she was straight." Tara never went around announcing her sexual orientation, nor did she believe in hiding it. She came out to her mothers when she was quite young. And although her revelation came as a shock, even an unwelcome one when the truth was first revealed, her mothers were wise enough not to impose a sentence of reeducation on their daughter. Tara was able to continue attending her regular middle school, go on to high school, graduate, serve time in the military, and go on to challenge uni at the great Augustus's halls of academia.

Tara was highly respected by her professors. She held a GPA of 94 percent. Although she did not qualify for a uni entrance scholarship, she did receive bi-annual semester uni scholarships that helped cover the cost of her tuition. Professor Politis referred to Tara as one of the most ingenious students she had encountered in years.

Tara was studying to be an educator. She would have made a fine teacher, too. Smart, witty, creative, and always ready with a jest if the mood of the room felt down, her goal was to teach high school history and politics. To quote Tara, "More than ever, it is critical for the minds of today's youth to be aware: aware of whom they are, aware of their surroundings, the decisions they make, and most especially, the decisions society is making for them." Never did words ring more true than these for the citizens of Hadrian. We are indoctrinated—from the moment we take our first breath, right through to the day we die—on the right way to live, the right way to think, the right way to feel, and the right way to love.

Tara chose to break the bonds of stereotypes and strove to be her own soul. She gathered to herself a small group of friends, who, like she did, believed in the concept of equal love. Her writing, her actions, her very words all expressed the idea that all members of humanity are equal and that no one—no one—be pushed aside. She fought for this belief, and, sadly, she died for it, too. For as much as Tara knew of the cruelties of this world, she had the deepest respect and hope for humanity. "Inside every intersex woman, man, and child," she would always say, "there is the truest desire to do what is good." When confronted with the questionable acts of her peers, Tara always found a way to justify them. "Misguided though many are, deep down, they all really want what is good and right in this world." Her solution to this conundrum was "Education." Tara's greatest hope was one day to walk into the classroom and provide opportunities for the students of our future to open their minds and learn to choose what is honestly best for humanity. For Tara, this best was acceptance. The kind of acceptance she didn't get when she exposed her sexual identity to two young women she had thought were her friends.

Tara didn't deserve such a brutal and torturous death. She was kind, gentle, and thoughtful of others' needs. That these women were able savagely to rape and murder her only testifies to the overwhelming hate that fills the very heart of our great country.

And even now, if Tara could speak to us from the grave, she would say these women who beat, raped, and murdered her, were merely a product of their environment. That society had educated them to hate and be cruel, and that, as a result of this lifelong indoctrination we have all endured, they actually believed that what they did to her was in the best interest of humanity. And we all know that isn't true. Let me give you one more taste of what Tara Fowler had to offer our world. The last poem she wrote was a sonnet. It was her plea to humanity—to all of us, whom she liked to call "Hum" titled "Frangible Essence." A copy of the poem can be found in Tara's memorial card you were asked to download. You may wish to follow along as I read.

Frangible essence, orb overflowing
With humanity's burgeoning presence.
Allotment tips, powder keg pulsate brings
Swelling waters bursting calescent.
Ripple waves erosion; giving slightly
Softly caressing cliff height's sandy shore
Aggressive breakers shatter human psyche;
Travail regardless all who may abhor.
O, humanity's ally! Occasion
All man. Vouchsafe commitment. Artisan
Logic, desiderata's nucleus:
Antecedent plenary devotion.
Recognize preservation is no crime.
Offensive forces one must needs defy.

Frangible essence. That indeed describes our Tara. It describes her awareness of humanity's great destruction. It describes her understanding of humanity's great potential.

Today, two mothers grieve the loss of a beloved child. Today, a brother grieves the loss of a beloved sister. Today, friends grieve the loss of a most steadfast companion. My name is Dean Stuttgart, and Tara May Fowler was my friend.

* * * * *

Tara's Welcoming Ceremony

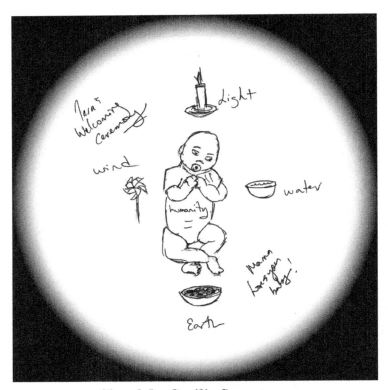

Sketch by Cecilia Sauveterre
Caption: "Mama loves you baby!"

* * * * *

Salve!

The Big Strai Lie[33]
HNN—Danny Duggin Reporting

If we all listen to those like Dean Stuttgart and Melissa Eagleton, everyone would foolishly come to believe that we should embrace our strai brothers and sisters. They claim we can successfully integrate heterosexuality into our mainstream culture. Well, I am sorry to disappoint those of you who have fallen for this nonsense, but this is nothing but a big fat strai lie! I do not say this because I hate strais. I am fully aware that the strais within our borders are our own children, which is why it is incumbent upon us to raise and educate our youth correctly. Allowing our youth to believe that opposite sex attractions are acceptable is simply wrong. They need to know that these abhorrent sexual desires are the very reason why Hadrian was established in the first place. This nonsense, this shilly-shallying around the idea that we are all the same, we are all one humanity, is both absurd and dangerous.

In fact, one key reason why the strai agenda has managed to garner popular appeal, especially amongst our youth, is the idea that strais are somehow the same as we are. They are not the same as the rest of us. Our youth do not understand how massively harmful and promiscuous the strai community is. Their inclination to procreate is the greatest threat facing our planet. The Big Strai Lie (BSL) has a number of facets including:

- that a lot of people in Hadrian are strai
- that being bisexual is okay
- being heterosexual is not a threat to the planet or the reason for the global population explosion
- and lastly, the most insidious lie of all, that strais are born that way

Let's break down these lies, shall we?

To begin with, there are not a lot of strais in Hadrian. No one under the age of twenty can claim to be anything less than a 2 on the Kinsey scale.

---

[33] http://www.americanthinker.com/articles/2015/07/the_big_gay_lie.html#.Vasqc1coXFc.mailto

That means, with the right education, no one in Hadrian need ever choose a straight lifestyle. The proponents of the BSL blatantly ignore all the evidence provided by our geneticists regarding the human genome and their success at having eradicated the heterosexual gene from Hadrian's procreation bank. No zygote lacking the homosexual gene is ever implanted into a female. No child in Hadrian is born straight. So this fact destroys both the first notion that there are a lot of strais amongst us, and lastly, that people are born strai. Not in Hadrian!

Next in the BLS is the belief that being bisexual is somehow okay. No, it's not! This whole notion of being bisexual is obscene. If you are with someone of the same sex, then you are gay, and great for you. If you are with someone of the opposite sex, then you are straight, and to those people, I say, "Stop putting yourself, the country of Hadrian, and the rest of the planet at risk of further population expansion!"

The third part of BSL suggests that heterosexuals can use birth control and Planned Parenthood to stop over-procreating. To that, I say, "Look outside our walls! There are over twenty billion pieces of evidence out there proving that heterosexuals are not capable of controlling themselves and holding back on over-procreation. If heterosexuals could control their sexual desires, the world wouldn't be in the mess it is in today!"

So, please, the next time someone tries to bamboozle you with the BSL—the Big Straight Lie—you refer them to this *Salve!* episode. And to that, I say

Vale!

Lying in Devon's Arms

As soon as he steps off the Nat tram (Hadrian's National transportation system—electronic trains that look like silver bullets except when moving), Devon feels like he is right back where he had left that very morning, The Northern Gate. The Midwest Gate looks exactly like every other gate where Devon has ever been stationed. All land gates are constructed of wood with decorative iron, illustrating Hadrian's fighting men and women combating the enemy, and they all rise to the daunting height of three stories. This, of course, is not for any practical reasons, just for a show of strength, and not just to the outside world; Hadrian's citizens need to be reassured of their safety so every time *Salve!* reports an attack somewhere against the Wall, its cameras always zoom in on these images pre- and post-newscast. The Wall extends beyond both sides of each gate and is built of thick concrete. The first few kilometers spanning left and right of the gate proper are compound headquarters and barracks housing both soldiers and civilian workers. Each gate is the equivalent of a small city, with housing, shops, theatres, and all forms of entertainment to keep the soldiers from going stir crazy during down times or to help them let off steam after an attack. Although Devon cannot see that far, he knows the Wall continues beyond the compound, in most places still three stories high, but with only the depth of one small room and hallway. This allows for provisions and armory to be stored and sparse accommodations for those soldiers stationed at each fifty-yard guard tower.

It really is amazing how much Hadrian's Wall has grown since Devon's eighteenth birthday, when he had been required to sign up to serve. Back then, there had still been hundreds of miles of open spaces with mere barbwire and electrical fencing. Now, most of the border has been walled off. *Salve!*'s call to arms a few years back wasn't so much for soldiers as it was for construction labor. Every new recruit spent the first year in the military doing "mortar and cement duty." Currently, there is only one section of Hadrian not walled in—the southern grasslands region along the borders of Quadrants One and Two, near where old Augustus City used to be situated. This entire area, including much of the richest grasslands in Hadrian, was contaminated by the dirty nuke set off by the fanatical Christian, Jeremiah F. Butler, that fateful day still referred to by all as 6-13. Very few of Hadrian's citizens are willing to work or live there because they fear radiation poisoning. The argument that outsiders aren't likely to care about the danger since their lives are so desperate anyway has been addressed by the extensive use of cameras and drone snipers on the guard towers along the southernmost border. The job of installing and maintaining these has been delegated to the least respected members of Hadrian's citizens—the re-ed faction. The least desirable jobs always go to those most desperate to find work.

And yet, not the entire Wall was designed strictly for defense. Stretches of the Wall between guard posts have been dedicated to sucking carbon out of the surrounding air and converting it into carbon neutral fuels, an energy source the military makes use of for many of its vehicles, guidance systems, and aircraft. Based on early twenty-first century technology, these unique sections of the Wall look more like giant stacks of cubes, each with an enormous fan inside it.[34] Devon had the unique opportunity to work on the construction of one such carbon capture zone of the Northern Gate wall. Being a part of securing the nation from outside attack as well as helping to cleanse the air of pollutants gave the young lieutenant a real sense of purpose and national pride.

As he walks towards the general's office to check in, Devon runs over his explanation for transferring once again. Although he has no viable reason for wanting to be at this particular gate, Devon had successfully convinced his preceding superior officer to release him. It's the "Birtbastard" (General Birtwistle—referred to as such, not so fondly, by the soldiers under him) that has Devon worried. Rumor and report suggest the man is not one to be so easily fooled. He knows he won't actually meet with the "Birtbastard," but his staff will have been trained to his idiosyncrasies. Whoever cross-examines him will be speaking in the "Birtbastard's voice." *Still*, Devon reasons,

---

[34] http://www.upworthy.com/meet-the-giant-air-sucking-wall-that-might-help-combat-climate-change?c=upw1&u=cc7589ff6eaf74ee71389382834b423ed4b2b2d0

there is nothing wrong with asking for a change. He sighs melancholically as he looks around him. *Not much of a change, really, but I could claim this gate sees more action. Or,* he considers, *I could say I suffered from a serious breakup and needed to get away from my ex.* Weak, but it is an excuse that has worked with others in the past, so it might just pass muster here.

Whether or not his story passes muster, Devon feels secure knowing his transfer was approved by Lieutenant-General Pauloosie. *That won't stop the "Birtbastard's" staff from grilling me,* Devon muses gloomily. Still, he needs to be here at the Midwest Gate. For some reason, a reason he can't even explain to himself, he needs to be near Frank Hunter. He needs to look into the eyes of the man who killed Todd Middleton. Even though he had been hurt by Todd's refusal to sleep with him, and claimed to be gleeful when Todd was exposed and sent away to reeducation camp, that never changed the fact that he had fallen deeply in love with Todd. Todd's death had come as a blow to his heart, one so painful that he found it impossible to continue seeing Frank's little brother, Roger. He tried not to blame Roger for what Frank did, but every time he looked at his young boyfriend, he saw Frank Hunter, and then the urge to kill began to well inside.

The last time Roger and Devon made love had ended in disaster—it ended their relationship. Devon knew he was being rough with the boy, but every time he looked into Roger's eyes, he saw Frank Hunter. When Roger begged him to stop, Devon slapped him across the face and told him to shut up. When Devon was finished and had finally rolled off him, Roger started to weep, "You promised me—"

"I promised you nothing." Now Devon cringes at the memory of his own insensitivity.

Roger bawling, muttered between sobs, "I said no S&M, and you said you'd never hurt me. You agreed. You promised me—"

Devon wouldn't even apologize; instead, he ended it. "I guess we're over then." Without even looking Roger's way, he ordered the young man to get dressed and go home.

"I hate you!" Roger cried. "You fucking Vibia bitch!"

These words still echo over and over in Devon's mind. *I wonder if he still hates me? He has every right to. Hadrian help me,* he muses, *I fucking hate myself. Hurting Roger like that when all I really wanted to do was hurt Frank—and myself. Is that why I'm here?* he wonders. *Just to hurt Frank?*

As soon as he was conscripted into the army, Devon began following

Frank's career through the military's data wave. *Career*, Devon muses. *More like stagnation.* It took Devon less than two years to rise from private recruit to second lieutenant while Frank Hunter is required by law to remain at the ranking of private recruit. As a result, Frank Hunter will always be a foot soldier. And yet, from everything Devon has read in the reports about the military's first penal private, Frank has managed to garner respect from the highest levels, and even though he can never carry the rank officially, it is said the "Birtbastard" considers Frank Hunter an elite sniper. Some even claim to have seen the "Birtbastard" actually talking to Frank Hunter, apparently to ask the private recruit for advice. That has never been proven, though. Still, Devon considers it a distinct possibility, remembering how strong a leader Frank was when he co-cap'd the Pride Panthers b-ball team.

* * * * *

The only way for someone to get close to Frank Hunter is to be assigned his guard or take up extreme running. Since becoming Frank's shadow would mean a demotion in rank, Devon decides it is time to get back into shape. Frank Hunter's legendary runs are common knowledge throughout Hadrian's military. It didn't take long for word of his incarceration and odd ways to reach the ears of nearly every soldier in Hadrian's army. Being privy to this knowledge before arriving at the Midwest Gate, Devon had already added running to his workouts. Running is hard for Devon even though he and Todd Middleton ran a lot together the one summer they dated. Knowing he has to be in prime shape if he is to keep up with Frank, Devon forces himself to run anyway, struggling all the while to push aside painful memories. Regardless of the fact that Devon began training for this task months prior to even applying for his transfer, he still finds that keeping up with Frank Hunter is a monolithic task. The man has been doing his run up and down and back and forth along the three-mile stretch of the Wall he is contained to by his tactile tattoo restraint for almost four years now.

Unfortunately for Devon, Frank can tell when someone is shadowing him on his runs. This only encourages Frank to push himself even harder so Devon will not have the opportunity to catch up. Frank's biggest fear is talking to anyone from his past, so when Frank runs, it is from his past. The last thing in Hadrian he will ever let catch up to him is his past, and Devon Rankin is a direct link to that past. To Todd Middleton. Even though it is common knowledge that no one can keep up with Frank on one of his runs, Devon is determined. Although he has never been successful as a long distance runner, Devon can sprint, so he determines shortly after arriving at the Southwest Gate, and after a few too many failed attempts at catching up to Frank, that he will catch Frank mid-run when he is on the ground running between stairwells. Devon lies in wait behind the central stairwell, the one leading up to the main gate guard tower. As soon as Frank lights off the stairs and begins running toward the next stairwell fifty meters away, Devon chases after him. The sprinting tactic works, but only momentarily. Devon knows he can't keep up the pace, especially since Frank, clearly annoyed at his presence, begins to run faster. It isn't long before Devon is left in Frank's wake without even being able to utter hello. Devon knows that the only way he is ever going to have his "talk" with Frank Hunter will be after he tackles and pins the man to the ground.

Tackling and pinning Frank isn't as easy as Devon thought. Although Frank never wrestled in high school, leaving Devon to think he has the edge, he was very quickly schooled in all the various maneuvers during hand-to-hand combat training. And Frank Hunter has always been a fast study. So, even though Devon tries to pin him face down by using the Double Leg Takedown maneuver, Frank, anticipating the move, is able to spin on his heels, press his hand down on Devon's head, grab his right arm, twist him around, and then slam his back down onto the ground, winding him. Before Devon can even catch his breath, Frank leaps down on him like a hawk. Flipping Devon on his side, Frank quickly slips his right arm between Devon's legs and his left arm under Devon's head and neck to clasp one tightly with the other. Devon is rendered immobile and barely able to breathe, let alone speak. This doesn't stop Frank from demanding, "What the *fuck* do you want from me?"

All Devon can muster in response is "I—want—you—"

"What? What?" Frank's rage has increased, his face reddening, his right arm painfully squishing against Devon's groin while the crook of his left arm digs deep into Devon's Adam's apple. Devon can no longer respond to any of Frank's queries. For a brief moment, their eyes meet. Devon's eyes are watering from the pain and frustration; this uncomfortable position in Frank's arms is oddly erotic, causing him to harden. Frank, feeling the sudden growth, squeezes Devon tighter for a millisecond before releasing him. Instantly, Frank grabs Devon's face in his hands and kisses him.

It isn't until much later, after the two men retreat to Frank's quarters, that Devon finally gets an opportunity to talk to Frank. By now, though, all questions about Todd's death seem moot. It is as if their lovemaking has cleared everything up for Devon. He isn't sure why or even how; he just knows that Frank killed Todd because he loved him. Frank Hunter had loved Todd so deeply he was willing to take the young man's life. Devon doesn't even want to know why anymore; knowing that is enough.

Strangely, it is Frank who initiates the conversation. "Why did you come here, Rankin?" Devon, resting his head on his right arm, looks over at Frank. Hunter is lying on his side with his back to Devon, his face towards the barrack wall. Using his left hand, Devon feathers his fingers over the small of Frank's back. Frank shivers. "Answer me, Rankin!"

"Call me 'Devon,'" seems to be the only answer the young man can give for the moment. Never in his wildest dreams did Devon ever envision himself with Frank Hunter, and then he had always figured Frank would be the aggressor, penetrating whomever he pleased, not being the one launched into. And yet, that was the very method of lovemaking Frank had insisted upon. Devon came at him from behind, and Frank had gripped both of Devon's hands tight against his throat. At one point, Devon felt as if Frank were trying to strangle himself with Devon's hands. It was highly erotic, and he knew he had to make Frank come before he killed him. Successfully freeing one hand, he gripped Frank's penis and brought the man to a climax. It was almost simultaneous, and Devon collapsed onto the small mattress with a satisfied groan. He didn't even notice how Frank slowly lowered himself into the fetal position away from him.

"All right, *Devon*, why did you come here?" The dry emotionless quality of Frank's voice and the sarcastic slur to his name causes Devon to pause. "It sure as Hadrian wasn't just to fuck me, now was it?"

"No—I mean—"

"No bullshit!"

"I did come here to see you. And, no, it wasn't to fuck you. I wanted to know—I—it doesn't really matter anymore."

"What?" Frank spits out derisively. "You think fucking heals all wounds?"

Even though Frank refuses to look at him, Devon shakes his head in response. "I guess I really came here because of those girls."

"What girls?"

"You know, the ones who murdered that girl." Devon doesn't know that Frank has little to no contact with the wave, being prohibited from wearing a voc lens or using any wall screens unless supervised. Frank has never missed any of that. It all belongs to a world he has chosen to be devoid of.

"No, Devon, I don't know."

Devon shudders. "It was brutal. They raped and beat her first." Shaking his head at the wonder of it, Devon adds, "Some folks think they'll get off, you know, like you did. I mean, I know you didn't get off—what I'm trying to say is there are those who think they should be sentenced like you."

"What do you think?"

"I think they'll get exile or henbane. If it's exile, they'll be leaving Hadrian here."

"I'll probably be on tower duty if they do."

"Why do you figure that?"

"I'm always on tower duty."

"You may have to be the one who has to—"

"Has to what? Shoot the bitches?" Cold and cynical Frank muses, "I suppose I will if they run back."

"You really don't know about what they did?"

"Nope. And I don't give a shit either."

"Wow." Devon is stunned. "This is like the biggest news since—" Devon cuts himself off. What he avoids saying is exactly what is on Frank's mind.

"Since my trial."

"Sorry, Frank; I—" There is a long pause while Devon waits for Frank to chastise or apologize. He gets neither. "It's just, well, their case is remark-ably similar—No, that's not right. They claimed their case was similar. You see, they raped and murdered some chick because she was strai, and then after killing her, they tried to use your case for precedence. They actually believed that they were right to kill her because she was straight. Can you believe it? And then they try to use you to get off. They actually thought they would get lifetime military service like you. I can't fucking believe it. There is no way in Hadrian that defense would ever work. I mean, your cases are so radically different. First off, you weren't the one actually to rape Todd; that was that...what was his name, the guy who ran the re-ed camp Todd was in?"

Frank's mutter is barely audible. "Gideon Weller."

"Yeah, yeah, that Weller dude; anyway, he was the one to rape Todd, so what you did was an act of mercy, an act of love. I can see that now. I couldn't before, but I understand now. I really do, Frank."

At this point in their conversation, Devon is leaning up on his left elbow, staring at the back of Frank's head. Frank's violent response so shatters Devon that he collapses back onto the bed in complete wonderment. And yet, Frank does not move. He just bellows from the depth of his belly. His voice ricochets off the wall, slamming into Devon's head. "You don't know anything! You don't understand shit!"

Memories start banging around Devon's mind; memories of that night Roger had him come over so Frank could show off his latest possession: Todd Middleton. They didn't have sex like Frank had claimed. Todd had been broken, shattered, terrified, and completely complacent to Frank's requests. Todd had been raped—and by Frank, by his best friend. "Oh, man. Oh, man, Frank." Devon just lies there, shaking his head, no longer looking at Frank but at the wall opposite him. Frank emits a pitiful moan. "Hadrian's Lover, Frank, how can you fucking live with yourself?"

Not his lover, Frank thinks ruefully, *his rage. I'm Hadrian's rage.* But Devon never hears those words as Frank only shouts a command, "Shut up and fuck me."

Devon, filled with anger and lust, wants to hurt Frank, and Frank, in self-loathing, wants desperately to be hurt. Roughly tossing Frank onto his back, Devon grips his throat with one hand and uses Frank's penis like a saddle horn with the other. It is like riding a brahma bull, with Frank bucking Devon at every thrust.

* * * * *

Hadrian's Martyrs

Hadrian's justice system is seldom cumbersome or overburdened. Only those few who contest the accusation laid against them find themselves inside a courtroom. Most are brought before Judge Julia Reznikoff after having confessed under interrogation while inside the temporary holding cells. Thus is the case with Angel Higgins and Grace Godoy. Neither girl denied her actions when informed that not only had the bartender seen them leave with Tara Fowler the night of her murder, but that a DNA match was found between that of Angel Higgins and the spit found on the victim. It was at this time that both girls admitted to the deed, but requested a trial by jury anyway. They had argued that their case was similar to that of Frank Hunter's, the only other known case in Hadrian where the guilty party had confessed to his crime, but due to the influence of his fathers' insistence that the act was assisted suicide and not murder, a trial had been granted. Angel Higgins also claimed assisted suicide and asked for their exile sentence to be converted into lifetime military service. Regardless of an outcry from the conservative right, causing their case to drag on through the summer months and well into fall, the two women were denied. This decision came about after Hadrian's head defense attorney held a brief interview with the young women.

* * * * *

Inside the small government office set aside for small meetings, Faial Raboud sits in wait for the arrival of the two young women who murdered her daughter's best friend in what was described to her as one of the most brutal forms of cruelty she has ever known to exist within Hadrian's walls. Looking about her, she notes how the room is similar to the one she sat in while awaiting the arrival of Graham Sabine, Crystal Albright, and her two mothers. *In fact,* Faial muses, *this is almost the same view.* The only difference is that it is now early winter; a slight dusting of snow covers the mounds of dirt that were once blooming with flowers and vegetables, as well as a thin powder coating the skeletons of a few leafless trees. Even in its state of hibernation, Hadrian's Central Government's rooftop garden is strangely beautiful. It speaks of loss and promise. Faial is brought back into the moment by the door opening. A civilian peace officer enters, escorting the two women into the room. Their hands are bound with plastic ties. These items have been recycled from the numerous mounds of plastic fished out of the Hudson Bay by detritus fishermen. Angel is the first to speak.

"Are you her?"

"Her, who?" Faial asks. Though she knows Angel means her, the lawyer who saved Frank Hunter's life, she harbors so much resentment towards Angel and Grace that she is determined not to give either girl any sort of break.

"Faial Raboud." "The lawyer." Angel and Grace both answer, their voices crawling over one another in desperate hope.

"I am she." Giving the women a quick glance, she points to their chairs with her eyes. "Sit down." They do as they are told, both girls locking eyes on Faial, who purposely ignores them. Turning to the peace officer, noticing he is about to leave, she advises, "Officer, you should stay."

Both girls start at this curt order. They were led to believe their time with their counselor would be private. What neither girl seems to realize is that Raboud has no intention of representing them. She is merely there as the Head of Hadrian's defense to determine whether or not another member of her team should be given the task of defending them. This decision, though already made up in her mind, is based on the facts of the case as presented by the interrogation team. In the voc vid, Angel confessed to getting Tara so intoxicated she could barely walk, to their stripping off her clothes, beating her, raping her with a beer bottle, then punching and kicking her until she is unconscious. When the investigator asked what she did after that, Angel said Grace was worried Tara might wake up and tell on them, so she hit her in the head three times with a brick. What really struck Faial as horrific was the cold and precise way in which Angel described the scene. When asked to give a reason for this attack and for spitting on the woman's dead body, she replied simply: "She was a strai" and then acted as if this justified the matter. Thus, as Faial sees it, this meeting is merely a formality; she could easily make her decision without talking to the guilty parties. Watching the interrogation, hearing both women confess, was enough upon which to base her opinion. And yet, Faial is suffering from a masochistic need to hear the girls' answers for herself. What she viewed seems too surreal. It is unfathomable that any human being could think this way and honestly believe her actions justified.

"So," Faial begins, "you admit to killing Tara Fowler." Faial isn't even bothering to put the question mark in her voice.

"Yes, ma'am," Angel responds first, "but it's like Frank Hunter, see; we were killing a strai and—"

Before Angel can finish, Faial cuts her off. "Like Frank Hunter? Tell me, when did Tara beg for you to take her life?" Angel stutters at this point. "No doubt," Faial responds for her, "Tara's life was so unbearable after being raped but—" here Faial pauses "—you were the ones to rape her."

Grace finds her voice. "I didn't!"

"No," Faial agrees. "You just held her in place so Angel could rape Tara with," looking Angel in the eyes, "what was it you used to simulate penile vaginal intercourse, a beer bottle?" Angel closes her eyes and sinks back into her chair. It is clear now Faial Raboud will not be defending them. "No, ladies," Faial points out to them as if speaking to children, "you cannot equate your crime to that of Frank Hunter's. Frank Hunter did not rape the victim. Frank Hunter did not beat the victim. Frank Hunter was the victim's lover and best friend. He acted out of a false sense of mercy. You two, on the other hand, raped, beat, and murdered Tara for one reason only—because she told you she was heterosexual." Glaring at the two girls now, Faial ends their meeting. "I will not defend you; no member of Hadrian's National Defense team will defend you. You may seek out a private lawyer if you wish, but it will do you very little good as my recommendation, along with that of Hadrian's National Prosecutor, Graham Sabine, is that you both be summarily exiled or offered Black Henbane for assisted suicide. Only one more voice is needed to seal your fate, that of Judge Julia Reznikoff."

Grace immediately bursts into tears as Angel cries out, "You can't do this to us!"

"I can and I will. You see, ladies, you both confessed, a witness connects you with Tara near the time of the murder, and your DNA, Ms. Higgins, was found on the dead girl's body." Faial turns cold. "In the name of Hadrian, why did you spit on the dead girl's body?"

"Because she was a fucking strai and strais make me sick!" Angel's voice hisses out like that of a snake.

Faial smiles grimly. "That ends this meeting. The facts of your case are simple. You are guilty. If Hadrian had hate crime laws, and I'm going to make sure we do *very soon*, I'd see to it that you were both executed. As the law currently stands, you get to choose between exile or assisted suicide."

Grace gasps.

Angel glares, her eyes filled with hate. "Fucking strai lover."

"Call me what you will," Faial sneers. "This meeting is over." Standing now, as she intends to leave, Faial places both hands on the table and leans in closer to Angel's face. "It doesn't matter to me which choice the two of you make, just so long as it means you will never again reside in Hadrian!"

* * * * *

Salve!

Survival Kit for the Exiled
HNN—Danny Duggin Reporting

Today's *Salve!* is going to look at the survival kit given to the exiled. As you know, when our citizens are exiled, they must head out into the unknown and find their own way in the outside world. The first few weeks are the most difficult as they trudge their way through the unruly terrain beyond Hadrian, which lies between our walls and the rest of humanity. As we know, this is to be the fate of two of Hadrian's darlings. We will be losing Angel Higgins and Grace Godoy as they walk through the Midwest Gate tomorrow morning, deep into the tree line, making their way through the forest and what little wildlife might exist in the neutral zone between our world and the masses. As our girls will be heading in a western direction, it is most likely they will end up living in the country of Alberta. Hadrian has had some positive dealings with Alberta in the past; its prime minister helped curtail the attacks against our Wall by the Manitoba brigade. This gives the young women hope that they will be embraced within this outsider world.

Honestly, I have no idea what it would be like to live amongst heterosexual barbarians. No doubt these two will have to hide their identities and pretend to be people they are not. This is something we have worked so hard against here in Hadrian, ensuring that no gay man or lesbian need ever have to hide whom he or she is ever again, and now two of our own are forced to venture out into that cold, intolerant world. It is sad irony, indeed, that they must now go live with the very people from whom they tried to defend Hadrian. Now, don't get me wrong, Hadrian. I do not condone murder, but their act was not so very different from that of Frank Hunter's five years ago. He, too, killed a strai, but he didn't get exiled or offered henbane. No, this man is still alive and a member of our society. Granted, he must remain a part of Hadrian's ground forces for the rest of his life, but even *that* is better than exile or death. It is the opinion of HNN and this reporter that Hadrian's justice system abandoned these girls. They, too, should be sentenced to life in the military given the opportunity to shoot heterosexual barbarians from the top of our walls as was the advantage granted to Frank Hunter.

Again, I veer off topic. Now I must race to tell you about the items that go into the survival kit for the exiled. Don't worry; these women are not going beyond our Wall empty-handed. Each girl will be given a pair of thermal underwear, long rain slickers, thermal blankets, a tarp, a coil of rope, one bowie hunting knife, matches inside a waterproof box, a paperback guidebook to surviving in the forest (both women lost their vocal contact lens when incarcerated), a paper version of Hadrian's most recent map of Alberta, as well as six weeks' worth of dehydrated rations. Hopefully, this will be enough to help Angel Higgins and Grace Godoy survive the challenges they will no doubt face during their trek from Hadrian to the nearest town or city in Alberta.

And now, a final word to the two women being exiled: Ladies, what you did was wrong. We all know that. I know you know that, and I am certain you feel remorse for your actions. Killing that strai was foolish. I wish there was a way to change the minds of Hadrian's justice system, but it appears your case has been irrevocably closed. Take care of yourselves out there in the wild terrain of the outside world. Be there for one another and stay strong. My thoughts, and the thoughts of Hadrian's citizens, go with you.

Vale!

Unexpected Encounters

After their night of violent lovemaking, Devon never goes out of his way to encounter Frank, or so he repeatedly tells himself. That night, as Devon sees it, was a mixture of anger and lust, and not one to be repeated. Regardless of his sadistic/masochistic nature, Devon acknowledges that their one night of battle-infused passion seemed to satiate both men, curing, for Devon at least, his anger and desire for revenge. As far as Devon is concerned, they need to go their separate ways and act as if their lovemaking never happened. Yet, as the days pass, the two men are always crossing paths. Devon finds this odd; the Midwest Gate is large enough for two men to go about their daily activities and never encounter one another, especially since one man is confined to a three-mile radius. Yet, somehow, Devon is constantly running into Frank. He can't blame this all on Frank either. Frank is the one limited to where he can go, but it always seems like Devon's duties bring him into contact with Frank. Devon is cordial every time he and Frank meet, and Frank always salutes as required as well as, oddly enough, offering Devon a shy smile.

Sometimes, these encounters don't even happen. Devon often finds himself seated at his assigned cubicle going over the schedule for an upcoming battle drill or reviewing the details of the last attack when he will suddenly look up and see Frank, except Frank isn't there. *What in Hadrian's name does this mean?* Devon wonders how he might rationalize either his encounters or daydreams. *The next time he is really here—when I really see him—I will have to ask him—get him to—what? Back off? He hasn't done anything. He's the one restricted. I can go wherever I damn well please. He sticks to his daily routine. When off duty, he runs back and forth, up and down, and back and forth again, and then on Sundays, his one enforced day off, he goes to the historical library to—wait—how do I know that?— Antinous help me.*

"Rankin!" General Birtwistle's voice is curt, ripping Devon roughly from his daydream. "Get your head in the game, Lieutenant!" Devon leaps up and stands at attention, saluting the general as per basic army regulations. "Sit down, Rankin. We were talking here, and suddenly, you stopped listening. Are you having some sort of stroke or seizure?"

"No, sir." Devon remains standing, clearly confused by how he managed to allow his mind to slip away during a critical meeting with the general. "I'm sorry, sir. I was just thinking about—"

"About what? Frank Hunter?"

Devon is shattered and stunned. "Sir?"

"Oh, don't play coy with me; the entire Wall is gossiping about your little tryst with him. How you tackled him in the dirt and got all hot and heavy until he dragged you back to his room. Don't worry. You can rendezvous with that private recruit all you want. He's been in the army longer than you and would have easily surpassed your rank had his sentence allowed for such promotion. I can make an exception for him on that account. Damn, I wish I had fifty more such men."

"Sir—I—we—don't—"

"Lieutenant-General Pauloosie led me to believe you were some crackerjack officer, career military and all that. Instead, I find myself saddled with a lovesick puppy."

"I am, sir—I mean, no, sir—"

"Just bloody well sit down!" Devon resumes his seat. He isn't even in his cubicle; he is in General Birtwistle's office. They have been discussing the upcoming battle drills, and when the general recommended they bring in Frank Hunter to develop the details of the mock attack, Devon drifted off. "Now, may we resume talking about Private Recruit Hunter without you cooing over him in a fantasy again?"

Devon blushes at the general's accusation and immediately chastises himself. *These random daydreams about Frank are getting out of control.* "Yes, sir, I will talk to Fra—Private Recruit Hunter and ask—"

"You are not going to ask him anything!" General Birtwistle is clearly annoyed. "He is your subordinate. You will order him to the task, and he will do it!"

"Yes, sir."

"Now, as I was saying, your ideas are all very well and good, by the book and all that, but there is nothing new or even dangerous about them."

"Sir, I—"

"Let me finish before you start defending yourself. I know it is standard practice to use laser light technology for skirmish practice, all very impressive-looking, but it does waste a lot of energy, and the President has 'requested,'"—here the general mimes quotation marks to show the order behind the President's word choice—"we reduce our power consumption."

"But the Wall's carbon capture units are constantly converting carbon dioxide into carbon neutral fuels—"

"Yes, yes." General Birtwistle is annoyed at this suggestion. "And all that carbon neutral fuel is reserved for the operating of our all terrain vehicles and aircraft. We cannot afford to use it for simulated attacks."

"We could use the urinators—" General Birtwistle raises a brow at the lieutenant's use of slang. The urinator is actually a urine-operated generator. It was first developed in the early twenty-first century by four Nigerian schoolgirls.[35] Little attention was paid to them at first, but the founders of Hadrian insisted they be one of the main sources of energy used. As practical as this form of energy is, most people are disinclined to use it since it requires an extraordinary amount of urine and, of course, there is always the smell. "Sorry, sir; that's just what everyone calls them." Devon coughs to hide his embarrassment.

"As you were saying?" The general isn't one for helping others save face.

"We could use the urine-operated generators. This base is quite heavily populated, so I'm sure we could easily acquire enough urine to run the simulations for the duration of the skirmish."

"Yes, yes, yes, but that still makes use of the wave and technology." And then in an aside, "Besides, they stink." Devon can't help but chuckle. As if offended, the general straightens his back and becomes even sterner, a feat Devon had thought impossible. "You don't see, do you, Lieutenant; we are constantly thinking and working inside the wave, but our enemies are not. They are not connected in the same way we are. And these laser light shows create a game-like atmosphere. Our soldiers look forward to these events. They are 'fun'!" Sarcasm and insolence drip. "No imminent danger is present. The end result is that our soldiers are no longer on their toes when a real attack happens. It is one thing to be shot through the chest with a beam of light; it means nothing if you can't be killed. And shooting

---

[35] http://www.asafeworldforwomen.org/global-news/africa/nigeria/3520-teen-girls-invent-urine-powered-generator.html

down a holographic man—where is the sense of reality in that? You see, this is why I brought up Private Recruit—don't you disappear on me!"

"No, sir; I'm paying attention." Devon is determined to gain control over his emotions and the longing he is experiencing for Frank Hunter.

"This is why I brought up Private Recruit Hunter. As a result of his sentence, Frank Hunter is in a unique position. Like the enemy, he thinks outside the wave. This is why he has proven to be such a great asset to this gate. Insisting he be transferred to my gate is one of my best maneuvers yet." Initially, Frank Hunter was sentenced to the Northern Gate, but when General Birtwistle learned of the private's extraordinary abilities as a sniper and tactical strategist, he knew he had to have him at his gate. The Midwest Gate suffers the greatest number of attacks. That piece of intelligence and the general's founding family status were all he needed to wheedle Frank Hunter away from Lieutenant-General Pauloosie. "That young man knows when an attack will occur even before our monitors do. He is always on his game, constantly peering into the horizon through his scope, attentive to nature's movements and manmade movements." The general pauses and looks Devon's way as if to ascertain comprehension in the youth. Devon merely looks bemused. The general harrumphs in response, creating even more confusion in the young man. "There is another aspect about Frank Hunter that distinguishes him from the rest of us."

"And what is that, sir?" Devon wipes away the sweat starting to drip down the back of his neck. He is beginning to feel like this meeting has become an interrogation.

"He reads."

"We all read, sir—"

"Not the way Hunter reads. He spends every Sunday in the historic museum, the library, as I'm sure you already know." Devon's blush deepens; is the general being coy with him? "He reads books, word for word, line by line, page by page. Most of us just skim the information we get on the wave, listening to the voiceover rather than actually reading anything. Frank, on the other hand," to Devon it seems like the general is referring to the private as a trusted confident, "well, he absorbs what he reads, thinks about what it all means. And, best of all, many of the books he reads are about the military strategies used over the ages. He studies war. And, like the enemy, he thinks outside the wave."

"What is the point of all this, sir?" Devon is still befuddled as to the general's intent.

"Young Hunter came to me with a brilliant idea." Actually, Frank Hunter has been coming to the general with this idea for over two years, but it wasn't until Colonel Guillaume de la Chappelle's last report that the general finally agreed to listen to the young man. Seeing a look of consternation on Devon's face, the general explains, "Don't be offended. He is not under your immediate charge, and I have made it clear to all the other officers that Private Recruit Hunter has free rein when it comes to bringing his ideas forth to me directly" (something he only recently agreed to, once again under the persuasion of de la Chappelle). "I will not waste Hunter's time with red tape and bureaucracy." The level of respect Frank has garnered from his superior officers stuns Devon. "Now, I was reluctant at first, but he has explained his reasoning quite well, and I am willing to give his idea a shot."

"And what idea is that, sir?"

"Live skirmishes using blank ammunition. He spoke of something called paint balls that will reveal when a person is injured or killed; some war game they used to play in the twentieth century. Said he'd read about it and thought it would be a great way to train new recruits. Sounds fascinating, really."

"But that would mean we'd have to base some soldiers outside the Wall?"

"Exactly! As Frank explained it to me, we never think like the enemy because we are always on the defensive."

"Well, we're not going to go out there and attack them. They're the ones always coming to attack us."

"Yes, yes, yes." The general is annoyed that Devon is not following his, actually Frank's, logic. "But we do not anticipate their moves because we never think like they do." Forgetting now what Frank had said, the general blinks up a cheat sheet to read off. "We never consider what their attacks might be like except based on what previous attacks have been. This is why our soldiers are stymied when an outside gang comes at us with brand new tactics. We must be able to respond to the unknown as quickly and as effectively as we respond to what we have come to expect from them." Having finished reading Frank's words, the general looks up momentarily to question Devon. "Are you following me now?"

"Yes, sir," Devon replies without complete certainty.

"So, we are going to have live skirmishes, two platoons pitted up against each other, with one platoon on the offensive whilst the other must repel it." General Birtwistle claps his hands together as if all is complete. "Now, you are to seek out Private Recruit Hunter and begin planning the first of these live skirmishes immediately. You are to report back to me as soon as the two of you are finished detailing the plans."

"Yes, sir."

"Now you can stand," the general orders. Devon obeys, stands to, and salutes his senior officer. "You are dismissed." With that said, Devon might as well have disappeared since the general dismisses him from his immediate attention; his eye blinks closed his notes on Frank's War Games scenario and blinks up an old report about the last attack against the Midwest Gate.

* * * * *

A turbulent explosion of energy forms a tight ball of hot ice inside Devon's stomach. He will not just be accidentally bumping into Frank; for at least two weeks, he will be working with him side-by-side. The tension is too much to bear, so Devon seeks Frank out, not to discuss their joint assignment, but to ask Frank whether he would prefer it if he were to ask for a transfer.

Devon finds Frank on one of his runs. Knowing he could never catch up with the man, Devon takes the local tram ahead one stop; this way, he can easily fall in line with Frank's pace. As a result of the run, Devon keeps his sentences short. "We have to work together."

"I know," Frank replies. "It was my idea."

Devon considers this for a moment and wonders whether Frank set this up intentionally. "Maybe I should transfer." When Frank doesn't respond, Devon persists, "What do you think?"

"Why do you want to leave?" Although subtle, Frank's demeanor suggests disappointment.

Devon is beginning to lag behind, so Frank slows his pace to accommodate him. This is something new. Devon is even more confused by Frank's body language than he is by his words. "I just thought I might be making your life uncomfortable, being, we, you know—and our connection to—and now we have to work together—and, well, anyway, if you would prefer it, I could—"

Frank stops running. Devon can't help but run past him a few paces before stopping himself. Suddenly, Frank reaches out and grabs Devon's arm, pulling him in for a kiss. When he finally releases Devon's lips, all he can say is, "Don't go."

Devon is stunned. It takes him a moment to regain his senses. "Okay—I won't."

The two men lock eyes—it is as if they have turned into one. Suddenly, Devon blurts out, "I want you." Three simple words, but poignant and strong enough to reach inside and touch the man Frank desperately tries to hide.

In response, Frank reaches for Devon's hand and whispers, "Come with me." Devon is taken aback when Frank leads him into the Historic Museum, through the displays of old northern Manitoba life, into more recent history explaining the purchase and transformation of northern Manitoba into Hadrian and, finally, into a small back room that just happens to be the library museum.

"Why are we here?" Devon asks, clearly baffled by this sudden turn of events.

The shy smile Frank reserves solely for Devon appears. "This is my sanctuary. This is where I come to read."

"Read?" Suddenly, the general's words are beginning to make sense. If an old library filled with dusty book has becomes Frank's sanctuary, then he doesn't just read; he must luxuriate in every word.

Suddenly, Frank lights up with excitement. "Yeah, the old fashioned way with a book in my hands, flipping pages instead of blinking to scroll. It's like nothing I've ever experienced before, the world around me vanishes, and my mind is drawn into the illusion created by these lines. I don't see words anymore; I—I see people, I see places, I hear conversations. I become the character, thinking and feeling and speaking." As he speaks, Frank's fingers softly caress the spines of books lined up like soldiers at attention on the shelf. He stops at one particularly large book, *War and Peace* by Leo Tolstoy. He pulls the heavy book off the shelf. Showing it to Devon, he exclaims, "It's absolutely brilliant. Nineteenth century warfare, but also love and complications in relationships and the whole social structure of society. Really, it's not very different from what we have here in Hadrian except for the obvious sexual orientation of the characters. That aside and, well, we're all alike; you know what I mean?"

Devon smiles as he places a hand on Frank's chest, feeling the man's heartbeat. "Here is your soul." So touched by Frank's essence, Devon pulls his face down and kisses him longingly. Frank embraces Devon, devouring his kiss, and then suddenly, he pushes him away. "No," he mutters. "Not here."

"Not here?" Devon is miffed at this rejection. "Why? Is this place so sanctimonious—Antinous's tomb or something?"

"No." Frank embraces Devon to appease him. Almost embarrassed now by what he has to say, Frank stutters slightly, "It's just that in here, every-where, except my quarters, they got vids on me 24-7. My room or yours, but never anywhere public. They're always watching me."

Devon pulls back. Looking up, he sees tears in Frank's eyes. So this is how General Birtwistle knew that he and Frank were intimate. "My place then," he whispers into Frank's ear. Then spinning on his heels and looking up at the ceiling, speaking to no one in particular, Devon winks, "Show's over boys and girls."

* * * * *

Once in Devon's quarters, the two men undress. At first, nothing hap-pens. Frank merely spoons Devon, and then very gently, without warning, Frank begins to penetrate his lover. Once immersed, Frank begins to pulse his penis in time with Devon's heartbeat. The pulsing, coupled now with Frank gently caressing his penis, causes Devon to moan in delight. This slow passionate lovemaking is such that all Devon can do is lie there and allow Frank complete control. Listening to Frank's gentle whisper, "Relax into it, baby," Devon allows his whole body to go limp. The intensity of Frank's motions brings on an orgasm so powerful that Devon cries upon climax. Lying enfolded in Frank's arms, Devon feels the safest he has ever felt his entire life. Then Frank pierces Devon to the quick. "Devon," he whispers, "I think I'm falling in love with you." Devon swallows hard. He tries to control his body's immediate reaction to clench, but Frank feels the tightness anyway. Frank appears to take it all in stride, as if Devon's reac-tion is natural and expected. "You don't have to respond, Devon. I don't expect anything—just—maybe, from time to time, come sleep with me?"

"I—" no thought goes into the response, "—of course I will." And he does, every night. Often not even to make love, just to lie there next to

Frank, feeling his body breathe, feeling his heart pulse and wondering whether he could ever learn to love this man.

* * * * *

Hadrian's Real News

The Exile of Angel and Grace
HRN—Melissa Eagleton Reporting

Earlier today, Danny Duggin shared with you the contents of the survival kit being granted to the exiled women, Angel Higgins and Grace Godoy. This is the first time in Hadrian's history that an individual being exiled has been given any sort of provisions to aid in her journey away from Hadrian. This is due to the high sentiment of sympathy being expressed for these two young women, regardless of the fact that they committed a heinous act of murder.

Many of Hadrian's citizens have answered my query as to whether or not this exile is warranted. And though many do see justice in the verdict handed down summarily by the defense, prosecution, and Judge Julia Reznikoff, some have responded with great vehemence against the court's decision. Zamira Lazami, for example, commented that the lack of a trial indicates a serious fault in Hadrian's justice system. Deidre Smith even went so far as to claim, "Angel and Grace did for Hadrian what should have been the justice system's job!" On the other hand, Walid Samra feels the justice systems works fine and that these girls, "having both confessed to the murder of Tara Fowler with both a witness statement and DNA evidence renders their verdict fair and impartial." He goes on to say that their situation in no way resembles that of Frank Hunter. "Frank Hunter was helping end his friend and lover's misery, whereas these women were the cause of Tara Fowler's pain and suffering." Âruna Gulovna also agrees with the verdict. According to Âruna, Angel Higgins and Grace Godoy's crime should be viewed as a wanton act of hate since they murdered the victim because of her sexual orientation. Finally, Jannack Mauritius stated, "Although I do not agree with Tara Fowler's choice to be heterosexual, her sexual preference in no way condones acts of violence that include rape and murder."

To Danny Duggin and his followers, Âruna's recognition of this crime as one motivated by hate is the deciding factor. Even if Hadrian had Hate Crime Laws, Angel and Grace would not have been tried under them. Sadly, Hadrian's Laws do not identify attacks against heterosexuals as acts of hate. And, yet, that their action was motivated by hate is evident. Also, Mr. Duggin, on the one occasion you mentioned the victim, you did not identify her as the victim, nor did you refer to her by her name. You simply called her "that strai." Well, Mr. Duggin, *that strai* had a name. Her name was Tara May Fowler. She was twenty-three years old, studying education, history, and philosophy at Augustus University. She leaves behind a younger brother and two loving mothers. Her family grieves her loss. So, rather than feel sorry for the ones who murdered this girl, believe that justice has been done. Two murderers have been exiled, and tomorrow we shall watch them walk through the Midwest Gate of Hadrian's Wall, carrying with them what no other exiled individual has ever received before, a survival kit complete with six weeks' rations.

TRUTH!

The Day of Exile

At the Midwest Gate, Private Frank Hunter is the sniper on duty in the main tower. Before climbing the three flights of stairs, he is informed by General Birtwistle that he is to shoot to kill if one or both girls should try to run back to the gate. "They know they are not allowed back in and know their fate if they try." Then pointing to his forehead, he adds, "Right between the eyes, Frank; make it quick and painless."

"Yes, sir," is Frank's response. He was anticipating this order since Devon warned him of his impending duty the first night they made—what, love or war?

At the ready, Frank waits for all the formality of the exile to end. First, they must read out the charges laid against the women, present them with their survival kits—this is the first Frank heard of the exiles getting survival kits—allow for the press to do their thing, and then watch as the gate is opened and the two women are ushered outside the Wall and left to their own defenses. Even three stories above in Watch Tower 1, Frank imagines he can hear wailing and moaning from below. *It won't be long now*, he muses. The sound of the gate reaches his ears, and Frank peers through his scope to wait for the two girls to walk into his sight. It takes a few minutes, long enough for Frank's mind to flood with memories.

Although this is his first exile, the reason for the banishment is too close to home for Frank. These girls had raped and killed a heterosexual. "Todd, forgive me," Frank whispers. But Frank knows it is not Todd's forgiveness he needs; it is his own, and that is something Frank ardently refuses himself. Suddenly, Frank's mind goes cold. All the tension his memories created in his body is gone. In the stillness of the moment, he watches the two women slowly make their way towards the tree line. As they draw near, one of the girls stops. *This is it*, Frank thinks. *She's going to turn back*. And

234

she does. He watches her mouth; she is shouting out something, probably "Mama" or "Papa." Frank has no idea who this girl is or what gender her parents might be, nor does he care. He simply has a job to do. He gives her one second to turn back, but she bursts into a run instead. Frank fires. A direct hit; right between the eyes, as ordered. The girl drops to the ground. Frank lifts his gun to bring the other woman into sight. He watches her drop to her knees. She appears to scream. Her face is torn by grief and horror. *Maybe now you know how the murdered girl's family feels.* This thought brings back the unwanted memories, and Frank wonders whether or not Todd's Papa Mike felt bereaved when he learned of his son's death. Not sure what this other woman might do, Frank decides to give her a warning. He shoots at the dirt in front of her, shaking her out of her current state of misery. She stares up at the tower. Still not moving, Frank fires another shot just a little closer this time. Dirt from the ground shoots up at her face. She winces. She stands quickly, turns her back on Hadrian, and begins running with all her might towards the safety of the tree line.

* * * * *

BOOK 4

NEW BEGINNINGS

Hadrian's Real News

The Need for New Beginnings
HRN—Melissa Eagleton Reporting

As the title of today's news report states, we are in desperate need for a new beginning, Hadrian. What our country has gone through in the past few years is akin to a seismic quake breaking the Richter magnitude scale. We have witnessed violence and murder resulting from hate. How have we managed to acquire so much bile while simultaneously convincing ourselves that we are a peaceful, loving nation that is working together to build a brave new world? Stop kidding yourself, Hadrian. You are no different than the fanatical Christians, Muslims, and Jews who berated, belittled, abused, mutilated, and yes, even murdered, and are still murdering, our lesbian, gay, bisexual, transgendered, and intersex siblings across the globe. No brave new world, no loving, peaceful people beats up a couple or berates and threatens them for walking arm-in-arm down the street. No peaceful, loving people beats a child to death for walking and talking "strai." No peaceful, loving people abandons their children and leaves them to fend for themselves in our cities' sewers. No peaceful, loving people turns a blind eye as these children are forced to work the sex trade for bits of food and pieces of clothing. No peaceful, loving people demands a transgendered woman prove she is male before providing her and her date service because they look straight. No peaceful, loving people gets a woman drunk in order to rape and murder her. No peaceful, loving people then touts those murderers as heroes of the people. In every possible sense, what we are doing to the straight, bisexual, and transgendered people in our community is wrong. I join Mother Stuttgart, one of our founding mothers, in reaching out to each of you, asking you to be a part of the movement that desires enlightenment, acceptance, and understanding. Hadrian, we need to embrace all of humanity as our founding families originally wanted us to.

Regardless of sexual orientation or gender identity, we all agree on the most critical of Hadrian's principles: maintaining a stable human population and reclaiming the natural resources of our planet earth. To this end, we can, if all are willing to set aside disparaging differences, work together.

TRUTH!

Dean's Speech

"Honored Madame President Stiles, quadrant officials, peace officers, key city council members, and fellow citizens, I stand before you today to express my fears and concerns for the majority of Hadrian's citizens. As many of you are aware, I am bisexual. This, in and of itself, is not deemed alarming or unacceptable in our culture as the vast majority of Hadrian accepts the idea that at least 80 percent of our population is somewhere between a 2 and a 5 on the Kinsey scale. What is deemed unacceptable, however, is for any of this vast majority ever to act upon their opposite sex attractions. That places any bisexual who falls in love with someone of the opposite sex in a very awkward and unfortunate position. This also includes our transgendered brothers and sisters. There are some, like my friend's girlfriend, who are afraid to transition into the bodies they would feel more comfortable in. My friend's girlfriend, for example, fears that the medical procedure required to provide her with her desired female body will exclude her from being able to be with the man she loves. People say that is foolish; we know she will be sterile and that transgendered women are free to date, make love to, and even register with a man—but are they really? Once the transition is complete, only those who know her from before her transition will treat her and her lover with acceptance. The vast majority of Hadrian's citizens, on the other hand, ignorant of her past, only see the lovers as heterosexual, and as a result, will attack them with verbal and/or physical abuse. One such case was that of Nadia Tornovoi and her registered mate Ichik Wongsuwon. As many of us know, Nadia was brutally beaten by a mob when the couple was seen walking arm-in-arm along Lesbos Boulevard in the city of Sappho.[36] This event occurred

---

[36] http://www.thelocal.fr/20130408/the-face-of-homophobia-in-france

only a few years ago during the debates leading up to the legalization of heterosexuality. Even though we claim to accept our transgender citizens, clearly any transgendered woman who falls in love with a man is at risk. No doubt the same can be said for a transgendered man who falls in love with a woman.

"What does this all add up to? Quite simply, that Hadrian citizens harbor a deep-seated hatred for heterosexuals. Hate may seem like a hard word to you, and I can tell by your facial expressions that many of you adamantly wish to deny the accusation. As much as you may want me to, I will not rescind my statement. Let me be perfectly clear; Hadrian citizens have been raised not only to disapprove of heterosexuals; we have been educated to hate them. We are actively and aggressively taught to hate heterosexuals. We are told to feel sorry for them, develop ways to reeducate them, and diminish their education and chances for advancement in life, leaving them to resort to menial, and often dangerous, labor. Nor do we deem them fit to serve in our military because they are perceived as aiding and abetting the enemy. Next come all the common hateful misrepresentations of the heterosexual. The women are selfish sluts, breeding humanity into extinction and having no regard for controlling pregnancy, willingly producing dozens of children each. It has even been cited that as recently as the twentieth century, it was common for families to have as many as ten or twenty children. While this may have been true at one time, it ceased to be the case for the First World countries by the end of the twentieth century.

"What is not spoken of and kept from the educational files used to instruct our youth, however, is that by the late twentieth century, Planned Parenthood had been successfully implemented in what used to be the European Union, old Canada, and the United States of America. By the end of the twentieth century, the average family consisted of one to three children, no larger than those we produce in Hadrian. The only difference is that we ensure that each adult is responsible for one child, and only one child, to be born into Hadrian. In this way, we maintain a stable population, whereas these lost civilizations had no structure in place to avoid a diminishing rate of citizens. As a result, they had begun depending on immigration to increase their populations in a desperate attempt to create a workforce capable of funding the pensions of their aging citizens. Do not misunderstand me; I am not purporting the notion that human population was actually decreasing in the days of population expansion—an expansion that we know reached detrimental proportions. I cite this fact merely to show that heterosexuals can control the growth of population through Planned Parenthood, just like the one we have here in Hadrian.

"Next I would like to address the issue of our attitudes towards male heterosexuals. These men, whom our society, along with female heterosexuals, says do not exist, do, in fact, exist and, like many of our bisexual and transgendered citizens, live a life of fear, resulting in anxiety, depression, and self-loathing. The first unfounded accusation against heterosexuals, men and women both, is that they choose to be straight. This is a misnomer, one the homosexual community, of all people, should understand. No one chooses to be gay, bisexual, or straight. We are born with our sexual orientation as was proved time and time again by the medical profession. One noted twentieth century medical practitioner, Dr. Kate O'Hanlan, provided what was then the American Medical Association with that very evidence. Allow me to quote her: 'Sexual orientation and gender are congenital.'[37] Now, many of Hadrian's genetic scientists claim to have eradicated the heterosexual gene from human DNA, but, as was proven in the trial of my son, Frank Hunter, there are no guarantees when it comes to manipulating genes. Just as pure homosexuals are born into this country, so are pure heterosexuals. We must learn to accept our sons and daughters regardless of gender or sexual orientation.

"One element of my research that I found both terrifying and fascinating is that the suicide rates amongst our heterosexual, bisexual, and transgender youth parallel those of the suicide rates of homosexuals living in those outside world countries that oppose homosexuality. Hadrian's bisexual, transgendered, and straight youth are fourteen times more likely to attempt suicide as their gay and lesbian peers. These suicides are linked to the bullying incurred by their peers as a result of being heterosexual, or perceived as being heterosexual. These figures parallel ones I found on the wave citing suicidal tendencies about lesbian, gay, bisexual, and transgender youths in what used to be our old Canada. Listen to what this historical document states: 'LGBT youth face approximately 14 times the risk of suicide and substance abuse than heterosexual peers.'[38]

"I call upon you, the leaders of our great society, to initiate educational

---

[37] http://media01.commpartners.com/AMA/sexual_identity_jan_2011/index.html

[38] http://ontario.cmha.ca/mental-health/lesbian-gay-bisexual-trans-people-and-mental-health/

programs that will help raise future Hadrian citizens to be more loving and compassionate towards all who are born and raised here.

"I would like to end my speech by quoting my mimi, my grandmother, founding mother Destiny Stuttgart. 'When the five families came together to acquire and create the country of Hadrian, we agreed on a series of basic principles to act as the foundation of our governance. First and foremost, we needed an environment where LGBTI citizens from across the globe could live without fear of recrimination, persecution, or abuse. This cornerstone, we assure ourselves and those who choose to join us, including straight individuals as well, was founded on the principle of love, acceptance, and equality for all.' What has happened to that founding ideal? Why do we no longer accept our bisexual, transgendered citizens, and why have we purposefully excluded and begun treating our heterosexual brothers and sisters in the very same manner our fellow LGBTI citizens were treated in the past and as many are still being treated in many outside world countries to this very day? As citizens of Hadrian, we need to rise above all forms of sexual bigotry and readopt our first principle: that we are all human beings regardless of race, religion, height, weight, and yes, gender and sexual orientation! I beseech you, listen to our founding mother."

* * * * *

Salve!

Stop Pandering to the Strai Agenda![39]
HNN—Danny Duggin Reporting

President Elena Stiles, Hadrian is disappointed in you! Why? might you ask. You are, after all, a genetic descendant of the Stiles founding family. But clearly, being a Stiles, or a Stuttgart for that matter, does not guarantee you will be a Hadrian patriot. My one apology to Gordon Stuttgart, who remains firmly entrenched in Conservative Right Politics. But back to you, Ms. Stiles; when the people of Hadrian elected you as our president four years ago, it was based on the understanding that you would continue to protect Hadrian's founding principles and carry on with the good work of reforming our wayward bisexual youth.

Instead, the first thing you did was to place strai sympathizer Jason Warith in charge of Hadrian's Reeducation System, who after turning our reeducation base camps into summer camps, announced his resignation as head of Reeducation. That's right, folks; the *Golden Boy of Reeducation* has just resigned because he's strai! Good work, President Stiles; you really know how to pick 'em. And now, word is out that you are seriously considering dismantling the reeducation system. Where are these strai sympathies coming from?

So, now that our reeducation system is in shambles, you propose to break your own Anti-Strai Propaganda Law, a law you signed into our constitution shortly after your inauguration, by funding educational changes that will allow our teachers to teach our youth about what it means to be strai. Well, the world already knows what it means to be strai. It means overpopulation and the inevitable polluting and destruction of our planet to accommodate twenty billion human beings. This is something Hadrian stands opposed to and must always stand opposed to!

---

[39] http://www.breakingisraelnews.com/46299/stop-pandering-to-the-lgbt-opinion/#CwiUC8xm-jqYt6L4d.97

Yes, I agree! Sorry, Hadrian; my production manager wisely reminds me to get back to the topic of Stiles threatening to dismantle the Anti-Strai Propaganda Law that strictly regulates the indoctrination of our youth by heterosexuals. Elena Stiles was recently quoted as saying the Conservative Right browbeat her into making this law. Well, I think it is time the Conservative Right really does do some browbeating. We need to browbeat President Stiles right out of office, making room for someone like Cooper Johnston, whose political campaign not only will maintain the Anti-Strai Propaganda Law, but return us to the day when being heterosexual was itself a crime, punishable by exile, and when all wayward youth who foolishly act on opposite sex attractions are reeducated for their benefit and the benefit of Hadrian!

The question that remains on the minds of every Hadrian patriot is why, and how, a founding family member becomes a turncoat? Not only has this happened to our President, but also, it is clear our founding mother, Destiny Stuttgart, heavily influences her. Mother Stuttgart, who is now, I'm sure, well over ninety, is clearly senile. Rather than take her ramblings seriously, we should be showing the old woman compassion and sympathy; she clearly needs proper medical care rather than the caregiving provided by her grandson, another out and proud strai! No doubt, Dean Stuttgart is the very root of all that is causing our government to betray our founding principles, the four cornerstones upon which our good country is based. We must never forget that ours is a nation intrinsically opposed to heterosexual propagation! To accept strais and bisexuals into our fold would only result in exasperating the world population and pollution problems the heterosexual barbarians have inflicted upon our earth!

So, then, why would two of our most respected founding family members turn on their country this way? After some work by HNN's research department, we discovered that President Stiles's leanings toward the strai agenda began with the death of little Fredrick Mustonen.[40] Being but four years old and suffering abuse at the hands of his mother because she feared he might be strai, she beat him to death; clearly, this was a case to pull at the heartstrings of all Hadrian citizens' hearts. But little Fredrick was the victim, not Hadrian. The woman who committed this heinous crime was sentenced to exile, but she wisely chose to drink Black Henbane. May little

---

[40] http://www.nydailynews.com/news/crime/oregon-mom-accused-killing-4-year-old-son-thought-gay-article-1.1738037

Fredrick rest in peace, but it is truly horrible to use his little death as a means to manipulate our citizens into feeling sympathy for all strais.

And, of course, there is the recent murder of Tara Fowler, an out strai at Augustus Uni, who actively fought for equal rights for strais as well as for the freedom for strais to marry and propagate at will. I am sorry she was murdered, as are all of Hadrian's citizens, but her death would never have occurred had Elena Stiles not encouraged strais to be out in the open, offending the sensibilities of Hadrian patriots, threatening to undermine the cornerstone that identifies our country as homosexual. And we all know what happens when one cornerstone collapses—the whole structure collapses. Under the old laws, Tara Fowler would have been picked up and placed in reeducation where she would have learned to love and embrace the only true loving expression, but instead, she was allowed to strut her heterosexual stuff and threaten Hadrian's homosexual lifestyle.

This brings us to the critical question: Where do we go from here? Do we reelect President Stiles, knowing full well her sympathies lie with strais, or do we look for new blood to come in and make Hadrian strong again? That new blood, though not having founding family genes running through his veins, has Hadrian's best interests at heart. Cooper Johnston promises to restore Hadrian to its former glory, fighting against the heterosexual barbarians and building this nation towards a better and brighter future.

Vale!

A Social Experiment[41]

Siddhartha Seshadri, Prasert Niratpattanasai, and Prasert's little sister, Kendra Schmidt (siblings seldom have the same last name since each child takes his or her genetic parent's last name), have decided to set up a little social experiment. Hadrian's historical archives are filled with vids and documents from the past, detailing the horrific crimes humanity committed against the gay community before the creation of Hadrian, and just last week, Sid found an old video shot by two men in Russia, dated circa 2015. The two men who created this video wanted to show the world just how horrible homophobia was in Russia at that time. And what the video revealed was pretty upsetting, evidencing why so many gay couples came together to create a safe haven in Hadrian. Even so, Sid found it sad, too, that what he was watching from years gone by was the very same as what he was witnessing today in his own country, except this time attitudes were reversed. In Hadrian, heterosexuals were reviled for being the "breeders" and "polluters of the planet." When he showed the old vid to Prasert, they both agreed a similar experiment needed to be done in Hadrian, on the streets of Augustus, and so Prasert, who had shared his bisexual identity with his little sister, found himself asking whether she would be willing to participate.

"Why me? Why not one of your straight friends?"

"Well, the two men in the Russian video were straight and their goal was to show Russia and the rest of the world just how homophobic their country was. I think we should use the same idea—have two homosexuals walking together like a straight couple—"

Kendra cuts him off. "Yeah, but the two guys in the vid are holding hands. Everybody in Hadrian holds hands. That just means you're friends. It won't work."

---

[41] http://www.telegraph.co.uk/men/the-filter/virals/11738047/Watch-what-happens-when-two-gay-men-hold-hands-while-walking-around-Moscow.html

"True." Prasert has to admit Kendra is right. Everyone holds hands in Hadrian. It denotes friendship. No one ever questions when a man and a woman are holding hands. More likely than not, two walking in such a manner are family or close friends. But that is not the same when it comes to two people walking arm-in-arm.

When Prasert brings up this point, Kendra ejaculates, "No way! That's gross." It takes a moment for Prasert's facial expression to sink in before Kendra realizes just how hurtful her sudden turn of phrase is. "I'm sorry, Prasert. I didn't mean to be so insensitive."

Prasert tries to swallow his disappointment, but he is still hurt. "That's all right. It just goes to show how deeply rooted Hadrian's prejudices are when your own sister can cut you to the quick without even realizing it."

This response cuts Kendra to the quick. "You're right, Prasert. I just blurt out an emotional response without any consideration to you or your friends. I'm sorry. How can I make it up to you?"

Prasert smiles. Kendra knows exactly what he is going to say. "By participating in Hadrian's version of a little social experiment."

* * * * *

The following morning, Kendra and Sid bravely wrap arms around each other. The physical contact denoting affection for someone of the opposite sex is foreign to both, but their intellectual understanding of the experiment allows both to overcome the oddity of the moment. Directing her attention to the back of Prasert's turban where he has adeptly hidden the small camera, Kendra giggles. "I can't believe we're actually using one of those archaic video devices."

"Hey," Sid reminds her, "some students need them. We can't all afford expensive vocs."

"No," Kendra agrees, "but a good voc cam records ten times better than that old thing."

"And how obvious would that be with Prasert walking backwards just to film us? You can't hide a voc cam in the back of a turban, now can you?" Kendra concedes the point and Sid shouts for Prasert to begin.

The couple walks casually through the Uni Park, taking a moment to enjoy the flowers, cross the small bridge over the babbling creek, as well as do a little bird watching, every movement calculated to reflect a young couple in love. It doesn't take long for the experiment to unveil some of the more guarded prejudices people hold. The people they pass begin to stop and stare. Someone even calls out to his friends, "Hey, look—it's a couple of strais!"

Laughter follows and someone else shouts, "You sick fucks don't belong here." "Yeah," another voice adds. "Leave Hadrian, why don't cha?"

And then someone purposely bumps into Sid. This happens a few more times, with men slamming into Sid's shoulder and women slamming into Kendra's. Suddenly, someone grabs Kendra and shoves her aside. The next thing Sid knows, a man twice his size in both height and weight has shoved his face up against his nose and started yelling, "What the fuck are you doing here, strai?" Much of the abuse blurs in Sid's ears, but Prasert catches it all on cam. Prasert's first instinct is to turn around and help his lover, but Kendra manages to extract Sid from a potentially volatile situation, so Prasert turns away again to continue capturing the event for posterity.

"We aren't strai," Kendra now pleads to the crowd. "We just lost a bet. We lost a bet. That's all. To pay up, we had to walk around Uni Park, pretending we were strais."

The big man looks Kendra's way before turning his scowls back at Sid. "That true?"

Sid picks up where Kendra left off. "Yeah, man; it's just a prank. We lost a bet. Our buddies made us do this."

"Fuckin' stupid bet. Your friends must hate you."

"Yeah," Kendra agrees, trying desperately to convince the man. "I would have been a lot happier having to down a dozen shooters or guzzle a mickey of rye."

This confession convinces the man and he laughs. Suddenly, he and Sid are best buds. He wraps an arm around Sid's shoulder and gives him a shake. "You two were really good. I really thought you were a knife and a stab walking that way."

"Yeah, well," Sid says as he breathes a sigh of relief, "that was part of the bet. We had to make it look real."

When Kendra is finally able to extricate Sid from his "new best friend," the three of them head back to Sid's place to debrief.

"Man, I'm telling you," Sid readily admits, "that man scared the shit out of me. I thought I was dead."

"I know," Kendra concurs. "The way he grabbed me and shoved me… Look." She points to the bruise on her left bicep. "That fucker really hurt me." Now looking her brother's way, she adds, "I had no idea what it feels like to be so hated. It's horrible." Shaking her head, looking directly into the vid cam Prasert is holding, she declares, "Everyone in Hadrian needs to know what this feels like." Now talking directly to their future audience, she says, "If you could feel what Sid and I went through today, just for walking arm-in-arm, you would never want—you could never want—no decent human being could ever justify treating another person that way ever again!"

* * * * *

Hadrian's Real News

Shocking News!
HRN—Melissa Eagleton Reporting

Jason Warith, the Head of Hadrian's National Reeducation System, has just resigned his post after exposing himself as heterosexual. This is perhaps the most shocking news to hit Hadrian's wave since the exile of Angel Higgins and Grace Godoy for the brutal murder of Tara Fowler. According to Jason, it was this very act of senseless violence, a vicious attack against a person resulting from hate, that inspired him to reveal his true orientation. He said he could no longer live with the pretense that he was gay. He had studied reeducation at uni and went on to bring in many of the humane reforms so desperately needed in our reeducation camps, but for Jason, that simply isn't enough. Jason turned down our offer to interview him, saying his coming out has brought with it a great deal of scorn and harsh words thrown his way. He wishes only to retire quietly now and avoid further bombardment of hate. But when he is ready, he promises to return to the forefront, or as he likes to call it, the front lines, in the fight for human rights in Hadrian, by joining forces with Dean Stuttgart and our founding mother, Destiny Stuttgart.

Although he is not here to speak these words, Jason Warith has given me permission to quote him directly. When asked why he was giving up on reeducation, as he is clearly the "poster boy" for the reformed heterosexual, one who lives a celibate lifestyle, his reply was simple. "I no longer believe reeducation is needed to help Hadrian remain strong in its intent to counter world population. Reeducating our youth—forever branding the unlucky ones with the stigma of being straight and, therefore, imperfect, someone needing to be fixed or cured—will never bring humanity together as a whole. We need to become one people, a collective willing to work together towards peace and harmony and the resurrection of the planet earth. If we want to create a sustainable world once more, we will have to learn to live and love and work together as one. Tara Fowler's death has convinced me that Hadrian needs to learn to accept all sexual orientations. I want to see a Hadrian that embraces humanity—not one that embraces hate."

Jason's words resound poignantly in the wake of the social experiment that has gone viral over the wave. Two young students of Augustus Uni, the uni considered to be the most liberal-minded in accepting open straight and bisexual students, decided to see how loving and accepting Hadrian's population really is. Siddhartha Seshadri and Kendra Schmidt, both gay, walked around Uni Park arm-in-arm. At first, they only experienced stares and the occasional glare. Fingerpointing and name-calling came next, and then the threat of violence ensued. The two had to lie their way out of being attacked by claiming to have lost a bet. If ever Jason Warith's words ring true, people, it is in the aftermath of this social experiment.

Truth, Hadrian! What you have just heard today is:

TRUTH!

Nothing Is Sometimes Everything

"What do you mean 'nothing'?"

"I mean 'nothing,' Sissy. I get nothing."

Sissy and Jeremy are holding hands across the small wood table that doubles as a kitchen table and coffee table. Her small home is a small one-room cabin. One room serves as a kitchen, living room, and bedroom. Only one other room is attached to the back—the toilet/washroom. Sissy has never wanted more. In fact, she actually found her living quarters quite spacious, even after her lover moved in. Sadly, Quinton had been perceived as strai and beaten to death two years earlier. No charges were ever made, and no attempt on the part of Hadrian's peace force or quadrant officials to investigate what happened was ever made. Even though this heart-wrenching experience taught her not to expect any fairness from Hadrian's legal system, Sissy still remains dumbfounded that Jeremy is being cut off without any recompense. "But you worked that ranch for close to thirty years now. You raised two children there. Surely that has to count for something."

Jeremy's voice is hollow. "If I fight him on this, he'll out me as bi and play on the idea of incest."

"That's ridiculous; we're not genetic siblings, and, besides, there are lots of gay couples out there just like we were. They met through their parents just like we did."

"Irrelevant. They can't procreate, whereas we can."

"Ridiculous. Besides, the odds of my getting pregnant at this age are slim to none."

"But not zero." With frustration building, Jeremy's anger bursts out. Letting go of Sissy's hand, he slams his fist on the table, shouting, "The law's the law, Sissy. I can't change that." Wisely giving her brother time to calm down, Sissy reaches across the table to rub Jeremy's hand. "I'm sorry I blew up. It's just, he's got me by the balls, and there ain't nothing I can do about."

Sissy refuses to give up. "Why not? The law's not immutable. The Stuttgarts and the Hunters changed it."

Jeremy harrumphs at that, "We're not the Stuttgarts or the Hunters."

"I know, but Mother Stuttgart, she'd support you."

"Get serious, Sissy. Who am I to go up to Mother Stuttgart and ask for help? Not only is she a national icon, but the woman doesn't even know me."

"Haven't you been watching *Salve!* and *HRN*? Mother Stuttgart's been on both, and she's a strong proponent for bi and straight rights. You should voc her."

"I wouldn't even know where to begin."

"START BY CONTACTING MELISSA EAGLETON!"

"Shit, Sissy; you think I know everybody."

"*HRN* has a contact button on its wave site."

"I know, but—"

"But nothing; contact *HRN* and ask Melissa Eagleton to connect you with Mother Stuttgart."

Jeremy shakes his head in defeat. "I might as well fart in the wind."

"What in Hadrian's name is that supposed to mean?"

"No one upwind ever smells the likes of me."

"What?"

"We ain't nobody, Sissy. Get that through your thick skull. Them folks live upwind of folks like us. They keep themselves sheltered from the wind so they don't have to smell us. When changes are made, it's because someone with money's got a strong arm and other folks are willing to listen. No one listens to the likes of us. Face it, Sissy; it's just you and me left. We cain't afford no help. No one gets paid no more."

Sissy looks dejected. "I guess that means letting go of all our hands?"

A depreciating nod precedes Jeremy's words. "I'm sorry, baby girl. We got no choice. All we got to make our living by is this small piece of rocky clay and grass we feed our sheep on. We make it based on this."

"That's not good enough. You can't let him win. You've got to fight, Jeremy."

"If he outs me, Teril and May'll find out."

"But they're your kids. They love you."

"Lots of families turn their backs when someone is outed. 'Member that

Middleton kid? And all them strai kids havin' to live in the sewers? Damn, I wish there were something we could do to help them."

"We can."

Jeremy looks up. Sissy sounds so confident that he can't help but be swept up. "How?"

"We contact *HRN*."

Both dejected and angry, Jeremy practically growls, "I ain't fighting Jake; I done told you that already."

"I know, but this isn't about Jake. It's about them kids. We could hire 'em on. Offer 'em a place to live."

"Sissy, be real. We just decided to lay off your entire staff and you want to hire these kids? We can't afford hired help; I told you that already."

"No, no, no, you don't understand." Smiling now, hoping to set Jeremy at his ease, she says, "We could offer 'em food and shelter in exchange for work. Surely living in the sheepherders' bunkhouse has got to be better than the sewers."

Flummoxed by the prospect, all Jeremy can sputter out is, "I don't know."

"Why not? Least we can do is offer. If they turn us down, they turn us down. But if they accept, well, then with the extra manpower, we could maybe break even."

"I reckon we could try. Kinda adopt 'em like."

"Yeah. Now yer thinkin'. We could give 'em a home, food, and clothes, something to work for and help keep this old sheep farm afloat." After a brief pause she adds, "Not everything's impossible."

Jeremy smiles. "That might work, and it sure would be nice helpin' them poor kids out."

"I'll contact *HRN*."

"No mention of my situation, mind you."

"I promise, Jeremy; I won't." Pausing briefly, Sissy brings up a truly sore spot for Jeremy. "What about Teril and May?" Jeremy's head sinks into his arms on the table. His sigh shudders with tears. "Don't let Jake be the one to tell 'em. If you tell 'em, I know they'll come around. If not right away, eventually. Trust them. Trust all them years you spent raisin' 'em and lovin' 'em." Running her fingers through Jeremy's hair, she adds, "I know them kids love you. Nothing can change that. I gotta believe that, Jeremy, and so do you."

* * * * *

Hadrian's Real News

Good News for Strai Youth
HRN—Melissa Eagleton Reporting

Hadrian, it is not very often these days that I am able to offer up some good news, especially news that pertains to our straight and bisexual youth. You may remember last year when I presented a *Salve!* on straight and bisexual youth living in the sewers of Hadrian. Sadly, I was still citing bigoted rhetoric and had even suggested that Hadrian's Peace Force needs to sweep all the sewers clean to bring these children out of hiding.[42] Well, as is evidenced by my *Hadrian's Real News* broadcast, I have come to see the ignorance of my previous ways. Fortunately, I have since gained the trust, unworthy as I am, of these abandoned and desperate children. Look to the right screen and you will witness footage of my recent visit to their underground home.

As you can see, I am being guided blindfolded down into Hadrian's sewer system by a youth whose face and all evidence of gender has been blurred to protect this child's identity. Once inside, with my blindfold removed, I saw before me these youth struggling to eke out an existence in a country that refuses to accept them for who they are. We were not allowed any sound, and the faces of all the youth are blurred out. But here, to my right, is a young heterosexual couple, the girl clearly pregnant. When I asked, she told me her last period was over six months ago. When I inquired into medical attention, her boyfriend sneered. He reminded me that doctors require credit, which none of these youth have, and Hadrian's current propagation laws would require the young girl to have an abortion.

The fact that this child was going to have a child in such horrific conditions encouraged me not to air this episode. All I could think of was how the peace officers would indeed sweep the sewers to find these youth and

---

[42] http://www.buzzfeed.com/lesterfeder/how-jamaicas-sodomy-laws-drive-gay-teens-into-the-sewers-of#.rrnZarwYP

impose an abortion on these children. She cried when she was reminded of that prospect and begged me not to let that happen. "Why," she asked, "can't we make our own baby? Why does everything have to be IVF?" As she was choking on her tears, her boyfriend finished for her. He made sure I understood that they were not interested in having dozens of babies. "We only want this baby. We are each responsible for bringing one child into this world; why can't a heterosexual couple bring two babies into the world the old-fashioned way?" When I inquired whether or not they could stop at two babies, he was adamant in the affirmative. "We'd use birth control if we could access it!"

Maybe Hadrian needs to revisit its birth control laws.

So why am I showing you this footage now? Because there is now hope for these youths. An individual who wishes to remain anonymous has offered food, clothing, and shelter to them in exchange for manual labor. When notified of this proposal, the youth were at first skeptical, but when they met with their benefactor, they accepted the kind offer, and now they are thrilled at the chance to start a new life somewhere where no one knows them as straight or bisexual. The young girl we saw will now be able to raise her child in a clean, loving home environment.

I know many people will want me to expose these youth and the person generous enough to save them from their current circumstances, but I cannot. When I met with the youth from the sewers, I was blindfolded, and no one revealed their real names to me. The individual who is taking these youth also managed to contact me anonymously. I have never seen this person's face, and I cannot even tell you the gender of the generous benefactor. Right now, I believe this is how it has to be. Until Hadrian's laws are more inclusive, the identity of these youth and their benefactor will remain a profound secret. Hopefully, as profoundly kept as the name of the young woman who seduced and later exposed Todd Middleton.

TRUTH!

36 Questions[43]

Dean and Geoffrey reconnect by using late twentieth century psychologist Arthur Aron's Experimental Generation of Interpersonal Closeness.[44] Dean had found this study on the wave while doing research for one of his psychology classes. When he first reached out to Geoffrey through the voc, he was saddened by how distant Geoffrey had become. Geoffrey's reticence is both natural and expected; Dean recognizes he must do more than just compromise. He must win Geoffrey's love. Woo him back. So he asks Geoffrey to start again. To this end, Dean commits to vocing Geoffrey every night. They both agreed that each night their voc convo will begin with one of Arthur Aron's thirty-six questions for generating closeness. Aron's study was brilliant and it has proven life-changing for Dean and Geoffrey. Dean started by asking the first question. *"Given the choice of anyone in the world, whom would you want as a dinner guest?"*

Geoffrey fumbles. To hide his discomfort, he picks at a fringe on his housecoat. Geoffrey is seated at his desk in his and Dean's bedroom. He was getting ready for bed when Dean voc'd in. "Geez, Dean. Can I say you? Are we allowed to say the other person, or are we supposed to pick someone famous?"

Dean's reply is equally confused. He too stumbles. Like Geoffrey, Dean is in bedclothes. He is wearing the maroon silk pajamas Geoffrey had given him for Hadrian's birthday a few years ago. Unlike Geoffrey, he is lounging on his bed. He runs his fingers along the buttons, causing the top one accidentally to pop open. Although Dean seems oblivious, Geoffrey notices. "To be honest," Dean replies, "I'm not sure. If we can pick each other, truth be known, your name popped up first for me, too."

---

[43] http://psp.sagepub.com/content/23/4/363.full.pdf+html

[44] http://www.nytimes.com/2015/01/11/fashion/modern-love-to-fall-in-love-with-anyone-do-this.html

Geoffrey catches himself smiling. He forces a frown, though, as the fear of being hurt is still prevalent. "Well," he says quickly to cover up his mixed emotions, "that was easy, then. What's question two?"

"Would you like to be famous? In what way?"

"Absolutely not!"

"Why not?" Dean was amazed at this sudden, very confident remark. Geoffrey was always the go-getter in their relationship. He ran a huge corporation, Hunter Detritus Fisheries, for close to twenty years, and then after selling majority shares to Hadrian's government, he became CEO for Hadrian's National Detritus Fisheries. Whether he likes it or not, he is at least somewhat famous in Hadrian.

"Famous people can't live human."

"That sounds strangely bigoted."

"It's not. I don't mean famous people aren't human. I mean that everywhere they go, they get recognized and can't just do normal things."

"Yeah, that's true." Dean is already learning so much more about his lover than even their twenty years of marriage had revealed.

"What about you?" Geoffrey asks. "I'm guessing yes for you since you've been fighting your way into the news so much of late."

"Yes, you're right. I do want to be famous, but not wave star famous like Eagleton or Duggin…"

"Especially not Danny Duggin," Geoffrey agrees. Both men laugh. Neither feels any level of respect for HNN's new newscaster.

"No," Dean agrees, "not like Danny Duggin. I don't mean big money fame, either. I guess, what I mean is, well, I spent the first half of my life hiding who I am, so afraid of being found out that I need to assert who I really am now." Dean watches Geoffrey's Adam's apple bob up and down as he swallows back his disappointment. "People need to know that I'm bisexual, and that it's okay." Geoffrey's eyes moisten. "There is nothing wrong with being gay, bi, or straight, and if making myself famous can help me share that with Hadrian, then fame becomes essential for me."

No longer interested in the topic of fame, Geoffrey mumbles, "You're bisexual? I thought you…"

Dean picks up where Geoffrey trails off. He knows what Geoffrey has been thinking. "Yes, Geoffrey. I'm bisexual." Dean sits upright, now cross-legged in the middle of his bed. "My time with you was not phony. I never faked loving you. I know when we separated I said I needed to be true to myself. I said I was straight, and I had to live a straight lifestyle, but these past two years have taught me something crucial."

"What's that?"

"I love you." Geoffrey breaks down at this point. The tears come freely. He covers his face with his hands and tries to control the emotion, but it is too overwhelming. Dean is also in tears. "I know I'm attracted to women, but there is something more."

Geoffrey barely manages to mumble, "What?"

"You. I'm attracted to you, too. It's you, Geoffrey. I love you. I want you. I desire you." Dean gets up from his chair and walks over to Geoffrey's voc image. He cradles Geoffrey's shimmering, holographic head in his hands, and then he rejoices in the electric sensation of kissing the man on the crown of his head. Geoffrey stands up and throws his arms around the shimmering holograph of Dean's body. The two men sparkle and snap with electrical energy.

Dean laughs. "So, I guess my original idea has fallen by the wayside."

"What idea was that?"

"That we only answer one question a night."

"Yeah," Geoffrey's laugh, though stunted by tears, is genuine, "that has definitely fallen by the wayside, as do all your forced plans." Now that his tears have abated, his laughter flows more freely. "You always did like to plan things out so perfectly, and then you'd get frustrated when things didn't turn out the way you expected them to. It is always best just to play things by ear, Dean. And, as it turns out, going through as many questions as we get through is what is working best for you and me."

Dean smiles in agreement. He lets go of the holographic image of his husband and makes his way over to his small bed. "Next question, then?"

Dean is almost a little too seductive in the way he lounges back onto his bed. Geoffrey watches Dean make himself comfortable on his bed in Destiny Stuttgart's home. Wistfully, he imagines Dean is really there in this room, making himself more comfortable on their bed. Geoffrey hardens. Not ready for any sexual play, Geoffrey crosses back to his desk and sits down in his desk chair. He swivels it so he is no longer facing the bed they used to share. Being anywhere near their bed, even just seeing it, feels too awkward for Geoffrey, especially with Dean's holographic image in the room. For a moment, there is a pause.

Dean's voice pulls Geoffrey out of his reverie. "Next question?"

"Yes, next question."

"*Before making a voc...*" Dean paraphrases the question since no one in Hadrian uses phones anymore—all communication is done through the wave; mostly through the vocal contact lens colloquially known as the voc. "*...do you ever rehearse what you are going to say? Why?*"

"Only if it's a business call. I figure if I can't be real with family or friends, then they're not family or friends."

"Good answer." Dean pauses before giving his response. "Please, don't judge me, but I rehearsed before this voc."

"I don't judge you, Dean, but why would you feel like you had to rehearse?"

"Because I hurt you too much to pretend I could just voc and things would be better, and I didn't know—I still don't know—what to say or how to act so I don't end up hurting you again."

"Just hearing you say that helps." Geoffrey sits up in his chair; he smiles at Dean's voc image. "All right, what question comes next?"

"*What would constitute a 'perfect' day for you?*" Dean doesn't even wait for Geoffrey to respond, leaping into his own answer. "For me, that would be a day where I didn't have to worry about studying."

Geoffrey isn't offended at the sudden reversal in turns, nor does it bother him that Dean's perfect day doesn't include him. "Yeah, I remember the uni days. Long days and even longer nights." Both men chuckle. "But," hoping to show Dean the light at the end of the tunnel, the one that is so dark and distant at this stage it is impossible to believe in, let alone see, Geoffrey adds, "the rewards are worth it in the end."

"Yeah, but," Dean counters, "you didn't have to worry about finding a job when you got out. You had your fathers' business to inherit."

"True." Geoffrey doesn't feel chastised in any way. "I can certainly understand how a Stuttgart might worry about his future chances in Hadrian." Dean smiles. Geoffrey successfully pops his "Pity me; I'm the poor student" bubble.

"My perfect day," Geoffrey offers up without request, "would be to have you, Frank, and Roger seated at the dinner table with me again." This seems so impossible that both men fall into a state of brief depression. "I'm sorry," Geoffrey begins...

"No," Dean insists, "don't apologize. It would make for a perfect day, and someday, Geoffrey, you mark my word, someday, it will happen."

Geoffrey's eyes have misted up again. "You promise?"

"I swear it on Antinous's grave, even if it has to happen at a barracks, the four of us will sit down for a meal again."

Geoffrey smiles, then bows his head. "I think I've had enough for our first kick at the can. I'm a bit of an emotional wreck." Wiping tears away, he stands up and motions towards what used to be their bed. "I need to sleep. I've a hard day tomorrow."

"All right, Geoffrey. I understand. May I voc again tomorrow night?"

"Of course, we still have—how many questions do we have left?"

Dean takes a moment to calculate. "Thirty-two."

"Seriously, we've only been through four?"

"Yeah," Dean agrees. "They're pretty intense, aren't they?"

"Maybe just for us, but it's good. I'm liking this. Voc me again tomorrow and we'll have a go at number five."

"I love you, babe."

Geoffrey smiles. He's not ready to say that yet, so he signs off with, "We'll talk again tomorrow night."

* * * * *

"When did you last sing to yourself? To someone else?"

"Hadrian help me, Dean; I can't remember. I guess, I think the last time I sang to myself was when I was two."

"Seriously, Geoffrey? Only two?" Dean smirks. "I seem to remember hearing you belt out a few when showering."

"I never—" Suddenly, Geoffrey blushes. He remembers. "Funny how the mind blocks out things like that. Especially if the event seems so trivial…"

"Or embarrassing," Dean finishes for him. "It's okay, Geoffrey; I always thought you had a beautiful voice. But you're not finished. When was the last time you sang to someone?"

"You, on your fortieth birthday." It was the last one the two men had spent together. Dean frowns. He holds back his tongue, though. He wants to ask, "Why not on Roger's birthdays?" but Dean could feel the same question haunting Geoffrey. Asking him this would only reopen the rift between, creating an even greater chasm. Right now, they are building a bridge, and moments like this prove just how fragile and precarious this building process is for them.

Geoffrey quickly shifts to Dean's turn. "And you?"

"I sing to myself almost all the time now."

"Really?" Geoffrey is both startled and amused. He also feels a tinge of regret. To sing to oneself suggests contentment. *Dean is happy now*, he thinks. His eyes grow dark as he mutters to himself, "Something you never were with me." Hoping to hide his disappointment, he feigns curiosity. "Interesting. Why?"

Apparently oblivious to Geoffrey's inner concerns, Dean answers, "It's when I study. I hum more than sing, really. It helps me concentrate. Relaxes me a little." Geoffrey's relief is audible. "Why? Did you think something different?" It dawns on Dean why Geoffrey might have been worried. "You don't need to worry, babe. Honestly, you don't need to worry. What we had was real. It's just, in many ways, I wasn't." Closing his eyes for a moment, Dean puzzles out his explanation. "I'm finally ready to introduce myself to you, and…" Now it is Dean's turn to show trepidation. "And, hopefully, you'll like me, love me, as much as you loved the scared Dean who had only clung to you for protection from the swirling world. I guess, what I mean is, I'm finally ready now to protect myself, and I still want to be with you." Coughing now, knowing he is being too pushy too soon, Dean leaps into question six: "*If you were able to live to the age of ninety and retain either the mind or body of a thirty year old for the last sixty years of your life, which would you want?*" Both men answer simultaneously. "The mind!" Then, "I knew you'd say that." Then a collective burst into laughter. Then both chant, "Next question," leading to more collective jocularity.

"*Do you have a secret hunch about how you will die?*" Dean answers instantly. "A bullet to the head like Harvey Milk."

"Hadrian's Lover, Dean, that's too fucking depressing. We're supposed to be connecting, not planning your funeral."

"Sorry; that's just the answer that popped into my head."

"Well, if you really believe that, then I'd have to say stop all this advocating because I don't like the sound of you dying that way."

"Well," Dean says, changing the direction of their conversation, "how do you see yourself dying?"

"With you cradling me. I'm old, weary, and you're holding my hand, telling me everything's going to be all right. We smile. We kiss, and I give you my last breath."

Dean raises his hand to his mouth. His eyes close. Tears stream naturally. "Thank you, Geoffrey; that is so beautiful."

* * * * *

"Name three things you and your partner appear to have in common."

"Easy," Geoffrey replies. "We both like horseback riding?"

Dean turns coy, "And sometimes on a horse." He gives Geoffrey a little wink. Suddenly, Geoffrey shuts down. Dean realizes he has moved too fast again. "I'm sorry, Geoffrey; I didn't mean to be too pushy; I just, I just, well, it just came out, you know, a blurt."

Geoffrey's voice lowers, bordering on a growl, "Do you even mean it?"

"Yes, I do." Dean's reply is honest, but Geoffrey is too enclosed right now to ascertain what is real and what is mere desperation on his part. "There were many times I enjoyed being with you, times when I let go of all my insecurities and misconceptions, and those times were beautiful. Like our first time together. I was scared, but you were so gentle, so understanding, so—" Dean just stops. He knows there is nothing he can say right now to right things with Geoffrey. He just waits for Geoffrey to find his voice.

"You know, Dean, these questions aren't working for me."

"Why not?"

"They're good. They're really good, but they are not addressing why you and I broke up. They are not helping us deal with the reason you left me and the scar, the bleeding, festering wound you left inside my heart."

"Oh, babe, oh, babe, I'm so sorry. I left you because I was angry at the world—and because I was confused within myself. I felt I had to be someone new. Someone I'm not."

"And what is that?" Geoffrey is no longer looking Dean's way. His left hand dangles over his left leg while his right hand cradles his face. His torso is slumped over while his upper back vibrates in a desperate attempt to combat his expression of grief.

"A straight man."

Geoffrey looks up, stunned. "I don't understand. You're not gay but you're not straight."

"That's right."

"Because you're really bi?"

"Yes, I'm bisexual, Geoffrey. It just turns out my first sexual attraction was with a girl. My second sexual attraction was with you. But this isn't just about sex anymore. This is about love, and I love you. I have loved you from the start. I just couldn't admit it to myself. I always said I loved you like a best friend, but if that was true, then I'd've been more like Will, wouldn't I? He never once reached out to Mike, and the one time they did have sex, Will was so drunk he didn't even know what was happening." Geoffrey almost laughs. Both men remember Will Middleton coming to live with them after that experience. He swore he would never go back to Mike, but then Mike had voc'd and shared the news that Will's application for a child had been approved, his sperm had been matched with an egg, and a surrogate goddess had been found for them, so Will had a change of heart. He wanted his child raised in a stable home, with two parents, so after Mike apologized and promised never to try to seduce Will again, he agreed to return home so the two of them could co-parent their child—the child who would become Todd Middleton.

"All right," Geoffrey whispers, "you're bisexual. So where do we go from here?"

Dean smiles, "Why don't we finish answering question eight and take it from there."

"All right," Geoffrey replies with a smile as he wipes his eyes, retrieves a handkerchief from his housecoat pocket (no wasteful tissues in Hadrian), and blows his nose. "But you have to promise that we move slow."

Dean nods and smiles in agreement. "Slow it is." His smile widens as he remembers, *Just like the first time we made love. Only this time*, he tells himself, *it is my turn to be gentle.*

* * * * *

Salve!

Hadrian Patriotism
HNN—Danny Duggin Reporting

Four years have passed since President Elena Stiles was elected as our president, and our country is gearing up for another election campaign with the hopes of our electing a president who will stand by principles established by the founding families. What we don't want, Hadrian, is another president like Elena Stiles, who, even though she may be the genetic descendant of one of our founding families, has been slowly whittling away at the four cornerstones of our great country. The legalization of heterosexuality is a blight on our country's good name. With heterosexuals feeling emboldened, it is becoming increasingly difficult to maintain control over population. Het'ros have called for equal rights in marriage and for the right to be able to propagate without government control. IVF isn't good enough for them. They want the "natural" approach. Well, we have seen what heterosexuality has done to our planet. The last thing our country needs to do is to embrace heterosexuals amongst our own, and yet, this is exactly what President Stiles is proposing. Even though she signed in the Anti-Strai Propaganda Law when she was first inaugurated, she slapped all good gay conservative folk in the face by changing the exile law for all but one form of strai behavior. Everyone knows strais can't control their libidos and that any strai behavior leads to the one sexual act that impregnates a woman.

As well, President Stiles, acknowledging heterosexuality as a viable sexual expression is putting Hadrian's female population, young and old, at risk. Have we forgotten the horrible attack? Although this attack took place almost thirty years ago, it should still burn indignation in the heart of every Hadrian citizen. The simple fact is, Ms. Stiles, we do not want heterosexual barbarians in our midst, which is why I, and all true blue Hadrian citizens, will be voting for Cooper Johnston come Election Day.

Cooper Johnston may not have pure founding family blood running through his veins, but he knows what Hadrian wants and needs most. Good old-fashioned Hadrian patriotism!

Vale!

War Games

Devon knows that if the games Frank devised are going to have any real chance of success, Frank must be freed of his ankle restraint. Convincing the general to deactivate the program controlling the tactile tattoo, however, will take a bit of verbal jostling on the young lieutenant's part.

"In order for these games to be as realistic as possible," Devon begins, "my team cannot know where or when this attack will occur."

"And you won't." The general isn't giving in.

"Actually, sir, we do know the where at least. Frank's team will have to attack somewhere in the three-mile circular radius of his prison zone." Devon sounds matter-of-fact about this, but deep down, he is motivated by the desire to give Frank something no one else can—freedom from his restraint. "His team won't even be able to go deep enough into the tree line to evade detection."

The general's head drops, his brow contorting in its usual manner when he wants others to believe he is thinking seriously. "Valid point, Lieutenant. I suppose this means Private Recruit Hunter will not be participating in the games because his ankle restraint is far too restrictive."

"But, sir." Devon is stunned that the general is actually considering leaving Frank out of the very training strategy he created. "You can't, in all good conscience, refuse him participation?"

"What are suggesting then? That we confine the attacks to Frank's— what did you call it—his prison zone? No, you are correct in your assessment. We need to think rationally about this and allow the attacking team to select a time and place to attack anywhere along our defense grid and, as you pointed out, that is a full fifty miles."

"No at all, sir. What I am proposing is quite simple."

"Well, go on, speak; I'm not a mind reader."

"I propose you release Frank from his restraint," says Devon, adding quickly and with hands up as the general's hackles are beginning to rise, "only for the duration of the war games."

Relaxing slightly, the general expresses some interest. "Go on; I'm listening." He retains an air of aggression by crossing his arms over his chest.

Taking advantage of the general's willingness to consider the possibility, Devon proceeds: "If Frank's team can hit us anywhere along the fifty-mile radius of our defense zone, then my team will have to react quickly; we will have to be on the ready at all times and everywhere in order to detect where and when his team might hit, as well as discover the attack before his team can do any material damage. These games," Devon stops and smiles; Frank's idea was brilliant, "will force our men and women to consider the possibility of an attack every second they are on duty, and even when they are not, they will know they must be ready without warning to be called upon for action."

"Yes, of course; I understand the pedagogy. I helped work it out with Private Recruit Hunter."

You did no such thing, Devon muses. *This is Frank's idea, and you just reap the credit by being his commanding officer—prison ward is more like it.* Still, Devon knows better than to deface a senior officer, so he responds accordingly, "Of course, sir. What I mean to say is that, in order for us to reap the full benefit of your plan, Private Recruit Hunter needs to be free of his restraint so his team can act and think exactly like the enemy. No enemy, of course, is restricted, so Frank can't be restricted. And having Frank out there is critical since—you said it yourself, sir—he thinks outside the wave." Then, pausing for effect, he adds, "If these training games prove as effective as we believe they will, then you will be presenting this strategy, no doubt, to the commanding officers at all the other gates. We both know Frank Hunter's genius, and if given free rein, he will provide you with excellent results, results which will no doubt elevate the Midwest Gate, under your command, as the most effective at repelling the enemy."

"Yes, yes, you are right. Hmmm…"

"What is it, sir?" The general's pause has an ominous air to it.

"I'm just wondering if I need to inform President Stiles of this decision, or at the very least, Judge Julia Reznikoff. She is the head of Hadrian's judicial system and the one who sentenced—"

To cut one's general off is a huge risk and a potentially career-ending move, but Devon does so anyway. "If you don't mind my asking, sir, were you not given sole charge over Frank Hunter? Is this not a decision for you to make?"

"Yes, yes, you're right." Tapping into the general's vanity proves useful. "Of course, this is my decision to make, and if you believe it is in the best interest of the games, then we must deactivate Private Recruit Hunter's ankle restraint for the duration of the mock attacks." And with that, Devon's reasoning prevails and General Birtwistle is persuaded.

The very moment when the general turns off the program for his tactile tattoo, Frank is filled with a flush of joy and anxiety. Close to five years of his life have been spent chained to this one restricted area, but now he is free to roam wherever he might, *for the duration of the games*, he reminds himself grimly. Funny how one simple thought can so easily deflate one's sense of joy, but Devon's glee on meeting him outside his "prison zone" more than makes up for the dour reminder. Devon lifts him up, swings him around, and starts dancing him around parts of the Wall he had never set foot on before. Frank is easily swept up by Devon's *joie de vivre* and is soon laughing and dancing freely.

* * * * *

Outside the Wall, deep inside the tree line, Frank has to contend with the grumblings of soldiers not used to any sort of deprivation. Their misery, however, fails to dampen Frank's thrill. Not only is he outside the Wall; he is free to think and act as he will. His first move is to speak to Mid about the attitude amongst the ranks. Mid is the commanding lieutenant of Frank's team. Mid is not her real name. Kimberly Westgate was dubbed "Mid" almost as soon as she stepped off the tram two and a half years ago when she first arrived for training. Not even her rise in rank could remove the "call sign" given her, so much so that the majority of soldiers only know her as Lieutenant Mid, forgetting she has both a first and last name attached to her person.

"Mid," says Frank, ignoring her rank and treating her like a subordinate. Mid is not in the least bit offended. Lieutenant Rankin and General Birtwistle both made it perfectly clear to her that this was Frank's platoon and hers in name only, despite the stupid laws pertaining to Frank's sentence that refuse him even a "mock" rise in rank. When approached, informed actually, about her role in the games, Mid readily agreed, even though her voluntary submission was far from required. The chance to work under the infamous "Shooter" (Frank's call name) and learn his strategies, techniques—just to catch a glimpse of this man's thought process is akin to being in Antinous's bed for Mid—is all the enticement Mid needs to agree to retaining only the guise of her rank. As explained by the general, Frank will give her the orders, and she will relay them to the platoon. But Mid had other plans. As soon as Frank approached her the first time out in the field, she cut him off in order to inform the platoon of their situation since she intends to run things.

"All right, you jarheads, listen up. Geller!" The sudden sharp whip of her tongue startles the youth, who is kicking at leaves beneath his feet. "Stand at attention when I address you." This curt reminder causes all the soldiers to stand even more erect. "We all know who Private Recruit Hunter is. You call him 'Shooter.' Well, out here, he is your commanding officer. Out here, you will call him 'Lieutenant'! You will salute him and do whatever he says, even if it means digging yourselves a latrine. Is that understood?" When she does not get an adequate response, she yells out the question, punctuating each word. "Is. That. Understood?"

"Yes, sir," the group of soldiers chime in reply.

"For the duration of the games, I will be acting as the lieutenant's first officer, so don't think I'm lower in rank than you. And if any of you step out of line, refuses one of Lieutenant Hunter's orders, or attempts to pull rank on him in any way, when these games are over, you will have me to contend with." Not a one in her platoon doubts the ramifications threatened. Lieutenant Mid is seen as a fair commanding officer compared with the rest, but when a recruit is out of line, she doles out severe punishment. No one in Frank's platoon is willing to risk Lieutenant Mid's threat of sanction.

"There," Mid says to Frank. "Now I won't have to play the fool and your leadership can run a lot more smoothly. I am your second lieutenant, sir. Please proceed to address your platoon." With that, Mid stands to attention and salutes Frank. When, noting through her peripheral vision that no one in the platoon has followed suite, she turns on them and shouts in her most commanding voice, "Salute your senior officer. NOW!" The entire platoon falls into line and obeys.

Frank smiles, returns their salute, and takes a moment to offer Mid his gratitude. "Thank you, Lieutenant."

* * * * *

Salve!

Cooper Johnston

HNN—Danny Duggin Reporting

Good evening, ladies and gentleman. Tonight's *Salve!* is going to be amazing. As you have come to expect, every so often, we bring on a special guest to interview. Tonight's special guest is none other than Cooper Johnston. Many of you already know that Cooper was recently elected as the leader of the Conservative Right Party. And I know with someone like Cooper at the helm, this ship called Hadrian is ready to sail into any mighty cyclone the Stileses and the Stuttgarts might have to throw at us.

With that said, it is important to remind our viewers that not all Stuttgarts have tainted blood. Gordon Stuttgart, head of Hadrian National Exports, has given Cooper Johnston his endorsement. And if anyone knows what it is like dealing with the outside world, it is Gordon Stuttgart. He is constantly in communication with the outside world, negotiating terms for the services we provide them. Thanks to Gordon Stuttgart, 14 percent of Hadrian's Gross National Income results from the exporting of fresh water from our numerous rivers and streams along with much of the grain and soya bean we raise. It is thanks to men like Gordon Stuttgart, who work tirelessly for our nation, that we can boast of having one of the strongest economic systems around the globe. Enough said on that front. It is time now to introduce you to tonight's guest: the Conservative Right's new leader, Mr. Cooper Johnston.

"Thank you, Danny."

"Welcome, welcome, Mr. Johnston. It is such an honor to have you on *Salve!*"

"It is an honor to be here. I appreciate having the great Danny Duggin, Hadrian's most beautiful lover, introducing me to our citizens who might not have heard of me yet."

"Oh, Cooper, you make me blush."

"Danny, you were amazing as Antinous. No one could have captured that role but you."

"Well, thank you. Playing Hadrian's one true love was indeed the role of a lifetime. But let's get back to the topic of you. You are so important, and everyone in Hadrian needs to know all about you, the man who will be our next president."

"Thank you for your vote of confidence, Danny, but we must allow for due process and the results of the election to make the final determination."

"Yes, of course. But I know you'll win. You have to win. The very security of our nation depends on you."

"You are right about that, Danny. Sadly, though, our founding mother, Destiny Stuttgart, in her declining years, is now being ruled by senility, and she has somehow managed to persuade a once-logical politician—did you know I voted for Elena Stiles?"

"Oh, me, too!"

"Well, somehow Mother Stuttgart has managed to indoctrinate even the likes of Elena Stiles into believing that Hadrian was established as a convalescent home for strais and bis. It saddens me to see such misguidance in both the Stiles and Stuttgart families."

"Oh, but not all Stuttgarts. That we both know."

"Yes, Gordon Stuttgart. Thank Hadrian for him. Now there is a man with Hadrian's best interests at heart."

"Undeniably! And you must be so proud to have a man like Gordon Stuttgart backing your political campaign."

"Yes, indeed. When Gordon Stuttgart approached me about running for the leadership of the Conservative Right Party, I thought I was dreaming, but with his financial support and encouragement, I have succeeded."

"Yes, and a lot of that is due to your vigilant stand on keeping Hadrian focused on the four cornerstones, the most important of which being that of a homosexual community working towards the diminishing of world population."

"Absolutely! You hit the nail right on the head there, Mr. Duggin. We in the Conservative Right know how critical it is for Hadrian to maintain a stable population and accept that the only viable, peaceful, and loving means to reduce excessive human population is through a homosexual lifestyle and in vitro fertilization. What Elena Stiles and Destiny Stuttgart are calling for is absolute anarchy. To allow for heterosexuals to copulate at will is utter insanity. Why, if we open the flood gates to allowing for heterosexual behaviours, then we are opening the gates to pedophilia and bestiality. These are not Hadrian's ways. We are a loving, caring country, and our hopes for the future are the hopes for mankind."

"Oh, Cooper, you are so right. So, what are your biggest fears if President Stiles is to be reelected this fall?"

"I think you know the answer to that. They are the same fears every patriotic citizen has: a return to the barbaric ways of heterosexuals and an opening of our gates to the world outside. And we all know what happened when we were open to receiving outsiders within our borders."

"Oh, Cooper, you are so right. Viewers, what you are seeing right now is a simulation of the nuclear attack against our fair country. That fateful day of 6-13 when Jeremiah F. Butler set off a dirty nuke at the border gate in Augustus City. So many lives were lost that day. So many others suffered the horrible after-effects of nuclear radiation."

"There is one thing I can guarantee the citizens of Hadrian if I am elected president—that never again will an outsider get close enough to our border to cause such horrific damage."

"Oh, Cooper, you are so right! And as if that weren't enough, there was that horrible breach of the Midwest Gate almost thirty years ago. Oh, viewers, it is almost too much, but as you can see by the grainy film, this attack was one of the most brutal. Our men were slaughtered and the women brutally tortured and raped. It's just sickening. Oh, please, we need to turn it off. I can't watch anymore."

"I understand your trepidation in viewing such horrors, but if we don't remind the citizens of Hadrian what those outsiders are capable of, what they have done to harm our very way of life, we may very well become complacent and allow the likes of Elena Stiles and Mother Stuttgart to convince others of the benign ways of the strai."

"But we know that's not true! Strais are anything but benevolent—especially the het'ro male! Such vile vicious creatures."

"Yes, Danny. Yes, they are! And it is the responsibility of Hadrian's government to ensure a strong military to better protect us from the very real danger they pose to our very existence. Outsiders are not only propagators and polluters; they are also extremely jealous of our natural environment, and they are determined to steal what precious bit of nature we have preserved inside Hadrian. Their ways are violent and vicious, and they will do whatever they can to destroy us. We saw that thirty years ago with the breach of the Midwest Gate, and we suffered horribly that fateful day of 6-13. We cannot trust anyone who is heterosexual. By encouraging our citizens to accept heterosexual ways, we are encouraging them to emulate those murderous marauding fanatics."

"Oh, Cooper Johnston, you have my vote."

"Thank you, Danny. And, now, I must ask you to replay that footage I voc'd your producer. I know how difficult it is to watch, but it is critical that we never forget what those heterosexual barbarians did to us."

"Hadrian, as hard as it is for us to watch and relive these horrific events, Cooper Johnston is right. We must never forget the crimes committed against our nation. Remember, when you voc your vote on October 28th, make sure your vote is for the betterment of Hadrian. Vote for the Conservative Right Party, and make Cooper Johnston our next president."

Vale!

Training for the Offensive!

"All right!" Frank's voice booms and echoes through the trees. "This isn't basic training, but it might as well be. We will be learning tactics no other recruit has ever seen before. Just being outside the Wall is a new experience and one that is both daunting and frightening for us all! We are in enemy territory now. Keep your eyes and ears open at all times. Even though no enemy has been sighted directly outside our main gate in over a year, that doesn't mean they are not out there." Frank pauses for a moment to allow that potential threat to sink in. "Embrace your fear! Don't pretend it isn't there. I don't want any fools under my command. Use your fear; let it light your awareness on fire." Turning now to direct Mid, he says, "There will be sentry duty. Recruits will work in pairs and be on guard duty for three-hour intervals. I want you to pick the pairs." Turning again to address the platoon, Frank bellows out, using all his authoritative powers, "Whatever camp we are at, and we are going to make many as we scout along our Wall's fifty-mile defensive perimeter, there will be sentry duty. You and one other will serve three-hour shifts, ensuring our camp remains safe and no outsider intrusions occur." Frank pauses for dramatic effect before continuing. He takes this moment to look into the eyes of every recruit. Many divert their attention; Frank makes note of these and those brave enough to hold his glare. "Now, we are going to teach ourselves what it means to be on the offensive so we can better anticipate enemy attack. Each of you was handpicked for your agility, intellectual skills, and effective use of weaponry. When we finish here, you will all go on to be instructors for the rest of Hadrian's army." Seeing a significant rise in swaggering conceit amongst the troops, Frank decides to remind them of their green status. "Assuming, that is, you *all* make it through training." Frank smirks slightly when the faces of a few recruits blanch. "Where we stand now will be our base camp as it is directly west of the main gate. This means we have two twenty-five mile stretches, one to the north, the other to the south, to scout out and determine the locations of our other camps. I want a camp established every five miles. Once all of our camps are established, we will determine our attack locations."

"Locations, sir?" Lieutenant Westgate, known mostly as Mid, is intrigued. "I wasn't aware that we would be attacking the Wall on more than one occasion."

"General Birtbas—" Frank catches himself, but not in time for the troops to snicker. Instead of chastising them, Frank can't help but smirk a little. "General Birtwistle has ordered us to attack the gate once, but he never specified how or when this attack is to occur. I have decided that it would be in our best interest to split our forces and attack the Wall multiple times and in multiple locations. Our initial attacks will be overt, the final one, and we will get to that later, will be covert. I intend for us to inflict as much havoc and confusion to Dev—Lieutenant Rankin's team as possible. With Antinous on our side, maybe we can deliver a blow hard enough to slap the complacency out of our military—shock us into preparing ourselves for any kind of attack, especially those least anticipated. Now," Frank lowers his voice to emphasize the gravity of their situation, "this little copse and the various camps we will be establishing are our new homes, and they will remain our homes until we can successfully fight our way back inside." This time, all the recruits blanch, and fear battles with confusion for control of their expressions. "That's right, boys and girls; you heard me. This is our home now. No one is letting us back in. We might as well be outsiders." Of course, Frank is exaggerating their situation as Mid, who was warned in advance about this scare tactic, knows full well they will all be welcomed back inside the gate should an emergency occur. Frank is not adding that piece of intelligence for a reason. He wants his troops to reconcile with their new environment and learn to adapt to the discomforts that are only going to get worse. "So, you must reconcile to the fact that we will be out here for some time, the duration of which will depend on how fast you learn. We may be here for days, weeks, maybe even months."

A communal groan ensues, and one youth steps out of the ranks to venture an opinion. "Why don't we attack now? We've all been through basic training. We're ready. Why make us live out here when we shouldn't have to?"

Frank smiles. He anticipated this sort of response. "All right then," he says in an encouraging manner, "attack." He turns to look in the direction of the Wall and motions for the young man to begin his assault.

Stunned, the young man mutters, "Alone?"

When the youth makes no effort to move, Frank grabs him by the collar and half-drags, half-pulls the boy through the trees towards no man's land, that two-mile stretch of wasteland where no life grows between the trees and the Wall. Behind them is a scuttling and muttering of troops wanting to see the outcome of this clash between ranks.

Once at the edge of the decimated tree line, Frank takes his gun and shoots twice in the air in rapid succession, followed by two shots with a two-second pause between each. As soon as the signal shots ring out, Frank turns, grabs the recruit, and shoves the boy forward. When Frank issues one curt command, "Run!" the boy races off in a mad dash towards the Wall. Frank begins to count down from five. When he reaches one, a shot rings out and the youth stumbles before falling.

One recruit screams, and another yells out, "Hadrian's Lover, they killed him!"

Frank snorts. He turns to the screamer and directs him, "You, go fetch our wayward recruit."

Mid turns to the troops to alleviate their fears. "He's not dead, just stunned slightly. He was shot with a paint bullet. It broke open on impact, splashing red paint like a blood-letting wound. Although it hurt, it is nothing compared to the feel of a real bullet."

When the screamer, Koman Samoei, finally reaches the downed recruit, he helps him to stand. When he offers an arm for the young man to hold, it is swatted away. Gripping his chest, the youth staggers back to the tree line.

Once the youth is back inside the tree line with the rest of the troops, Frank stops him. His eyes are immediately drawn to the red stain. Had it been a real bullet, it would have pierced the young man's heart. Frank's smile suggests pride. "Nice shooting, Devon!"

"Who's Devon?" the injured youth inquires.

"Your shooter," Frank answers. "What's your name?"

"Private Recruit Atherton."

"Your first name, recruit," Frank clarifies.

"Brian."

"Well, Brian, do you still want to attack the Wall right away?" Mid laughs, as do the other recruits.

"No, sir! We will attack when we are ready and no sooner."

"When do you think we'll be ready, sir?" Private Samoei asks.

"When I say we're ready. In the meantime, we have a camp to establish."

With that, Frank turns and marches back to the copse they will begin preparing for base camp.

* * * * *

Salve!

Hadrian Needs You!
HNN—Danny Duggin Reporting

Citizens of Hadrian, our military is calling out to you to join forces with us to help stem the tide of barbarian heterosexual hordes. We need a strong show of strength to keep these desperate marauders from executing an attack that would lead to the end of everything we hold dear. All we have worked so hard to build and create within the walls of our fine country is at risk. We cannot allow close to fifty-five years of toil and dedication to humanity and the planet to be suddenly ripped away and stolen from us. Our very lives are at risk, our children's lives are at risk, our ideals are at risk, and the very cornerstones upon which we built this good country are at risk of being torn out from under us. Hadrian, our military needs you.

Yes, it is true that our military has seen a marked growth with Hadrian's new penal system diverting exile for many of our citizens who have committed three minor offenses, but the military still needs to grow. Citizens between the ages of twenty-two and forty are asked to find their inner patriots and pledge at least one tour of duty at the Wall. And, if being a part of the military full-time is beyond your personal scope, consider joining the militia. Your weekends will be best served retraining your body for combat so you can answer the call when Hadrian's Wall suffers from another brutal attack. According to General Birtwistle, numbers for Hadrian's militia are down since most who heeded the first call to arms were in fact members of the militia. So, if you can't commit yourself full-time to Hadrian's National Army, you can at least step up and answer the call for our reserves.

Remember, Hadrian is *our* country and we are all responsible for its safety!

Vale!

Two-Mile Dash

Frank is horny. He's been this way for over a week. Slapping the monkey isn't doing it for him. He needs to feel his cock inside Devon. He desperately wants to feel Devon inside him. The problem is that he is out here, in the tree line of the neutral zone, and Devon is back inside the Wall.

Both men are strategically trying to outwit the other. Thus far, Devon's team has successfully been able to repel all of Frank's renegade attempts to infiltrate the Wall. Frank is not worried. He has been using all of the strategies previously utilized by outsiders since the beginning of Hadrian's existence. One advantage to being off voc and restricted to the historical library and wall screen is that Frank has a lot of time for reading. He has studied and restudied every attack made against his country since its inception. Frank isn't even going to try to exhaust reenacting all of the various attacks made against Hadrian since its inception. The attacks all have had one thing in common: they have been en masse, whether it be broad daylight or in the darkest hour of night. Very few of these attacks have been skill-driven. Only the few who succeeded in breaching the Wall were of that caliber; even then, the damage wrought by the enemy was contained to the Wall itself. Never once has the enemy penetrated the Wall and made its way inland.

Frank, however, knows that penetrating the Wall is possible, and all it will take is for one daring individual to do exactly what he has planned. Frank's first goal was to get Devon and his team complacent. That, he believes, has been accomplished. Frank staged these easily anticipated strikes, some close together, some sporadic, but all found within the training book outlining previously known attacks to give Devon the idea that his team is winning this war. But Frank knows it doesn't matter how many battles an army wins before he makes his final strike: the one he believes will lead to a revamping of Hadrian's military and rethinking of how they go about defending the border lands.

Tonight's the night, Frank decides. He has been keeping cover at the edge of the tree line, camouflaged and just beyond the extension of light from the Wall's search beams. Frank has been timing the lights—where they flash, how long they take to crisscross over the neutral zone, and how long empty spots of land remain in pitch black. Knowing how fast he can run, and having added two-mile dashes to his and his troops' training, Frank is confident he can make it to the Wall between the passing of the lights. Tonight is perfect. There is no moon, no stars, no "husbandry in heaven," as the Bard would have put it. Frank smirks at this knowledge. *Go figure, I'd remember a line from* Macbeth. *I hated the play when I was in high school. Hadrian's Lover, I hated Shakespeare when I was in high school.* Not anymore, though. Frank has acquired so much knowledge since being in the army—no years of schooling, uni or higher, could compete with the extent of reading Frank has accomplished. *The best thing that ever happened to me was the loss of my voc*, he reasons.

But he does worry about the heaviness of the cloud cover. Rain would slow him down since mud is slippery and harder to run through than hard dry earth. And lightning—lightning would expose him. *Hopefully, not for too long*, Frank muses. It's a risk, one worth taking. The last thing anyone at the Wall is expecting is one lone figure making its way towards the Wall—that only happens during the day when the individual is looking for assisted suicide.

Having made his decision, Frank gets up and crosses over to Lieutenant Westgate. "Mid."

Lieutenant Westgate turns to face Frank. He offers her the requisite salute, and she returns it. "Have you decided?"

"Yes, ma'am."

"Tonight?"

"Tonight."

"When?"

"Within the hour."

"How soon before you signal the team to advance?"

"Not sure. First I have to get in. Kill off the tower guards, make my way down the Wall, killing everyone as quickly and as silently as I can, and then..." Here Frank trails off.

"Then?" Mid suspects Frank has plans beyond just overtaking the Wall. She keeps her smirk well-hidden. She'd do the same in his place. *And, why not? He's the one taking all the risks. What I wouldn't give for a quickie with Lillian.* She arrests that thought quickly as she begins to feel the beginnings of a smile creeping over her lips.

Frank returns to the moment. "And, then, when the Midwest Gate is secured, I'll return to the center gate guard post and flash the signal. Does the team know what is expected?"

"Of course they do, Frank. You've drilled it into them a hundred times."

"I just hope it's enough," Frank mutters.

Mid, sensing trepidation on Frank's part, reassures him with a punch to his shoulder. "It'll work. It's a brilliant plan. We're just damn lucky an outsider hasn't thought of it first."

"Yeah, it'll work." Looking back to the Wall, Frank walks towards the edge.

Mid follows, feeling the need to reassure Frank of his upcoming success. "You can make the time. I've timed you over and over. You can make it to the Wall before the lights come back." Frank frowns. He knows she's right. He can do the two-mile stretch in less than two minutes; one minute and twenty-two seconds in fact; five seconds faster than the lights take from dispersal to return. But running against a clock in trails does not always equate to real time when up against the enemy. The nervous tingle is unavoidable. Frank takes a moment to breathe deeply, putting himself into that Zen-like moment that always comes before, and especially during, a run.

Crouching down now, Frank prepares himself for the sudden sprint that will come when the lights veer away from each other. The very second the darkness opens up before him, Frank is off. Mid stares, amazed by how fast Frank dashes out of sight. And it seems too fast in her mind when the lights return and wave over the ground before her. There is no sign of Frank. "Yes," she ejaculates. "He did it." With an exuberant spin back towards the camp, Mid decides it is time to tell the others.

* * * * *

Salve!

War Games
HNN—Danny Duggin Reporting

We have some exciting news to share with you today, Hadrian. Our military has been working overtime to ensure our safety. When not encountering the real threat from the outside, a platoon of highly trained infantry men and women at the Midwest Gate have been simulating attacks against the Wall to keep our defenses finely tuned and razor-sharp. I know I feel a lot safer knowing our brave soldiers are on their toes and ready for whatever the enemy may throw at them. I am pleased to report that all, and simulated, attacks have thus far been successfully repelled by the finely tuned military men and women at the Midwest Gate.

You may wonder why these simulations are occurring at the Midwest Gate and not at any of the other gates. Well, to begin, the Midwest Gate suffers the greatest degree of incursion, and the idea behind these games comes from Lieutenant Devon Rankin, who is currently stationed there. He has taken it upon himself to challenge the security forces we have in place, not because he mistrusts our military forces, but out of concern for military complacency. As the good lieutenant explained it to me, our military has become too used to the same strategies being used over and over by the enemy. Lieutenant Rankin is convinced that one of these days, our enemies will come up with a strategy no one has previously thought of, either on the inside for defense purposes, or from the outside in terms of aggressive offensive maneuvers. When asked to elaborate, Lieutenant Rankin became circumspect. He reminded me that our wave links are often monitored by outsiders, and the last thing he wants to do is to give our enemies new ideas. The purpose of these games is for our military to explore all possible forms of attack against our walls, both those that have been used in the past as well as consider new strategies the enemy might very well consider in the future. To that, I say, "Good on you, Lieutenant

Rankin; you exhibit the finest traits of leadership and military prowess we like to see in the men and women who guard our country."

These war games will not remain restricted to the Midwest Gate, either. After a series of simulated attacks evidences the impenetrability of the Midwest Gate's wall, these games will be shared with all the other gates. Lieutenant Rankin will be required, at that time, to travel from gate to gate, administering these games and ensuring equal success at each as well. And Lieutenant Rankin has been extremely successful. Thus far, his team has successfully repelled eight separate attempts by its counter team, under the charge of Lieutenant Mid—sorry, that appears to be the lieutenant's call name—her real name is Kimberly Westgate, which explains why they call her "Mid." Mid comes from Midwest Gate, and her last name is Westgate. I just love the sense of camaraderie and jocularity exhibited by our brothers and sisters in arms.

Citizens of Hadrian, it does my heart good knowing that our national security, our very lives, are in the capable hands of military personnel like Lieutenant Rankin and Lieutenant Westgate. In fact, if you elect Cooper Johnston as your next president, I guarantee he will pursue these war games with the due diligence they deserve!

Va—

Breaking news! This is just in—Oh, dear!—Oh, no!—Oh, Hadrian, my production manager, Darien Dumas, just informed me via my voc transmitter of some truly dreadful news. As we all remember on that sad day when Angel Higgins and Grace Godoy were exiled, Angel Higgins, in what was very likely an overwhelming sense of fear and panic, turned and ran back towards the gate. She had been crying for her fathers. Well, sadly her life ended that day as the sniper on tower duty shot her. We then watched as the sniper shot warning shots at young Grace, who then ran for cover in the tree line. Oh, forgive me, Hadrian; this is heartbreaking. The soldiers currently deployed to participate in War Games, those stationed outside the Wall to create mock attacks against the Midwest Gate— it turns out they have discovered Miss Godoy's body. She had barely made it into the forest before some wild animals attacked her. Hadrian's top forensic anthropologist, Giselle Barre, was immediately called to the scene. According to her released statement "All evidence points to an attack by a pack of wolves." And, yes, they consumed most of her flesh. Very little remained of the young woman's body. She was initially identified by—by her backpack, the survival kit, her identity later being corroborated with DNA evidence. Hadrian still has Grace Godoy's DNA on file. Her backpack, too, had been ripped apart by the wolves. No doubt to gain access to the dried food inside—six weeks' worth of food rations. Oh, Hadrian, this is too horrible, too dreadful—too, too—Huh? Oh, yes, sorry, Hadrian,

Vale!

At the Wall

As soon as Frank reaches the Wall, he stops to catch his breath. Resting his backside up against it, he leans forward to place his hands on his thighs. For a brief moment, he works at controlling his breath as his flesh vibrates with excitement. Frank has just run his best time ever. For a moment, he caught himself wishing he had his old voc back so he could have timed himself. Even without quantifiable evidence, Frank knows he just bested his best. He smiles, more confident and sure of himself than ever.

His next step is to scale the Wall. Part of his training included wall climbing. Unlike many of the other recruits, Frank took this training seriously. Actually, Frank took all his training seriously. Giving complete concentration on whatever task was at hand was one way for Frank to forget what he had done. With 100 percent devotion to the military, Frank could avoid thinking about Todd until he finally went to rest his head on his pillow. The harder he worked during the day, the more likely he would fall asleep before his thoughts could haunt him. Even then, there was no escape as memories of Todd and the assisted suicide lingered as a recurring dream. A good night for Frank was when he had slept soundly, dreaming nothing at all—leastwise, nothing he could remember.

Things have changed, though, with Devon's arrival. For the first time since he killed Todd, Frank has given himself to another man. Frank has allowed someone to reach inside and hold his heart. And although the nightmares have yet to cease, Frank has finally begun feeling a sense of joy returning to his life. In moments like these, guilt overwhelms him. Shuddering, feeling that he is somehow betraying Todd by learning how to love again, Frank pushes all thoughts to the back of his mind and concentrates on the task at hand. The first stage of the plan is complete. Time for stage two: scale the Wall.

From a distance, Hadrian's Wall looks impenetrable; its sheer glassy surface would hinder even the most skilled of climbers from attempting this feat without proper equipment, but Frank intends to do this by feel alone. He will not even risk using a flashlight, even though he has one strapped to his forehead, since he does not want to give away his position. Nor did he bring rope and hook so he can climb the Wall with relative ease. Mid had recommended this approach, but Frank refused, fearing the noise of the hook clanging against the stone wall would cause an alert. No, Frank knows these walls. He has scaled them many times in the past, on the inside, to the chagrin of the MPs unfortunately assigned as his "prison guard." Though he had precious little time to study the outside wall when he and his team first left the comforts of their military base, Frank suspects that the exterior of the Wall will have even more chinks in it as a result of previous attacks and harsh weather. *Too bad there isn't any of that carbon-sucking wall closer to the Gate*, he muses. *That would much easier to scale with its building block structure. But,* he reminds himself, as Mid had rightly pointed out, *that section of the Wall is far too dangerous.* "No doubt," she had said, "the same huge fans used to suck in the air could very well suck you in and spit you back out in shreds." Just the thought of being so thoroughly mutilated caused Frank to shudder. Thus the decision had been made for Frank to scale the part of the Wall closest to the Gate; the cement wall that, from a respectable distance, looks as smooth as glass but, as Frank believes, will, upon closer inspection, prove to be pitted and cut into with tiny chinks.

Frank is right. He has little trouble finding ridges, deep grooves, and on the odd occasion, even small craters, some big enough for Frank to insert his whole foot. When he finally reaches the parapet, Frank listens carefully for footfalls. One of the night guards is making the rounds. Frank waits for the individual to pass him, giving enough distance for him to slip over the edge unnoticed, and then he strikes. Using his "paint knife," a small pen-like weapon that leaves a line of indelible red ink on the victim, Frank "slices" the night guard's throat. As soon as the young man feels Frank's hand and the cool sensation of the ink drawn across his neck, he begins to groan. Frank turns the young man around and motions for him to be silent, mouthing the words "You're dead, remember." The young man then allows Frank to direct his "dead body" to the Wall where he proceeds to drop down the side and slump over in an acceptable dead man position. *First blood. Now for the tower guards.* Between where he stands and the first guard tower, Frank knows he must make at least three more kills. He accomplishes each as quickly and as quietly as the first downed soldier using his "paint knife." The tower guards, though, he takes out using his paintball pistol. Both women take a shot to the chest. Being in such close proximity causes both soldiers to experience substantial pain upon impact. Frank shrugs an apology as both glare his way, slowly lowering themselves to "die."

"Time for stage three," Frank whispers.

"Stage what?" one of the downed soldiers enquires.

In harsh, low tones, Frank scowls at the girl. "You're dead, or have you forgotten? Do I need to shoot you a second time?" Not wanting to experience another sting at even closer range, the soldier wisely closes her eyes and plays dead. Frank turns to face the spotlight control panel. After a few taps to the main board, Frank successfully hacks his way into the military wave link and reduces the spotlights' timing by sixty seconds. This will give his team enough time to make the dash to the Wall. He has trained them well, and after two weeks of pushing them as hard as he pushes himself, Frank is confident they can all make the dash in less than three minutes. It will be Mid's job to fix the timing issue Frank just created. The goal of these games is to reveal weaknesses in Hadrian's security, not to put her in actual peril. Next comes the signal and he is off to kill more sentinels and the other watchtower guards. Frank's last task before he can slip away to be with Devon will be to sneak into the general's quarters and "kill" Birtwistle. No doubt, he will have to slaughter quite a few soldiers between here and there, but that does not seem daunting to Frank. Just the thought of "slitting" the general's throat with indelible ink that will stain his neck for days brings a smile to Frank's otherwise stern expression. "I better get to work," Frank reminds himself, "or I'll run out of time to see Devon." Anticipation of lovemaking with the "enemy" has Frank highly motivated to get the job done fast.

* * * * *

Hadrian's Real News

Hadrian Is All a Titter
HRN—Melissa Eagleton Reporting

Hadrian is all a titter with talk of these war games being played at the Midwest Gate. Contrary to popular belief, Lieutenant Rankin—and he willingly admits to this fact—is not the brainchild of these games. The idea was merely brought to General Birtwistle's attention through Lieutenant Rankin because the individual who both conceived and planned nearly every detail of these games is nothing but a lowly private. And yet, he is not so lowly, as this "private" has been in the army for an even longer stretch of time than Lieutenant Rankin. The good lieutenant informed me that he was jostled awake, having been given quite the fright and delight, on the last night raid made by this "private" and the "enemy" team.

One lone man scaled Hadrian's Wall, took out the upper sentinels, changed the timing of the spotlights so the rest of his team could cross the divide between the tree line and the Wall, and successfully scaled it without impediment. This enemy team went on to "kill" General Birtwistle, whom I hear is still bristling from reports of this incident. As the story goes, and it comes direct from the horse's mouth, the unnamed soldier woke the general so he could inform him he was dead. From all accounts, the general was not very impressed with having his "beauty sleep" disturbed or having been incorporated into the games. Yet his "death" is justifiable in that it really brings home the fact that there can be no complacency regardless of rank. If the real enemy ever does infiltrate any of our gates as deeply as these war games proved probable, the general may very well find himself killed in his sleep.

The last stage in this well-executed coup of the Midwest Gate was for the "enemy" team to corral the remaining soldiers who were not "killed in battle" into the main compound while the "subordinate private" and his team claimed victory. This test, I assure you, proves this soldier right. We cannot rely on old tactics and stratagems to work forever as repellents to the enemy. We must start thinking like the enemy in order to curtail future potential advances.

The military refuses to release this private's name to the media because he is one of the many "subordinate privates" sentenced to the military for crimes that can range anywhere between a misdemeanor and major transgressions. Depending on the case, and the abilities of your defense lawyer, you, too, may find yourself once again reporting to duty at any one of our military gates rather than suffering the pangs of exile or the obvious danger of henbane, otherwise known as "black death."

Yes, Hadrian, our military is fast becoming the penal colony we swore we'd never have inside our country. The fact that our legal system has been far too black and white for far too long is not the key issue that needs addressing. What worries me, and many of you, my viewers, is that the shades of gray long desired and needed in Hadrian's courts are now being haphazardly drawn into reassignment to the military. That our military is in dire need of men and women in arms ready to fight, even die, for our safety, is not, nor should it be, contingent on those citizens who break the law.

When I interviewed President Stiles about this issue, she felt it better for the military to "stock up on soldiers through the penal system" rather than impose even longer conscription time on our youth. As it stands, all youth between the ages of eighteen and twenty-one are required to serve in the military before reentering Hadrian's society upon coming of age and swearing fealty to our union. Yes, we need soldiers. We need men and women of strong mind and body to protect us from the constant attacks the military report daily. But are we truly getting these kinds of men and women when they are being forced into service as a result of wayward behavior—crimes committed against our society?

Laugh along with me, Hadrian, as I come face to face with the very irony of my assertion. The "subordinate private" about whom I opened this show is one of these individuals who broke society's law and, though remaining a private all his days in service, he is indeed one of the men and women we so dearly need in our military. But will all these imposed-upon soldiers be as useful as this one man? Will they, like him, give their entire hearts and souls to the military in dogged determination to protect, honor, and serve our country? This is a question that cannot be ignored,

Hadrian, for as it stands, with a huge push from powerful officers in our military, such as General Birtwistle, our military will comprise more MPs than actual soldiers, for each imprisoned military man or woman must come complete with a twenty-four-hour watch. I think our government needs to review the legal code binding this country together and rethink the ways it is helping to burgeon the number of privates in our military.

Truth, Hadrian. There is nothing wrong with asking for, nay, even demanding, nothing less than the truth from our government.

TRUTH!

Death Is Orgasmic

Frank's victory over General Birtwistle (he never even considered this a defeat for Devon) was so intoxicating that when he finally made his way into Devon's room, he could barely contain himself. The lovemaking was so intense that both men reached a pinnacle of sexual pleasure neither had known was possible for the human body. Spent, but not tired, Devon lay with his head cradled in the soft alcove just beneath Frank's shoulder.

"Man," Devon pants, "you can kill me anytime. With you, death is orgasmic." His fingers trace the indelible ink that marks the spot where Frank had "slit" his throat. He treats the marking as a badge of honor. Frank smiles one of his rare smiles. Devon, relishing this atypical moment, proclaims, "I wish you'd smile more often, Frank; it lights up your eyes." As if on cue, as happens with any sort of compliment made Frank's way, the light in his eyes dims. No longer joyful or victorious, the morose Frank Hunter reemerges. "Why is it," Devon demands, "that every time I compliment you, you turn dour?" Frank just closes his eyes and turns his head in reply. "Come on, Frank. You can be happy. It's allowed."

In a rare moment of honesty, Frank reveals himself. "I don't think I can...ever be truly happy. The guilt. The guilt is too much."

"Frank," Devon remonstrates, "Todd would want you to forgive yourself."

"It doesn't matter what he would or wouldn't want, Devon. It just is what it is." Frank shudders as the memory of Todd's death begins to asphyxiate him. "It sure as fuck wasn't orgasmic."

Devon, a little miffed and confused, demands, "What are you talking about?"

"Todd's death." Shaking his head morosely, he repeats, "It wasn't fucking orgasmic." Staring now into Devon's eyes with a look so chilling

Devon's testicles recoil, he adds, "I did it coldly. We both looked at his heart monitor just before I—uh, took the patches off him and put them on me, and for a brief moment, the line went flat. That should have stopped me, but it didn't. I think I saw fear in his eyes, but I—but I—but I did it anyway. I took his pillow out from under his head and suffocated him. You know he was strapped down so his body couldn't move around much, but I can still feel the jerking movements. I can still feel when his body went limp. I smothered the life out of him."

"You did it because he asked you to." Even as he says this, Devon knows his words sound hollow.

"I did it because I loved him." Turning now, tears swelling up from pleading, Frank rants, "I fucking loved him and I murdered him, so you can't—you can't fall in love with me. I won't allow it."

"It's too late to warn me of that, Frank."

"I can't love—I can't love—I can't love—"

"But you can, and you do. You love me as much as I love you."

"I'll only end up hurting you."

"And I'll only end up hurting you. So what? That's life, and beside the point. We still love each other. In the end, that's all that really matters."

"Don't you get it?" Frank is only whispering, but there is fire and ice in his voice. "Nothing matters to me anymore."

This conversation isn't over, and even though Devon knows Frank's slight opening up is something that needs nurturing, he persists. "Todd could never live in this world after everything that happened to him. You and I both know that." Not even trying to tread carefully, knowing full well what he is about to say is going to remind Frank about his having been the first to rape Todd Middleton, Devon reminds him of the other horrors Frank's best friend suffered. "I mean, everything he went through at re-ed. No one would want to live after that. Todd knew that, and so did you! You felt responsible. Fuck it, you *were* responsible! But you've atoned. Hadrian's Lover, Frank, you can't keep sentencing yourself to life over this."

Frank's eyes darken. "There is nothing in this world that can ever undo what I've done."

"The past is the past, Frank." Devon is pleading more than counseling at this moment. "You have to move on."

"The past is dead," Frank replies dryly. "I murdered it."

At first, Devon has no idea how to respond. He lets the silence sit between them like a knife poised and ready for blood. He knows that whatever he says next will either sever their fragile relationship or set a flame to the knife's edge and cauterize the wound.

"Is that why you never ask about any of the people we've known?" Frank remains stolid. Devon persists. "Did you know T'Neal is famous? Well, almost famous." Pretending that Frank is expressing interest, Devon continues, "Yeah, Pepper Tibbits signed him. Can you believe it? He's gonna be a famous drag queen. And," now elongating his vowels as if the intrigue is too much for Frank to bear, "he's also a makeup artist for the Hadrian Broadcasting Corporation." Devon shakes his head in mock disbelief. "I know. I couldn't believe it either. The HBC. Pretty cool." Behind the cynicism, Devon is seething. "For Hadrian's sake, Frank. Open up to me." No burst of ire is having any impact on the now encapsulated soul of Frank Hunter. Devon is relentless; he has fallen in love, but the man of his longings is completely shut off. "Okay, fine, no T'Neal. How about we talk about Roger? You know, your little brother, the man I dated for over year! Have you told him about us yet?"

Franks leaps off the bed, shoving Devon aside in the process. "*Us*? There is no fucking *US*! In order for there to be an *US*, there has to be a me, and Frank Hunter died the same day I killed Todd Middleton."

"Then let's talk about Crystal."

Frank is shocked into silence. He can't even respond because Devon has just side-swiped him.

"Surely you'd like to know what happened to Crystal? Be privy to whatever personal hell her life has turned into?" Instead of empathizing with Frank's confused expression, Devon snorts derisively. "I mean, she's just as guilty as you are when it comes to Todd's death." He harrumphs, "Maybe even more so. She fucked him and betrayed him. She's the one who landed him into the shit in the first place." Knowing he has touched on something deep inside Frank, Devon carries on. "I still remember that day in Sterne's math class when the old bitch exposed him and accused him of raping Crystal, and that fucking little bitch said nothing in Todd's defense."

Frank turns now to face the Wall. His naked body soaks in the chill of the cement. Desperate for any kind of relief, Frank is suddenly wishing the cement were wet so it would entomb him. Without realizing it, he asks, "What happened to Crystal?"

Devon is stunned. He hadn't expected that he would actually pull Frank out of himself, but bringing up Crystal and the pivotal role she played in Todd Middleton's incarceration at the Northeast Reeducation camp and his ultimate suicide (assisted suicide) has seemed to spark something in the self-condemned man. "No one knows for sure. She just disappeared. It's like she got exiled without any of the fanfare."

"She'd never be exiled!" Albeit, his tone is bitter, but Frank is finally engaged. He is no longer pressing his face against the cold wall. He has turned and is now looking (glaring actually) at Devon.

"No one knows for sure, but that's the scuttle butt."

Frank shakes his head. "No one knew."

"No one knew what?"

"Her mama is Elena Stiles, pure founding family bloodline and Hadrian's President."

"No shit!" Crystal's connection to that family, though pre Todd Middleton's exposure and Frank's trial, wasn't a profound secret; it was simply little talked about. Crystal's mothers had decided that in order for Crystal to experience a normal adolescence, the less people knew of her fortuitous connections, the better. And then after the Todd Middleton debacle, they deemed it wise that no one ever knew she was in any way related to the woman who was, at that time, running for president.

"So what? She just disappeared then?" Frank asks without really expecting a reply. "Lucky little bitch!" Suddenly, all the pent up rage, guilt, and despair Frank has been holding in for years bursts out of him. Screaming at the top of his lungs, he crumbles to his knees and begins to cry.

Devon leaps from the bed and instantly wraps his arms around his lover, cradling him, allowing him as much time as it takes until Frank is emotionally spent. When finished, Frank whispers, "I do love you, Devon. Hadrian help us both, I do love you."

* * * * *

Hadrian's Real News

Who Is She?
HRN—Melissa Eagleton Reporting

One of Hadrian's greatest mysteries is the name of Todd Middleton's young lover. When Todd Middleton's exposure first hit Hadrian's media wave, the whole of the nation was confounded. How could one of our elite be straight? Todd Middleton, son of Will Middleton, both Hadrian's finest b-ball player to date and the brilliant bio-engineer who altered the genes of the soya bean so we could grow the protein rich legume here, was exposed as a straight man, an active heterosexual. It was even intimated that Todd Middleton had raped the girl, and yet no one in Hadrian seems to know her name or even her whereabouts. I have dug deep into this mystery, Hadrian, but have yet to unveil the truth. It worries me how such a significant detail about one of the most important cases in Hadrian's history can remain veiled to the populace. Why is this woman's name so carefully hidden? Whose daughter is she? How powerful is this man or woman to be able to silence individuals who must surely be in the know?

When word of this case first hit the media wave, we learned of a video-tape recording the sexual act. I inquired about this tape only to discover that it had been destroyed. Gideon Weller, then warden of the Northeast Reeducation Camp, deemed the tape's evidence no longer necessary since Todd Middleton had confessed to being straight and having been sexually active. Although Mr. Weller is no longer here to question, I was able to interview Dean Stuttgart, then Dean Hunter, dear friend and father figure to Todd Middleton. He informed me that Weller deemed the video nonessential and that it only served to hurt the young girl and her parents, thus he had it and all traces of it on the wave, destroyed. When Mr. Stuttgart told me this, I immediately inquired into the name of the young woman. He apologized for keeping it secret, but he had agreed to sign papers that would keep her identity a secret. "To reveal her name," Mr. Stuttgart suggested, "would have a profound impact on our country at this time." When I questioned further, Mr. Stuttgart did admit that he had originally wanted the girl's name splattered all over the wave, but after deliberating the issue with their lawyer, Faial Raboud, he and all others with knowledge of this event had signed waivers agreeing never to speak this girl's name or mention her involvement. I was surprised to learn that key members of the radical new human equality movement actually agreed to such terms, but Mr. Stuttgart believes this will all come to light soon and their reasons for being circumspect will be understood and respected.

I have come to admire Dean Stuttgart and the efforts he has made to bring light to the abuses committed against many of Hadrian's citizens, but I must admit, my dedication to revealing truth to our nation has me uncomfortable with my current failure to unveil this mystery of who this young woman is and the real role she played in exposing our country's once beloved golden boy, Todd Middleton.

Truth, Hadrian; bringing light to the truth will always be my goal.

TRUTH!

Christine Sterne

Christine Sterne smiles grimly at her reflection. She is tall now, 6'1". After she stopped taking heterosexual birth control, she grew another two inches, allowing her to achieve her youthful longing to be over six feet. She gives her head a slight shake to make her long mousey blond hair, which dangles in false curls around her neck, more airy. Her black eyebrows contrast in jarring juxtaposition. She muses over the irony of not being allowed hair products to hold her hair in place (in Hadrian what hair products are available are all natural since chemical gels and aerosol sprays are illegal) when she is forced to dye her hair every three weeks and do root touch-ups at least once a week. The natural products available in Hadrian were never effective at disguising her looks enough, so her aunt arranged for a black market supply of an Ultra Blonde Highlighting Kit that did not meet Hadrian's environmental standards act. It sickened Christine to use it, but she conceded to the need. After what had happened in her final year of high school, it was evident that she had to present a new self to the world.

Another sacrifice Christine is forced to make for this new look is wearing her hair long with permanent curls. Again, her aunt went through the black market to obtain hair products with strong enough "illegal chemicals" to ensure long-lasting and natural-looking curls. But when Christine asked her aunt for a hair product that would help her keep her hair in place, she was met with ardent refusal.

"It is bad enough we have to participate in damaging the environment to cover up your stupidity. It is bad enough I risk every day being caught committing illegal acts to save your sorry ass. It is bad enough that I could very well be exiled. But you want more illegal products. And why? For selfish, vain purposes? Absolutely not! You can do what normal Hadrian citizens do!"

Those "normal" Hadrian citizens, like Christine, who prefer their hair well-kept, either wear their hair short or, if their hair is long, put it up in a ponytail or bun. Anyone wanting to add flare to his or her hair has to rely on natural hair oils and teasing to keep a style from falling apart. Christine hates that approach. Teasing creates knots, and the natural oil route means she has to avoid washing her hair less than once a week. She can't stand the greasy, gritty quality that accompanies the required buildup of natural oils, so she has conceded to her conceit and wears her hair as open and free as she can make it. As she studies her form in the mirror, she mourns the loss of her natural dark brown hair, cropped short so it was always perfect.

Again, as always happens if Christine takes too long observing her reflection, her mind places her in front of the podium at Hadrian's National Council for open debate. She never smiles at her audience. She addresses it formally with humility and reserve.

> Good evening, men and women of Hadrian, venerable intersex. I stand here today to make a full and frank confession. My name is Christine Sterne, but I was born and raised Crystal Albright. Though my real name holds no rank or distinction in our country, there are those of you out there who know me as the secondary child of our President, Ms. Elena Stiles. I changed my name, and my overall physical appearance, in order to hide my shame from my family. I did not want Mama Stiles's Presidential campaign to be destroyed because of my foolish mistakes. You see, I am the one who really killed Todd Middleton. Frank Hunter was only the physical agent that brought about Todd's death, but I smothered him just as surely as Frank did. I knew Todd was in love with me. I knew he was sexually attracted to me. I knew that I could easily seduce him and win sexual favors from him with just the right glance. I determined to use him for my heterosexual fling before finally settling down and marrying the right woman. And I did just that. I seduced Todd Middleton. I made love to Todd Middleton. But when we were found out, the threat of my exposure and what that would mean for Mama Elena was so great I allowed the machinery of our government to plough over Todd. And although I never accused him, I let

the insinuation that he had raped me stand, thereby adding further to his misery while he suffered at reeducation camp. I stayed in the shadows. I remained anonymous. My name was never mentioned in court or through national media. Such is the power of high-end politics. And, so, I remained silent behind my wall of protection. I can no longer bear that silence. All I hope for now is that my admission of guilt will help Hadrian's citizens look more kindly on those of us who are marginalized as a result of our differing sexual identity. I am bisexual and my name is Crystal Albright.

This is the speech Christine Sterne makes every time she studies her reflection in the mirror.

This is the speech Crystal Albright lacks the courage to utter.

* * * * *

Hadrian's Real News

An Interview with President Stiles
HRN—Melissa Eagleton Reporting

"President Stiles, thank you for honoring me with an interview. I know my viewers are anxious to hear you outline the platform for your political campaign."

"Thank you, Ms. Eagleton. Let's dispense with all the pleasantries and get right into it."

"I concur."

"Hadrian, during my four years as your president, I have brought about a few changes that have disgruntled a few of our citizens. The first serious change was to appoint Jason Warith as head of our National Reeducation System. Granted, he just stepped down after exposing himself as strai, but no one can deny the more humane procedures he instigated in our reeducation system. The use of corporal punishment, a system of punishment much abused, is no longer administered at any of our camps. Another unsavory practice administered against our students was 'Medicinal Sexual Relations.' Rape would be a more accurate term! Thanks to Jason Warith, rape is no longer a part of our youth reeducation. I was disappointed to receive his resignation and felt his exposure only verified his ability to run our reeducation camps, he himself being a prime example of how heterosexual tendencies can be controlled."

"So is that a focus for your political campaign, Madame President? Do you intend to place an emphasis on teaching members of our society about controlling their heterosexual tendencies?"

"It is one focus, but not the only one, and it is certainly not limited to encouraging celibacy amongst the heterosexual community. Though, I do believe self-imposed chastity is the best approach for heterosexuals to take, I am unwilling to enforce that as law."

"Why, Madame President?"

"Because chastity is a personal decision and not one of the State. Ms. Eagleton, I think it is time Hadrian's government got out of the bedrooms of our citizens."

"How, then, do you propose population control? It seems counter-productive to allow heterosexuals sexual freedom when the ultimate outcome of their sexual expression is pregnancy."

"It was pointed out to me, Ms. Eagleton, and quite wisely, too, by Mother Stuttgart, that there is only one type of heterosexual sex that induces pregnancy: penile vaginal intercourse."

"Of course, and that form of sexuality is illegal. If people are caught in the act or it is discovered through an unwanted pregnancy, then the guilty parties are subject to exile."

"Yes, that is correct."

"Do you plan to remove that law?"

"No."

"I don't understand, Madame President. Birth control is a viable solution. Any heterosexual engaging in sexual acts that could induce pregnancy can avoid that outcome with the use of condoms, spermicidal jelly, the pill our doctors still prescribe to young women who could potentially suffer from gigantism, as well as diaphragms, even the female condom."

"Yes, Ms. Eagleton, I am aware of the varieties of birth control heterosexuals can have access to; however, there is only one guaranteed approach to avoiding pregnancy and that is through abstinence. In the case of heterosexuals, abstinence need only be exercised with penile vaginal intercourse. This will not change, not during my tenure as president."

"Then what will change, Madame President?"

"I will remove the Anti-Strai Propaganda Law I signed into being when I was first elected president. This law is wrong, Ms. Eagleton. It is a form of censorship unbecoming of Hadrian. We have always valued full disclosure and honesty above all, and I wish to return our country to that state. I have pledged funding for reeducation and a better understanding of the whole of human sexual expression. Our children need to learn that it is okay to be different and not have to fear bullying simply for being who they are. With that in mind, the Anti-Strai Propaganda Law must be revoked and a series of informative sex-education lessons need to be developed so our children can learn to understand and accept a variety of sexual identities."

"Including heterosexuality?"

"Including heterosexuality. We must never forget these are our children."

"So, under your leadership as Hadrian's President, no one will ever be expelled for being heterosexual."

"No one ever was, Ms. Eagleton. That is the biggest misconception of our governing laws. The only way one would ever be expelled was if there were concrete evidence of heterosexual intercourse or the individual confessed to having had said intercourse."

"Then why the new law, Madame President? Why legalize heterosexuals?"

"Again, another misconception. I never actually input a new law into our system, Ms. Eagleton. I merely reminded people of what the law already states and insisted no one be unreasonably persecuted. It has always been legal for a person to be openly straight, even to engage in a variety of sexual acts with someone of the opposite sex. All I did was remind the nation that the only illegal form of coitus in Hadrian is penile vaginal intercourse. What has evolved, or perhaps I should say mutated, from this one law is a deep-rooted belief that all forms of heterosexuality are dangerous and thus any acceptance of opposite sex attractions and behaviors must be quelled."

"So what do you propose to do about Hadrian's misconceptions and overwhelming prejudices towards our straight and bisexual citizens?"

"I believe education is the answer. We must create education packages that will help our teachers better instruct our students in the full spectrum of human sexual expression as well as promote understanding and acceptance amongst ourselves."

"What about the issue of sterilization? Even with all the reforms Jason Warith brought into reeducation, I understand sterilization is still being imposed upon any youth sent to these facilities."

"Sterilization is based on the idea that there is a heterosexual gene that must be eradicated from the human genome."

"Do you agree with that idea?"

"No, I do not. I have put forth a bill that would make the sterilization of our reeducated youth illegal, but it has yet to pass the House of Commons."

"So, I guess this is proof positive that the President doesn't have complete control."

"That is correct. Hadrian is a democracy, not a dictatorship. And within a democracy, rules need to be in place to help abate one person controlling everything."

"Will you continue to push for this much-needed change in our laws?"

"Yes, I will."

"So, along with sexual reforms, or rather informing Hadrian of the true nature of its the laws, and improving the quality of our educational system, what else do you hope to accomplish as Hadrian's President, if elected for a second term?"

"I hope to increase funding to Hadrian's military. Though we have experienced fewer attacks these past few years, the war games scenarios held by the Midwest Gate have clearly identified potential weaknesses in our security system. We need to better train our soldiers for all conceivable contingencies, even those that seem the most unlikely."

"Good answer. So, tell me, Madame President, how do you feel about the schism in the Stuttgart family. Mother Stuttgart has thrown her weight and backing into your ring whilst her son, Gordon Stuttgart, is propping up Cooper Johnston as the leader of the opposition. Can you give any rational explanation for how this one founding family could become so polarized for this electoral campaign?"

"Yes, good question. It seems the Stuttgart family is a microcosm of our nation. We, too, are divided on the issue of sexual equality. Nearly twenty-seven years ago, we, as a nation, grieved along with Gordon Stuttgart when it was announced that his son had died in a car accident, having hit a moose; the bubble, supposedly being driven by the boy, had been completely demolished and the teen's remains were so mutilated that only a DNA test could identify him. Dean Stuttgart was positively identified as the youth in that bubble, and yet Dean Stuttgart is alive today. When it was first announced to the world that he was alive and a graduate of our reeducation system, people were shocked and stunned. Many even exonerated Gordon Stuttgart for having created this fiction. So, though the only legal action taken against this man for fabricating a lie was a hefty fine of a million credits, which was allocated to reeducation reforms, it would be wise of Hadrian's citizens to consider the morality of the man behind Cooper Johnston. This is a man who abandoned his own son and imposed a hateful lie on Dean Stuttgart's life."

"Good point, Madame President."

"Destiny Stuttgart, Gordon's mother, on the other hand, is our founding mother. She helped draft the original constitution and, though close to ninety, she still has all her faculties. She tires quickly and is easily distracted, which are both normal considering her age, but she is far from senile and as she likes to say, she 'knows a hawk from a handsaw' if you know what I mean."

"Yes, indeed. For those viewers unfamiliar with William Shakespeare's work, this is a line from *Hamlet* where the titular character is warning his friends that he is not what he appears to be, in Hamlet's case insane, in Mother Stuttgart's case, senile. And, like Hamlet, Mother Stuttgart is reminding those who pretend to be her friends that she knows who her enemies are. Don't be fooled by the Conservative Right in its determination to undermine our founding mother's intellectual skills. She may be old, but she is certainly not stupid!"

"Agreed; all one need do is spend a half-hour in her presence to know our founding mother's faculties are all there."

"Now, Madame President, no doubt you watched the *Salve!* interview with Cooper Johnston."

"Yes, Ms. Eagleton, I did."

"Any thoughts on Cooper Johnston's use of terrorist footage to win over the voting populace?"[45]

"Yes, that was rather unseemly of him, and HNN, for that matter. After that horrific attack, it was decided at the highest levels of government to make known the details of the footage but not to air it over the waves. Such footage is far too graphic and gruesome for younger, sensitive minds to grapple with, which is why we left viewing to the discretion of the parent, rather than mandatory viewing for all to endure. The footage itself is stored on the Hadrian gov site and the address made widely known so anyone over eighteen can access it, but it was never intended that the footage be used by social media."

"And yet, Cooper Johnston had *Salve!* air it twice. Why do you suppose that is?"

"I'd rather not speculate as to the motives of the Conservative Right, Ms. Eagleton. My campaign is based solely on what I, as leader of Hadrian's National Party, will do for the development of Hadrian and for the improvement of the quality of life for *all* our citizens."

"That is as safe a response as it gets, I suppose, but at least you aren't stooping to the level of the Conservatives, whose entire campaign seems

[45] http://www.cbc.ca/news/politics/conservative-video-spreads-isis-propaganda-to-make-justin-trudeau-look-weak-1.3133039

built upon a malignant spirit determined to foul your reputation and terrify the masses."

"I am not interested in pointing out Cooper Johnston's flaws, Ms. Eagleton. I prefer to let his words and actions speak for themselves."

"And they do speak quite loudly for all those not taken in by his excessive use of fear tactics. I hope the majority of Hadrian's citizens are rational and aware enough to know that any leader who condescends to terrifying the populace for votes is only evidencing how his rule is equally likely to be based on keeping people's emotional senses heightened in order to prevent the intellectual neurons from working inside the brain. Fear tactics are used by governing powers that want only to control the mass populace, not work with them for the country's overall betterment."

"Madame President, thank you so much for joining me today. I appreciate the candor of your responses, and I wish you luck in the upcoming election."

"Thank you, Ms. Eagleton."

"To all my viewers, good night; may the media and your government always present you with the truth."

TRU—!

"No!"

"I'm sorry? Is something wrong Madame President?"

"Yes, it's me. I haven't been entirely truthful to the electorate."

"What do you mean, Madame President?"

"My campaign manager warned me against doing this."

"Doing what?"

"Granted, I have never lied, but I do feel as though an omission is equivalent, or rather that somehow one is playing a dangerous game when always equivocating."

"And, what is it you have omitted to announce to the electorate, Madame President?"

"That my daughter is bisexual. People are constantly asking me where my sympathies for strais comes from, and the fact is, though all my other answers have been truthful, the real truth lies a lot closer to home."

"I see."

"There is a lot more to this story. You see, my daughter, Crystal Albright, was having relations with a young man."

"And who was this young man, Madame President?"

"Todd Middleton."

"The boy whose murder case set this country on fire?"

"The boy, who, I believed at the time, had raped my daughter."

"When did you learn otherwise?"

"Just prior to Frank Hunter's trial."

"Please, Madame President, continue."

"I received a text message between Crystal and Frank Hunter's papa, Dean Stuttgart. We only knew him then as Dean Hunter."

"What did this text message say?"

"Well, it turns out Crystal initially thought she was texting Todd since Dean Hunter had the boy's phone. This message happened before Todd Middleton died."

"And, in it?"

"In it, Crystal admitted that Todd and she had had consensual inter-course. She was never raped."

"Why did you not share this evidence in the trial, Madame President? It certainly would have made a huge difference in the outcome of this case."

"At first, Crystal refused to affirm that she had been the one to make the text. She neither refused or denied complicity, and our lawyer encouraged us to leave this information out."

"And Faial Raboud, Madame President, how did she respond to your decision not to allow this critical piece of evidence to be used?"

"At first, she fought to have it subpoenaed, but she soon realized she could win this case without having to drag my name through the mud so close to the election."

"So, Madam President, why are you dragging your name through the mud now, so close to another election?"

"Because it is the truth, Ms. Eagleton, 'May the media and your govern-ment always present you with the truth.' If by acknowledging my failings when it comes to my daughter, I lose this next election, then I lose. But if I am to return to office, I must do so honestly. I want the electorate to know that I have come by my sympathies for the strai community honestly in the same way the majority of Hadrian's parents should come by them too. We promote the Kinsey scale as the basis for our reasoning behind the country's focus on homosexuality, but how many people have really thought about what that means?"

"What do you think it means, Madame President?"

"It means that the majority of Hadrian's citizens exist anywhere from a 1 to a 5 on this scale. From a one to a five! That is almost 85 percent of our population. Eighty-five percent of Hadrian's citizens whether they are willing to admit it or not, experience both same sex *and* opposite sex attractions. We have to stop condemning the bulk of our citizens; we have to stop forcing them to live their lives in fear, and most importantly, we have to stop encouraging them to abandon the ones they love just as my daughter did with Todd Middleton. She confessed to me that she loved him. I couldn't understand at first, especially when she refused to leap to his defense. But then I realized that our entire culture is based on the condemnation of anyone with opposite sex feelings. She was terrified not only for herself, but for me. She refused to step up and defend her boyfriend because she didn't want what she had done to affect my political career. That's when I realized that, although my daughter was wrong, what we do to make our citizens think and act the way she did is also immoral. Loving another human being is not, and should never be deemed, criminal.

"I am sorry I kept this information about my private life a secret, but sharing one's private life is never easy."

"No, Madame President, it is not. And I must say, it is refreshing to have a politician open up as honestly as you just did. That alone establishes you as the better candidate.

"There is very little left to say, except that this might very well be an historic moment when a politician has provided the electorate with the 'whole truth and nothing but the truth.' This, Hadrian, is the very least we should expect from those whom we place into positions of power."

TRUTH!

Third Party Politics

Telling Matt about Stephanie is one of the hardest things Wolf has ever had to do. That Matt will be unreceptive, Wolf anticipates, but he has to broach the subject anyway. Stephanie was going to break up with him because she knows how important their friendship is to both men. Wolf, not wanting to lose either and confronted with the inevitable loss of his lover, has decided telling Matt is the only thing he could do. He knows it could mean losing both his best friend and lover because Stephanie doesn't want Matt to know.

"It will hurt him too much, and I've already inflicted two lifetimes' worth of pain on him."

Although Wolf understands Stephanie's reasoning, he can't bear the thought of losing her, so he makes the most important decision of his life, and the riskiest, too, by choosing to tell Matthew.

Matt's response is as expected, expressing hurt and betrayal. "I can't believe you're asking me this."

"I just, I need your blessing, Matt."

"Are you fucking insane? You want me to say, 'Great'? Or 'I'm happy for you'? Well, I'm not! I fucking hate him. You know what he did to me. What he made me do. I told you everything, man, and now you want me to bless your union. Fuck, man! I thought you were my friend!"

"We are friends, Matt."

"Not as long as you're with him!"

"Her."

"Fuck! Don't give me that! *He* abused me."

"I know, but Stephanie's not the same girl as the boy you knew. She's— well, she's sorry for what she did to you."

"And that's supposed make it all okay? *She's sorry*. It doesn't work that way, Wolf!"

"I know, but she's gonna leave."

"Good!"

With eyes red and tears refusing to be held back, Wolf pleads with his best friend. "But I love her. And she won't stay with me because she knows we're friends. She says she won't hurt you again." Tears overwhelm him and Wolf sobs with abandon. Finally back in control, Wolf adds, "Stephanie was a girl pretending to be a man in a fucked up world. Now she's just a woman. And she loves me. And I love her. And she's leaving me. For the first time in over fifteen years, I'm actually happy, and I'm about to lose everything 'cause Stephanie's leaving me and now I've lost you, too. I'd never have risked our friendship if I didn't love her, Matt."

Matt, with his back turned, hands on his hips, one knee bent and head bowed, shudders, "Do you really love her?"

"I love her as much as Hadrian loved Antinous."

"And she makes you happy?"

"As happy as Antinous made Hadrian."

"Fuck." Matt turns to face his friend. "You love her and she loves you?"

Feeling almost hopeful, Wolf can barely whisper his response. "Yes."

"You deserve to be happy."

"We still mates?"

Matt almost smiles. "Yeah, man, we're still mates."

"Will you tell Stephanie you're okay with her and me?"

Matt groans. "Fuck, Wolf, you're pushing it!"

Despair reopens both men's wounds. "She won't believe me."

Matt harrumphs, "She'd be a fucking moron if she did." Turning now, expressing all his disgust and hate in two glaring red eyes, eyes filled with tears that, for Matt, too, also refuse to be denied, he concludes, "I don't ever want to be in the same room as her."

"Just a voc, a voc message, that's all."

"Cam it now before I change my mind."

Wolf quickly wipes his eyes, hoping to keep the film from being blurry. "Ready."

There is a brief pause as Matt stands, hands on hips, head bent, then utters, "Stephanie." Now Matt stares into Wolf's eyes; one of them is operating the cam, and his glare is directed at her. "For some reason unfathomable to me, this mother fucker Wolf loves you. He fucking loves you so you better not leave him because he's my best mate, and I swear on Antinous's tomb if you ever hurt him—just don't leave him. Not because of me." Matt spins on his heels, giving the cam his back. "All right, I'm done. We're still mates regardless of what she decides. I just don't ever want to see her." Turning now to speak one more time to Stephanie, he adds, "Don't you fucking break his heart!" Turning away again, Matt orders, "Turn it off."

* * * * *

Telling Faial about their relationship is one of the hardest things Jason and Cantara ever have to do. Jason is both confused and embarrassed. In fact, he is terrified at the thought of how Faial might respond. The last time he saw her, he had confessed a strong attraction for her. Faial had responded with compassion and understanding, but not with similar feelings, for which Jason will always be grateful. Although he didn't know it at the time, he was forging a true bond of love with Faial's daughter, Cantara. On that fateful night when Jason cradled Cantara, helping her overcome suffocating grief, the two discovered themselves kissing. When they stopped to look deep into one another's eyes, they knew they were going to build something important together. It turns out that "something" is a life together.

For Cantara, although she knows how supportive her mother is, she deems herself one of the lucky ones. Regardless, Cantara is still unsure how Faial will react to her making a lifelong commitment to a man—and not just any man, the very man who once professed his love for Faial.

Faial's silence causes both Jason and Cantara to despair. Just when both are convinced she is going to explode with ire, Faial steps forward to embrace them both. Her words, "Welcome to the family, Jason" fill the young couple with warm bliss. "You know," she adds, "I've always wanted a son."

Even so, it isn't completely easy. Faial, after all, is a lawyer schooled in the ways of Hadrian's legal system. Her initial reaction (albeit hidden)—fear—is consistent with that of any good parent. Fear for her child's safety. Thus, as a result of, and against her better judgment, she blurts out a reminder of the law, "Penile Vag—"

Cantara quells that potential onslaught. "No, Mom. No spouting the law. We know it. We know what we can and can't do. We're not fools."

Faial saddens. "You know you won't be able to have children. The state won't allow it. Any confessed—"

"Yes, Faial." It is Jason's turn to cut her off. "We know that law, too. I burned that bridge when I came out as straight. But if Cantara wants a child, she is still able to. I've told her I'm willing to keep our love a secret; that way she can raise a baby and I can be our child's 'uncle.'"

Cantara immediately launches the counter-attack, "And I told Jason I'm not hiding anything. We love each other and have the right—"

"—should have the right, but we don't."

"—to express our love openly. And if that means we can't have children, then we can't have children."

Faial's mood is somber. "Or grandchildren."

Cantara softens to her mother's grief. "I'm sorry, Mom."

Faial steels herself to her new reality. "Well, it looks like you two have just placed another challenge on my plate."

Cantara and Jason beam, asking in tangent, "What's that?"

"I'm just going to have to present a bill to the government allowing for straight couples to raise children."

"Good luck with that, Mom."

Jason's love and confidence in his soon-to-be mother-in-law flows freely. "If anyone can help change history, Faial, it's you."

Smiling, Faial reminds him, "Please, Jason, call me 'Mom.'"

* * * * *

Telling Roger is one of the hardest things Frank has ever had to do. He anticipates that Roger will be unreceptive, but Frank has to broach the subject anyway. Devon is going to break up with him because he doesn't want to come between the two brothers. Frank, not wanting to lose either and confronted with the inevitable loss of his lover, decides telling Roger is the only thing he can do. He knows it could mean losing both his brother and his lover because Devon doesn't want Roger to know.

"It will hurt him too much, and I've already inflicted two lifetimes' worth of pain on him."

Although Frank understands Devon's reasoning, he can't bear the thought of losing him, so he makes the most important decision of his life, and the riskiest, too, by choosing to tell Roger.

Roger's response is as expected—expressing hurt and betrayal. "You've got to be fucking kidding me?" Dumbfounded and outraged at what Frank is revealing, Roger cuts him off. "Do you know what that man did to me?"

Frank shudders in shame. "Yes, he told me."

"And you still want my blessing? Are you fucking insane?"

"I'm sorry, Roger."

"Sorry doesn't cut it. He turned fucking brutal. He couldn't have sex without beating me. The last time we were together, I told him to stop, but he kept right on battering me. He fucked me even after I said, 'Stop'!" Staring at his brother in disbelief, Roger concludes, "He's not a nice man, Frank."

"A man can change."

"That's all you've got for me? 'A man can change'?" Pointing now to his body, Roger declares, "The bruises have healed, Frank, but the scars he left are deep! I fucking hate him!"

Frank's tears burst forth as he proclaims, "But I love him, Roger. And he loves me."

Roger is having none of it. "He made my life a misery!"

Frank pleads with his little brother. "But I love him. And he won't stay with me because he knows I want to marry him and he thinks that will hurt you. He says he won't hurt you ever again." Overwhelmed, Frank sobs with abandon. Finally back in control, he adds, "Devon was angry back then. Angry at me for killing Todd. He wanted to strike out and hurt me, and you were the closest thing to me he had. He wasn't functioning on reason, just anger and spite. But he doesn't hate me anymore. He loves me, and I love him. And now he's leaving me because I asked him to marry me. For the first time since Todd—since being in here, I can finally say I'm happy. He makes me happy, and now I'm about to lose everything."

"What do you mean everything?"

Frank's hopes rise slightly. "'Cause Devon's leaving me, and now I've lost you, too. I'd never have risked losing you, Roger, if I didn't love him as much as I do."

"Fuck!" Turning his back on his brother, with hands on hips and head bowed, Roger shudders. "Do you really love him?"

"I love him as much as Hadrian loved Antinous."

"And he makes you happy?"

"As happy as Antinous made Hadrian."

"Fuck." Roger turns. "He doesn't beat you, does he? He's never hurt you?"

Overwhelmed with hope, Frank can barely whisper his response, "No."

"He makes you happy?" The very thought is unfathomable. "He really makes you happy?"

"Yes."

Roger ponders this for a moment. "You deserve to be happy."

Frank slumps over. "I know I don't deserve happiness, but I love him."

Roger turns and crosses over to his brother, placing his hands on his shoulder. He shakes Frank slightly to get him to look in his eyes. "No, Frank, I said you deserve to be happy, and," closing his eyes while pausing for a breath, "if Devon makes you happy, you should marry him." Frank leaps into Roger's arms, crying too hard even to respond. Roger understands. "It's okay, Frank. You'll always be my brother."

"Will you—" Frank trips over the words, "—will you tell Devon you're okay with him and me?"

Roger groans. "Fuck, man; don't push it!"

Despair begins refilling both men's wounds. "He won't believe me."

Roger harrumphs. "He'd be a fucking idiot if he did." Turning now, expressing all his disgust and hate through two glaring red eyes, eyes filled with tears that, for Roger, also refuse to be denied, Roger admits, "I don't ever want to see him again!"

"Just a voc, a voc message—that's all."

"You better cam him now before I change my mind."

"I—I can't." Frank lost his vocal contact lens when he was incarcerated.

Roger squirms before reaching deep inside for the never-ending well of brotherly love. Quickly, to avoid changing his mind and hurting his brother, he wipes his eyes. The last thing Roger wants is for Devon to see him cry. He blinks, nods once to Frank, and then begins. "Devon," Roger shakes and thrusts his hand palm out in front of him, "don't talk; just listen!" Staring dead ahead, no doubt deep into Devon's eyes, Roger hopes to ascertain any sign of reform; begrudgingly, he admits to seeing some. "For some reason unbeknownst to me, this mother fucking brother of mine says he loves you. He fucking loves you so much he's willing to risk losing both you and me! Don't you fucking say a word! You don't deserve him! And I damn well know he deserves a lot better than you. But he loves you." Roger shakes his head, dumbfounded. "I can't fucking believe it, but he loves you, so you better not hurt him like you did me because he's my brother, man, and I swear on Antinous's tomb, if you ever hurt him—*if you ever hurt him*—I will hunt you down and make the last few hours of your life a living fucking hell!" That said, Roger severs the connection with one quick blink of an eye. Looking back at Frank, Roger reassures him, "We're still brothers, regardless of what that bastard decides."

* * * * *

Forgiving Frank for his role in Todd's death is one of the hardest things Dean has ever had to do. After Frank killed Todd, albeit in an act of assisted suicide, Dean couldn't even look his son in the face. Dean knew in his heart he was abandoning his son, and he knew Frank must have been badly hurt by that abandonment, but for Dean, grief and disappointment masked Frank's pain. As hard as he tried to fight against this most unnatural parental act, he could not wrap his brain around the fact that Frank had, according to the presiding judge, murdered his best friend's son, a young man Dean had come to love as much as his own children. Todd Middleton was Dean's adopted, though not legally, son. Todd's exposure, the abuses Todd had suffered in reeducation under then warden, Gideon Weller, compounded with his sudden death by asphyxiation, severed the cord of love that had bound Dean to Frank. Loathing had replaced love when Geoffrey explained how Frank had forced Todd to have sex in a desperate attempt to tame him and avoid his being sent to reeducation—a sadly futile act. Dean wishes Geoffrey had left him in ignorance, and yet, knowing the truth is the only way one can ever truly obtain true forgiveness. When Dean and Geoffrey finally set the date for their reregistration, Dean is confronted with the reality of having to accept Frank back into his life.

"Dean, I want Frank at our wedding. I want him to sit at the head table with us. Roger can stand up for you, but I want Frank to stand up for me."

Dean is stunned. Of course, Geoffrey wants his eldest son at their wedding. Seeing how important this is to Geoffrey causes Dean to wonder about his own feelings for Frank. "Geoffrey, I need a little time to think about this."

"Take all the time you need, but know this, I can't see myself reentering our relationship without the full acceptance of our family. You once loved him as a son. Please look inside and try to find that love again."

"I don't know if that's possible, Geoffrey."

"If not, then meet him on neutral ground and try to build a new connection. I can't, as much as I love you, Dean, consent to remarry you if that means leaving Frank in the background. He's our son. I know he's done horrible things, but he is paying for those, and he will continue to pay his dues for the rest of his life. But I cannot, I will not, countenance a continuance of judgment thrust on him on our part." Sighing, knowing that Dean's decision in this matter will determine whether or not they can live their lives together, Geoffrey adds, "One does not abandon one's child, no matter what the circumstances are." And although Geoffrey is taking a huge risk playing this next card, he knows it might be the only way to get through to Dean and bring him back to accepting and loving their son. "I am not Mike Fulton." Looking directly into Dean's eyes, he asks, "Are you?"

Dean turns white, his breath catching painfully in his chest. Mike Fulton. He abandoned his son, Todd Middleton, the boy Dean loved like a son. "I'm not..." Dean desperately wants to say he is nothing like Mike Fulton, but the facts have just punched him in the heart. "Oh, Geoffrey, forgive me."

"I have." Feeling love and empathy, but refusing to give in to pity, Geoffrey clinches it for Dean by saying, "Now it is up to you to forgive Frank."

Dean finally admits to his own personal truth. "I abandoned Frank, just like Mike abandoned Todd."

Geoffrey does not dispute him. "Yes, you did."

"Can he—will he—forgive me?"

"Roger and I are scheduled to visit him next Sunday. Come with us. What you and Frank need is for someone to make the first move. He can't, not where he is. But if you forgive him, maybe he can learn to forgive himself, and then learn to love you as his papa again. You'd like that, wouldn't you?"

All Dean can do is nod, words choked by emotion, but when he finally gets his voice back, he answers Geoffrey's behest. "Yes. I want that."

* * * * *

Salve!

Stiles Takes a DIVE!
HNN—Danny Duggin Reporting

Oh, people, did you watch yesterday's *Real News*? I did; well, not when it was broadcast, but as soon as I heard about what was said on it, I blinked right into that newscast, and all I can say is "Madame President, THANK YOU!" This is just too good to be true. Not only did she admit to having lied to our country, having been voted in under false pretense, but she also admitted to having brought her own personal strai agenda to the table. You know, she claims that 85 percent of the population is bi—well, that sounds like a confession to me. I always knew Stiles was straight. She just has that strai look about her, something in her eyes. And here I was worried that Cooper Johnston was going to have a fight on his hands. Prior to yesterday's stunning announcement, Elena Stiles was winning in the polls. I don't even have to look at the polls now to know that she just handed over the office of the Presidency to Cooper Johnston. She might as well step down now.

Cooper Johnston really is the best choice for President. He is not harboring any deep dark secrets, nor is he willing to give any credence to the strai agenda, which is, as we all know, to turn everyone in Hadrian strai so we can join up with the rest of the world in polluting and overpopulating our planet. The soon-to-be Mr. President's platform is simple and easy for all of Hadrian to understand: strengthen our military; strengthen our education systems, and reestablish the laws mandating that all youth who display heterosexual tendencies be incarcerated into reeducation and all citizens of age be expelled; and, of course, investing heavily into pollution clean-up and environmental restoration here inside our walls. Cooper Johnston also promises to keep the Wall closed, blocking entrance to "emissaries" from the outside world. Nor is he prepared to create a whole new government plutocracy to send Hadrian citizens to other countries as ambassadors.

We know full well that the lives of these "ambassadors" would be at risk, not just from violent barbaric heterosexuals, all of whom are rabid homophobes, but also at risk of catching any of the multitudes of diseases that ravage the outside world. Cooper Johnston will not expose anyone from Hadrian to that!

So we all know how to vote next month when we are asked to voc into our individual election links. When you cast your ballot into the virtual basket, make your vote count. Vote for Hadrian, not for the barbaric strais!

Vale!

A Campaign Ad!

Elena Stiles walks forward out of the dusk. Dark clouds slowly dissipate into the background as she is slowly engulfed by a rainbow. Behind her, Hadrian's government building's solar panels shimmer with new morning light.

Directing her attention to the camera, Elena Stiles asks, "What is the rainbow?" She pauses briefly to allow her viewers time to ponder this question. "When we first look upon a beam of light, we see stark white, but when the storm passes and the light shatters through infinitesimal dew, what is revealed is its true spectrum." Here, Elena opens her hands to gesture to all that is inside the rainbow. "And that, my friends, is humanity. When we embrace the rainbow, we embrace humanity, not just one facet. This is what our gay and lesbian brothers and sisters fought for, still fight for, outside our walls. but they didn't fight alone. Included in their ranks were bisexuals, transgendered, the intersex, and their straight allies. Together, they fought for equality amongst humanity. And this is what we must fight for inside our walls. Look at our rainbow. It is not one mere stark band of bright white. It is, like the human race, a multifarious display of color."

Destiny Stuttgart emerges from the storm that is receding in the background. Walking forward into the light, she joins Elena Stiles. The two women stand engulfed in the rainbow.

"Mother Stuttgart stands firmly beside me, inside the rainbow."

Destiny Stuttgart holds Elena Stiles's hand. Also walking out of the dark clouds in the background are citizens of Hadrian who step forward to join them. Two men enter, both wearing the traditional symbol for gay men, followed by two women wearing the traditional symbol for lesbians. Next, a dozen men and women join them, all wearing shirts with the symbol for being bisexual. A transgendered man enters wearing a shirt that proudly proclaims his trans status, and a trans lady emerges wearing the same. An intersex then joins the collective, followed by a man and a woman, arm-in-arm. All reach out together, holding hands, forming a semi-circle behind Elena Stiles and Destiny Stuttgart. Each woman walks to one end of the human rainbow's spectrum and links all of humanity into a circle.

The camera homes in on Destiny Stuttgart's face. She smiles. "Hadrian, join us in holding hands with all of humanity."

The camera returns now to Elena Stiles, who finishes with, "Join us in accepting the true diversity of the human condition."

* * * * *

Hadrian's Real News

Happy Fifty-Fifth Birthday Hadrian!
December 31, 21__.
HRN—Melissa Eagleton Reporting

A lot has happened in the last five years when I helped you all ring in Hadrian's fiftieth birthday. We have seen the exposure and death of one of Hadrian's favorites, young Todd Middleton, son of the great Will Middleton, both known for their exceptional skills on the b-ball court, and Will Middleton known as the agricultural engineer who genetically altered the soya bean so we could grow it here in our northern climate. We also learned that Will Middleton was straight, that one of our finest was not gay as all had presumed, but a heterosexual. That, in no way, lessens his accomplishments and all he strived for in making our lives easier in Hadrian. Rather, what it illustrated for many conscious and thinking citizens is that we may be harboring too much prejudice towards those of a differing sexual orientation.

After Todd Middleton's unfortunate demise, all of Hadrian watched the Frank Hunter trial with bated breath. Hunter was found guilty of murder under unique circumstances, and rather than be exiled, he was sentenced to a lifetime of military service. This set a dangerous precedent for Hadrian, opening the door to our military growing in numbers by sentencing citizens to military service. That Private Frank Hunter's military service record is so exemplary was compounded by the fact that the military came to like this new means of recruiting.

From here, we began witnessing a rash of strai-bashing incidents, culminating in brutal murders, one of a four-year-old boy, another of a detritus fisherman, who was murdered and burned inside his bubble, and most recently, the horrific rape and murder of uni student Tara Fowler.

Considering the vile turn our country has taken, President Stiles felt the urgent need to reeducate all our citizens about our laws and what they are really saying. And, though I personally believe these laws need refining,

President Stiles at least refused to allow our citizens to blatantly abuse the system to harm our neighbors. The reeducation system was changed for the better, initially under the guidance of Jason Warith, and continued under the leadership of Adrian Adams, the man Warith claims should have been given the position in the first place. Adams, like his predecessor, works tirelessly to create a more humane approach to reeducation. Warith and Adams have introduced such reforms as the removal of corporal punishment and also of the questionable practice of medicinal intercourse.

Jason Warith, exposing himself as a celibate strai, also took Hadrian aback. This announcement was unexpected, and the backlash of hate speech and threats made against his life was only further evidence to support President Stiles's concern regarding the level of bigotry we harbor in our nation towards our own children who are born bisexual or straight.

There is another piece of news with respect to Hadrian's former minister of reeducation. He recently announced his engagement to Cantara Raboud. Of course, the union between a man and a woman has no legal status in Hadrian; still, the two lovers will be sharing vows and dedicating their lives to one another at a private ceremony to be held in an unknown location. They naturally fear repercussions if the day, time, and place of their wedding are publically publicized.

Lastly, perhaps the most important piece of information to date was the stunning revelation President Stiles made on this very news show. She revealed to Hadrian that her daughter, one Crystal Albright, is not only bisexual, but that she played an intricate role in the case of Todd Middleton's exposure. That was a daring, brave, and extremely risky move on the part of our President. She illustrated for us how family supersedes everything, even one's political career. She knew full well that revealing her personal truth could very well be the end of her political career in Hadrian.

I am proud of our nation. Not only was President Stiles not wiped off the face of the political map as Cooper Johnston had predicted, but she was elected for a second term by a majority vote. Thank you, Hadrian, for showing compassion, understanding, and, most of all, integrity during this time of tribulation for our country. You made the right choice in electing Elena Stiles to work for us over the next four years to restore balance to the planet's ecosystem, accepting all our children regardless of gender or sexual orientation, and further strengthening our military so our country's defense will allow for the opening of our gates once more to the rest of humanity. We are entering into a new age Hadrian, one in which we can proudly say we are on the right side of history![46] [47] And, as our founding mother, Destiny Stuttgart, said, one that will see us "holding hands with the rest of humanity," and, as our President wisely states, will help us learn to accept "the true diversity of the human condition." To you and all who believe, it pleases me to say happy fifty-fifth birthday, Hadrian.

TRUTH!

---

[46] http://www.amazon.ca/The-Right-Side-History-Activism/dp/1627781234

[47] http://shop.hrc.org/right-side-of-history-t-shirt.html/

The Human Pentagram

President Elena Stiles stands on the steps of Hadrian's capitol building. Before she begins her inauguration speech, she looks out at the crowd. Never would she have imagined, just a few years ago, that she would be giving such a speech, and yet, she feels completely at peace, as if her destiny is being fulfilled. Smiling at her supporters, she begins:

> It is customary for a newly-elected President to extend her thanks to the people for having been chosen for such an auspicious and critical role in the governing of our nation. Hadrian, I thank you for electing me for a second term as your governing head. It is also customary that the President's inaugural speech outline the key focus for the upcoming four years of service. I intend to do so now, but in a way not seen in our nation in over four decades. Today, for my inaugural speech, I will read to you from the original document that forms the very basis for our country's constitution. For it is upon the words of this document that we have laid the basis for our laws and treatment of our fellow citizens. This document will not sound like the document we all believe to be the founding families' original constitution. That is because this document is the original constitution of our nation.
>
> Like you, Hadrian, from my childhood, I was raised and educated to believe that our great nation was founded on four ideals—the four ideals that create the four cornerstones, or as they are sometimes called, pillars, of our community: Hadrian's sexual preference is homosexual; Hadrian is a safe haven for homosexuals from around the globe; Hadrian

establishes as its goal to restore balance to nature and learn to live in harmony with our planet; and lastly, that Hadrian's population will never exceed that of ten million. All of these sound good, do they not? But sadly, Hadrian, this is not true. Our country was not founded upon these four cornerstones. Rather, our country was founded upon the Human Pentagram.

Needless to say, we have all been educated, perhaps I should say inculcated, to believe that the first and foremost of these four cornerstones is that homosexuality is the preferred and acceptable sexual orientation of our nation. Nothing could be further from the truth. This cornerstone, in fact, the pinnacle point, the very head of our pentagram, is the point which recognizes and accepts all forms of gender diversity, gender expression, and identity as well as the full spectrum of consensual human sexual orientation. What this means, Hadrian, is that our founding families never excluded bisexuals or heterosexuals, nor did they ever recommend that we strive to rid our country of anyone expressing opposite sex attractions. Rather, we have allowed our fear of overpopulation to govern our irrational behaviors for too long. As a result, inspired by the guidance and wisdom of both Jason Warith, head warden of Hadrian's Reeducation system, and our founding mother, Destiny Stuttgart, I have disbanded the arm of Hadrian's educational system that indoctrinated our youth towards a sexual lifestyle foreign to their very being. No longer will Hadrian be home to the tormentors we formed this country to escape. No longer will Hadrian judge our children for whom they are and press them through the mood of an unfair, unjust educational system. We must learn to love and embrace our own without fear or reservation.

Does this mean Hadrian is suddenly going to embrace a population explosion? No, I assure you it does not. The second point of the pentagram, that being on the right-hand side, is the expressed need to quell and control human population through planned parenthood with each of Hadrian's citizens being responsible for bringing one child into this world and to register that child through the government census so a firm grasp can be held on population growth. Hadrian is, and always has been, firmly committed to a ten million-population mark, and nothing changes that.

On the left-hand side of the pinnacle is the promise to the people of Hadrian that whoever lives here, regardless of his or her cultural heritage, race, faith or non-faith, gender or sexual orientation, will be allowed to live in peace and with acceptance. Hadrian is to be a safe haven for humanity. No one faith supersedes another, no one race dominates another, no one gender subjugates another, and no one sexual orientation takes precedence over another. Let me repeat that last phrase: No one sexual orientation takes precedence over another! These are the original words of our founding families' constitution! No one sexual orientation takes precedence over another.

The right leg of our pentagram points directly to our country's pledge to move forward as a species towards ecological restoration and living in harmony and balance with our natural environment. Arresting and reversing climate change, along with all of the other catastrophic damages resulting from humanity's raping of our Mother Earth, to our excessive use of her atmosphere, land masses, and waters as our collective dumping grounds will forever be the focus of our people.

The left leg—sadly, the left leg was severed. This point on the Human Pentagram points to the need for humanity to work together as one. Hadrian once had an international policy. Our founding families believed it was critical that Hadrian retain communication with the international community. For that is the only way we can ever fully restore balance to our planet and help diminish human population. We are meant to be the model upon which other nations can see how it is possible to maintain a stable population, run a healthy economy, avoid entrapment, and live in harmony with Mother Earth. We have not been that model, Hadrian. It is time we try to live up to our own standards. In keeping with this idea, I intend to open communication with the outside world, allowing back inside our borders emissaries from other countries, as well as sending our own ambassadors abroad. We must work together as a human species if we are ever going to get a handle on the numerous problems our forefathers created for our generation and for future generations yet to come. I don't know about you, but I want my children to live in a clean world, one rid of hate and prejudice. And, even though this is an ideal that humanity may never achieve, I will work to my dying breath to strive for nothing less.

Our country was not founded on four cornerstones! Our country was founded on the Human Pentagram. Knowing this, I will not, in good conscience, sign any laws that allow for the domination, subjugation, and/or eradication of any human being! No human beings will be exiled or forced to learn how not to be themselves. Never again, Hadrian!

Many of you may ask why I have embraced what seems to be a radical departure for our country's ways? I do not depart from our nation's purpose, as stated in its original constitution, to embrace humanity as a whole and rectify the damages we have committed against our once beautiful earth. Not only do I not depart from them, but I turn the light back onto this document and invite all from our good nation to open this file and read it. This is Hadrian's true intent. And as your President, I not only hold these words to be true, but I will govern our nation according to its true intent!

But you're right. I haven't answered the question. Why was I willing to listen to Mother Stuttgart? Beside the fact that she is one of our founding mothers, she also took me on a virtual tour of Hadrian's National Archives. It was there she revealed to me the original founding documents. It was there that I learned the true intent of our nation. And it was there I learned I could no longer turn my back on my daughter. My daughter—as I shared with you in an interview with Melissa Eagleton on Hadrian's Real News—my daughter is bisexual. My daughter had a male lover. His name was Todd Middleton. Just as I no longer deny my daughter the right to be who she is, I will no longer deny that right to any of Hadrian's citizens. We are all human!

Look again at our pentagram: The Human Pentagram. We have the head, the right hand, the left hand, the right leg, and the left leg. Humanity stands strong in Hadrian!

* * * * *

Epilogue

Presidential Pardon

General Birtwistle's office, though the largest in the complex, is far too small for the ceremony taking place. Crammed into the small room (8' by 10') standing in a semi-circle behind the general's extremely large mahogany desk (the desk itself taking up close to one-fourth of the entire space) are Danny Duggin from *Salve!*, Melissa Eagleton from *Hadrian's Real News*, President Stiles, Colonel de la Chappelle, whose beaming smile is seraphic, Lieutenant Kimberly Westgate (known as Mid by her peers), Lieutenant Devon Rankin, Geoffrey Hunter, Dean Stuttgart, and Roger Hunter.

General Birtwistle is seated at his desk, staring intently at the door, awaiting the anticipated knock. He, too, is grinning, but rather than looking seraphic, his expression simply looks goofy. No one in the room, especially the officers of lesser rank, is willing to inform him of this, though. Across from him, standing on either side of the door, are a cameraman (for *Salve!*) and a camerawoman (for *HRN*). Each holds steady a miniaturized version of the old-fashioned movie camera. This particular style is for appearances only, but it lends an air of authenticity to their role as camerapersons. Both could use their voc lens, but the union of photographers and filmmakers has proved that the handheld device is capable of producing a higher resolution than even the most expensive of vocal contacts.

Soon the knock arrives, and General Birtwistle attempts to compose himself in a serious manner, failing miserably and only adding to the clownish representation of his character.

"Enter!" His attempt at sounding stern fails as his voice cracks. The two lieutenants standing behind and to the right of the general desperately try to stifle their laughter. It is difficult since the overall mood of the room is jocular. General Birtwistle wisely chooses to ignore them. This is Frank Hunter's day; nothing and no one is going to spoil it.

Frank Hunter opens the door and walks into the room. He walks directly to the center of the room where he stands at attention and promptly salutes the general. The general stands and salutes the young man.

"I am certain you are curious as to why I summoned you here today." Once again, the general's goofy smile slips out as his attempt to be stern and stolid fails.

Frank notices how foolish the older man looks, but he doesn't feel inclined to laugh. He is confused. He was certain he was in for a reprimand. After having successfully seized the gate and "killed" the general in his sleep, it seemed like Frank was always managing to annoy the general. But that is clearly not the case or the old man wouldn't be grinning like a monkey right now. Nor would there be such an unusual array of individuals present. He mouths the word *Dad* and then notices the woman standing immediately to Geoffrey Hunter's right. *Hadrian's Lover*, he muses, *is that the President?* The dumfounded look on Frank's face causes much mirth to explode in the room, even from the President and the general. Devon is laughing outright, along with their cohort, Mid.

"Yes, son," General Birtwistle finally answers the quizzical look in Frank's face, "that is the President." Sitting back down at his desk, the general continues, "She is here today to present you with a Presidential Pardon." Frank's expression merely grows in confusion, going from mere befuddlement to being outright flummoxed.

"A—a pardon, sir?"

"Yes, private, a pardon." The general looks the President's way. "Madame President, if you please."

But before the President can begin, Frank interjects, "But I don't deserve a pardon. I killed a man. I killed—I killed my best friend." Devon's heart clenches tight; it is agony for him to watch Frank suffer from pangs of guilt.

"Yes, Private Hunter," President Stiles remarks, "but in the past five years, you have proved yourself more than worthy of this parole. You have helped to strengthen Hadrian's security with the War Games scenarios you produced, and if you are to travel from gate to gate continuing with this good work, then I have no choice but to pardon you." Madame President, unlike the poor general, is able to maintain a strong sense of authority while simultaneously expressing her pleasure in today's proceedings. "I have great plans for this country of ours, Private Hunter, and in order for me to follow through on my campaign promises, I need to be able to reassure the electorate that our Wall is impenetrable. Your War Games scenarios will help me do that. The citizenship of this country deserves to have our soldiers being trained by the very best in order to anticipate the unexpected and that, Private Recruit Hunter, is exactly what I want you to do." Ceremoniously, Madame President steps out from the semi-circle and approaches Frank. Standing before him, and with all the authority and strength seen only in the rare few who become the great leaders of all time, President Stiles announces, "Private Frank Hunter, you are officially pardoned of your crime against the state. You are free to live your life as you see fit without hindrance by the state or our military." She hands Frank a small box. Inside is a vocal contact lens. "It is a small gift from your friends. Rather than show you your pardon on a wall screen, we thought you might like to link up and view it by using this instead."

Frank's fingers shake as he reaches inside the little box and retrieves his vocal contact lens. He places it in his right eye and blinks. Appearing on the main drive is a file title "Presidential Pardon." Frank blinks it open to read the very words the President just vocalized.

As the tears stream free from Frank's eyes, Devon rushes forward to give his fiancé the biggest bear hug of his life. Even though this action has brushed the President off to one side, she shows no sign of annoyance, so the general allows for this momentary bit of indiscretion. He can appreciate the joy of the moment, but since this ritual is not yet finished, he clears his throat and orders Lieutenant Rankin back into line. "Private Frank Hunter, attention!" Frank obeys instantly. Standing now, the general walks around his gigantic desk and stands before Private Frank Hunter. "You have been given the opportunity to leave the military, if that is your choice, though I do hope you decide otherwise. If you are interested in becoming career military, I will then present you with the rank of lieutenant." Smiling, General Birtwistle waits for Frank to nod before pinning on his lieutenant's badge. "One last thing," the general says with a wink. "Colonel de la Chappelle, please step forward." The colonel obeys with starch formality and a sparkle of a smile in his eyes. This is a day he has been waiting for for close to two years. He salutes the general and then turns to face Frank. The general then orders, "Open tactile tattoo restraint control FH001." Simultaneously, the two men blink open the doc that runs the program controlling Frank's tactile tattoo restraint. Neither man needs to say anything, just blink the scroll to off, and it need not happen concurrently either. It is a military ceremony, though, so they follow procedure to the letter. "Blink off." Frank feels a slight tingle in his right ankle where the tactile tattoo sits. The sudden realization that he is no longer condemned to a three-mile stretch along the Midwest Gate brings tears of joy to his eyes. General Birtwistle and Colonel de la Chappelle salute Lieutenant Hunter. All military personnel do the same. Frank returns their salute.

With all ceremony complete, the room explodes with the formerly suppressed jocularity, and everyone engages in the full gaiety of the moment. Once again, Devon rushes to his lover. They hug. They kiss. Frank's family joins them. All cry freely—tears of joy.

* * * * *

Bibliography

Anti-Reflection Coatings. PV*EDUCATION.ORG*. Retrieved from: http://
pveducation.org/pvcdrom/design/anti-reflection-coatings. Retrieved on:
March 23, 2014.

Aron, Arthur, et al. "The Experimental Generation of Interpersonal
Closeness: A Procedure and Some Preliminary Findings." *Personality and
Social Psychology Bulletin*, SAGE journals. Retrieved from: http://psp.
sagepub.com/content/23/4/363.full.pdf+html. Retrieved on: February
21, 2015.

Barrett, Stephen. "Glare Factor: Solar Installations and Airports.
Industry at Large: Environmental & Sitting Issues." Retrieved from:
http://www.solarindustrymag.com/issues/SI1306/FEAT_02_Glare_
Factor.html. Retrieved on: March 23, 2014.

Belge, Kathy. "Jane Addams: Social Worker, Political Activist, Nobel
Peace Prize Winner." About.com: Lesbian Life. Retrieved from: http://
lesbianlife.about.com/od/lesbiansinhistory/p/JaneAddams.htm.
Retrieved on: April 11, 2015.

Bennett-Smith, Meredith. "Why do Virginia, 13 Other States Want
to Keep their Anti-Sodomy Laws a Decade after SCOTUS Ban?"
Posted: 04/09/2013 7:27 pm EDT. Updated: 04/09/2013 7:30 pm
EDT. *Huffington Post*: Politics. Retrieved from: http://www.huffington-
post.com/2013/04/09/virginia-anti-sodomy-laws-supreme-court-
ban_n_3047489.html. Retrieved: February 23, 2014.

Brooks, Adrian (author). Katz, Jonathan (Foreword). *The Right Side of History: 100 Years of LGBTQ Activism*. Paperback – June 9, 2015. Retrieved from: http://www.amazon.ca/The-Right-Side-History-Activism/dp/1627781234. Retrieved on: August 11, 2015.

canada.com.: CLASSIC EDITION. "8 great Manitoba hikes." By Travel Manitoba. June 8, 2005. Retrieved from: http://www.canada.com/story.html?id=91a5f5c6-841d-453a-9334-4ea877ccdf55. Retrieved on April 11, 2015.

Canadian Mental Health Association. Ontario. *Mental Health*. "Lesbian, Gay, Bisexual & Trans People Mental Health." Retrieved from: http://ontario.cmha.ca/mental-health/lesbian-gay-bisexual-trans-people-and-mental-health/. Retrieved on: August 6, 2015.

Carton, Mandy Lee. "To Fall in Love with Anyone, Do This." January 9, 2015. nytimes.com. Retrieved from: http://www.nytimes.com/2015/01/11/fashion/modern-love-to-fall-in-love-with-anyone-do-this.html. Retrieved on: February 21, 2015.

CBC News. "Gay–straight alliances subject of debate in Saskatchewan: While politicians spar, Regina student tries to launch group." Posted: April 16, 2013 2:30 p.m. CT. Last updated: April 16, 2013 2:28 p.m. CT. Retrieved from: http://www.cbc.ca/news/canada/saskatchewan/gay-straight-alliances-subject-of-debate-in-saskatchewan-1.1357369 . Retrieved on: February 23, 2014.

CBCnews/Politics. Analysis. "Conservative video spreads ISIS propaganda to make Justin Trudeau look weak." By Eric Blais. Posted June 30, 2015 12:22 p.m. ET. Retrieved from: http://www.cbc.ca/news/politics/conservative-video-spreads-isis-propaganda-to-make-justin-trudeau-look-weak-1.3133039. Retrieved on: September 23, 2015.

Corneal, Devon. "The Talk My Preschooler Wasn't Too Young To Have." Posted: 04/18/2013 3:29 pm. *Huffington Post*: Gay Voices. Retrieved from: http://www.huffingtonpost.com/devon-corneal/the-gay-marriage-talk_b_3111122.html?ir=Gay%20Voices. Retrieved on: February 23, 2014.

David Suzuki Foundation. Issues. Climate Change. "What is climate change?" Retrieved from: http://www.davidsuzuki.org/issues/climate-change/science/climate-change-basics/climate-change-101-1/. Retrieved on: February 23, 2014.

Delay, Tom. "Why is there no Manhattan Project to tackle climate change?" ENVIRONMENT BLOG: The World's Leading Green Journalists on Climate, Energy and Wildlife. *The Guardian*. Retrieved from: http://www.theguardian.com/envi:ronment/blog/2014/mar/11/why-no-manhattan-project-climate-change. Retrieved on: August 6, 2015.

Facebook, Gay Middle East Identities. "Arsham Parsi and the Iranian Railroad for Queer Refugees." qualiafolk.com. "State-sanctioned sexual reassignment." Retrieved from: https://www.facebook.com/photo.php?fbid=427917150647459&set=a.408602162578958.1073741851.399207883518386&type=1&theater. Retrieved on: February 22, 2014.

Feder, Lester J. "Why Some LGBT Youth in Jamaica are Forced to Call a Sewer Home." BuzzFeedNews. Retrieved from: http://www.buzzfeed.com/lesterfeder/how-jamaicas-sodomy-laws-drive-gay-teens-into-the-sewers-of#.rrnZarwYP. Retrieved on: August 6, 2015.

Francis, Merlin. "Climate change is caused by nature, not human activity." Tuesday, February 1, 2011 11:52 IST | Place: Bangalore | Agency: DNA. KIRKUS: INDIE REVIEWS. Retrieved from: http://www.dnaindia.com/scitech/report-climate-change-is-caused-by-nature-not-human-activity-1501621. Retrieved on: February 23, 2014.

Government of Canada. Statistics Canada. Police-reported hate crime in Canada, 2012. "Overview of Hate Crime by Motivation." Police-reported hate crimes motivated by sexual orientation. Retrieved from: http://www.statcan.gc.ca/pub/85-002-x/2014001/article/14028-eng.htm#a8 Retrieved on: February 19, 2015.

Heller, Aron. Associated Press. "Israel City unveils gay Holocaust victims memorial." Friday, January 10, 2014. LGBTQ Nation. Retrieved from:

http://www.lgbtqnation.com/2014/01/israel-city-unveils-gay-holo-caust-victims-memorial/#.UtAd9hHTYWw.facebook. Retrieved on: February 23, 2014.

Hinnant, Lori and Corbet, Sylvie. 04/23/13 06:46 p.m. ET EDT. "France Legalizes Gay Marriage after Harsh Debate, Violent Protests." *Huffington Post*: Gay Voices. Retrieved from: http://www.huffing-tonpost.com/2013/04/23/france-gay-marriage-law-_n_3139470. html?ir=Gay%20Voices&utm_campaign=042313&utm_medium=e-mail&utm_source=Alert-gay-voices&utm_content=Photo. Retrieved on: February 23, 2014.

Huckabee, Charles. S.C. House Keeps Penalties on Colleges that Assigned Gay-Themed Books." *The Chronicle of Higher Education*. March 11, 2014. Retrieved from: http://chronicle.com/blogs/tick-er/s-c-house-keeps-penalties-on-colleges-that-assigned-gay-themed-books/74099?cid=at&utm_source=at&utm_medium=en&ir=Gay%20 Voices. Retrieved: March 11, 2014.

Huffington Post: Gay Voices. "Amy Grant Talks Gay Fans and Being Invited to Perform at Same-Sex Wedding." Posted: 04/23/2013 12:30 pm EDT. Retrieved from: http://www.huffingtonpost.com/2013/04/23/amy-grant-gay-fans_n_3139505.html?ref=topbar. Retrieved on: February 23, 2014.

Human Rights Campaign. Right Side of History T-shirt. "I Stand on the Right Side of History." Retrieved from: http://shop.hrc.org/right-side-of-history-t-shirt.html/. Retrieved on: August 11, 2015.

"IPCC and climate science." Home. Opinion. Your Say. Posted on Tuesday, 21 January 2014. *Otago Daily Times*: Online Edition. Retrieved from: http://www.odt.co.nz/opinion/your-say/288838/ipcc-and-cli-mate-science. Retrieved on: February 23, 2014.

IPCC: Intergovernmental Panel on climate change. Retrieved from: http://www.ipcc.ch/index.htm#.UwqGa15kKOh. Retrieved on: February 23, 2014.

Kauffman, Alexander, C. "The CEO who Took On Indiana's Anti-LGBT Law—And Won." *Huffington Post*: The Third Metric. Retrieved from: http://www.huffingtonpost.com/2015/04/07/marc-benioff-indiana_n_7017032.html. Retrieved on: April 24, 2015.

Kinsey, Alfred et al. *Sexual Behavior in the Human Male*. Philadelphia and London: W. B. Saunders Company, 1948.

Kuruvilla, Carol. "Oregon mom accused of fatally beating 4-year-old son until his bowels tore because she thought he was gay." Posted Friday, March 28, 2014. *New York Daily News*. Crime. Retrieved from: http://www.nydailynews.com/news/crime/oregon-mom-accused-killing-4-year-old-son-thought-gay-article-1.1738037. Retrieved on: August 6, 2015.

LeBlanc, Denis (editor), Tomlinson, Maurice (journalist). "Jamaican Youth Minister to develop plans for LGBT homeless youth." Erasing 76 Crimes. Retrieved from: http://76crimes.com/2014/04/17/jamaica-youth-minister-to-develop-plans-for-lgbt-homeless-youth/. Retrieved on: April 18, 2014.

Mayo Clinic. "Healthy Lifestyles: Getting Pregnant." Answers from Roger W. Harms, M.D. Retrieved from: http://www.mayoclinic.org/healthy-living/getting-pregnant/expert-answers/pregnancy/faq-20058504. Retrieved on: April 18, 2014.

McGonnigal, Jamie. "'So…Who's the Bride?'" Posted: 04/22/2013 11:50 am. *Huffington Post*: Gay Voices. Retrieved from: http://www.huffingtonpost.com/jamie-mcgonnigal/so-whos-the-bride_b_3114070.html. Retrieved on: Feb. 23, 2014.

McPartland, Ben. "Beating reveals 'the face of homophobia' in France." *The Local: France News in English*. Published: 8 April 2013 13:31. Retrieved from: http://www.thelocal.fr/20130408/the-face-of-homophobia-in-france. Retrieved on: June 15, 2014.

Military.com. Army Weapons Qualifications Course. Retrieved from: http://www.military.com/join-armed-forces/army-weapons-qualification-course.html. Retrieved on: July 11, 2015.

Moore, Chadwick. "Love in Putin's Russia." Posted January 14, 2014 2:05 p.m. ET. ADVOCATE.com. Retrieved from: http://www.advocate. com/print-issue/current-issue/2014/01/14/love-putins-russia. Retrieved on: February 23, 2014.

Morgan, Glennisha. "Isaak Wolfe, Transgender High School Student, Denied Use of Assumed Name at Graduation." *Huffington Post*: Gay Voices. Posted: 05/09/2013 11:13 AM EDT | Updated: 05/09/2013 11:42 AM EDT. Retrieved from: http://www.huffingtonpost. com/2013/05/09/isaak-wolfe-graduation-transgender-_n_3238947. html. Retrieved on: February 23, 2014.

NASA Earth Observatory: Where every day is Earth Day. "Is Current Warming Natural?" Retrieved from: http://earthobservatory.nasa.gov/ Features/GlobalWarming/page4.php. Retrieved on: February 23, 2014.

National Defence and the Canadian Armed Forces. Honours & History. Rank Appointment Insignia. Retrieved from: http://www.forces.gc.ca/ en/honours-history-badges-insignia/rank.page. Retrieved on: July 5, 2014.

NIPCC: Nongovernmental International Panel on Climate Change. Retrieved from: http://climatechangereconsidered.org/. Retrieved on: February 23, 2014.

Nobel Prizes and Laureates. Jane Addams – Biographical. Retrieved from: http://www.nobelprize.org/nobel_prizes/peace/laureates/1931/ addams-bio.html. Retrieved on: April 19, 2015.

Nowysz, Karina. "Adidas creates shoe made from recycled ocean trash and illegal fishing nets: Sports apparel company partners with Parley for the Oceans environmental organization. Daily Buzz. Yahoo! News. Retrieved from: https://ca.news.yahoo.com/blogs/daily-buzz/adidas-creates-a-shoe-made-from-illegal-fishing-171835933.html. Retrieved on: August 6, 2015.

Nunavut Tourism. People of Nunavut. The Inuit of Nunavut are a very young ancient culture! Retrieved from: http://www.nunavuttourism. com/about-nunavut/people-of-nunavut. Retrieved on: April 10, 2015.

"Oceans North: Protecting Life in the Arctic, Hudson Bay Estuaries." Retrieved from: http://www.oceansnorth.org/hudson-bay-estuaries, Retrieved on: January 27, 2014.

O'Hanlan, Kate, M.D. "Origins of Diversity of Sexual Orientation and How Discriminations Impacts Health." AMA: Helping Doctors Help Patients. Retrieved from: http://media01.commpartners.com/AMA/ sexual_identity_jan_2011/index.html. Retrieved on: February 16, 2014.

"'Oh my' – George Takei is peeved over Arizona's anti-gay religious freedom bill." Staff Reports. Sunday, February 23, 2014. LGBTQ Nation. Retrieved from: http://www.lgbtqnation.com/2014/02/oh-my-george-takei-is-peeved-over-arizonas-anti-gay-religious-freedom-bill/. Retrieved on: February 23, 2014.

OnSourceShakespeare. *The Tragedy of Hamlet, Prince of Denmark* (1600). Retrieved from: http://www.opensourceshakespeare.org/views/plays/ playmenu.php?WorkID=hamlet. Retrieved on: August 15, 2015.

OnSourceShakespeare. *The Tragedy of Macbeth* (1605). Retrieved from: http://www.opensourceshakespeare.org/views/plays/playmenu. php?WorkID=macbeth. Retrieved on: August 15, 2015.

Paton, Callum. "Mr, Mrs, Miss…and Mx: Transgender people will be able to use new title on official documents." MailOnLine. Retrieved from: http://www.dailymail.co.uk/news/article-3066043/A-new-title-trans-gender-people-join-Mr-Mrs-Miss-used-driving-licences-bank-details-gov-ernment-departments.html. Retrieved on: May 3, 2015.

PinkNews: Europe's Largest Gay News Service. "Russia: Identity of man killed and raped with beer bottles revealed." Retrieved from: http:// www.pinknews.co.uk/2013/05/13/russia-identity-of-man-killed-and-raped-with-beer-bottles-revealed/. Retrieved on: January 10, 2014.

Potential Impacts from the Reflection of Proposed Solar Panels. Retrieved from: http://www.oregon.gov/ODOT/HWY/OIPP/docs/solar_glarepotentialwl.pdf. Retrieved on: March 23, 2014.

Reid, Graham. "The Double Threat for Gay Men in Syria." *Washington Post*. April 28, 2014. Retrieved from: https://www.hrw.org/news/2014/04/28/double-threat-gay-men-syria. Retrieved on: August 14, 2015.

Rubin, David. "Stop Pandering to the LGBT." BreakingIsraelNews: Latest News Biblical Perspective. August 4, 2014. Retrieved from: http://www.breakingisraelnews.com/46299/stop-pandering-to-the-lgbt-opinion/#CwiUC8xmjqYt6L4d.97. Retrieved on: August 6, 2015.

Safe World For Women. "Teen Girls Invent Urine-Powered Generator to Tackle Nigeria's Energy Problems." Source: GPI/ Temitayo Oloinlua. Retrieved from: http://www.asafeworldforwomen.org/global-news/africa/nigeria/3520-teen-girls-invent-urine-powered-generator.html. Retrieved on: August 3, 2014.

Sample, Ian (Science Correspondent). "Male sexual orientation influenced by genes, study shows." Friday, February 14, 2014. *The Guardian*. Retrieved from: http://www.theguardian.com/science/2014/feb/14/genes-influence-male-sexual-orientation-study. Retrieved on: February 22, 2014.

Scheinert, Josh, D. "Why do We Still Allow Religious Schools to Bully Gay Kids?" Posted: 03/25/2013 12:34 p.m.. *Huffington Post* Politics Canada. Retrieved from: http://www.huffingtonpost.ca/josh-d-scheinert/gsa-in-catholic-school-manitoba_b_2946292.html?just_reloaded=1. Retrieved on: February 23, 2014.

Self, Wayne. "Listen Up, Boy Scouts: Gays aren't Pedophiles, and Pedophiles aren't Idiots." Posted: 04/22/2013 4:07 p.m.. *Huffington Post*: Gay Voices. Retrieved from: http://www.huffingtonpost.com/wayne-self/boy-scouts-gays-pedophiles_b_3119530.html?utm_hp_ref=gay-voices. Retrieved on: February 23, 2014.

Shabazz, Abdul-Hakim. "Indiana lawmakers advance gay-marriage ban amendment." Reuters. Wednesday 22 January, 2014. YAHOO! NEWS Canada. Retrieved from: http://ca.news.yahoo.com/indiana-lawmakers-advance-gay-marriage-ban-amendment-022837758--finance.html. Retrieved on: February 23, 2014.

Staff Reports. "Federal prosecutors charge Texas man with hate crime in attack on gay man." Friday, February 21, 2014. LGBTQ Nation. Retrieved from: http://www.lgbtqnation.com/2014/02/federal-prosecutors-charge-texas-man-with-hate-crime-in-attack-on-gay-man/. Retrieved on: February 23, 2014.

Stewart, Colin. "2 Ugandan men face trial on gay-sex charges." Erasing 76 Crimes. Retrieved from: http://76crimes.com/2014/04/18/2-ugandan-men-face-trial-on-gay-sex-charges/. Retrieved on: April 18, 2014.

Stewart, Colin. "For assaulted LGBT, Uganda medical care must be anonymous." Posted on September 6, 2012. Erasing 76 Crimes. Retrieved from: http://76crimes.com/2012/09/06/for-assaulted-lgbt-uganda-medical-care-must-be-anonymous/. Retrieved on: February 23, 2014.

Stewart, Colin. "Zambia risk: Clerics with gays' blood on their hands." Erasing 76 Crimes. Posted on April 13, 2013. Retrieved from: http://76crimes.com/2013/04/13/zambia-risk-clerics-with-gays-blood-on-their-hands/. Retrieved on: February 23, 2014.

Tashman, Brian. Right Wing Watch. "Fischer: Gay activists should support Russia's anti-gay laws in the name of diversity." Monday, August 5, 2013. LGBTQ Nation. Retrieved from: http://www.lgbtqnation.com/2013/08/fischer-gay-activists-should-support-russias-anti-gay-laws-in-the-name-of-diversity/. Retrieved on: February 23, 2014.

The Literature Network. Charles Dickens. *Our Mutual Friend*. Chapter 48. Retrieved from: http://www.online-literature.com/dickens/mutual/48/. Retrieved on: August 15, 2015.

this (+) life. Thinking of Matthew. Retrieved from: https://thisposi-tivelife.wordpress.com/2011/10/09/thinking-of-matthew/. Retrieved on: August 13, 2015.

Tomlinson, Maurice. "Homeless Jamaican LGBT Youth Live in Sewers." YouTube. Published December 1, 2013. Retrieved from: https://www.youtube.com/watch?v=9SI2gmUlszI&noredirect=1. Retrieved on: April 18, 2014.

Vascular Flora of Manitoba. Retrieved from: http://home.cc.umanitoba.ca/~burchil/plants/. Retrieved on: April 11, 2015.

Whalen, Jenni. "Meet the giant air-sucking wall that might help combat climate change." UPWORTHY. August 28, 2015. Retrieved from: http://www.upworthy.com/meet-the-giant-air-sucking-wall-that-might-help-combat-climate-change?c=upw1&u=cc7589ff6eaf-74ee71389382834b423ed4b2b2d0. Retrieved on: September 18, 2015.

worldatlas, ARCTIC MAP. Retrieved from: http://www.worldatlas.com/webimage/countrys/polar/arctic.htm. Retrieved on: January 27, 2014.

CPSIA information can be obtained at www.ICGtesting.com
Printed in the USA
BVOW08s1206180416

444626BV00002B/29/P